A Whirlwind Of Rapture
Engulfed In Fear

Elsie Cooper

willingly traded her carefree role of New York debutante to be the wife of the handsome Russian aristocrat. She followed him from New York to London to the court of the Tsar— where pomp and pageantry masked shuddering terror.

Count Alexander Martynov

adored her, possessed her . . . and drew her into the circle of evil that had long cursed his royal family. In a palace that had seen assassinations, suicides, and evidence of a ghost, nothing seemed unreal . . . though even ecstasy was often an illusion.

Rasputin

the wild peasant of towering form and vulgar appetites, became a monk and won the favor of the Tsar and Tsarina to become the most powerful man in Russia. His hypnotic eyes bore into Elsie's soul with satanic fervor . . . and a darkness portending her doom.

CLARISSA ROSS

MOSCOW MISTS

AVON
PUBLISHERS OF BARD, CAMELOT AND DISCUS BOOKS

MOSCOW MISTS is an original publication of Avon Books.
This work has never before appeared in book form.

AVON BOOKS
A division of
The Hearst Corporation
959 Eighth Avenue
New York, New York 10019

First Avon Printing, March, 1977

AVON TRADEMARK REG. U.S. PAT. OFF. AND IN
OTHER COUNTRIES, MARCA REGISTRADA,
HECHO EN U.S.A.

Printed in the U.S.A.

To Beatrice Bourke who lived and danced in Paris in the period in which this story is set. An American girl who became a ballet star in Paris, she studied with Mathilde Kschessinska, and knew many of the Russian aristocrats as refugees. For her generous help in giving me authentic details for this story and for her continuing beauty as a person.

To Marilyn who gave me the title and much help.

To Nancy without whose faith and encouragement I could not have written the book.

MOSCOW MISTS

❧ Chapter 1 ❧

SOME OF THE TERRIFYING MOMENTS she had known were to stay with her a lifetime. Elsie Cooper had made a determined effort not to think of those days in that other far-off land. But they stubbornly remained part of her life experience. They could not be erased however much she might wish it.

Moscow.

The very name of the ancient Russian city was enough to fill Elsie's mind with a succession of vivid tableaux! Suddenly she saw the faces of people almost forgot and scenes of horror and majesty such as she was never to know again.

She recalled standing on the bank of the Moscow River on an early evening in May when the cool air and the warm spring flood waters of the river had mixed to create a mist fine and white and impenetrable to her eyes. And then suddenly a twisted, phantom figure had appeared from the mists and began shuffling toward her.

Elsie had traded the carefree, charmed lifestyle of a New York debutante to be the wife of a handsome Russian aristocrat without knowing the change this marriage was to bring to her life. Without guessing the terror awaiting her in that new existence in a grim old palace in a decadent world which was crumbling all about her!

Did she believe in ghosts? Perhaps not as many people understood ghosts, but the phantoms that crowded her mind when she remembered were terribly real. So were the flashes of scenes that still returned to haunt her.

The Russia of 1913, trembling on the brink of revolution, would always live in her memory. Moscow, with the great medieval city of the Kremlin standing grimly amid

1

the newer city, its walls marking the borders of the city of Moscow of the fifteenth century. Moscow, the city of many churches. Rising higher than the maze of rooftops shone the blue-and-gold onion domes of the church towers. It was the holy city of Russia. Yet it seethed with turmoil, injustice, decadence. A city of great avenues along which stood the elegant palaces of the royalty and the fine houses of the rich. Blocks away were the two-story wooden buildings and the log cabins that housed the city's ordinary people.

Elsie remembered her first time in an Orthodox church with her new husband. She had stood beside him, enchanted with the great cathedral. Peasants were present in heavy work clothes and rough boots; the women wore shawls over their heads. The royalty wore furs and jewels and stood shoulder to shoulder with the poor. People of every rank stood together holding candles, lost in the fervor of their worship. Everywhere about the cathedral golden icons glistened; there were the miters and the crosses, the bearded priests in their golden robes, the swirling pots of incense and the glorious surge of the music. The myriad of voices rising in tribute.

But these memories were of the earlier days only. And when she thought about those days she started with that evening in the first week of 1912 when she attended a performance of "The Bird of Paradise" with Laurette Taylor, Guy Bates Post, and Lewis S. Stone. She had been more excited about seeing Laurette Taylor than in the play.

Elsie's doting uncle, Gordon Cooper, and his wife, Jane, had purchased tickets for the performance as a New Year's gift for her. A wealthy clothing merchant with a fine brownstone house on East Forty-second Street, Elsie's uncle and his wife had brought her up following the death of her parents. As a result, Elsie grew up with the children of the rich and socially prominent in New York. At 21, she was one of the beauties of the town with pert, Gibson-girl good looks and her auburn hair wound about her brow in becoming coronet braids. She had large blue eyes, perfect lips and a warm smile.

Seated in a lower box directly across the theater from the one Elsie, her Uncle Gordon, and Aunt Jane occupied were Mrs. Gilbert Wilberforce, a bejeweled matron of mammoth proportions; and her thin, white-mustached husband, who perpetually wore a vague look. In the box with them were two handsome well-dressed young people; the young woman wore a glistening diamond tiara on her jet-black hair and the dark-haired and mustached young man was impressive in white tie and tails.

Elsie asked Aunt Jane, "Who is sitting with the Wilberforces?"

Aunt Jane was of sturdy Yankee stock with a long, plain face and lanky body that no amount of jewelry or expensive gowns could much decorate. Now she pursed her thin lips and said, "They're those Russians!"

Uncle Gordon, broad and beaming, with a kind face and a warm nature, raised a plump hand in protest. "Not mere Russians," he said in his deep, baritone voice, "they are special, the Count Alexander Martynov and his sister, the Countess Olga."

"I've heard about them," Elsie said. "They are Mrs. Wilberforce's prize attractions for the season."

"Russian royalty," Uncle Gordon said with a note of meaning in his voice.

"Royalty, fiddlesticks!" Aunt Jane said with a quick, disapproving glance at her husband. "Don't try to turn the girl's head!"

Uncle Gordon showed modest surprise at his wife's remark, but argued mildly, "A count and a countess, surely that must mean something?"

"Very little if you ask me," Aunt Jane sniffed. "Russia is full of counts, dukes, grand duchesses, and all that nonsense. Back in my hometown in New Hampshire the local banker owned most of the land and money. My father and everyone else always called him squire. I don't expect the title of count means much more in Russia."

Uncle Gordon chuckled. "As usual, you are closer to the truth than I like to admit."

Elsie gave her Aunt Jane a small smile of rebuke. "I think you like to make little of people, Aunt Jane. Mrs. Wilberforce is merely trying to be social; I don't think we should criticize her for that."

Aunt Jane said, "I can see it's the young man who interests you. I declare you're not able to take your eyes off him."

Elsie blushed. "Well, he is handsome."

After a while, Uncle Gordon let them know of his preference. "The young man has good looks and a kind of easy charm. But if you want my pick of the two, I'd vote for the girl any time. She has an interesting face, a serious beauty. Give me the Countess Olga."

"Well, some day," Elsie mused, "I'd like to meet the count and his sister!"

Aunt Jane gave her a cynical look. "And I thought you plagued us to come here and see Laurette Taylor! It seems you've forgot all about your favorite actress!"

"I haven't," Elsie said with a small smile. "I'm loving the play. I think Miss Taylor is wonderful; so is Lewis Stone."

"The cast is better than the play," Uncle Gordon said.

"And the audience more interesting than either," Aunt Jane said with a hint of sarcasm. "Well, don't fret, Elsie. We have all been invited to the ball Mrs. Wilberforce is giving next Saturday night. The count and the countess are the guests of honor."

Elsie couldn't hide her delight. "Why didn't you tell me before?"

"I decided to wait," Aunt Jane said with a smirk. "Let you rave on about those anarchists."

Uncle Gordon shook his head. "You mustn't call them that. They are of the aristocracy, and very few of that class are anarchists."

Aunt Jane was primly adamant. "To me Russians and anarchists are one and the same!"

"The lights are dimming," Elsie said. "Thank goodness, the play is about to begin again."

People settled back in their seats and the curtain rose on the final act of the South seas' story. Elsie tried to keep her mind on the play, but found her thoughts kept wandering off. Count Alexander Martynov kept flashing before her eyes. What would meeting him at the ball Saturday night be like?

After the final curtain came and the company had taken its curtain calls, the lights in the playhouse went up again; and the audience prepared to leave. As Elsie rose from the cane-seated chair, she saw that Mrs. Wilberforce and her party had already gone. They must have left during the curtain calls, thought Elsie as she found herself feeling disappointed that she'd not had another glimpse of the handsome young man.

Saturday night seemed a long time coming. On Thursday afternoon it rained and Elsie's best friend, Marjorie Judson, came for lunch. Later upstairs in Elsie's room they talked.

Marjorie was a lively blonde who wore her hair coiled at her neck in large braids and liked to wear gaily colored dresses. On this dark afternoon she had chosen a flowered print with a trim of white lace at the neck and sleeves.

Elsie asked her friend if she'd heard Aunt Jane making those sour comments on the Russians at lunch?

"Yes," answered Marjorie. "But what brought your aunt to talk about Russians?"

Elsie laughed. "She thinks I've fallen in love with one."

Marjorie's shapely eyebrows rose. "A Russian? Where would you ever meet one?"

"Mrs. Wilberforce had a count and a countess as her guests at the theater the other night. I was impressed by the count and said so. I'm sure it upset Aunt Jane."

"Of course it would. Me as well," Marjorie said, coming over to her. "If you fell in love with a Russian and married him you'd move to the other side of the world!"

"Would that be so awful? We're bound to marry one day."

"But we'll marry someone here in New York and live here," Marjorie said, seating herself on the bed beside her. "I don't want to lose you; neither does your aunt."

Elsie replied, "I say if you're enough in love with someone, it doesn't matter where he wants to take you."

"Anyway, you're practically engaged to Tom Holmes!"

Elsie pouted. "That banker! All he thinks about is money! I'm sure if I married him we'd spend all our evenings discussing our budget."

Marjorie gave her an accusing look. "You seemed satisfied enough with him until you saw this Russian. What is your count like?"

"Gorgeous." Elsie said. "And I'm to meet him at the ball Mrs. Wilberforce is giving on Saturday night."

"My parents are taking me," Marjorie sighed. "Chaperoned."

5

Elsie put an arm around her friend. "Don't worry! If I meet my count, I'll have a special afternoon tea for him; and I'll sit you right next to him."

Marjorie smiled. "You are excited about him, aren't you?"

"I am," Elsie said. "I am."

When Marjorie left, Aunt Jane said, "I noticed you couldn't wait to rush upstairs after lunch to gossip."

Elsie stood before her aunt smiling, her tone mocking, "How could you think such a thing, Auntie dear?"

"I know you both," Aunt Jane said, putting down her knitting needles and sitting back in her chair. "Just as I've come to know your generation."

"Our generation?"

"Yes," Aunt Jane said. "You've grown up with many things I didn't have when I was a girl. You have the telephone, the electric light, the trolley car, the typewriter, cash register, subway, Graphophone, camera, motion pictures, airplane and the automobile, and girls like you now have taken their places in business offices."

"Don't you approve?" Elsie wanted to know.

"I don't know," her aunt confessed. "Though I do know that beef has raised from fifteen cents a pound to twenty-eight and the salary of a good cook has gone up from sixteen dollars a month to thirty-five! There has to be an end to it!"

"I think it's a marvelous new age for women," Elsie said.

"I believe one of the reasons things have changed so fast is because of those self-starters on the new automobiles," Aunt Jane declared.

"What bearing do they have on it?"

"Made women more independent. They can now drive a car without having to get someone to crank it. And gives them an excuse to shorten their skirts so they don't get caught in the gas pedals!"

Elsie laughed and went to sit on the arm of her aunt's chair. She said, "You really don't disapprove as much as you try to make on."

The older woman sighed. "Are you still determined to go to the Wilberforce party on Saturday night?"

"Of course! Don't you want me to go?"

6

Her aunt's plain face shadowed. "I don't know. I'm almost afraid to take you."

"Why?"

Aunt Jane glanced at her worriedly. "Because I think you have an unhealthy crush on that young Russian count."

"Aunt Jane!"

"Well, you went on so about him at the theater the other night."

"I couldn't help noticing him," Elsie protested. "He was nice looking. And I've met so few European men of his age."

"The fewer the better," Aunt Jane said. "You know things are bad over there. Many people think a war is brewing now that King Edward is dead. The Kaiser is mad, and they say Tsar Nicholas is a weakling ruled by his German wife. Russia could have trouble at any time. You read every week of the political unrest and the bombings there!"

"I only want to meet Count Alexander," Elsie said. "I don't plan to go off to Russia with him."

"I have known cases where a meeting led to something like that," the plain-faced woman warned her.

Elsie affectionately placed an arm around the shoulders of the older woman. "You're worrying over nothing. I've never even met the count. He may not notice me on Saturday. You're making a fuss about something that will never happen."

Aunt Jane sighed. "I hope so." She glanced up at Elsie sadly. "You must realize that you are all that your uncle and I have. We love you and are dependent on your love. I think your Uncle Gordon would take it worse than I if you ever decided to marry and go a long way off."

She was touched by these words, in a way a paraphrase of what Marjorie had said. Impulsively she told her aunt, "You know that I love you and Uncle Gordon more than anyone else on earth. I would never deliberately hurt you."

"Not deliberately," Aunt Jane agreed. "But if you felt deeply in love you might think yourself justified in anything you decided."

"I hope not."

Her Aunt Jane gazed down at the carpet with a tone of

7

despair in her voice, "I suppose it is silly of me. But I have a strange feeling about your meeting this young man. It sends a chill down my spine. Don't ask me why? But whenever I've had this feeling of dread before I've seldom been wrong."

Elsie listened and tried to discount her aunt's words, to push them aside as the fearful comments of an adoring relative upset at the possible prospect of her going·far away with a man she loved. And yet, at the same time, a tiny warning voice within her kept telling her that her Aunt Jane might be right.

Elsie made it a point to avoid any further talk about Saturday night as the week went on. At last the special night came, and she was in her room putting the finishing touches on her makeup. She had chosen a pale blue, low-cut gown which she thought would do justice to her auburn hair and blue eyes. And she wondered about the count and whether he knew the latest American dances. She was adept in the turkey trot to the lively music of ragtime, she also did the waist-bending maxixe and the bunny hug. She had learned the slinking steps of the tango and expected that at least the count would know that step.

There was a knock on her door. She threw on her wrap and went to answer it. Her stout Uncle Gordon was standing out there in white tie and tails and wearing a black cape. He had his tophat in his hand and beamed at her.

"You look beautiful, Elsie," he told her. "You'll be the sensation of the evening."

She leaned close and kissed him on the cheek. "It sounds lovely even if I know it isn't true!"

They went downstairs where a prim Aunt Jane waited for them. She had on a long coat of white fur over the plain black gown which she invariably wore to balls. Rising from her chair, she gave Elsie an approving look.

Aunt Jane said, "The car is waiting. We should get on our way."

Elsie's eyes twinkled as she told her Aunt Jane, "After all your talk, I do believe you're excited to get there!"

"We know who's excited," was Aunt Jane's comment.

They went outside to find Henry, who was making the difficult adjustment from coachman to chauffeur with some reluctance. The old man in his new uniform was standing on the sidewalk waiting for them. He opened the rear door, and they all stepped inside, Aunt Jane first, Elsie taking her place in the middle of the rear seat, with Uncle Gordon flanking her on the other side.

Uncle Gordon leaned toward Elsie and with a chuckle said, "I'm sure Henry is annoyed that the rain took off all the snow. Otherwise, he could have used one of the sleighs tonight and been a lot more happy."

"Just so long as he gets us on our way," Elsie said, as the old man crawled gingerly behind the wheel.

Henry managed to start the car almost at once, although he sent it into a startling jerking motion before they moved ahead.

The Wilberforce mansion was on Forty-seventh Street a block closer to the East River. Henry drove the car along at a good speed, careful to avoid the other automobiles and horse-drawn vehicles they encountered along the way. Although electricity had come to New York, this part of the great city was still lighted by gas lamps. On this dark night, the lamps sent off a yellow glow that could be seen for a good distance. Elsie sat very still and silent between her aunt and uncle, her heart pounding with excitement at the expectation of the evening ahead. Henry outdid himself as chauffeur, and they shortly reached the entrance of the Wilberforce mansion.

"Heavens!" Aunt Jane exclaimed as she peered out the side window.

"Must have invited half of New York," Uncle Gordon chuckled amiably.

"I just know it's going to be a wonderful party!" Elsie said, awed by the number of carriages, hansom cabs, and automobiles, lining up before the towering brownstone mansion. Servants with lanterns in hand were there to direct the traffic and others saw that the arriving guests were conducted safely to the wide red carpet that covered the sidewalk and led up the entrance steps to the large double doors of the house. A steady stream of guests made their way up the steps and inside.

"The Wilberforces are making all this special show to impress the count and countess," Aunt Jane said acidly.

"Can you blame them?" Uncle Gordon said. "It's not every night we get to hobnob with Russian nobility!"

9

"And that may be a very good thing," Aunt Jane said, giving him a reproving glance in the dark rear seat of the auto. "Be sure that Henry knows when to pick us up."

"I'll attend to that," Uncle Gordon rumbled.

Elsie made no comment as the first big moment of the evening had arrived. A servant in uniform opened the door and assisted Aunt Jane and her out. Uncle Gordon followed and briefly discussed the business of Henry's returning for them later.

Uncle Gordon then joined the two women to escort them inside. The entrance foyer was brilliantly lighted with the newest electric fixtures hung from the high ceiling. Inside other servants directed the ladies to a dressing room at one side of the entrance and the men to one directly opposite. Later, they would join each other to be presented at the entrance of the ballroom upstairs.

Aunt Jane allowed a maid to remove her cape and gave Elsie a warning glance. "You're much too pretty for your own good tonight, young lady. I want you to forget any notions you may have about that Count Alexander Martynov!"

Elsie blushed and laughed. "You're being silly."

"I think not," Aunt Jane said with a knowing look on her plain face. "Fix your hair in the mirror, and then we'll go join your uncle."

Elsie obediently pushed through the group of chattering, elegantly gowned females of all ages to the big wall mirror and managed to find a portion of it to study herself and fix up loose wisps of her auburn hair. Then she hurried back to Aunt Jane, and they both went out to the entrance foyer where Uncle Gordon, hugely magnificent in his evening dress and white tie, awaited them.

They took their places in the line, which seemed unending, and gradually made their way up the broad, curved stairway. Along the way, Uncle Gordon exchanged friendly nods and brief words with some of the other men. Aunt Jane looked prim and almost disapproving of the whole affair. Elsie spotted her friend, Marjorie Judson, a distance up the stairs ahead of them. She waved and Marjorie, who was in the company of her mother and father, waved·back excitedly.

At last they reached the reception line, and Elsie felt almost faint amid the crowd and the heat of the room. Mr. Wilberforce greeted them in his friendly, vague way, and then they moved on to the domineering, overweight Mrs. Wilberforce, whose ample figure was festooned in a shimmering gold gown and whose thick fingers were aglitter with huge diamonds.

"How nice of you to come," Mrs. Wilberforce said in well-rehearsed tones. "And how lovely Elsie looks tonight."

Elsie bowed demurely. "Thank you, Mrs. Wilberforce."

The stout woman turned to the handsome, tall, dark man standing beside her and said, "Count Martynov, I'd like you to meet Miss Elsie Cooper, niece of two of my dearest friends."

Count Alexander Martynov smiled politely and took Elsie's hand. "Delighted, Miss Cooper," he said in perfect English, with hardly any accent. The voice was warm, rich.

"I saw you at the theater the other night," Elsie said, aware that Aunt Jane was impatiently waiting for her and Uncle Gordon was in line to be introduced.

"Ah, yes, the theater," the count said. "Good actress, your Miss Laurette Taylor."

Then Elsie moved on as the count warmly greeted her Uncle Gordon. She was sure that the young Russian had not noticed her at all. His response had been automatic, and he'd barely looked at her as he spoke. Next she greeted the Countess Olga who again was wearing her diamond tiara. She was a beautiful young woman with the same good looks as her brother, but with a touch of sadness in her young face.

She studied Elsie much more closely than the count had and said, "I remember you! You sat in the box across from us at the play the other night."

"Yes, we did," Elsie managed, still somewhat unhappy at the lack of impression she'd managed to make on the count.

Countess Olga told her, "I think you are the typical American girl! What is it they call her, the Gibson girl?"

Elsie didn't know whether it was a compliment. She said, "Charles Dana Gibson draws many girls for our magazines."

"Of a special type," Countess Olga said. "Your type. You should be flattered."

"Thank you," Elsie said politely and moved on as her Uncle Gordon boomed his appreciation of the dark-haired young countess and warmly shook her hand.

The orchestra was already playing and dancing was in progress. Many of those arriving were seeking out chairs along the walls of the great ballroom before joining the dancers. Uncle Gordon saw Elsie and Aunt Jane to chairs, and they were barely seated when waiters arrived with trays of champagne.

Elsie sat with her Aunt Jane sipping champagne and taking in the festivities as Uncle Gordon stood posed with his glass in hand, ready to fend off any unwelcome interlopers, or to greet old friends.

Aunt Jane gave Elsie a glance and said, "You seemed to get along better with the countess than with her brother."

Elsie blushed. "She's very friendly."

"I'm glad it turned out that way," her aunt told her. "I've already warned you that I have a strange feeling about that young man. I think he could bring you great unhappiness."

"That's nonsense!" Elsie protested.

"I never ignore my instincts," Aunt Jane said firmly. "I had an Irish grandmother, and this gift came from her. It has been a mixed blessing, but I have learned to heed it!"

✑ Chapter 2 ✎

"EASILY THE BEST AFFAIR of the season," Uncle Gordon said as he sipped his drink and approvingly eyed the dancing couples.

Elsie was sure that he was right, but felt like a wallflower seated there next to her Aunt Jane. Her state of mind was not improved when she noticed the handsome Count Martynov dancing by with an attractive blonde girl. The orchestra seemed never to stop and the music was lively and pleasing.

Most of the guests had arrived now and those not standing in the upstairs foyer were dancing in the huge ballroom with its wall of mirrors on one side. Elsie saw her friend Marjorie dancing by with a short, jolly looking young man and then a few couples later it was the turn of the brunette Countess Olga to dance by in the arms of a bearded young man in a red military uniform with dark blue stripes along the trousers. Elsie began to feel she was the only one of her own age not on the floor. It was humiliating!

Just then Aunt Jane tapped her arm with her fan and in a low aside, warned her, "You are soon going to have a partner!"

A certain something in her aunt's tone gave a warning, so Elsie glanced up to see her tall, mustached host coming straight toward her. And she murmured a panic-stricken "Oh, no!"

"May I have this waltz, Miss Cooper?" Gilbert Wilberforce asked.

"Thank you," Elsie said, rising. Her Uncle Gordon was watching with a twinkle in his eyes, while Aunt Jane had her usual dour expression.

Elsie's head was reeling. Her elderly partner had a dis-

13

tinctive and showy style of waltzing that quickly whirled them by many of the more sedate couples as he led her into the dancing throng. Before she knew it they had gone the length of the ballroom and were on their way back. During this sweep of the big room, they passed the count and his blonde companion.

She said, "I see the count has found a charming partner."

"Wife of the Russian military attaché visiting here from Washington," Mr. Wilberforce explained. "The fellow in uniform dancing with Countess Ogla is the attaché."

Somehow Elsie felt better for this, although she knew it didn't make any sense. But she drew some small comfort from knowing that the count was doing a duty dance with one of his government people. Gilbert Wilberforce became even more fancy and energetic in his waltzing, but she didn't mind as long as she managed to keep up with him. She noticed that many of the others had ceased dancing to watch them and offer admiring comments on the remarkable agility of their aging host.

Then a dreadful thing occurred. She was suddenly aware that something had happened to one of her shoes. The heel felt distinctly wobbly. She tried to ignore this and compensate for it by shifting her weight a little. Unhappily, Mr. Wilberforce chose this same moment to become more daring in his intricate steps. Elsie struggled to follow her partner's lead gracefully, despite the panic within having reached a peak! The heel felt less stable every second. She was about to give up and tell the happily unaware Gilbert Wilberforce that she'd had an accident with her shoe. But she had waited too late!

The heel came off completely! And at exactly the wrong moment, she whirled gracefully and then somehow lost her balance altogether and tripped the exuberant old man who held her in his arms. The shattering result was that they both went crashing to the floor. It happened so swiftly she was hardly aware of the exact train of events.

She heard screams and saw the unbelieving look on the face of the vague, mustached Gilbert Wilberforce. In the next second, they were inextricably entangled in the middle of the ballroom floor with the other dancers halted and staring at them. The orchestra went blithely on.

There were offers of help from all sides. Willing hands lifted both Elsie and the shocked host to their feet. A rumpled Gilbert Wilberforce asked, "Are you all right, my dear?"

"I lost my heel," she explained, blushing fiercely.

Seeing that they were not hurt, the other dancing couples, with true social aplomb, resumed dancing again as Gilbert Wilberforce, more than slightly off his usual dignity, escorted her back to her aunt and uncle. She had to limp beside him as if one leg were shorter than the other as the heel had vanished in the melee.

"I'm terribly sorry," she apologized to him as they made their ignoble retreat.

"Nothing at all, dear girl," her host said, always the gentleman. "Could have happened to anyone."

She gave him a solicitous glance. "You didn't hurt yourself, I hope?"

"Not at all," he assured her. "What about you?"

"Just my heel," she said miserably, feeling she had made them both look like utter fools.

Aunt Jane was on her feet to greet them. "Whatever happened?" she wanted to know.

"My heel," she murmured, aware that the music had stopped and the other couples were coming off the floor. Sure that all eyes were on them, that they had become the laughing-stocks of the occasion.

It was then that the real magic of the evening began for her. A pleasant, male voice from behind her said, "I think this belongs to you."

She turned, her lovely face still crimson and saw it was none other than Count Alexander Martynov who had rescued her heel and was now holding it out to her. "Thank you," she said, in a small, shamed voice.

The count said, "The heel is useless without being attached to your shoe. I suggest you give me the shoe, and we shall have it repaired."

She hesitated. "I doubt if anything can be done."

"Then you must have another pair of shoes," the young Count said. And he turned to Gilbert Wilberforce, "Surely you have someone on your household staff who can take care of this emergency?"

Mr. Wilberforce nodded in a kind of stunned fashion.

15

"Yes, I would hope so." He turned to her. "If you will let me have your shoe, Miss Cooper."

"I'm too much bother," she protested, as she sat down. The handsome count was already on his knees beside her removing her shoe gently and smiling up into her face. "One way or another the damage shall be repaired," he promised. Then he stood up and gave the shoe and heel to Mr. Wilberforce.

As their host vanished clutching the heel and shoe, Uncle Gordon reintroduced himself and Aunt Jane to the count, who now showed a real interest in them. Uncle Gordon said, "And this unfortunate accident victim is my niece, Elsie."

The count offered her another of his brilliant smiles. "The young lady who attended the Laurette Taylor play, of course."

Elsie sat there beginning to think that her accident had been much less of a calamity than she'd first decided; for it had brought the count to her side, and he was now giving her his full attention.

Uncle Gordon asked, "Are you and your sister going to be in America long, count?"

"Only for a few weeks more," the young man said. "I can not remain away too long. Since my brother's death I have been head of the family. There is a responsibility."

"You must visit us," Uncle Gordon went on. "We do not live far from here."

Count Alexander smiled, "You are very kind."

Aunt Jane remained cynical in manner as she dismayed Elsie by asking the handsome young man, "Do you not have a great deal of trouble in your country? A lot of unrest?"

The count did not lose his amiable smile. "I think that might be said of half of Europe today, Mrs. Cooper. My own country does have some distressing problems."

"Yet you don't mind going back there?" Aunt Jane said, pursuing the subject.

Uncle Gordon spoke up with some embarrassment, "My dear Jane, you are talking about this young man's homeland. We do not desert our country whatever internal problems we may have."

"Exactly!" Elsie chimed in ruefully.

"My forbears didn't," Aunt Jane said sternly. "They came to this country as revolutionaries."

"Then you would be most at home in Russia today," the count said with good humor. "The place is alive with revolutionaries."

Even Aunt Jane joined in the laughter at his so neatly having turned the tables on her.

Then Mr. Wilberforce returned with Elsie's heel at least temporarily mended. He said, "I make no promises. But several strong nails have been put through the bottom of the shoe. The heel may hold."

"Allow me." Count Martynov said with another of his warm smiles for Elsie, as he knelt and fitted her shoe on. "Is that all right?" he asked anxiously before he rose.

"Yes," she said. "You are too kind!"

The count stood up. He nodded toward the orchestra and said, "The music has resumed. Will you do me the honor?"

It was utter bliss. "Are you sure you haven't promised to dance this one with someone else?" Elsie hesitated on the brink of complete delight.

He shook his hands. "I am quite free, if your aunt and uncle will permit us."

Aunt Jane waved them off with her fan. "Go ahead! Or the music will have ended again! And if you feel your heel coming off again, for goodness sake remove yourself from the floor."

"I will," Elsie promised as they went out to join the others in a lively one-step.

The Count said, "I'm amazed at the amount of social life here in New York. I had no idea."

"You can be no stranger to dancing," she said. "You dance well."

"Thank you," he said. "I have done a great deal of it. We do not spend all our time living in terror of the anarchists as your aunt seems to think."

"You must forgive her," Elsie said. "She has had little firsthand experience of Europe."

The dark-haired count smiled down at her as they danced and said, "I consider your accident most fortunate. Otherwise, I might not have noticed you."

"I have been thinking the same thing," she declared

happily. "I call it a kindly stroke of fate and not an accident at all."

"Dating from the moment the cobbler imperfectly constructed your shoe," the count said. "Knowing that it would give way at the precise second when I might retrieve it."

"You speak English so well," Elsie marveled.

"English is a second language among the more fortunate classes in Russia," he told her. "Most of us also speak French, since many of the aristocracy spend much time in Paris."

"Russia excites me," she said.

His face showed a rueful smile. "Poor Mother Russia! So much beauty and so much to offer, and yet mine is a country on the abyss of disaster. I did not give your good aunt the satisfaction of agreeing with her, but I know her to be right."

Elsie's eyes widened. "If you are so aware of this, can you not do something to help the matter?"

"One has hopes and then they are crushed," the young count said earnestly. "Because I am of the aristocracy does not mean I am ignorant of the excesses of our government, or of the fact that the tsar and his empress have been badly advised."

"Is there not a mad monk named Rasputin who has an evil power over them? At least I seem to have read this somewhere."

A shadow crossed the count's face as he almost angrily declared, "Do not place the blame on Rasputin! There are others who bear the true guilt. Rasputin is worshipped by the peasants! The monk Iliodor spread much of the gossip about Rasputin! They were associates and then Iliodor turned on him because he was becoming more popular. It is very complicated! You cannot possibly understand."

"I'm sorry to be so badly misinformed," she apologized.

He smiled again. "It is enough for you to be as lovely as you are. How could you be expected to know the tormented political state of my country."

The music ended when they were close by the orchestra. Count Martynov turned to the musicians and applauded them directly. He said, "I would like to import all of you to Moscow."

As he turned back to her they were joined by the military attaché from Washington. The bearded man had the Countess Olga on his arm. He bowed to them, and the countess eyed her brother with an anxious look.

Her lovely black eyes fixed on him in reproach as she said, "I have been trying to find you. There are things to be discussed and settled before the evening is older."

Count Alexander looked slightly embarrassed. "I'm sorry. I planned to look for you in a moment."

Countess Olga turned to her. "The young woman from the theater?"

"Yes," Elsie said, nervously. It seemed clear the countess did not much enjoy having her brother in her company.

Countess Olga went on to explain, "My brother and I have an important family matter to discuss. A message must be sent home tonight. You will excuse him, won't you?"

"Surely," she said.

The count bowed to her and took her hand and kissed the back of it. "Thank you for the dance. I shall see you again."

"I hope so," she said quietly.

"Meanwhile, I shall leave you to dance with Colonel Peter Simmars," the count said with a faint smile. He gave the man in the elegant red uniform a warm glance. "Peter's job is to look dashing and be the best of dancers."

Countess Olga impatiently took her brother's arm and led him off, beginning to talk to him seriously even before they were more than a few feet away.

Colonel Simmars showed a resigned look on his bearded face. "You must forgive the countess, Miss Cooper," he said. "They are facing a family crisis."

She stared at him in amazement. "You know my name and the count didn't tell you."

The big man in the red uniform smiled. "No magic about it, dear young lady. The countess had you identified before we came to join you."

"I see," she said.

The music resumed with another romantic waltz and Elsie found herself dancing with the dashing colonel. He was truly as good a dancer as the Count had suggested. But despite his dancing ability and the excellent music, she found herself still thinking of the handsome, dark count who had made such a strong impression on her. And perhaps the thing which had struck her most was that he was troubled. Beneath his seemingly calm exterior, the count was tense and confused He was aware of his country's predicament and appeared to have some very original ideas about the cause of the trouble.

Realizing suddenly that she was neglecting her partner, Elsie asked the colonel, "Are you permanently stationed in Washington?"

"More or less," he said. "I journey to other parts of the United States when there is a need. We have a large embassy in Washington. I am far down in the scale of importance."

She said politely, "I'm sure you all have your work to do."

The colonel continued waltzing with her as he said, "There are times when I would prefer to be home. It is a period of rapidly moving events, and I would like to be closer to my parents."

Elsie sensed the same sort of tension in him that she had in the young count. She wondered if his political views were similar and guessed they would be. As a test, she asked, "What about Rasputin?"

The colonel frowned. "A villainous scoundrel! He is causing my country a great deal of trouble!"

She raised her eyebrows. "You surprise me. I spoke of him to Count Alexander just now, and he seemed to have a great admiration for him."

"A misplaced admiration!" the colonel fumed. "Let me say I esteem the count and his sister. But the Martynov family are known to have some strange opinions politically. That is our great problem in Russia, we are so divided!"

They danced on and when the music came to an end, the colonel took her back to her aunt and uncle. To her surprise she saw Tom Holmes standing there with them, evidently waiting for her. He was a tall, thin young man with wavy chestnut hair who looked splendid in his white tie and tails.

Colonel Simmars thanked her warmly, then vanished in the crowded room.

Aunt Jane asked, "What happened to your count?"

"His sister swept him away," Elsie said with a wan smile.

Tom Holmes spoke up, turning to her aunt and uncle. "But surely you have heard?"

"Heard what?" Uncle Gordon asked with his broad, ruddy face all attention.

Tom Holmes went on in a worldly drawl, "There was an assassination back in Russia. Word came tonight after the ball began. The uncle of the count and countess was blown to bits while driving through the streets of Moscow in his sleigh."

Elsie was shocked. Now she understood the count's and countess's behavior. "How awful for them!"

"And for poor Mrs. Wilberforce," Tom said. "You know she spent a fortune on this party. The count and countess have probably left by now. The word came through a little while after the reception line ended. But they remained for a time with the understanding that nothing be said. Of course, once the story got out, it spread from person to person like wildfire."

"I can imagine," Elsie said dryly. "Especially if everyone was as quick to detail the bad news as you."

Tom Holmes showed hurt on his pleasant face. "Would you have preferred that I not tell you?"

"I don't think you should be so eager to repeat it," Elsie told him.

"That's all the thanks I get," the young banker said with mild annoyance. "You wanted to know where the count had gone?"

Aunt Jane spoke up quickly. "It really doesn't matter. And I'm glad to know what happened. I imagine those two poor young people have left by now."

"I think so," Elsie said. "I could tell the count was upset."

Tom Holmes in his superior fashion informed her, "I've met both he and his sister before, and I'd say they were strange."

"Strange?" Elsie repeated. "In what way?"

The young man touched his white tie nervously. "It's hard to explain. They're different."

"Don't you mean foreign?" she suggested with a hint of sarcasm.

Her uncle cleared his throat and said, "It is bound to put a damper on the party. Especially if everyone hears about it." He glanced around and, noticing there were not too many dancing couples, added, "I think the word has spread."

"Poor Mrs. Wilberforce is upstairs having a fit of hysterics," Tom Holmes said. "At least she was when I last heard. And I doubt if she has come back down."

Aunt Jane gave Elsie a knowing look. "In the face of all this calamity, your losing your heel was a small matter."

"I'm beginning to think so," she agreed.

Uncle Gordon said, "In my opinion it is our duty to try and keep the party going. I suggest we dance, Jane!" And he stood ready for her to join him.

Aunt Jane considered for a moment and then closed her fan and put it down. She said, "You're probably right." And she went out onto the dance floor with her husband for the fox-trot in progress.

Tom Holmes turned to her, "Can we do less?"

"I suppose not," she agreed and allowed him to take her out onto the floor.

As they danced, he said, "I didn't know you were going to be here tonight."

She said, "You were out of town when we were invited. I haven't had a chance to see you since."

"I only returned from Chicago this morning," he told her. "I hadn't time to get in touch with you and make it here. I was late as it was. I hoped you might be here."

She tried to resign herself to his expected line of talk. She said, "I hope your trip was a success."

"The bank seemed to think so," he said proudly. "I'm beginning to have some weight around there. I expect to have my own office soon."

"That will be nice," she said, offering a smile to her friend Marjorie, who was dancing by with the stout young man again.

"You don't seem much interested," Tom told her with an offended tone of voice.

"I am," she made herself say. "I can't think of anything more thrilling than to have your own office."

Tom scowled at her. "I know what's wrong with you.

22

You are still dreaming about that count, someone who probably has never done a day's work in his life."

"Tom!" she said, "Please don't be offensive."

"I mean it," he went on angrily. "No wonder they blow those fellows up. They aren't any good."

"You don't know what you're talking about."

"They're just plain useless. And why don't they stay home."

"Tom!" she reproved him. "Unless you stop, I'll have to ask you to lead me off the floor; or better still, I'll leave you and walk off myself!"

"And start a scandal!" he said, aghast. "You wouldn't!"

"I'm sure I saw the president of the bank here," she went on mischievously. "Think what an impression that would make on him. He'd have you before him for questioning in the morning."

"Don't do it!" Tom said, almost pleading.

"Not as long as you behave," she told him. And through this blackmail she managed to finish the dance with him without any more unpleasantness.

Elsie was concerned by the news about Count Alexander's uncle. There was no sign of the young count or the others of his party now. They had undoubtedly left as soon as the Countess Olga had come for him.

The buffet was being served in an adjoining room, and she went with Tom and her aunt and uncle to stand in line for the elaborate food offered. Mrs. Wilberforce was still not present, and the word went around that she had been given a sedative and sent to bed by her physician, who was also a guest at the ball. So the party ended on a somber note. Mr. Gilbert Wilberforce was at the door to say good night to his departing guests. Elsie thought he looked more forlorn than usual.

Tom insisted that she join him for dinner the next evening, and although she was not too enthusiastic about the idea, she finally agreed. The place was to be Delmonico's and the time seven. Tom would come by for her in a hired coach at six-thirty and by her aunt's' strict rule, she would have to be home by nine-thirty at the latest.

It rained again the next day; and the dark, gloomy day matched her own mood. She was sure that if the news of the tragedy in Russia had not arrived she would have had

23

a long evening in the company of Count Alexander Martynov. And she also was certain that he would have wanted to meet her again. But alas, it was one of those brief contacts she would treasure for the rest of her life, but which would become nothing more than a memory.

Elsie blushed. The count had been more attractive to her than any man she'd known previously. And he had seemed to like her. Perhaps he would contact her before he left New York. Or if he didn't have time, he might write her. This thought offered her solace, and she clung to it.

The telephone in the downstairs hall was enough of a novelty to still make any call important. And all through the long, wet day she hoped that the telephone would ring and it would be Count Alexander on the other end of the line. She even rehearsed what she would say to him.

Aunt Jane had come upon her staring out the window of the living room at the downpour. The grim Yankee woman had told her in her crisp way, "I think you're mooning over that count. And I hope I'm not right."

She'd turned to the prim, older woman with a thin smile. "And if you are?"

"I'd say you should forget all about him. I have a feeling about your count. And the news of what happened to his uncle last night didn't do anything to make me feel better."

"That had nothing to do with Count Alexander," Elsie had protested.

"I'd say it had a good deal to do with him," was Aunt Jane's grim reply.

When the telephone did ring, it was not the count, but her friend Marjorie. Elsie had rushed to take the call and when she heard her friend's voice she was unable to stop herself from saying, dismally, "It's only you."

Marjorie chuckled. "I know who you hoped it would be. Sorry! But you did make a handsome couple when you danced together. I think you did that heel thing on purpose to attract his attention."

"I did not," she said. "And he left early as you know."

"I heard the secret reason," Marjorie said through the crackle on the line. "I guess everybody did."

"I doubt that I'll ever meet him again," Elsie told her friend disconsolately.

"He's charming, but maybe it is for the best," Marjorie said. "Russia is a long way off. And things are getting worse there."

"I think a lot of it is exaggerated," Elsie said. "We have bombings and shootings here, too."

"I don't think it's quite the same," Marjorie said. "Who was the man in the red uniform you were with later. I'd have settled for him."

Elsie laughed. "He has a wife. He's a member of the Russian Embassy at Washington. I believe it was he who came with the news of the assassination of the count's uncle."

"I suppose they will go straight back to Moscow."

"I'd imagine so. I'm having dinner with Tom tonight. We're going to Delmonico's."

"Now, that sounds better to me," Marjorie said. "If you change your mind, tell Tom I'd be glad to take your place."

"I'm going," she said. "I've already promised. And after this dreary, disappointing day, I'll probably even enjoy hearing about his chances of being promoted."

Marjorie chuckled at this. And they talked a few minutes more about what she was going to wear before they ended the conversation. Elsie stayed close by the telephone for the rest of the day, but no calls came for her.

Tom was punctual as usual. The rain had ended, but it was cold, so Elsie wore a heavy cape. The cabby lost no time rattling the ancient vehicle over the cobblestone streets until at last they came to a halt before the splendor of the glowing entrance of Delmonico's.

They entered the plush crimson of the noted eating place. The lights were softly yellow in their illumination to give it all a romantic aura. Many of the men were in evening dress and the women wore fine gowns; some had ostrich feathers in their hair.

Elsie left Tom to put his coat in the gent's checking, while she went to the ladies' room to leave her cloak with the attendant and freshen up. Just as she entered the busy anteroom, she found herself face to face with a startled Countess Olga Martynov!

⊷§ Chapter 3 §⊷

COUNTESS OLGA SPOKE FIRST, in her soft voice with its slight accent. "You are, of course, startled to see me here."

She stared at the shapely olive face of the dark-eyed young woman. "Yes," she admitted.

"I would prefer that you do not mention it to anyone," the countess said.

"As you wish," Elsie replied, still not recovered from the shock of the meeting.

"My brother was fortunate in arranging a last-minute booking on the *Lusitania* which sailed this morning. He is on his way back to Russia."

"And you are remaining here?"

The countess nodded. "Yes. Alexander will return for me in mid-April. I happen to know that he has written you a message which you will no doubt receive tomorrow."

Elsie couldn't hide the pleasure this news gave her. She said, "How kind of him."

"He was deeply impressed by you," the other young woman said. "Only the sad news of our uncle's tragic death prevented him from seeing you again."

"I'd say you were both brave to remain at the party after you had heard the news," Elsie said. "Everyone admired you for it."

The countess brushed this off. "We did not stay all that long. And we do owe a great deal to Mrs. Wilberforce."

"Will you be staying with her?" Elsie asked.

"No," Countess Olga said. "I have taken a suite at the Waldorf-Astoria Hotel."

Studying her in a somber fashion, the countess said, "After you receive my brother's message I should like to have a private talk with you."

26

Elsie's heart pounded with pent-up excitement. She wondered what this meant. Trying to appear calm about it, she said, "Would you come to my house for tea one day?"

"I would prefer that you visit me at the hotel," Countess Olga said. "It would insure us more privacy."

"If you like."

"Tea is an excellent idea," the young Russian woman went on. "Shall we say three-thirty, day after tomorrow. Colonel Simmars and his wife are still here with me. They will not be taking the train back to Washington until tomorrow night."

"Very well," Elsie said. "I shall call on you at the hotel the day after tomorrow."

"I shall have tea ready at three-thirty," the countess said. "And again, please do not speak to anyone of our meeting here tonight."

"You have my word," Elsie assured her.

The countess left the ladies' room, and Elsie saw that the colonel's wife had been waiting for Olga by the exit door. The two went out together, no doubt to join the bearded, young colonel. Elsie moved on to the cloak room attendant and gave her the cloak which she'd taken off and been carrying on her arm.

As she studied herself in one of the mirrors of the ladies' room, Elsie found herself wildly speculating about it all. Why had the countess remained in New York? What had Count Alexander written in his letter to her? And why did the countess wish to talk with her?

Of one thing Elsie was certain. The countess was no happier now about the interest which Count Alexander had shown in her than she had been at the party. Elsie was positive the countess did not want her brother becoming romantically involved with any American girl. She found herself annoyed by this and vowed she would not allow herself to be frightened off by the assured countess, who was likely no older than she was.

When she left the ladies' room and rejoined Tom in the foyer, Elsie half-expected him to mention having seen the countess and her party. But he didn't; so she decided he'd probably missed them while checking his coat. Tom had an awkward way of asking questions about things that didn't concern him. She had an idea that the countess and her friends had probably taken one of the small private dining rooms upstairs; therefore, they would not likely encounter her again unless they all decided to leave at the same time.

Because Tom knew the headwaiter at the famous restaurant, he was able to get a very good table at the rear of the big main dining room. Tom studied Elsie across the table. "After last night, I think we should seriously discuss our future."

"Our future?" she repeated, slightly surprised.

"You know what I mean," the young man said in his overbearing way. "Our families have expected us to get married for years. I didn't like the way you threw yourself at that count fellow last night."

"I did not throw myself at him." Her cheeks were burning.

Tom looked down at his plate. "You drew a lot of attention. Several people mentioned you two today. I wasn't much pleased."

"And I'm not much pleased at your possessive attitude toward me." Elsie sat back, her eyes bright with anger. "I have always thought of you as my friend. I enjoy us having that relationship. I hope you're not about to spoil it."

The waiter brought the champagne Tom ordered and opened it. He filled their glasses and put the white-clothed bottle in the cooler of ice he'd brought to the table for it.

The moment the waiter left, Tom raised his glass and offered Elsie a toast. "To our friendship then," he said in a milder tone.

She summoned a small smile for him and sipped the bubbling wine.

Tom said, "I had a talk with the bank's manager today. I shall have my own office within the month. Suppose I celebrate the occasion by offering you a diamond?"

"No, Tom," she said quietly. "I'm not ready for marriage yet. I want more time to decide exactly what I wish to do with my life."

The curly headed young man across the table from her looked disconsolate. "My mother blames it on the motor car! She says that now you young women have learned to drive these horseless vehicles, you've become much too independent! And I'm inclined to agree."

28

Elsie smiled. "Whatever the reason, I'm not ready to marry yet."

The waiter arrived with their first course. From then on through the fish course, the pheasant and the dessert, Elsie managed to keep the conversation on other things of interest to Tom. She even endured another long account of his self-appraised brilliance and what he had promised himself he would do in his banking career.

On the ride home in another hansom cab, he took the opportunity of the darkness and privacy to place an arm around her and kiss her. She found his attentions a nuisance but managed to keep him reasonably in hand without having to appear too prim and proper. She did not want to break the friendship between them and knew if she completely repulsed him he would be bound to be in a rage. At the same time she made a mental note to avoid such compromising situations as much as possible in the future.

He saw her to the door and they said their good nights. Then he retreated to take the cab to his home while she went inside. The house was quiet with most of the lights out. She made her way up the stairway and was confronted by her Aunt Jane in a dressing gown on the landing.

"Did you have a pleasant evening?" her aunt wanted to know.

"Yes," she said, thinking that it had all been worthwhile if only because of her meeting with the countess and the news that Count Alexander had sent her a letter.

"Did you see anyone we know?" Aunt Jane asked.

Because of her promise to the countess, Elsie said, "No one really important."

"Tom is a nice young man with wealthy parents and a good future," Aunt Jane reminded her.

Elsie smiled bleakly. "So he has told me. Good night, Aunt Jane." And she kissed her aunt on the cheek before going on to her own room.

If Aunt Jane suspected anything she didn't show it. And she didn't seem to notice the letter that came in the mail for Elsie along with some others the next morning. The count had not written any return address on the envelope. But Elsie was expecting the letter and noticed the bold handwriting at once, which she knew must be his. She quickly took it, along with the rest of her mail, and went up to her room to read it in privacy.

Her fingers trembled with excitement as she tore open the heavy fawn envelope. The message inside took up most of the page of folded sheet of notepaper, but the handwriting, like that on the envelope was bold, so the message was not all that lengthy.

She read: "My Dear Miss Cooper: Meeting you was the highlight of last evening's party. I write this in haste as I'm shortly sailing for Europe because of the tragic murder of my uncle. Olga has chosen to remain in New York, and I shall return in a few weeks to meet her and spend a little more time in your country then. I shall look forward to seeing you again and getting to know you better. I'm a great believer in fate, and I'm convinced the heel business was meant to bring us together. I shall think of our pleasant moments often, and I apologize for not being able to deliver this message in person. Yours most sincerely, Alexander."

Elsie read the brief letter over several times, and each reading gave her happiness. She knew her aunt and uncle did not approve of this new friendship she had made. She also realized that Countess Olga was opposed to her having a romance with Alexander. She could only assume that the countess felt her brother should date only the nobility in his own land. Perhaps the countess was justified in this feeling.

Elsie determined she would see.

The next day Elsie made an excuse of meeting Marjorie to her aunt. Then to further protect the secrecy of her destination, she drove herself to the Waldorf-Astoria.

The elegant lobby of the famous hotel was properly subdued. The desk clerk inquired her name, then telephoned the countess before giving Elsie the number of the suite. After getting the countess's approval, he gave Elsie the floor and number.

Countess Olga herself opened the door in answer to Elsie's knock. The dark girl was dressed in a plain black dress and looked wan. She did not smile, but in her grave fashion said, "Do come in."

"I'm a few minutes early," Elsie apologized as she removed her coat.

The countess took it and hung it in a nearby closet. "It doesn't matter," she said. "It will give us more time together. The waiter brought the tea tray a few minutes ago; so everything is ready."

They sat on a divan with the tea tray before them, and the countess poured their tea and served the light food on the tray. During this time the dark-haired girl talked only about the weather and of how pleased she was with the good service in the hotel.

Elsie glanced about the room as she put down her empty tea cup. She said, "It is a fine suite. I'm sure it is also very expensive."

"That does not matter," the countess said with a weary wave of her graceful hand. "Will you have more tea?"

"No, thank you," Elsie said nervously. She knew they had exhausted small talk and now the moment of truth must emerge.

The countess folded her hands in her lap. Then with another of her serious glances at Elsie, she said, "Very well. So now we shall talk."

"Yes," Elsie said in a small voice.

"You received my brother's letter?"

"I did."

The keen black eyes of the countess were fixed on her. "I have no idea what was in it. Nor do I wish you to tell me. But I do know that the count found you interesting. He talked about you more than I expected considering the crisis we were facing."

"I enjoyed meeting him."

"I'm sure you did. Alexander can be charming, even when under a severe strain, as he was at the party. The word of our uncle's assassination was not all that much of a shock. We had assumed for some months that he was a doomed man. But the timing of his murder was most unfortunate for us. You may think I'm referring to his death coldly and wondering why I did not decide to return to Russia for the delayed ceremony of his funeral, which Alexander shall attend."

Elsie said, "It is no business of mine."

"You are quite right in that," Countess Olga said. "But I'm most willing to tell you. Our uncle was not friendly toward either Alexander or me. He was our mother's

31

brother, not our father's. And since the death of our own parents we have lived with our father's brother, Count Andre Martynov; his wife; and our cousin, Timofei. Our mother's brother resented this and treated us as strangers. Still, for appearances' sake Alexander felt he should attend the funeral."

Countess Olga looked more bleak than ever. "You might even count him among our enemies. He was opposed to our political views. We are somewhat more moderate in our ideas than most of the nobility; and when my brother, Basil, was murdered in St. Petersburg three years ago, our Uncle Ivan did not attend his funeral."

"I did not know you had lost a brother," Elsie said with sympathy.

"Another assassination victim," the girl in black said bitterly. "His body so mutilated that when Alexander went and brought it back the casket could not be opened."

"Dreadful!"

"Many dreadful things happen in Russia," the countess assured her. "And I see no hope of times becoming better."

Elsie said, "Last night I mentioned Rasputin to your brother and I was surprised to hear him come to the monk's defense."

A strange expression crossed the face of the countess. She said, "I warned you that our family is somewhat radical in our views. I happen to be of the aristocracy, but I also am one who believes that there must be a change of government in our country. I do not, like Alexander, give my full support to Rasputin, but the so-called 'mad monk' has much to be said for him. Yet I fear he is too powerful in his influence over the royal family, and through them, over the government. The other revolutionaries are seething with anger at his ascent to power. Yet many think of him as holy."

"I know very little about him," Elsie admitted.

The countess sighed. "I do not want you to think of me as an enemy."

"Why should I?"

"You may after you hear what I have to say."

"Oh?"

The lovely, oval face of the countess showed a frown. "I

listened to my brother last night. And I'm certain when he returns to this country, he will want to renew his friendship with you. I'm convinced he is infatuated with you to the point where he might one day decide to ask you to be his wife."

Blushing, she said, "That is taking a great deal for granted, countess."

"No matter," the other young woman said curtly. "I'm sure you are equally enthralled by Alexander. I can understand an American girl being charmed by him. He has good looks, fine manners, and a title."

"I'm not interested in titles," Elsie protested.

"Most American women are."

"You need not fear that about me," she said. "But I do think that what may happen in the future between your brother and me is our private affair."

Countess Olga gazed at her with what almost might be construed as pity. "I almost knew that would be your answer."

"Then why go on with this discussion?" Elsie asked.

The slender Russian noblewoman rose and moved to the center of the room facing her. "I hope to save you from tragedy. I do not think Alexander should plan to marry. It is not you I oppose, but his possible marriage to anyone."

"Why?"

"Because I do not think he is sure of himself at this moment. Nor is he sure of what may happen to our family and its fortunes. Russia is very different from America. We have a city place and a country place. The city house is what we call a palace, situated on the shore of the Moskva River. It has been the palace of the Martynovs for centuries."

"And?"

The slender young woman in black began pacing slowly back and forth in the dusk-ridden room. "Let me tell you something about our family. My father's line was a noble one, but in common with other noble families a strain of insanity cursed us down through the years. A Count Nicholas Martynov married and murdered three wives within a matter of five years. His crimes and insanity were found out in due time and he cut his own throat. His ghost still stalks the palace in Moscow, so they say."

"Ghosts do not terrify me," Elsie said. "I do not believe in them."

Countess Olga halted in her pacing to give her another sharp glance. "If ghosts do not terrify you perhaps madness does?"

Then in a grim tone, the countess said, "The madness that may have filtered down to our generation."

Shocked, Elsie asked, "Are you saying your brother may be insane?"

"No," she said. "But he is a man of violent tempers, as was my late brother, Basil. I put it down to Basil's strong passions that he exposed himself to needless danger and was murdered. I fear that one day Alexander may do the same."

Elsie hesitated and then reasoned, "You say you do not want Alexander to marry. Yet would not the proper wife have a restraining influence on his tempers?"

"I was afraid you would miss the point of what I've been trying to tell you," Countess Olga said.

"What you have said does not make reason."

"I have spoken as plainly as I can," the woman in black said. "You live in a happy land here with a good future. I'm sure you have many fine, young men wishing to marry you."

"And so must you have," Elsie said.

The countess shrugged. "In Russia it is different. My brother and my Uncle Andre must approve any suitor of mine. And my choice is not apt to be theirs."

Elsie said, "Then you should understand how I feel. I must make my own choice."

"Of course! And you shall, I'm sure of that," the woman in black said, crossing to her. "But I beg of you to think about what I've said. Do not see my brother again. It would be most discreet if you were out of the city when he returns."

Elsie shook her head. "I won't make that promise."

"Don't decide now. Think about it," said the countess. "I'm only warning you for your own sake. I do not want to see you put your life in the same tragic situation of Alexander and I and all the other Martynovs."

"I thank you for your good intentions," Elsie said in a

quiet voice. "If you have nothing else to tell me I should be on my way."

"Nothing more," the countess said with a sigh and went to the closet and brought out Elsie's coat and helped her on with it.

"Thank you for the tea," Elsie said.

The sharp eyes of the girl studied Elsie with what almost seemed like pity. She said, "You are most welcome. We will no doubt meet at various social occasions."

"No doubt," Elsie said.

"I wish us to be friends."

"I would like that."

"Do not reply to my brother's letter."

"He gave me no address."

"That is fortunate," the dark-haired girl said. And then she leaned over to Elsie and gave her a cool kiss on the cheek. "I wish you well."

"Thank you," Elsie said, happy to escape the gloomy living room of the suite. The countess, dressed in black, had seemed more bleak than before. While waiting for the elevator, Elsie found herself wondering why the lovely dark girl was so opposed to her having a romance with her brother? Why tell her of the history of madness in the family? A thought came to Elsie: Could Olga be touched with the taint of madness? Did this madness take the form of an incestuous love for her handsome brother?

The possibility shocked Elsie, and she could not get it out of her mind. Despite the countess saying she wanted to be friends, Elsie had not been convinced of the sincerity of her words. Was it possible that Olga hated anyone who threatened to take her brother from her?

Elsie drove back home with this alarming business troubling her thoughts. And this continued to bother her for the days that followed. Then about ten days later, she received a letter from Alexander. It had been written in London and was more ardent in tone than the first one she'd received. In it, the young count told her of his constant thoughts of her and gave her a London address at which to write him. He planned, according to his letter, to hastily cross the channel and take a train in Paris that would eventually take him to Moscow.

He planned to stay in his native city only long enough to

attend his uncle's funeral. Then he would return to London, look after some business matters there, and take the first available ship back to New York. With luck he would be in New York in late February or early March. Meanwhile, he would continue to write to her and look forward to her replies when he returned to his hotel in London.

She wrote him a friendly, but what she felt was a discreet, letter, and mentioned that she'd had a visit with Olga. She felt it was best to let him know. If he had any suspicion of his sister's possible behavior to her, he would realize that they had met and he had been discussed. She sent the letter to his London hotel.

Almost at the same time a third letter reached her. It had been mailed in Paris. In it, he spoke of thinking of her almost constantly; and he hinted that when he returned to New York he would ask her hand in marriage. Elsie was truly surprised by the tone of the letter. But she was more upset by one of his paragraphs near the end of it in which he warned her, "Say nothing of this to my sister. Olga is a strange, moody girl, and she might not understand."

The letter bothered Elsie so much that she knew she must talk with someone. So she phoned Marjorie and asked if she might come over for dinner and the evening. Marjorie was delighted to have her come; so it was arranged.

Aunt Jane worried, "How will you get home?"

She said, "If I remain late, I could stay at Marjorie's all night."

Her aunt shook her head. "No. I'd rather you didn't. Her mother has not been well. You should not impose yourself as a guest if there is no need of it."

"Marjorie's father will summon a hansom cab for me and accompany me home, I'm sure of that."

"If he doesn't offer, you must telephone us," Aunt Jane said. "Your Uncle Gordon will have the chauffeur get out the car and pick you up."

"I'm sure that won't be necessary," Elsie said.

When she reached Marjorie's house on Twenty-sixth Street, she found her friend in a state of excitement. They at once went to the sewing room and closed the door for privacy. Then Elsie gave her friend Alexander's letters to read.

Marjorie quickly went through them and when she'd finished the third one, she exclaimed, "I vow he intends to ask you to be his wife."

Elsie showed a strained smile. "You really think so?"

"Don't you? It's all here in the last letter!"

"I have worried about it," Elsie said. "That is why I wanted you to read the letters."

Marjorie gave her a knowing look and handed the letters back to her. "If you want my advice, I'll give it. Send your count a letter to London and tell him you're thinking of marrying Tom. That it's almost all arranged."

She gasped. "Why?"

"To discourage him. It's apparent that the longer he is away from you, the more he thinks he cares for you. You have to end it."

"But maybe he is in love with me?" Elsie said, sinking back in her chair with dismay.

Marjorie stood before her. "Are you in love with him?"

She hesitated. Then she nodded, "I think so."

Marjorie groaned and turned away. "It's his glamour, his title."

"His sister suggested that. It's not so. I really do think I care for him."

"The Countess Olga." Marjorie said with disgust.

"Yes."

"That's another good reason for giving up any romantic ideas about Alexander," her friend said. "That countess is so odd. Since she's been alone in New York, she rarely sees anyone. And those who have seen her think she's strange."

"I don't understand her," Elsie sighed. "I've been forced to wonder if there could be an incestuous love for her brother on her part."

Marjorie's eyes widened and she sank down on a nearby sofa. "Incest!"

"She told me there was a taint of madness in their family," Elsie went on. "I'm not sure I believe the story."

"I do!" Marjorie exclaimed. "And I think you've hit on the truth! She's in love with her own brother! And from

what he said about being discreet in his letter, I'd venture
that he isn't all that innocent either!"

"No!" she protested. "I don't want to think about it any
more."

"You'd be wise to," Marjorie said. "I've heard of such
cases right here in New York City. If you went off to Russia as his bride, you might find yourself in terrible trouble!"

"Olga warned me of that. But I think she's bluffing! She
wants him to marry some girl of the Russian aristocracy,
or she wants him for herself."

"Either way she is going to cause you trouble. Remember that." Marjorie warned.

Elsie remained at her friend's house until nine. And
then because Marjorie's father was still at his club, she had
her friend telephone for a cab. She knew her aunt and
uncle would not approve of her riding back alone in a
cab, but she was certain there would be no danger.

The cabby was an elderly man who drove her to her
door and waited until she was on the steps. Then he drove
off. As she unlocked the door, she was startled to hear a
moan from behind her. She quickly turned, but it was a
dark night, and no street lights were near the door. She
saw no one.

She took a step down and then without warning a figure
sprang from the shadows, and she felt hands cruelly seiz-
ing her throat. With a strangled cry of alarm, Elsie staggered back in the grip of her attacker.

ᵕᵌ Chapter 4 ᵌᵕ

THE STRONG HANDS continued to tighten on Elsie's throat, and she knew she would soon lose consciousness. Because of the darkness, she had no idea what her attacker looked like. The suddenness of it all had left her in a stunned state. But realizing the desperation of her plight, she now began to claw and try to struggle against the figure which had sprung at her from the shadows.

Most of her efforts were to no avail. But as her panic mounted she made an attempt to bite the wrist of her attacker. She managed to do this once and he let out a howl of pain and a rapid flow of words in some language which she did not understand.

She tried to bite him again, but this time she didn't succeed. Happily the moment when the attacker had removed the bitten hand temporarily from her throat had given her a chance to breathe a little. Now the terrible pressure on her throat was resumed and she felt she could not survive!

Suddenly, there was a burst of light before her eyes, the attacker uttered a loud oath and ran off down the street!

"Elsie!" It was her Uncle Gordon Cooper's voice as his ample figure came lumbering down the front steps to give her support in time to keep her from collapsing on the sidewalk.

When she opened her eyes again, she was on a divan in the living room with her Uncle Gordon and Aunt Jane hovering over her, plus a shattered looking old Henry and Mary—the cook—standing in the background.

Uncle Gordon held a brandy glass to her lips and told her, "Take some of this."

She took a mouthful and coughed as she swallowed it.

Her throat still ached and her head was reeling. She looked up at her Uncle. "Did you see him?"

"Only got a brief glimpse of him as he ran away," her uncle said with an angry look on his ruddy face. "Seemed a sort of vagrant in near rags."

Aunt Jane asked, "Were you able to get a good look at him?"

She shook her head. "No."

Uncle Gordon continued to tilt the brandy glass to her lips as he used his other arm to support her in a sitting up position. "Take another swallow. Doesn't matter whether it makes you choke a little. It will do you good."

She obeyed him and took another mouthful. And although it burned all the way down, she did feel better for it. She said, "I had the key in the door. Almost had the door unlocked. In another moment, I'd have been inside."

"Henry thought he heard a cry in the street," Uncle Gordon said. "He and Mary share the bedroom in the front of the basement, so they were nearest to you."

Henry's wife, Mary, who had been the cook in the household for longer than Henry had been chauffeur, said, "I knew it was a woman's voice crying for help! I told Henry so!"

Uncle Gordon nodded approvingly. "And you were right, Mary. Henry rushed upstairs and turned on the outside lights and roused your aunt and I."

Elsie told her uncle. "I can sit up by myself now. The brandy helped." Then she added dolefully, "So he managed to escape."

"No question of that," Uncle Gordon said, standing there with the empty brandy glass in his hand and a frustrated look on his broad face. "He ran into an alley and made his way into the next street. Henry ran after him, but lost sight of him. He could be anywhere by now!"

The ancient Henry in his threadbare dressing gown over a flannel nightgown, said, "What about the police, sir?"

"They must be informed," her uncle said, and he moved away to look after this.

Aunt Jane sighed. "You came back alone in the cab, didn't you?"

"Yes," Elsie confessed.

"I knew it," her aunt declared. "If you'd only learn to listen to your uncle and me."

"I'm sorry," she said.

"Much good that would have done if you'd been murdered on the doorstep," Aunt Jane said with a reproving look on her face.

From the hall, Elsie heard her uncle calling the police. Henry and Mary went downstairs to dress for the arrival of the police and Aunt Jane remained standing near her with a dejected air.

By the time the police arrived it was almost thirty minutes later. There were three of them, two in the familiar blue uniform and a third in a dark suit, a wing collar, flashy green tie, and a green bowler hat. The three held a hasty conference with Uncle Gordon, then the two uniformed policemen accompanied by Henry went off to investigate the alley where the criminal had vanished. The plainclothesman removed his bowler hat and entered the house.

Uncle Gordon led him into the living room where Elsie was still resting on the divan. Her uncle said, "This is Captain Patrick Harrigan of the Police Department. He is a friend of mine and he wants to ask you a few questions."

Captain Harrigan bowed slightly. "If I may, Miss Cooper."

"Do you feel well enough to be questioned?" Aunt Jane hovered by her in worried fashion.

"I'm all right now," Elsie assured her. And in truth she did feel much better.

"Just what time do you think it was when it happened?" Captain Harrigan asked Elsie.

She considered, "Probably around twenty minutes to ten," she said.

The florid-faced, balding man nodded and made some notes. "You say you were on the doorstep when you heard a moan?"

"Yes. Directly behind me."

"What did you do?"

"I turned, but I could see no one. Then I decided to step down onto the sidewalk. It was very dark and difficult to see."

The captain wrote briskly. When he finished, he said, "It

41

is still a dark night, no hint of a moon or stars. Good night for burglars and hold-up men. We are getting enough of both in this city just now. Can you tell me anything about this fellow?"

"I didn't get a decent look at him," she confessed. "But Henry did and my Uncle Gordon saw him running off."

"In the distance," Uncle Gordon said unhappily. "So I could make out nothing beyond the fact it was a man who seemed to be in rags."

Captain Harrigan listened and wrote something else down. He said, "Miss Cooper, you must realize it is very dangerous for young women to travel about the city on their own at night."

"I know," she said.

"You suffered the consequences," the balding man said gravely. "You say you didn't see this fellow. Did you hear him? You claim you bit him."

"I did," Elsie said.

Captain Harrigan asked, "What was his reaction?"

She said, "He screamed!"

"What did he scream?"

She hesitated for she had been thinking about it all. The man had uttered a long sentence of rage in some foreign tongue after the scream. And she had begun to worry that this was no ordinary criminal at all, but an agent sent by Countess Olga to murder her. It could be by now that the countess had heard from her brother and that she'd guessed his romantic inclinations.

After a few seconds' delay, she said, "I don't remember what he screamed—something foul. I sort of closed my ears to it." She hoped he would believe her. It wasn't that she wanted to protect the countess if she had initiated a murder plot against her, but she didn't want to jump to rash conclusions without giving herself more time to think. Yet it gave her a guilty feeling to know she was hiding facts from the police who were trying to help her.

Captain Harrigan frowned as he wrote down her answer. "I don't suppose it really is important. But sometimes a shout of anger can betray a man's nationality if he has an accent. But that would be little to go on."

Uncle Gordon asked, "What can be done?"

The captain stood up. "Not a great deal, I'm afraid.

We'll make the usual inquiries. I doubt if my men will find any trail to follow in the alley. But I'll see the block is patroled more often after dark."

"We would appreciate that," Aunt Jane said, also getting to her feet.

"New York is a great city now," Captain Harrigan warned them. "Great cities always are plagued with crime. We do our best, but at times it seems a losing game."

"I thank you for coming so promptly," Uncle Gordon said.

The balding Captain assured him, "You know we are always at your service, sir." And with his notebook and pencil still in hand, he glanced at Elsie again. "Is there anything else at all you recall about the incident?"

She was sure her cheeks were red from the shame she felt. Yet she had taken her stand, and she could not change it. She said, "Really nothing, officer. I had an idea he was about the same height as myself and his hands were wiry and terribly strong."

The captain gave a satisfied nod. "All helpful," he told her. "So the man likely was short, thin and at least had strong, muscular hands." He wrote it down.

"I'd say so," she agreed, feeling a little less guilty. "I was very confused."

"I'm sure you were, Miss," the Captain said, putting his notebook and pencil in an inside pocket. "If we round up any likely suspects we may want you and the chauffeur, along with your uncle, of course, to come down and take a look at them."

Uncle Gordon said, "Just let us know, and we'll be there. I would like to see the scoundrel caught and placed in prison."

"We'll do our best," the captain said. He glanced at Elsie again. "Odd that he didn't take your purse."

"I thought about that," Uncle Gordon said, his brow creased. "I found the purse near where he attacked her. He left it there on the sidewalk."

Elsie said, "The lights came on very swiftly. He may have dropped it and been afraid to wait and pick it up."

"Likely," the captain said, his bowler hat in hand. "But why did he continue to throttle you when he'd already snatched your purse? If he were an ordinary thief, he'd have taken the purse and run."

"I agree," Aunt Jane said with a frightened look on her usually expressionless face. "That's why I think he meant to kill her rather than rob her."

"Why?" Uncle Gordon wanted to know.

Captain Harrigan looked down at his bowler, which he was twisting uneasily in his hands. "There are maniacs about, sir. Some of them wanting something else from women than their money, if you know what I mean."

Uncle Gordon nodded in reply. "I follow you, captain. And it makes me doubly nervous to think that we may be contending with a dangerous maniac."

"True, sir," the Captain agreed. "They can be a lot more difficult to catch. Anyone might be a suspect—one of your respectable male neighbors for all you know. These fellows are cunning at concealing their true natures. Only after dark and in the shadows do they attack their prey."

"I declare I shall have nightmares for a month," Aunt Jane said unhappily. "Now we are dealing with a maniac!"

"Don't let your nerves take over," Uncle Gordon urged her. "It isn't like you, and it isn't becoming."

The questioning was climaxed by the return of Henry with the two policemen. Of course, their exploration of the alleys and the street beyond had produced nothing. The criminal had seemingly escaped without leaving a single clue to his identity—except for the one Elsie knew, but which she had determined to keep to herself.

Uncle Gordon thanked the three members of the police department and presented them each with one of his best Havana cigars. Then he saw them out. When he returned he told Henry and Mary to go back to bed. Next he directed his attention to Elsie and Aunt Jane, saying firmly, "We must also go to bed and try to put this out of our minds until we have some rest."

"Go to bed," Aunt Jane said in disbelief. "How can you expect to sleep tonight, Gordon Cooper!"

Uncle Gordon looked determined. "I intend to and I will. And so will both of you. We will not help ourselves by losing our rest and becoming ill."

Aunt Jane started out toward the stairway leading up from the hall. "I'll never feel safe here again."

"Nonsense," her husband said. "This was probably one of those once in a lifetime things. There may never be anything like it happen on this street again."

"Better not," Aunt Jane said grimly as she started up the stairs.

Uncle Gordon waited for Jane to join him. "Come along, young lady," he said. "And don't forget you helped bring this about by taking a needless risk. I trust you have learned your lesson."

"I will be more careful," she said dutifully as she went to him. "I don't want to put you through anything like this ever again."

The big man gazed down at her with tender eyes. "You mean everything to your Aunt Jane and me. When I heard you were out there in danger, I wished that it had been me rather than you. I thank Heaven you came out of it safely." He kissed her tenderly on the temple and placed his arm around her as they mounted the stairs.

The more practical Aunt Jane was on the landing waiting with a bottle of white liniment in her hand. "I want to rub some of this on those marks on your throat before you go to bed," she said.

And so the eventful night came to an end. At least it did for Elsie an hour or so later when she finally fell into an exhausted sleep. But the frightening experience had taken its toll of her and she had terrifying nightmares in which a wicked looking stranger attacked her while a smiling, malevolent Countess Olga looked on.

She slept until late in the morning. By that time her Aunt Jane had telephoned Marjorie; and as a result, Marjorie and her parents were stunned and guilt-ridden. Mary brought a breakfast tray up for Elsie to have in bed while Aunt Jane looked on.

"I'm really all right," Elsie protested. "I don't need to remain in bed."

"You'll stay in bed for at least a day, or I'll call in Dr. Russell," her aunt said. "I really should do that any way."

"Don't do that." Elsie wailed, knowing that conservative old Dr. Russell would be apt to condemn her to bed rest for a week.

"Then do as I say," Aunt Jane said, sitting by her bed. "How is your throat?"

"Much better." She said, starting on her breakfast.

Aunt Jane said, "I telephoned Marjorie. Her parents feel very badly about what happened. They were shocked."

Elsie paused over her porridge. "You shouldn't have told them."

"I did what was proper. They had a right to know. They shouldn't have let you start home alone."

"Marjorie's mother was in bed, and her father hadn't arrived home," she protested.

"Well, they're sorry; and Marjorie is coming over and bringing you flowers," Aunt Jane said.

"Gracious! You'd think I were dead."

"Not your fault, you aren't! I warned you!"

"Aunt Jane, please! You know how guilty I feel."

Uncle Gordon appeared in the doorway with a smile on his broad face. "Thought I'd look in before I left for the office. You seem a lot better."

"I am," she said. "Aunt Jane won't believe me."

Uncle Gordon said, "I talked with the police just now. So far no suspects. But they'll keep looking."

"Much good that will do. It's probably some maniac living right in this block, peering out from behind closed shutters at us as we innocently walk down the street," Aunt Jane said dramatically.

Uncle Gordon shook his head in resignation. "You're making far too much fuss about it. My guess is it will never happen again." And he left the doorway to start downstairs.

"That's a man for you," Aunt Jane sniffed. "He can be brave when he knows this maniac's prey are women!"

"We don't know that," Elsie protested. "Captain Harrigan only offered that as a suggestion."

"I think he was right," Aunt Jane said firmly.

It was the start of a difficult day for Elsie. Aunt Jane was determined to punish her for her lack of caution by keeping her in bed and popping by to see her every half-hour with a new lecture. The afternoon was brightened by the arrival of a radiant Marjorie bearing a dozen red roses.

Marjorie gave the roses to Aunt Jane, who hurried off to arrange them in a vase. Then she kissed Elsie and doffed her coat and wide-brimmed hat and seated herself in the chair by the bed.

Elsie groaned, "I'm more than glad to see you. Aunt Jane is treating me alternately like a criminal and an invalid."

"She seems to be enjoying the excitement," Marjorie laughed. But she at once became serious again. "It's no joking matter. You might have been killed."

Elsie touched her throat and agreed, "No, those hands were not at all gentle!"

"And you had no warning?"

"I heard a sort of moan. Stupidly I went back down the steps to find out what it meant. I found out!"

Marjorie's eyes were wide with the horror of it all. "Was he awful looking?"

"Probably."

"You didn't even get a look at him?"

"No."

At this point in their exchange, Aunt Jane returned with the flowers; then left them to advise Mary about the evening meal.

Alone again, Elsie said to Marjorie, almost in a whisper, "I have something important to tell you. And no one else must hear me."

"Is it about Count Alexander?" Marjorie asked.

Elsie hesitated, and then said, "Yes and no," a little surprised at her friend's question.

"What do you mean?"

"It may have something to do with Alexander, but it has more to do with last night."

"I don't understand."

"You won't give me a chance to explain."

"I'm sorry."

"I lied to the police."

"You what?"

"I held back information from the police about what happened last night."

An astounded Marjorie demanded, "Why?"

"I had to."

"Go on!"

47

Elsie said, "During the struggle I managed to bite the man on one of his wrists."

"Good for you."

"He howled with anger and released me with that hand for just a few seconds. And then he came at me again letting out an angry accusation in a torrent of foreign words."

"Foreign words."

"Yes."

"What language?"

Elsie said, "He didn't speak French, German, or Italian. I have a smattering of all of them. It was something different."

Marjorie stared at her. "Such as?"

"I'm almost sure it was Russian. I don't know the language, but I've heard it spoken before."

"Russian!"

Elsie's eyes met those of her friend. "Does that suggest anything to you?"

"It couldn't have been Alexander. He's still in Russia. Or is he?"

"Probably somewhere on the way back. It wasn't Alexander."

Marjorie's attractive face took on a wise look. "I know what you're thinking. That it was Olga. That she hired someone to try and kill you!"

"Yes."

"That's shocking!" Marjorie said with a tremor in her voice. "You honestly think she'd go that far?"

"I'd say she's a very determined person," Elsie replied. "If she's made up her mind to eliminate me I think this man may have been her agent. And since he failed last night, he may try again."

"Then you must tell the police," Marjorie urged her.

She shook her head. "It's too risky."

"You can't chance not telling them."

Elsie said seriously, "I don't want to accuse the countess if she's not to blame, or even if she is. She would be able to prove her innocence, you can be sure of that. And it could put me in a bad light with Alexander."

"Who cares," her friend exclaimed. "I'm all against your romance with him anyway."

48

"I know that," she said. "But you must see I'm right. Since I do care for him."

"If you don't tell the police, I will," her friend said promptly.

"If you do I'll swear the man spoke in Italian, and it won't do any good," Elsie promised her.

"But why are you so stubborn? You admit if the countess is behind this she may try the same thing again."

"I'll be much more cautious from now on," Elsie said. "I'll not go out of my way to make myself a target."

"I think you should forget all about Alexander. From all you say Countess Olga must be a thoroughly evil person."

"We could be all wrong about her," Elsie argued. "And that man last night might have spoken Norwegian, or Danish, or who knows what. I was panic-stricken. I can't take an oath on his being Russian."

"You suspect it."

"Frankly, I do," Elsie agreed. "And when Alexander gets back, I'll tell him all about the incident and how the countess has behaved toward me."

"And you'll keep quiet about it until then?"

"Yes. I've told you. If anything happens you can tell my Uncle Gordon."

Marjorie paled. "If anything happens! You make my flesh creep!"

"Nothing will," Elsie promised with a smile. "And who knows, maybe in the meantime the criminal will be located by the police. But I'll be interested in meeting the countess again and noting her reaction."

"Saturday afternoon!" Marjorie exclaimed.

"What do you mean?"

"Mrs. Wilberforce's friend Mrs. Ryan is having her annual tea and charity sale for orphans at her home on Fifth Avenue. I'm almost positive the countess will be there. Mrs. Wilberforce takes her to all the various social events."

"Are you invited?"

"Yes," Marjorie said. "And so is my mother. But she is not well enough to attend. You can come with me in her place."

Elsie's eyes sparkled. "I'd like that! You're sure it will be all right?"

"Of course," Marjorie said. "I'll come by for you in our carriage, and we'll show up in style on Fifth Avenue. We'll see how your countess behaves when she sees you."

"I can hardly wait," Elsie said.

Elsie was impatient as the several days went by until it was Saturday. There had been no developments in the case, and everyone in the house seemed to be getting over their shock and focusing their attention on other things. Aunt Jane made a small protest about her attending the charity affair, but relented since the affair was to be held in the afternoon and Marjorie vowed not to leave Elsie's side.

Saturday was a bright early March day with warm sunshine and the streets clear of ice and snow. Marjorie came by promptly at three in a fine carriage drawn by two shining bay horses. The coachmen helped Elsie into the carriage, where she took a seat beside Marjorie.

As the carriage rolled along the cobblestoned street Marjorie laughed and said, "What price autos? I still like my horses and carriage. Much more romantic."

"I think you're right," she agreed.

They drove downtown on Fifth Avenue until they came to the brownstone mansion of the Ryans. On the bright afternoon the charity affair was being well attended as evidenced by the line of carriages and autos on either side of the street. Carriages were still predominant in a ratio of about three to one.

As they alighted from the carriage, Marjorie suddenly tugged at Elsie's arm. "I told you it would be an interesting party."

Elsie looked in the direction Marjorie indicated. Entering the Ryan house was Mrs. Gilbert Wilberforce accompanied by the Countess Olga Martynov.

◆§ *Chapter 5* §◆

MRS. JAMES RYAN was at the peak of the New York social world.

The ballroom of her mansion had been set up with tables for the tea. Despite the hugeness of the room, it was filled with chattering females in the latest styles as Elsie and Marjorie entered to be received by the poised, gray-haired Mrs. Ryan. She greeted them both pleasantly and then quickly gave her attention to the next guests in line without seeming hurried about it.

As they moved away Marjorie whispered to Elsie, "They say she was once a musical comedy actress on the West Coast. But no one has been able to prove it."

"I think she's very nice," Elsie replied.

"And Mr. Ryan has made so much money with his contracting firm," Marjorie went on. "My father claims Mr. Ryan and the mayor are cronies; so he gets all the really good contracts."

Elsie made no reply, for she had suddenly spotted Countess Olga Martynov a short distance away talking to an older, stout woman. Suddenly, she realized the emotional scars the attack had left on her and began to tremble.

"Is anything wrong? You're deathly white!" Marjorie told her in a low voice.

"I'll be all right," she said. "I see she isn't wearing mourning today." And she indicated the countess with a slight movement of her head.

Marjorie gazed down the room. "I should say not! That yellow dress is striking!"

Elsie said nervously. "At least you were right about her being here. But now that I'm this close to her I'm filled with panic."

51

"You're actually trembling."

"I know and hate myself for it. Why should seeing her make me feel this way?"

"You had a bad experience and you connect it with her. But remember you came here for a purpose: to try and catch her up. And that is what you must do. I'm not afraid of her. I'll stay with you while you talk with her."

Elsie held back. "I don't know whether I can. I know I'm being foolish. But she seems to give this whole room a sinister atmosphere. That's how I react to her."

"The room is filled with women here in the interests of a good cause. There's nothing sinister about this occasion."

She told her friend, "There is about her. Maybe I should avoid her. I can easily do it in this crowd."

"But you came here to see what she'd say and do when she met you?" Marjorie lamented.

"I know," she sighed, thinking she might faint in the heat of the room and the press of people around her. She was sorry she'd decided on the scheme.

"You can't back down now."

Elsie saw the rebuke on Marjorie's face and knew she was right. If she drew back from the arrogant Countess Olga now, she would continue to be in fear of her. She must gather her courage and challenge Alexander's possessive sister.

She took a deep breath. "All right," she said. "Stay by me."

"Depend on it," Marjorie said grimly.

Elsie walked slowly toward the countess, feeling that she was playing a role in a macabre drama of some sort. She wondered if all her suspicions about the young noblewoman were unfounded and inspired by her knowing that the countess opposed her romance to Alexander. Had the countess tried to have her murdered? Why?

Elsie halted as she reached the countess. At the same time the dark-haired woman turned so that she suddenly saw Elsie.

"Miss Cooper," she said, "you look very well this afternoon."

There had to be irony in the remark. Elsie thought the words were too carefully chosen for anything else. She forced a wan smile. "Thank you. Your dress is lovely."

"I've been doing some shopping during my stay in New York," the countess said, her keen black eyes studying Elsie.

Marjorie spoke up, "I'd say you found the right places."

Elsie said, "This is my friend, Marjorie Judson. You undoubtedly have met before."

"Yes," the countess said, giving Marjorie one of her cool smiles.

The countess turned to Elsie again. "What was this I heard about your being the victim of a street attack?"

Elsie had an idea the countess could not resist bringing the subject up. It seemed the tables were to be turned, that she was the one to be tested. She said, "Yes. A thug tried to strangle me."

"You weren't hurt badly?" the countess asked.

"No, fortunately one of the servants heard me cry out. I was rescued in time."

"But the man escaped?" the countess asked with great interest.

"Yes."

"Have they no idea who it was?"

"I was able to offer them a few clues," Elsie said, wanting to worry the countess, if she were the one behind the attack. "The police hope to catch him."

"What sort of clues?" The countess sounded suddenly uneasy.

Elsie smiled. "I'm sorry. I'm not allowed to repeat the information to anyone. I'm sure you understand."

The countess looked disappointed. But she said, "But of course. I suppose you have had letters from Alexander?"

Elsie said, "Yes, several." She was not going to lie about it.

The countess nodded. "I know. He has also written me and mentioned his letters to you."

"Did he?"

"Yes," the dark girl said. "So it seems that in spite of everything, you two are destined to be much better friends."

"I look forward to his return to New York," Elsie said boldly.

The countess showed mild surprise. "Then you don't know? You haven't heard?"

Elsie said, "I don't know what you're referring to."

"No doubt you will get a letter tomorrow," the countess said. "I received one just before I left this afternoon. I barely had time to read it before I came out. Alexander is already on his way back. He's on the *Mauretania*, which will be docking in New York on Thursday morning."

Elsie could not hide her excitement at the news. "I had no idea he'd be here so soon."

"Yes," the countess said. "Some of my friends are joining me at the dock to meet him. I'm sure Alexander would be much pleased if you were on hand to greet him when he lands. Why don't you and Miss Judson join us at the Cunard Pier?"

Surprised by this friendly move, Elsie hesitated. Turning to Marjorie, she asked, "Will you be free on Thursday?"

"Yes," Marjorie said at once. "What time?"

"The ship should dock at noon. We plan to arrive there a half-hour early, around eleven-thirty," the countess said. "It is such an interesting sight to see the ship come in and the actual docking."

Elsie said, "It's very kind of you to invite us."

"Alexander might chide me if he found I neglected to ask you," his sister said. "So we will expect you."

"I am anxious to see him again," Elsie said.

"I'm sure you are after all those letters," Countess Olga said with a wise look on her lovely face. "I'm not saying I think either of you are right in this. But obviously, you do not need my approval.

"You must forgive me for some of the things I said the other day. I was still shocked by the news of my uncle's murder. Not at all myself. I shall expect you both on Thursday morning." And with that the countess walked away.

Marjorie waited until she vanished in the crowd and then said, "I can tell you one thing. She's a sly lady."

"You noticed?"

"How could I help it? I'm almost sure she was behind that attack on you. She acted strange and all those questions."

"But she invited us to the pier to welcome the count," Elsie reminded her.

"She did that to cover up," Marjorie said with disgust.

"You think so?"

"I'm sure of it. You frightened her when you said you were able to give the police some clues."

"That did seem to upset her."

"It certainly did. It was after that she asked you to the pier."

Elsie frowned. "Perhaps I should have told the police about my suspecting the man was a Russian."

"I've said that from the start."

"It can wait now," she sighed. "Alexander will be here in a few days! It's so wonderful. I find it hard to believe. And I want to talk it all over with him first."

Marjorie said, "If he didn't want his sister to know about his letters and the romance between you two, why did he tell her?"

"He must have changed his mind. Decided it would be best to be frank. I'm in favor of it."

Her friend eyed her bleakly. "You're always too open. Your countess friend isn't given to that. His writing her about you may have driven her to the desperate act of hiring the thug."

"We can't be sure."

"I'm more sure all the time."

"Well, is it important now?" Elsie asked. "Alexander will be here to take care of the decisions. I'm sure he'll be able to handle his sister."

"I hope so. But I wouldn't count on it," was Marjorie's opinion.

"I can wait the few days left," Elsie said. "And just to spite her we will accept her invitation to the docking."

Marjorie said, "I think you'd be wise to forget your count and accept Tom's ring."

"Stop!" Elsie protested. "You sound like my aunt and uncle. Let's have some tea before everything is gone." And they went to the opposite side of the room to join the line of ladies waiting to be served.

Tom called on Elsie on Sunday, but her mind was too filled with romantic notions of her count for her to pay much attention to him. She and the young banker sat on a love seat in the living room and struggled through an hour or so of conversation. Her Aunt Jane and Uncle Gordon had discreetly gone out to make a Sunday afternoon call on an ailing friend.

Tom in his dark suit and high collar looked awkwardly young. He said, "I took collection at the morning service. I'm on the vestry committee now."

Elsie tore her thoughts from a fancy of the handsome Alexander leaning on the rail of the *Mauretania* and staring at the ocean while he dreamt of her. In a vague voice, she said, "You are what?"

Tom looked at her with mild annoyance. "You weren't listening to me! I said I've been appointed to the church vestry committee, and I soon expect to be treasurer."

"That will be nice," she said, trying to make up for her lack of attention by sounding enthusiastic about it.

The young man eyed her warily. "I don't think you care. I don't think you are interested in me anymore."

"Tom!" she reproached him as her mind drifted to that other young man on the *Mauretania* again.

Tom got up indignantly and took a stand in the center of the smallish room. He pointed an accusing finger at her. "I know when it began! When you met that Russian count!"

"Tom," she said, "we don't want to quarrel, do we?"

"I don't care," the young man said unhappily, a curly lock of brown hair falling down on his forehead. "You've had nothing but bad luck since you met him. You were almost killed by that thug!"

"It's nonsense to blame that on Count Alexander," she said.

"And the police haven't found the criminal."

"I know."

"It should be a lesson to you," Tom told her. "Make you see that you need a husband to protect you and a home of your own. You're wasting your time dreaming about someone who is thousands of miles away in Russia."

Elsie couldn't resist saying, "He's not in Russia! He's on his way here. He's arriving in New York Thursday, and I'm going to be at the dock to welcome him!"

Tom was rigid with surprise. When he finally spoke, he said, "That's a nice thing to tell me."

"There's no need to be jealous."

Tom was purple with rage. "Let me tell you just one

thing, Miss Elsie Cooper. If you go to that dock to meet him, that's the end of us! I'm finished! I'm not going to be made a fool of by that crazy Russian!"

"Tom!" she said, getting up.

"You've had my final word on the subject!" Tom declared angrily. And he dashed from the room, slamming the door after him.

Elsie went to the window to see the disgruntled young man slipping into his long overcoat as he strode down the street away from the house.

Within seconds, Mary entered the room with a tray of cookies, cocoa, and a baffled face. "I brought up Mr. Tom's favorite snack, and I arrived just in time to see him go out and slam the door."

Elsie smiled ruefully at the cook. "I'm sorry, Mary. He had one of his temper fits."

"What a pity!" Mary said, staring down at the tray.

"Never mind," Elsie said. "I'll have some anyway."

"Very well, Miss," Mary said. "I'll place the tray on the table by the divan." As she turned to leave, she hesitated to ask, "Do you think Mr. Tom will be back?"

"I don't think so, Mary," Elsie told her.

The next day, Elsie got a letter from Alexander advising her that he was leaving London and would be in New York almost as soon as she received his letter.

In this letter, Alexander devoted a good part of the message to his state of mind. He indicated that he was in a very troubled mental condition. He was honest in advising her that Moscow had been seething with unrest when he left it. He was tormented by the dreadful conditions in his country, and yet he found himself among the privileged aristocracy.

Alexander pointed out that it was ironic that he was not satisfied, like so many of the others, to take the wealth which came his way and ignore the plight of the ordinary people. Unhappily, he had been born with a conscience, and he was being torn this way and that. So buffeted was he by the storm of anarchy brewing around him that he felt he could no longer face it alone.

He needed a wife and adviser, someone to give him comfort and counsel. And he was of the opinion that she, coming from the freedom of the United States, was the ideal person to give him personal happiness and a new perspective on his situation. More than that, he was deeply in love with her, certain of this after his long weeks of thinking about her during their separation. It was his hope that she would accept his offer of marriage soon after he arrived in New York and that she would return to Russia with him as his wife when he left for home in early May.

It was unthinkable.

This was already early March, and he was blithely suggesting that within two months she become engaged to him, marry him, and leave the country! Most girls of her social position took a year or more between the period of their engagement and their marriage. It was the accepted thing. Alexander could not be expected to know that.

Also he did not have the time. He clearly had to return soon to Moscow. And it was obvious he did not wish to go without her. His confession of love had been touching, and he feared that another long separation might mean his losing her. Also he'd indicated that he was suffering great inner turmoil. He badly needed someone to share some of his personal problems. In all this there had been not a single reference to his sister!

Elsie found herself wondering if the Countess Olga and his relationship to her might be one of his personal problems? She feared this was possible, although she hoped not. It was a strange situation in which she found herself. She could not imagine marrying and leaving her aunt and uncle so soon. On the other hand, she was beginning to think of life as bleak without the companionship of the handsome count.

She knew her Aunt Jane would declare this nonsense. That it was not possible she could be so in love with a man she'd seen only one evening—and for a brief time at that. Of course, there had been the letters, but again, Aunt Jane would sniff at them and say they counted for nothing.

Elsie knew she would never agree to that. In his letters she felt Alexander had revealed more of his real self in a short while than might have taken months in person. She was sure that she knew him as well as if she had dated him for that long. She realized she had to prepare her aunt

58

and uncle for what was ahead, but didn't know how to go about it.

She waited until Wednesday evening after dinner. Then casually over her coffee, she said, "I'm going to the Cunard Line docks tomorrow. I want to see the *Mauretania* coming in. I'm going with a party to greet someone. Marjorie is coming along. I'd like to take the car, if I may."

Aunt Jane asked sharply, "Who are you going to meet?"

"Count Alexander Martynov," she said nervously. "His sister invited Marjorie and I. There'll be a lot of people there. You remember the count and countess."

Aunt Jane gave her an accusing look. "You've been receiving letters from that man!"

"A few," she admitted in a small voice.

"I knew it!" Aunt Jane declared. "You cannot trust these foreigners!"

Uncle Gordon gave her a mild smile of rebuke. "You're being silly, Jane. No harm in the girl having a few letters from that fellow. We all were young once."

Aunt Jane stood up angrily. "I will not have my niece hypnotized by the false charm of that count. If you don't care, I do!"

"Why make such a fuss?" Uncle Gordon wanted to know.

"Why this underhand business about the letters," Aunt Jane said, her face pale with rage. "Elsie is not in the habit of concealing things from us. I'm sure he encouraged her not to tell us."

"You're wrong!" Elsie protested. "You can read the letters if you like. I have nothing to hide."

"I'd like to believe that," Aunt Jane snapped. "And if you go to the dock tomorrow morning, you do so without my approval."

Before she could make any reply to this, her Aunt Jane went out of the room and upstairs. Elsie turned to her Uncle Gordon. "I didn't mean to upset her. But she's so unfair in this. I like Alexander, and I know he is fond of me."

Uncle Gordon's broad face was sad. "Did he write you that?"

"Yes."

"What else?"

"He wants me to marry him and go back to Russia with him," she said, bursting into tears and leaning hard against her uncle.

He patted her head as he had done when she was a tiny child and with the same gentleness as in those long-ago days. For all his size and gruffness, he was a kind man. He spoke to her reassuringly, "You mustn't upset yourself. Try to understand that your Aunt Jane is upset because she doesn't want to lose you. Neither do I."

"But if I'm in love with Alexander," she sobbed.

"We'll have to find that out," Uncle Gordon said. "And we'll also have to learn a few things about him. But one thing is certain, your aunt and I will never stand in the way of your happiness, however difficult it may be for us."

She looked up at him with a tear-streaked smile and kissed his cheek.

"You say his sister invited you to be at the pier?"

"Yes," Elsie said.

"So she must approve of the interest you two are showing in each other," her uncle suggested.

"I hope so," she said. "It's hard to be sure."

"I tell you what," Uncle Gordon said. "I can take a little time off in the morning. Why don't I drive you and Marjorie to the docks. I'd like to meet this count again, and it would be an ideal opportunity."

She hesitated. "I don't know."

"I won't ask him his intentions, or anything like that," her uncle said with a chuckle. "I'll just greet him. And if a party of people are there, I'm sure he wouldn't mind. There are bound to be other groups waiting for friends and relatives. I won't stand out in the crowd."

Elsie smiled at him, "I know you won't. And it probably is a good idea."

He gave a nod toward the stairs. "If I'm able to give your aunt an account of it afterward, it might make her feel better."

She said, "I'll honestly be glad to have you there. I'm still a little awed and frightened by it all."

"Then that settles it," Uncle Gordon said. "As for the

business of your marrying him, that will have to be thought about later. How long before he leaves again?"

"About two months."

Uncle Gordon shook his head. "Your Aunt Jane couldn't even decide what to put on the wedding invitations in that short a time."

"I know it isn't long," she agreed, unhappily.

"Hardly reasonable."

"But he has to leave, and he can't return for a while," she said. "I think he's very unhappy and needs someone."

Uncle Gordon's broad face showed a wry smile. "Everyone does, my dear." And he held her close to him again as he had when she came to him as a child.

Elsie slept little that night. And Aunt Jane refused to talk with her at breakfast. But Uncle Gordon was as good as his word. He drove up at the door a few minutes after eleven with Marjorie in the front seat of the car beside him.

Elsie hurried out and joined them. Marjorie was wearing a heavy coat and had a wool scarf around her broad brimmed hat and tied under her chin to keep the hat secure in case of a strong breeze and keep her warm. Elsie was dressed in an almost identical fashion, with a scarf tied around her head. Uncle Gordon was wearing a jaunty cap rather than his usual Homburg and had on a heavy tweed coat.

As they drove off, Elsie said, "I'm glad it's a fine day."

"Fine but cool!" Uncle Gordon said. "But then it is only March. We could have snow. It will be good to see the sun sparkling on the Hudson."

Marjorie gave her an excited glance. "I'll bet you are all goose pimples."

"I am nervous," she said, blushing.

Uncle Gordon said, "It shouldn't take too long to get to the Cunard Pier if the traffic isn't heavy."

It didn't. They parked the car a distance from the pier, in an area where many other cars and carriages had been left. The drivers of the carriages sat bundled well against the cold morning.

When they reached the pier, they found it busy and confused. Her uncle made some enquiries and learned that

61

the *Mauretania* was already in sight, coming in by the Statue of Liberty, at that very moment.

"Miss Cooper!" It was the familiar accented voice of Countess Olga that came to her above the clamor of voices and other sounds in the pier terminal. And the dark young woman emerged from the crowd and crossed over to her. "We've been looking for you."

"We just arrived," Elsie said. "My uncle drove us."

"How nice!" the countess said with a smile for her uncle and Marjorie. "Our party is going out to one of the open wharves to watch the liner coming in. It seems silly to wait inside the whole time in spite of the cold."

"We did come to see the ship docking," Elsie agreed.

"I'm glad you see it my way," Countess Olga said. "I will round up the others, and we will all go out together. And then return later to greet my brother."

So it was that a few minutes later Elsie found herself out at the edge of a nearby wharf with the others watching the majestic liner coming slowly up the Hudson toward them. Other parties were on the wharf, and everyone was in an excited, jovial humor. Elsie was flanked on one side by her uncle and on the other by one of the women in the party of the countess.

"It's a beautiful sight!" she enthused as she watched the ship approach.

Then, without warning, she felt her purse tugged from her hand. She wheeled around in surprise to see herself facing a middle-aged woman in a shabby coat with a shawl on her head. The woman snarled something at her and at the same time shoved her hard and ran. It had all happened in a quick second, and a shocked Elsie toppled backward to the wharf's edge!

◦§ Chapter 6 §◦

ELSIE SCREAMED as she fell backward. Her cry was taken up by the others near her as they saw her about to topple over into the water far below. Elsie hovered over the brink of the wharf for a second or two before she felt herself clutched by the arm and swung back to safety. She gazed into the face of her uncle, sobbed, and fell against him.

"You're all right!" he said, his arms protectively around her.

In the confusion, no one was watching the *Mauretania* any longer. The drama taking place on the wharf was the focus of everyone's attention. She vaguely heard cries a distance away from the street, but was still not composed enough to leave her uncle's arms.

Marjorie was there, her angry face poked close to Elsie's. "They didn't manage it this time!" she announced. "The police caught the woman in the street! She didn't get away!"

"Good," Uncle Gordon said. And he told Marjorie, "You look after Elsie. I'll go speak to the police."

Marjorie's comforting arm replaced her uncle's as her friend said, "I was sure you were going over into the water and be drowned."

Elsie nodded and lifted her head. "Let's go inside!" she said.

Then Countess Olga came up. "What a dreadful thing to happen. I'm so glad you're safe."

"Thank you."

Countess Olga went on, "I feel personally guilty. It was my idea for you to be here and even to come out on the wharf."

"You could not foresee anything like that would

63

happen," Elsie said stiffly, but wondering if it had been another planned attempt by the countess to get rid of her.

Marjorie gave the countess a defiant look. "They caught the woman. I expect they'll find out why she did it and make her pay for it."

The young countess showed a disconcerted expression. "Did they catch her? The police?"

"Yes, the police," Marjorie said grimly.

"Well, I'm glad," the countess said, although she didn't sound all that convincing. "It is time to go inside. I'm sure you won't mind that, Miss Cooper."

"No, not at all," she said. Still pale-faced and trembling, she told the countess, "Please don't mention any of this to your brother when he lands. I don't want to spoil things for him. He can hear about it later."

Countess Olga regarded her with a strange, wary look. "If that is what you'd prefer. I'll tell the others not to mention it."

"Please do," Elsie said.

The countess left them to rejoin her party. The *Mauretania* was close to the dock now, and both the great ship and the tugs were letting out signal blasts as the business of bringing the vessel to her berth was looked after. Marjorie and Elsie slowly made their way back toward the terminal. Uncle Gordon joined them at the entrance.

As they went inside, he told Elsie, "The woman is foreign."

Elsie gave him a troubled look. "What nationality?"

"Polish as well as they were able to make out," her uncle said. "She either can't speak any English, or refused to."

"Sounds familiar," Marjorie commented.

"What about my purse?" Elsie asked.

Uncle Gordon's broad face was grim under the motoring cap. "The police will have to keep it for a while as evidence. You will get it back shortly. I made a complaint against the woman and gave them the name of Captain Harrigan. Hopefully, he will look into the matter."

"Let's hope he has better luck than last time," Marjorie suggested.

"I can't imagine how the incidents could be related," Uncle Gordon said.

Elsie gave her friend a warning glance to say no more. Then she told her uncle, "I quite agree. There couldn't possibly be any link between the two attacks on me, simply coincidence."

"I would like to think it was the end of it," her uncle grumbled.

Of course, Elsie knew there was a strong reason to believe the attacks were motivated by Countess Olga and the hatred she felt for her. But she could not discuss this until she had a chance to ask Alexander's opinion about it all. Now was not the time to dwell on it. She must contrive to appear as untouched by the experience as she could and be on hand to greet the young Russian count.

Uncle Gordon found benches for his niece and her friend then went to watch for the appearance of the count.

Marjorie's pert face showed anger. "You should have told your uncle."

"What?"

"You know! The countess led you out there and then arranged for that weird old creature to attack you."

"We can't be sure."

"Elsie! I could tell from her manner! I guess she's nervous enough now. I saw her face shadow when I told her the police had captured the woman," Marjorie said.

"We'll have to let it wait," Elsie said with a weary sigh. "I don't want to think about it now."

"You must tell the count; and if he's any kind of a man, he'll end these goings-on," Marjorie said. "And if that woman tells the police who hired her, your Russian may have a bad time defending his sister."

"Please let's not go over it all," Elsie begged her friend.

Marjorie made a face. "I know! You don't want to have a scene spoil the count's return! I wouldn't care!"

The huge frame of Uncle Gordon came hovering over them. He said, "Better come along now! I think you'll be able to greet that young man in a moment or two."

Elsie rose from the bench feeling a little giddy from excitement. Everything else was forgot in the delight of knowing that in a short time she would be facing the man she had come to believe she loved. Dazed, she let herself be guided to the gate through which he would emerge, her Uncle Gordon on one side of her and Marjorie on the other.

By the time they reached the gate, Alexander had already appeared and was affectionately greeting the Countess Olga. He made a dashing figure in his long black coat with its black Persian lamb collar and a fur cap of the same curly fur. Others in his sister's welcoming party came to shake his hand. He was cordial to them and then he began looking around and saw Elsie where she waited a short distance away.

The count excused himself from his sister and the others, and removing his cap, he came toward Elsie with a warm smile on his face. Reaching her, he bowed and kissed her on the back of the hand. Then he told her, "I wanted you to be here."

Elsie was ecstatic. In Alexander's presence, she felt nothing could be too wrong. She managed, "You know my uncle and Marjorie."

"Certainly," Alexander said and greeted them both in a friendly manner. Then he said to her, "I will be going directly to our suite at the Waldorf-Astoria. But with your permission, I would like to call on you later this afternoon."

She nodded. "I will be at home."

"Around four?" the handsome count suggested.

"Fine," she said.

He gave them all another of his warm smiles and said good-by for the moment. Then he left them to rejoin the countess Olga and her party. Elsie noticed that the countess was standing awaiting her brother's return with a look of disapproval on her attractive face. Alexander took his sister's arm and moved off toward the street exit of the noisy terminal.

Marjorie gave her a surprised look. "You didn't ask if he had a good trip?"

She smiled wanly. "I didn't need to make small talk. They were waiting for him."

"And impatiently if I read the look on his sister's face," Uncle Gordon said. "We may as well leave also."

Marjorie was still looking disappointed. "After all those letters he ought to have taken you in his arms!"

"He's a Russian not a Latin," Elsie teased her. "You've been reading too many romantic novels."

They left the terminal and drove Marjorie home first. She promised her friend a full report on the count's afternoon call and assured her she was going to make no hasty decisions. Then she kissed Marjorie good-by and got back into the front seat of the car beside her Uncle Gordon.

As they drove on toward the house, he said, "I'll have to do some fancy talking to get your Aunt Jane in the mood to allow that young man to call this afternoon."

"I've promised he could," Elsie said, giving the stout man at the wheel a look of pleading.

Uncle Gordon sighed. "I was there and heard you."

"I do need to talk to him," she said. "Alone."

"Yes," her uncle said. "I know that. I'd say the best thing is to offer your aunt a shopping expedition to Bloomingdale's. I'll also try to reason with her about your count."

"Please do," Elsie said.

They had agreed to say nothing about the unhappy incident on the wharf, feeling that it would only serve to make her Aunt Jane more confused and adamant against the count's afternoon visit. But they had not counted on the efficiency of the New York police and more especially that of Captain Harrigan. By the time they reached the house a hansom cab was waiting outside.

Uncle Gordon turned the car over to Henry and asked him, "Whom do we have as a visitor?"

"Gent from the police department," old Henry said. "That's his cab by the door."

Uncle Gordon and Elsie exchanged glances. She said, "Well, that ends keeping the wharf thing a secret!"

"I'm afraid so," Uncle Gordon said as they reached the door.

Aunt Jane let them in with a satisfied expression on her face. "You must have had a fine time at the docks," was her greeting. "Captain Harrigan is in the living room waiting to talk with you both."

"No reason to make a fuss, Jane," Uncle Gordon told his wife who responded with a stony look and silence.

The balding Captain Harrigan greeted them respectfully. "Sorry you had another nasty experience, Miss Cooper," he said, standing, his bowler hat in hand.

"Yes," she said. "I seem to attract criminals."

Uncle Gordon scowled. "I can't understand it at all, captain. My niece never had any such troubles before. Then we have two incidents like this!"

"Very odd," Captain Harrigan agreed.

"Has crime become so much more common?" Uncle Gordon wanted to know.

"Far too common," the captain said. "But that is not the explanation for Miss Cooper being the victim in these two recent incidents."

"What is the explanation?" she asked, aware that Aunt Jane was standing in the background and worried that he might say something to link the Countess Olga with it. Then the trouble would be there to stay.

The balding Harrigan was serious. "I talked with the woman through an interpreter. She is Polish, you know."

"The police told me that," Uncle Gordon agreed. "What did she have to say for herself?"

"Nothing rational," the captain said. "I probably might have done better could I have conducted the questioning in English."

Uncle Gordon wanted to know, "Why did she shove my niece in such a vicious way? Elsie nearly went off the wharf because of it. Wasn't it enough to snatch her pocketbook?"

"I went into that," the inspector said. "In the woman's muddled mind it was a natural action, meant to keep your niece from coming after her."

"That makes no sense," Uncle Gordon complained.

"I know that, sir," Captain Harrigan said.

"Does the woman have any previous police record?" Uncle Gordon wanted to know.

The inspector nodded. "Yes. The officers in the precinct in which she lives say she has been arrested twice before for petty thefts. This was her boldest attempt."

Elsie said, "What will happen to her?"

"She will go to jail," Captain Harrigan said. "Nothing will prevent that. It depends on the judge how long a sentence she gets."

Elsie said, "Then it is your opinion that the woman is

not a true criminal, but some unfortunate who is a little mad?"

"You have said it very well, Miss," the captain told her. "That would be my almost exact description. Some of these older immigrants become confused and lost here in a strange city and find themselves driven to deeds they wouldn't be capable of at home."

Elsie turned to her uncle. "I think in the circumstances we oughtn't to press the charges."

Uncle Gordon shrugged. "The woman could be dangerous to others."

"That is right, sir," Captain Harrigan agreed. "The young lady need not appear in court. It would be best for you to come, sir. I will let you know the time."

"I shall be there," Uncle Gordon promised.

Captain Harrigan removed her pocketbook from his coat and said, "Meanwhile, I'm happy to be able to return this."

Elsie took it with gratitude. "I had no idea I'd get it back so soon."

Captain Harrigan showed modest pleasure. "I was able to use some small influence, Miss. The item was noted and its contents taken down. And I will ask you to sign a receipt for its return."

She signed the receipt. Uncle Gordon thanked the captain again and then saw him out. Aunt Jane came into the living room when her husband returned. She gave them both one of her bleak Yankee looks.

Aunt Jane said, "Well! I won't say I told you so."

Uncle Gordon didn't give her the opportunity to say much else, at least not before Elsie. He inquired if Mary had lunch underway and when he was answered in the positive, he led his wife into his study, shut the door behind them, and presumably had his down-to-earth talk with her.

At any rate, at lunch, they seemed to have arrived at some conclusion. Aunt Jane was restrained and said little. Uncle Gordon talked about what a fine ship the *Mauretania* was. He went on to discuss the Cunard line and the new flagship they were launching on her first trip to New York in a few weeks. This ship was the mightiest ship ever to serve on the Atlantic and was called the *Titanic*.

When lunch was over, Aunt Jane went upstairs and changed into a different dress. Uncle Gordon summoned the carriage and he winked at Elsie over his shoulder as he escorted Aunt Jane on the promised shopping spree. At least for the present, he had somehow won.

Except for the servants, Elsie was alone in the house. As four o'clock approached, she began to feel terribly nervous. She had put on a favorite green dress and been especially careful with her hair and makeup. She'd even arranged with Mary for some special food to be served later. And she checked that wine and liquor was available on the dining room sideboard.

The captain's explanation that the Polish woman who'd robbed her had a record with the authorities and was a little mad had eased her mind. She no longer blamed Alexander's sister for concocting a plot against her. And it made it seem more likely that the countess had been innocent of having any hand in the first attack on her either. For this reason she decided not to mention her suspicions to the young count. It seemed that her suspicions had been unfairly grounded and she would do well to dismiss them from her mind.

The doorbell rang at four sharp; it was Alexander. Mary answered the door and took the young man's hat and coat. Elsie led Alexander into the living room; and the moment they were alone, they were in each other's arms. Alexander's kisses were ardent and lingering.

When he did stop, he took her hands in his and smiling at her, said, "That is what I wanted to do when I saw you at the pier. But for purposes of propriety it had to wait."

"Can I get you a drink?" Elsie asked. "Some wine?"

"Just seeing you is enough for me now.

"I've dreamt of this moment," she said, her eyes shining.

"Then your answer is yes?"

She nodded. And he once again embraced her. She felt it was surely the happiest moment she had ever known. Later, they sat on the divan and discussed the more practical side of their romance.

The handsome Alexander said, "I have it all planned. We will have a simple marriage ceremony here, wherever you like."

"My aunt and uncle would want Grace Church," Elsie said.

"So it shall be! Then when we arrive in Moscow, it will still be only early spring, and we shall have an Orthodox ceremony in one of the cathedrals there. You will love it! Our weddings are very colorful with incense, candles, and the priests wearing robes of golden cloth. The church windows are masterpieces of color and the icons are the sort of art you don't see often in churches here!"

"Two weddings! And I know nothing of the Orthodox faith!"

"You will learn," he promised. "It is an offshoot of Rome. In the cathedral my family attends, and where we will be married, there is a great icon of *St. George and the Dragon*, surrounded by a set of miniatures showing the life of the saint. When we were small boys, my father used to take my brother Basil and me to look at it. He would explain the story of the saint from the various sections of the icon."

"Your brother Basil was also murdered," Elsie said. "I had tea with your sister, and she mentioned it."

A shadow crossed the face of the handsome young man. "What did she say about it?"

"Not too much. That it happened in St. Petersburg and you went to accompany the body home. That you had to keep the casket closed because his body had been so mutilated."

Alexander nodded grimly. "Basil made a noble sacrifice. We honor him in death. He dared to speak the truth as he saw it. I'm not sure I have the courage."

She was at once anxious, touching his hands with hers. "If anything should happen to you."

"I have not my brother's courage," Alexander said grimly. "And I am the only young man of the family left to carry on. So I cannot follow in his footsteps, although I might wish it."

"Is the political strife that bad?"

"It has never been worse," he sighed. "I need you to give me hope. To distract me from the horror and cruelty which fills my country at this moment. I cannot risk dwelling on the human state in Russia, nor the political injustice. It so happens I have to be part of this system which I despise."

"I will help you in every way I can," she promised.

"You will have a great palace to supervise and many servants," he told her. "You will have to preside over many family and social occasions with me. But I know I can be proud of you."

She gave him a rueful smile, "You have still to win the consent of my aunt and uncle to this marriage."

"Will they be difficult?"

"My uncle won't," she said. "I can't answer for my aunt. You will have to be tactful with her."

"I shall be all tact," he promised.

"The thing she will resent as much as the idea of my going so far away is the short time for the preparations. You plan to return late in April."

Alexander smiled. "Yes. I have a special surprise for you."

"What?"

"You have heard there is to be a new liner on the Atlantic, finer than anything yet built. She is making her maiden voyage here early in April, and we are booked to sail on her on the return voyage later in the month. I have already paid for our passage. The ship is called the *Titanic*."

"My Uncle Gordon was speaking of this new liner at lunch," she recalled.

"Everyone who travels is excited about the *Titanic*," he said. "People are offering premium prices to be on her maiden voyage to New York. And I think there will be the same pressure for tickets for the voyage back to England. That is why I booked early. It will be our honeymoon ship."

"Exciting," she said.

"Then we will cross to France and take the train from Paris. A few changes along the route and we arrive in Moscow, your new home."

She said, "What about your sister?"

"Olga?"

"Yes. She does not want me to marry you. When she had me to tea she warned me it would be bad for both of us. What did she mean?"

Alexander's handsome face darkened again. "She said that to you?"

"Yes. Why?"

He hesitated and then got up and began to pace before her, walking slowly as he attempted to explain. "Olga is a sensitive, moody girl."

"She does not seem to want you to marry me."

Still pacing slowly, he said, "It is not so much that she doesn't want me to marry you, but that she opposes my marrying anyone."

The thought of incest struck her again. In a taut voice Elsie said, "It isn't natural for her to feel that way."

He halted and stood staring at her. "I know that. It is hard to explain."

She said, "I do not feel I should marry you and go to a distant country to live in the same house with her unless I know she has changed her attitude toward me."

"She will! She must!"

"But why has she acted this way in the first place?"

Alexander hesitated. "I have always been her favorite brother. When Basil was murdered she became closer than ever to me and more possessive of me."

"To the point where she forbids you a wife?"

"She fears that one day I will suffer the same fate as my brother. She knows the desperate conditions in our country. She may feel you will not be able to stand up to the test of them. That you will decide to desert me and I will be left badly hurt."

"You think that is her reason?"

"It has to be," Alexander said. "I will talk to her and explain that nothing will change between her and me. We will be as close as ever. And in you she will gain a sister. She should be thankful."

Elsie was not sure she understood, or liked, all Alexander had said. She still feared an incestuous relationship. But she dared only hope for the best.

Mary served the lunch Elsie had ordered and wine. Then Alexander left before her aunt and uncle returned, promising to see them the following evening and to talk seriously with his sister at once.

Things turned out better than Elsie had hoped. The next day she received a warm, sisterly letter from Olga, in which the Russian girl apologized for trying to discourage the romance. Olga wrote that she found happiness in the coming marriage between Elsie and her brother. And she vowed to do all she could to help Elsie adjust to her new life in a foreign land.

Elsie thought the letter could not be more perfect. But Marjorie's response to the letter was different. "I think it is a shade too perfect. Too sweet to be the real Olga. She has claws, that girl. Like any smart feline, she has retracted them until the best moment to strike."

"If I listened to you I'd never get married," Elsie teased her friend.

"That might not be such a bad idea," was Marjorie's comment.

Alexander visited Aunt Jane and Uncle Gordon as he had promised. And it was a minor miracle that he achieved their agreement to the marriage. Aunt Jane moped and wept for a few days until Uncle Gordon warned her they had only a short time for the wedding preparations and no time at all for self-pity. Yet he began to eye Elsie wistfully when he thought she wasn't aware of it and to be much subdued.

Elsie knew it was going to be hard on them. She would miss them, but they were already talking about visiting her and Alexander in Moscow and Elsie faithfully gave her promise that she would always make an annual visit to New York.

There was the usual round of parties for the prospective bride and groom. Only the parties were crowded into an abnormally short space of time. The wedding was set for April 19 at Grace Church, and Aunt Jane was already involved in getting out invitations and making arrangements with the vicar.

Because Alexander was of the Russian nobility, it became an item for the newspapers, beyond the society columns where the round of dances, teas, and dinners at Delmonico's, Sherry's, and other places were reported. Feature stories in all the papers told about the Cinderella-like romance between the Russian count and the pretty New York girl whose heel he'd rescued at a ball. It was the sort of story loved by sentimental readers, but which annoyed Aunt Jane to a fury.

As Aunt Jane and Marjorie slaved along with Elsie addressing the wedding invitations, she fumed, "I heartily dislike the spectacle the newspapers are making of this wedding!"

Elsie looked up from her writing to give her a wry smile. "There's nothing we can do about it, Aunt Jane."

"I think you are enjoying it," Aunt Jane said primly. "Next thing we'll be characters on the comic page with 'The Yellow Kid.' "

Marjorie couldn't control her laughter. "I think Elsie would make a good addition there."

"It's not a laughing matter," Aunt Jane warned Marjorie. "All sorts of dubious strangers will be turning up at the church to try and crash the wedding. The vicar is very worried."

Elsie paid no attention to her aunt's cranky spells, since she knew it was mostly a way for the older woman to relieve her nervous tension. And she was having such a blissful time going to the many lively parties with Alexander that she couldn't be angry at anyone.

Being the guest of honor and fiancée of the charming young nobleman was a heady business. And it was to the credit of the Countess Olga that she did not try to share the spotlight of the occasions with them, remaining in the background as much as possible. Some of the papers included her in the romantic story, but only in a minor way.

But from Alexander's return his sister had behaved most properly and friendly toward Elsie. Sometimes Elsie had doubts about whether the girl's attitude was genuine, but everything was going so well that she dared not dwell on them. It seemed nothing could shadow the perfect romance and wedding.

Then four days before the wedding, on the morning of April 15, 1912, Elsie received a telephone call from Alexander. The moment she heard his voice, she sensed something was wrong.

He told her, "Darling, I have some tragic news for you."

"What?" she asked, frightened that it might have to do with Olga.

He said, "We will not make our honeymoon trip on the *Titanic*. The ship sank early this morning with a loss of more than two thirds of the passengers and crew. Struck an iceberg off Newfoundland. My cousins were passengers aboard on their way to the wedding. I don't know whether they were lost."

The shadow had fallen.

Chapter 7

ELSIE TRIED TO BLOCK the tragedy from her mind, to think that it had no bearing on her wedding. But she soon knew this was untrue. From the moment the news of the harrowing sea disaster broke, it cast a deep shadow over everything. News of the survivors came scantily and when the list of the drowned became known, many of her friends' families were affected.

Elsie began to wonder whether it was some kind of an omen, a sign that her marriage was doomed to disaster. She didn't dare betray any of these doubts to her aunt or uncle. And she didn't say anything to Marjorie either.

A hurried conference was held at Elsie's house, with Alexander and his sister present. Aunt Jane told them, "If you think we should, there is still time to cancel the ceremony."

Count Alexander frowned, "The invitations are all out. It would be impossible to notify everyone. And I want the marriage to go on."

"Our cousins were not known to anyone here," Countess Olga said. "It is a sad ordeal for us, but no one else will be touched. And those who have lost someone will simply not attend the ceremony."

Uncle Gordon gave the count a questioning glance. "What about your passage to England?"

"I've talked with people at the Cunard Line," Alexander said. "They can book us on the *Lusitania* which sails a day later than the *Titanic* was scheduled to leave."

Aunt Jane showed concern. "I hate to think of you taking a liner after what has happened."

Alexander said, "A disaster like that of the *Titanic*'s sinking may never happen again. The *Lusitania* is a fine ship, and I very much doubt if she will ever see the bottom of the Atlantic."

"I sincerely hope not," Uncle Gordon said. "I'm sure there must have been negligence on someone's part in the *Titanic* business. The news suggests they deliberately ignored the warnings of icebergs."

Aunt Jane sighed. "At least it has taken the interest of the press in another direction. We should be able to get through the wedding without a lot more drivel being written about a royal romance."

Countess Olga said, "I agree. We will benefit from that."

"You have our deep sympathy in the loss of your cousins," Uncle Gordon told the two young Russians. "They were a young married couple, weren't they?"

"Yes," Alexander said. "I imagine Irena refused to leave her husband; otherwise, she would have been in one of the boats picked up by the rescue ship. They were deeply devoted."

Elsie said, "So it is agreed. We go on as well as we can."

Alexander nodded. "Yes. It means our wedding will be smaller and quieter, but that may not be all bad."

For the most part, smiles were the order of the day. Count Alexander looked handsome, and the red-bearded colonel came up from Washington to act as best man to replace Alexander's cousin.

The reception was held at Elsie's uncle's club on Thirty-sixth Street. And she and Alexander spent their wedding night in a special honeymoon suite at the Waldorf-Astoria. It was a night of blissful happiness for her, and she temporarily forgot all the tragedy that had threatened her and Alexander becoming wed. He proved himself a gentle, but passionate lover; and any doubts she may have had about her new husband and his sister were forgot. She had no fear that at this moment he loved anyone but her alone.

Countess Olga had been sad and reserved during the day of the ceremony and afterward, but Elsie attributed this to the Russian girl's sadness at the loss of her cousins. Both Alexander and Olga had attended a small, private service in one of New York's Eastern Orthodox churches

the morning after the drowning of the two had been officially confirmed.

Then it was the morning of the sailing of the *Lusitania*,
a time for frantic embraces and tearful exchanges with her
Aunt Jane and Uncle Gordon, a long moment spent
promising to write Marjorie faithfully and scattered fare-
wells to many others. Then Elsie boarded the great liner
with its four funnels, which so resembled the sunken *Titanic*. Much of the celebration and gaiety usually shown at
these embarkations was missing on this cool, sunny morning. People were still shocked by the tragedy of the sister
ship.

Elsie and Alexander, along with Olga, took their places
at the rail of the majestic ship and waved to those on the
dock until the ship was too far out in the Hudson for
them to see the wharf.

The handsome Alexander turned to her and said, "Well,
my dear, our journey begins."

"I wish we could be in Moscow tomorrow," she said.

Countess Olga, standing at her elbow, showed a wry
smile on her lovely face. "Never fear, you will get there
soon enough."

The voyage proved pleasant and uneventful. Elsie felt it
was an extension of their few honeymoon days at the hotel. The only thing that bothered her was the way Alexander's sister began to show her possessiveness of him again.
At first Elsie tried to ignore this, but it continued until she
had to make a small protest to her new husband.

She did not mind Olga having her cabin next to them,
her dining at their table, or her remaining with them all
during the days and many of the evenings. If they went to
the ballroom to dance, Olga came. It was the same when
they played shuffleboard on deck; Olga almost always
managed to be present.

What did upset her was that on several occasions, Olga
came to Alexander and requested that she have a moment
alone with him for discussion of some personal problem.
Each time this happened Alexander excused himself and
left Elsie alone in her deck chair or in her cabin and went
off for a conference with his sister.

Irked to the point that she could remain silent no longer, Elsie challenged her new husband one evening as he re-

turned to their cabin after being with his sister for an hour or so.

Elsie halted in her dressing for dinner to face him in her robe and ask, "What was it this time?"

The dark, sensitive face of the handsome Alexander showed guilt, and he apologized. "Olga is very disturbed about something at home, a family thing. She doesn't want you to be bothered about it. We've been trying to find a solution to the problem."

"I can't help feeling shut out," Elsie told him. "I think she is making these problems up to take you from me." She did not dare speak of the suspicions she'd harbored about them, still hoping they weren't true.

Alexander came to her and took her gently by the arms. "I promise you that she urgently needs my help. I cannot go into the matter without her permission. You must trust me. It is silly to be jealous of my sister."

"I'm not jealous. It's just that I feel she has always been against our marriage and that already she is trying to separate you from me," Elsie explained.

Alexander showed astonishment. "I can't believe you could entertain such childish notions."

"I don't see it as childish."

"Olga has always depended on me. She has no one else to turn to."

"What is this dreadful problem that takes so much of your time?"

"I can't tell you," he said with an unexpected firmness. "I have to ask you to have faith in me and overlook this whole affair."

She looked up at him wistfully. "You know I don't want us to quarrel."

"Then we won't," he said with a smile, "for I certainly don't want it."

"Try and discourage her from these secret interviews," she said. "Surely you must have talked whatever it is out by now."

He sighed. "I will do my best. You should make other friends among the passengers. Then if we're apart for awhile you won't miss me."

"I don't mind being alone," Elsie said. "It's just that I feel Olga is trying to exert an undue influence over you."

"And that is nonsense," he said. "But I will try to avoid this sort of thing for the rest of the voyage. I didn't realize you were so upset about it."

"I am," she said.

He kissed her. "Worry about it no more. Finish dressing and let me escort the most beautiful woman on the ship to dinner."

Elsie found it hard not to accept Alexander's explanations, especially when she wanted everything to go well. But something was wrong. What was this mysterious relationship between her husband and his sister?

They were all three seated at the captain's table. The various stories about the romance in the press had done its work and Elsie was conscious of stares and whisperings whenever they walked through the main dining salon on their way to the table. Several people had approached both Elsie and her husband on deck with an awed excitement and asked for their autographs. In all cases Alexander had refused the request.

To Elsie he had complained, "We are not to be bothered in this way. It would never happen at home. I'm not a theater count willing to greet his admirers at the stage door."

The captain was well aware of Alexander's desire for privacy and saw that it was carried out. While he had them at his table, he treated them with deference and asked no special liberties. The other guests at the table had apparently been similarly advised by some proper authority and also behaved most discreetly.

The main dining salon was reminiscent of a fine hotel room with elaborate wood paneling, great chandeliers that never seemed to sway regardless of the motion of the vessel, a string orchestra, and impeccable service in the pure white linen and sparkling silver tradition. The food also was excellent.

On this particular evening Elsie was surprised to find the elderly Oxford don who had normally sat on her right absent and a young, brown-haired man with a shrewdly intelligent yet kindly face seated next to her. He made a handsome figure in his dinner jacket.

The captain at once rose and told the group at his table, "I know you will be sorry to hear that Professor Baker has suffered a minor heart seizure and at the doctor's advice will remain in his cabin for the balance of the voyage. Any messages you may care to send him will be much appreciated, I'm sure." He paused and smiled at the young man. "May I now introduce Mr. Ralph Manning, an overseas correspondent for the Hearst Press, and presently on his way to act for them in Moscow." After this, the captain introduced each of them to the young man.

When the introductions were over and they were served dinner Ralph Manning smiled at her and said, "I feel myself extremely fortunate to be seated next to you, countess."

Elsie smiled. "I haven't become used to the idea yet. I can assure you I don't feel like a countess."

"But you are," the young man said.

"I still have the average American's wariness about titles," she told him. "I'm happy to meet you because we are also going to live in Moscow. My husband's family palace is there."

"I have seen the Martynov Palace," Ralph Manning told her. "You will have a beautiful home with a view of the river and more servants than any mansion in New York, if that's any satisfaction to you."

She laughed. "As long as I'm not responsible for them."

The young man glanced across the table where the Countess Olga was engaged in a serious conversation with an older man, an American stockbroker. He said, "I think the Countess Olga will be required to turn over the reins to you."

"I won't insist on it."

"I have an idea the count will. It will be expected."

"Have you spent much time in Russia?" Elsie asked.

"Several years."

"It will be all new to me."

"You will be exposed to the better side of things," he told her.

Her eyebrows lifted. "You're telling me that there is another side to the country?"

"Yes."

"Even my husband says that Russia is in a chaotic state," she said worriedly.

"Moscow is the hub of Russia, but no longer the capital;

the tsar rules from St. Petersburg. Yet Moscow still is the greatest city, and the pulse beat there lets you know what is happening in the rest of Russia. This is why my employers wish to have me there."

"I shall have a second wedding when I reach Moscow," she said. "In the Orthodox church."

The young man nodded. "Then you will in truth be a countess. Moscow might be called another Rome. It is the heart of the Orthodox church. People of every class worship in the great cathedrals. I'm always fascinated by the golden icons glittering in the soft lighting."

She stared at him. "You find Russia very colorful then?"

"Colorful but tragic," he said. "The inequities of our own country are much more obvious in Russia. The moujiks live in spartan silence waiting for the next onslaught of the tax collector, meanwhile the wealthy and noble ride by swathed in furs in their troikas. If the moujiks rebel, groups of Cossacks ride down on them and use their whips and sabers until the rebellion is crushed. There is little justice for the poor and less hope."

"You sound bitter."

"I can't help it," Ralph Manning said with a sober look on his pleasant face.

"I'm sure that my husband, although of the nobility, shares your concern for the average people."

Ralph Manning nodded. "I'm aware that the Martynov family is unique in its class. You may be happy about that. They treat their servants well and have spoken up against increased taxes and other injustices. They are a different example of the nobility."

"I'm glad of that," she said. "I hope to help Alexander bring about more reforms for his country."

"There will have to be many, or the pot will boil," the young newspaperman said. "Mr. Hearst is extremely worried about the anarchists and feels they may easily succeed in destroying the present government and taking over."

"What do you think personally?"

"I hope he is wrong," the young man said. "But all I see and hear makes me more fearful that he is right. With the situation as explosive as it is now, it would take only a tiny flame to ignite it."

"So my husband says," she sighed.

"I must try and get an interview with him," the young reporter said.

She glanced in the direction of Alexander, who was seated beside the stockbroker's wife and nearer the captain. "Have you ever talked to him?"

A strange look crossed the young man's face. "Once. When his brother Basil was murdered."

"I've heard about that."

"He refused to discuss the matter with me," Ralph Manning told her. "So the encounter was brief."

"I'm sorry. I know he was very upset about his brother's murder. You should be able to understand that."

"I was fully sympathetic. But I also felt, because Basil had been something of an individual, there could be a good story for our papers. Your husband didn't agree."

She sat back for her dessert to be served by the silent and efficient steward. "My husband didn't want his brother written about."

"He would not answer my questions concerning the murder, or what Basil had been doing in St. Petersburg," the young newspaperman said. "Perhaps it was the wrong time. Very often we lose a good story because of a mistake in approach."

"I'm certain that must have been it," she said, beginning the dessert.

Elsie's meeting with Ralph Manning helped her to enjoy dinner and feel less upset. She made an attempt to introduce Alexander to him, but her husband was busy talking with the captain. The introduction, therefore, had to wait. But later, when the couple was in the ballroom at a table near the oval dance floor, Elsie told Alexander about the young man.

Alexander showed a shadow of annoyance. "I wish you wouldn't discuss me with members of the foreign press."

Mildly surprised, she said, "It wasn't intended to be a discussion of you. I knew he had been in Russia before, and I asked a few questions of him in a social way."

"How did my brother come into it?"

"He said that he had tried to interview you once concerning your brother's murder."

Her husband scowled. "I was tormented at the time."

"I suggested that."

"What else did he say about Basil?"

"Nothing other than that he was a unique member of the nobility and that the Martynov family was much more generous to those on its estates than most. That you were generous with the poor."

Her husband's mood remained suspicious. "I would say that he was buttering you up to get at me. Pry us both with questions. And as for Basil, why not let the dead rest."

"I'm certain he was trying to be nice to me," she said unhappily. "You don't approve of anyone I meet, it seems. I felt he might make an excellent escort and dancing partner for Olga. It might make her less demanding of you."

"So that's it!" Alexander said coldly. "May I remind you that Olga is a countess, a woman of position. I do not care to have her in the company of a mere reporter."

She stared at him in astonishment. "You can't be serious!"

"I am."

"This is a fine, clever young man representing an important newspaper chain. In America he would be received anywhere."

"My sister is not an American," was her husband's cutting reply. "And in a sense, neither are you since your marriage to me. You must become aware of your position."

Elsie could not help becoming angry. She grasped the stem of her champagne glass so viciously she might have broken it in an attempt to control her emotion. "I am an American and I always will be. Please remember that. And I cannot share such snobbery toward one of my fellow countrymen."

Evidently her husband saw that he had gone too far. He at once smiled and leaned across the table in a placating mood. "Come, my dear, we are quarreling about nothing. I'm sorry I did not choose my words better."

"You ought to be." She was still angry.

"It is only that people in my position have been plagued by the press, especially the foreign press," he said. "And Olga is not in a good frame of mind to meet young men; she is very worried about her own future."

"Does she fear I will take her position as head of the palace? If so, she needn't worry."

"That is not her concern. It is a more personal thing that I cannot talk about," he said easily, returning to his old ploy of avoiding talking about his relationship with Olga. "Come, the orchestra is playing, let us dance."

So they danced and had more champagne and became more like true lovers again. Then Olga joined them at the table and sat there quietly for a few drinks and a dance or two with her brother. Elsie watched them together on the floor and again wondered about the two. But the rest of the evening went well, and the couple said good night to Olga at the door of her cabin, with everyone happy.

Elsie felt that her new husband always made the most passionate love to her following some sort of difference they might have. And so it proved again tonight. When she lay back delightfully weary and satiated from his caresses she once again felt that she had been unjust to him in her dark suspicions. It was merely that she did not understand him.

She fell asleep shortly, but it was then that her subconscious took over and she descended into a torment of dreaming. She had nightmares about the attacks on her in New York, she experienced the horror of the near fall from the wharf; and she always was aware of the slender, black-robed, sullen-looking Countess Olga watching all these attempts on her life. Olga, the dark shadow in the background, directing the threats against her.

She awoke to the silence and darkness of the luxurious cabin in a sweat! She reached out to touch her husband, thinking to find solace and perhaps be able to return to sleep. But no one was at her side, only emptiness. Shock followed fear.

"Alex!" she called out.

There was no reply. Next she swiftly threw back the bed clothes and went to the small bathroom. The door swung open, no Alex. Then she noticed that some of his clothing was gone. He had dressed and left the cabin while she slept.

Was he in Olga's cabin? All the suspicions of incest came rushing back into her mind.

At Olga's cabin, Elsie pressed the buzzer and knocked

on the door. Then she waited impatiently, wondering what was going on in there at this moment.

She pushed the buzzer again and was about to knock on the door more furiously when it suddenly opened and Olga appeared in her nightgown. Olga did not not seem at all sleepy, or even too surprised that she should be at her door at this past midnight hour.

Olga stared at her. "What do you want?"

"Where is Alex?" she demanded.

"Isn't he with you?"

"No. I woke to find myself alone in my cabin."

Olga hesitated. "You must not be concerned."

"I am concerned," she said firmly. "Is he in there?"

"In here?" Olga repeated. "Why should you think that?"

"You're always seeking him out and taking him away with you," Elsie accused the other woman.

Olga showed the first signs of being upset. She made a move to close her cabin door. "Good night!"

Elsie was too quick for her; she pushed her way through the door and into the cabin, the mate of the one she and her husband occupied. There was no sign of anyone in the bed. She then went to the bathroom, which also was empty. She now began to think she might have acted too hastily. She halted in the center of the stateroom.

"He isn't here!" she said in surprise.

Olga's look was as cold as her tone. "I said not."

"But where can he be?"

"I have no idea."

Elsie stared at her. "Why would he go out at night and not let me know?"

"Perhaps he felt ill. Decided a stroll on deck would do him good," Olga suggested. "There could be any number of reasons. Alexander is not used to having to account to a wife."

Elsie felt this was a barbed accusation. She said, "He owes me the consideration of not frightening me in this fashion."

"He probably thought you wouldn't wake up."

"But I did," she said.

Olga's tone was close to a sneer. "And you decided he had come to me?"

Her cheeks burned. "I'm sorry," she said in a low voice and hurried to the door.

Olga spoke out, halting her. "You have many things to learn. My brother is much different from the man you think! He is upset and full of dark moods. You will do well to remember that and not be shocked by whatever may happen."

"Thank you," Elsie said bitterly. "I'm sorry I disturbed you." And she went back out into the corridor and closed the door after her. She at once heard the lock on the other side of the door snap into place. And this made her worry whether she had searched the cabin thoroughly enough. She had not bothered with the clothes closet, or under the bed; she had not wanted to appear ridiculous. Still, he well might have hidden himself in either of those places.

She went back to her own cabin hoping he might be there, but he wasn't. There was no question of sleep now. She stood considering her next move for a moment or two. And it seemed to her that Olga had been telling her the truth. Perhaps Alex had gone up on deck. She crossed to the porthole and drew back the curtain to see there was a moon, and the sea looked calm. But it must be very cold on deck.

It took her ten minutes to dress warmly in her heavy coat and tie a scarf around her head. All during this time, she listened for her husband. But he did not return. So as a last desperate move she decided to try and find him on deck. If he were in a depressed mood, he might need her.

She made her way up a gangway and then out onto the deck. She was at once more aware of the gently rocking movement of the great liner. The deck seemed completely deserted. A ghost place! She shivered as she glanced out at the waves with the moon reflected on them. They looked icy cold! She could not help thinking of how the other great ship, the *Titanic*, had sunk in water like this and of the chorus of moans from the hundreds cast into the freezing waters to die almost at once. Life belts were no protection from the cruel, icy sea.

Elsie forced herself to dismiss such thoughts and start a search of this main deck. If he were not here, she would have to try the one above. Or one of the main cabins where people gathered. She did not think the lounges were kept open all night; at least she doubted that they sold liquor in the small hours, although the bars must shut very late.

The cold was getting to her. She tightened her coat about her and started down the long section of abandoned deck. She had never realized what a haunted sort of place the empty deck of a great liner could be at this hour of the night. She glanced up and saw the light in the bridge where the liner was being controlled. High above her in the dark blue of the night loomed the giant funnels.

She felt small and insecure. She glanced at the railing and thought how easy it would be for a would-be suicide to ease himself over it and be lost forever! Or what a prime choice for a murder. With no witness around it would only take a moment for the killer to swing his victim overboard. Would the watch on the bridge notice and sound an alarm? She doubted it. And would it help the unfortunate victim if such an alarm were set off?

Not likely. The cruel sea would have devoured its victim by that time. She shuddered again and told herself she could not indulge in such grim thoughts. She was simply terrifying herself needlessly when she needed all her wits to try and find her missing husband.

Olga had suggested the deck. And this set off more thinking. Suppose she had purposely done so to get her out there in this deserted area. Get her out here to become an easy victim.

It was at this moment Elsie heard footsteps behind her. She almost cried out. But with a gasp of fear, she began to hurry along the expanse of empty deck, which seemed to loom endlessly ahead. The footsteps seemed to gain on her, but she didn't dare look over her shoulder! She didn't dare!

Chapter 8

ELSIE KEPT RUNNING down along the deserted deck, the sound of her heels mixing with the relentless clattering of the shoes of her pursuer! Breathlessly she reached a turning point from which she could make the passage to the other side of the ship. Without hesitating she wheeled around it, made her way along a shadowed, narrow corridor, and emerged on the opposite deck. She now made a right turn and found herself racing along in the direction from which she'd come!

All at once she saw the solitary figure of a man coming toward her in a long, dark coat. She halted in her panicky flight and leaned against the cabin trying to catch her breath as the figure drew nearer. She did not know whether it might be friend or foe, but surely it was not her phantom pursuer. She had somehow left him behind.

The man came up to her and to her relief it was Ralph Manning. He was wearing a heavy coat and a black, peaked cap and his pleasant face showed some concern as he recognized her.

"What are you doing out here alone at this hour, countess?" he wanted to know.

"You may well ask," she said grimly. "You're the first person I've encountered on all this wide expanse of deck." She did not include the phantom who had chased her down the other deck.

He said, "Very few venture beyond the enclosed deck at night," he said. "I think they miss something. I enjoy the solitude and the night air. On the other hand it is rather lonely for an unaccompanied woman."

She was still breathing heavily. "I'm glad we met."

"So am I," the young man said, studying her with a concerned look on his nice face. "You'll excuse my saying it, but you appear to have had some fright."

"You are perceptive."

"Not especially so, although it is supposed to be part of my business," Ralph Manning said.

She hesitated and then decided to be completely truthful with him. It struck her that it was time she had found a friend in whom to confide. This young American was going to be stationed in Moscow and might be someone whom she could turn to if the romance she had embarked on so hopefully should turn into a grim disappointment.

She said, "I wakened and found my husband missing."

Ralph Manning said promptly, "I saw him on deck."

She was at once interested. "How long ago?"

"Perhaps five minutes ago," he said. "Actually, it was on the other deck. We passed and nodded to each other. He was wearing a coat just as I am and I intended to stop and chat with him for a few minutes. You don't get too many companions at this hour. But he did not appear to be in a friendly mood. He kept straight on, showing no desire to chat with me."

"And?"

"Perhaps a moment later I heard him speaking to someone else behind me. From a fair distance behind me. I turned to see who it was, but by that time they had gone inside. The deck was empty."

Embarrassed but determined to find out all she could, she forced herself to ask, "Did he meet a man or a woman?"

The young man shrugged. "I wish I could answer that. But they only spoke for a moment in low voices. Your husband's voice overshadowed the other one. I can't be positive, but I'd say it was likely a man."

She looked at the young newspaperman with consternation. "But why would my husband leave his bed in the middle of the night to come up here and meet some stranger?"

"Sorry. I wouldn't know that."

"He should have at least wakened me and let me know," she went on with growing concern.

Ralph Manning said, "It may be that he decided you would not waken. That he could go out on whatever errand he had in mind and not have to explain it to you. By the time you were awake he would be back in bed."

"I think it very strange."

"I agree it is worrisome. But I'm sure he's all right. He went somewhere inside, countess."

Almost irritably, she told him, "I wish you wouldn't go on calling me countess. I feel you're talking to someone else."

He showed bewilderment. "What do you want me to call you?"

"My name is Elsie," she said. "We're both about the same age, and I hope we're going to be friends. Call me Elsie."

He smiled. "Delighted to. But then you must call me Ralph."

"Very well, Ralph," she said. "I'm being completely honest with you in this, because I think I may need a friend before or after I reach Moscow. I'm troubled by the behavior of my husband and his sister, Countess Olga."

Ralph said, "The Martynovs are not easy to understand."

"Why do you keep harping on that?"

"Because it is so," he said gravely.

She gave him an ashamed look. "I should have told you before. When I first saw you I had raced across from the other deck. Someone was chasing me."

The young newspaperman at once registered alarm. "Chasing you?"

"On my heels!"

"Who?"

"I don't know. I was afraid to take the time to look back. I wound up in a panic, just racing on, until I met you."

"There was no one else in sight when I first saw you."

"No. Whoever it was didn't cross over to this deck. I lost them when I came here."

He stared at her. "Could it have been your husband?"

"Why wouldn't he identify himself?"

"True," he agreed. "That's very odd."

"Especially since you claim you saw him on the other deck a few minutes earlier."

"Yes."

She sighed. "I went to his sister's cabin. It is directly adjoining ours. She seemed surprised at my wakening her and didn't give me any suitable explanation of where he might be, although she did hint he could be on deck."

"Did she say why?"

"I think she mentioned that he often had insomnia and went out to get the air."

"And so you followed?"

"Yes. I was worried about him," she said.

"Normal enough," he agreed.

She looked down with a tiny shudder. "My marriage has already turned out differently from what I expected. Alex seems so confused and moody most of the time. And he goes away with his sister, sometimes for fairly long periods. The two of them seem to be conspiring and planning against me. I feel like an outsider."

"That is too bad," Ralph said to her. "But you must keep one thing uppermost in your mind. You have married a Russian. These people are not quite as we are in their customs. Also at this particular time the Russian nobility have grave problems to contend with. They are actually fighting for their existence."

She eyed him seriously. "You're saying that Alex and his sister may be discussing things which I would not understand?"

"Precisely."

"But as the wife of the head of the Martynov family, I will have to learn these things."

"No doubt you will," Ralph said. "But your husband may not think the proper moment has arrived for this."

She sighed. "I'm confused and frightened."

"Don't allow your imagination to run away with you," her new friend advised her. "It will surely work out all right. I have watched the count at the dinner table. There can be no doubt he is in love with you."

"Thank you," she said. "Have you also watched the Countess Olga? What do you think her feeling is toward me?"

The young man shrugged. "She is a very hard person to fathom. I would not venture a guess as to her thoughts."

"Nor would I," she said. "I think she hates me."

"Why?"

93

"Because she has a strange, possessive love for her brother."

Ralph Manning nodded slowly. "There again we come back to the strangeness of the Martynovs. There are many eccentrics among the Russian nobility. It is probably the most decadent in Europe."

She gave another tiny shudder. "I'm already beginning to fear life in Moscow."

"You mustn't jump to conclusions," the young newspaperman warned her. "Give yourself a chance to adapt to these people and their country. Do not think because they speak English so well they are just like you and I."

"I'm discovering that."

"You seem cold," he said. "Let me escort you back to your cabin."

"I do not want to be a nuisance," she protested.

He smiled, "My dear Elsie, we are now friends on a first name basis; there is no imposing on true friends. Come along." And he let her link her arm in his.

She thought how lucky she had been in meeting him. And how important he might be in her new life. He was one of her own who in the course of his profession had made a study of Russia and things Russian. He could guide her through the treacherous shoals which surely lay ahead. For some reason she had full trust in him, although he was little more than a new acquaintance. She felt they had been friends for a long while.

As they walked along the empty deck on their way to her cabin, she said, "It is eerie out here at this hour."

"Strange," he agreed.

"We are to reach England the day after tomorrow, they promise."

"Yes."

She glanced up at him. "Will you be in England long?"

"I will check with the Hearst Bureau in London for further briefing," he told her. "I'm most directly answerable to the London office. Then I'll cross to France and take the train from Paris to Moscow."

"That is exactly our plan," she said. "At least I mean we'll be spending a few days in London and then taking the Paris to Moscow train. Alex mentioned having to look after some business in London."

"The Paris-Moscow Express is an excellent one," Ralph told her. "You will wine and dine as well as on this ship and your private compartment will be comfortable. Where are you staying in London?"

"The Savoy Hotel."

"Very grand," the young newspaperman said as they went inside to go down the gangway and walk the length of the corridor to her stateroom. "My news syndicate doesn't encourage such expensive hotels. But I'm staying at a very good one nearby, called the Picadilly, in the center of the theater district. You must see some theater while you are in London. They have the best."

"I hope I can," she said.

"I'm sure your husband will want to take you. And if he cannot find the time, because of his business appointments, I'd be most happy to escort you and Countess Olga to a performance."

"You are very kind," she said. For a moment she had forgot it was in the small hours of the morning and she was still in search of a missing husband.

They reached her cabin door and the young newspaperman removed his cap and said, "I shall look forward to seeing you tomorrow. Our deck chairs are rather close together, and I shall not be afraid to approach you in the future."

"Please don't be," she told him. "And thank you."

"My pleasure," he said. And then in a rather mocking, yet pleased tone, he added, "Elsie."

She smiled. "Good night, Ralph."

He went on down the corridor and she tried the cabin door. It was not locked although she was sure she had locked it before leaving. Still, she had been in a troubled mental state and might have overlooked it. She turned the handle and slowly opening the door went inside. The cabin was still empty.

She stood there, trying to decide what to do next. As she did so, she heard the door open and turned to see Alex come in. He was wearing his dark coat with a cape and his Homburg hat, just as Ralph had described him.

Alex came across the cabin to face her. In an even voice, he said, "What are you doing out of bed and dressed?"

"You can ask that? Where were you?" she challenged him.

He removed his hat and coat casually and threw them on a chair. "I took a stroll on deck."

There was something in his manner which she did not understand. He was standing there cold and aloof, nothing like the lover of a few hours earlier. That man and the one she faced now might have been different people who simply bore a slight, outward resemblance to each other.

She said, "You should not have gone out without telling me."

"Why?"

"You are my husband. I expect it. I wakened and was frantic about you."

The count's face was expressionless. "You behaved most stupidly. I understand you awakened Olga and bothered her for no purpose."

"She told you that?"

"Yes."

"I did not consider it to no purpose," she rebuked him. "I was worried about your safety."

"I am a grown man and capable of taking care of myself. I am also used to making my own decisions as to what I do in the day or night. You must learn that."

"You gave me a bad time."

"Your own fault. You should have remained in bed and gone back to sleep."

"I couldn't."

"Then you were wrong."

She said plaintively, "If you care for me, you must understand. I dressed and went up on deck to find you. I was pursued by some phantom, and I don't know what would have happened if I hadn't run into Ralph Manning."

Alex smiled coldly and went to her and said, "Since it is not likely you will be involving yourself in any more nocturnal adventures tonight, I shall help you off with your coat." And he did, taking it. As she undid the scarf on her head and passed it to him, he said, "So you and this Manning fellow are becoming fast friends."

"He rescued me tonight. I'm grateful."

"I'm sure you are," Alex said as he went to the closet

and hung up their outer clothing. When he returned he said, "Don't become too close to him."

"Why not?"

"He is assigned to Moscow by the Hearst syndicate. Those fellows are always looking for stories. He might eventually do us some harm."

"How?"

"Moscow is a place of gossip these days," he warned her. "A lot of the things which are happening should not be reported in the American press."

"I disagree with you there," she said stoutly. "I intend to have Ralph as a friend, and I hope you will also be friendly toward him."

"If his behavior allows it," the count said. "I think you should try and put a curb on your too-vivid imagination. You seem to always be in trouble because of it. There was the incident when you claimed to be attacked in the street, your near-accident on the deck, and now this. You are not a child."

She was near tears. "You have no thought for me at all."

"On the contrary," he said, embracing her. "I think a great deal of you. But you must learn to be strong."

"You turn to your sister before me," she cried.

"Petty jealousy on your part," he reproved her. "You must settle your nerves and go to bed. Think nothing of all this."

She leaned close to him, felt the warmth of his arms and his body against her. Knew that she still loved this strange, aloof, young man, but did not understand him. She asked, "How can you expect that of me?"

"I do," he said. "I have my own habits and my own reasons. Whatever I may do, there is a reason for it. I ask you to remember that."

"I love you," she said.

"And I love you," the young count told her. "But I have other grave responsibilities beyond those I have to you. I own a great estate on which many families depend. I am involved in the sickness which is Russia's today."

"Whom did you go out to meet?"

"I cannot tell you," was his firm reply. "I ask that you have faith in me. And I in turn demonstrate my own confidence in you. You may have this newspaper chap as a friend; he may be good for you. At least he can tell you something about what to expect in Russia. And he will be one of your own people to turn to when you are lonely."

She leaned back in his arms and studied his handsome face. "You are being most generous. Is it true generosity or that you have ceased to care for me?"

"How can you think that?" he asked, his face softening as he kissed her once more.

So the lover she knew in him returned and remained thoughtful and considerate of her during the following morning. The sun was shining, the sea calm; and when Ralph Manning came and asked her to join him in a game of shuffleboard, it was Alex who encouraged the idea.

Alex at once got up from his deck chair and said, "I think that an excellent plan. Elsie becomes bored and mopes, Mr. Manning. You shall keep her busy while I attend to writing some urgent letters."

Ralph smiled, "I would consider it a great privilege."

She glanced down the line of deck chairs and saw that the one occupied by the Countess Olga was empty. She turned to her husband and asked, "Where is Olga?"

He eyed her with what seemed sardonic amusement as he said, "She complained of being sleepy. I understand she had a broken night's rest last night. She has gone below to enjoy a nap."

"I see," she said, knowing that he had gone beyond giving a reply to her question. He had managed to insert a reprimand for her having wakened Olga in the night.

Ralph led her to the shuffleboard area where they found an elderly British couple waiting to be their opponents. They played a long game and won. After which Ralph suggested they go to the forward lounge and have a cocktail before lunch. Since Alex was nowhere in sight and made it a habit of lunching late, Elsie felt there could be no harm in the idea.

She said, "Very well. It sounds like fun."

The lounge was crowded, and they had some difficulty locating a table. At last they were forced to share one with the couple with whom they'd played shuffleboard and who had gone to the lounge ahead of them. The man was a tall, well-preserved Britisher in his sixties; his wife was a shorter petite woman probably in her forties who had a round face, outstanding only because of alert hazel eyes and a warm smile. She was overweight, but pleasantly so, resembling a well-turned-out English china lady in her deck coat and wide brimmed hat.

The two were Sir Peter and Lady Hazel Monteith.

"We do so like your country, countess," Lady Hazel beamed at her over her Scotch and soda.

Elsie was having a martini. She said, "You mean America, of course."

"Most emphatically," Sir Peter said with a nod of his silver head. "Russia is a different cup of tea. We've been there; but in spite of the beauty, we were distressed by much we saw. I do not imagine we shall visit it again."

"Not if the newspapers are right," Lady Hazel said with a sigh. "Winston Churchill had a letter in the press recently in which he said Russia was like a tinderbox and the anarchists would soon apply the match to set it in flames!"

Sir Peter's aristocratic face showed annoyance. "My dear, you must learn to take Winston's utterances with a grain of salt. He is not the man his father was—not even that. Too much bombast!"

Sir Peter said to Elsie, "You need have no serious concern, countess. You have married into a noble and wealthy family. If revolt comes to Russia, he can simply take you away from it and come to England and America as many wealthy refugees have before."

She wished that Alex were there to take part in the serious talk, but then decided against the thought. Her husband was quick-tempered and might have snapped back some hasty reply to the elderly British couple.

She said, "I hope it will not come to that."

"I'm sure that it won't, my dear," Lady Hazel said patting her with her plump hand.

Sir Peter pushed aside his empty glass. "Time for a quick stroll around the deck before lunch," he announced. "Must not waste this excellent food."

Lady Hazel gazed at him, showing resigned admiration. "Lord Peter has so much energy. And the food is excellent. I love the *Lusitania*, don't you?"

"It is a fine ship," Elsie agreed.

Lady Hazel sighed. "I cannot imagine her ever going to the bottom of the Atlantic as the *Titanic* did."

Sir Peter gave an angry snort. "The inquiries were stupid. Both the American and the British ones. When a vessel sails directly into an iceberg and takes three hundred feet out of her bottom there has to be negligence. I doubt if the like will happen again in our time." He rose. "Well, no matter. We must have our stroll."

Lady Hazel rose as did Ralph. She said wistfully, "It has been a pleasant morning. Too bad we are docking tomorrow. We could do it all again." And she waddled off after her husband.

At last they had the table alone. Ralph sat down and said, "They are amusing."

"I like them," Elsie said.

"Very definite in their opinions," he suggested.

"Most middle-aged people are. I know my uncle and aunt are very strong in their views," she said.

"Tell me about them," he suggested, smiling at her across the table.

"Not much to tell," she protested. "They are ordinary, good people." But she did go on to give him a background on them and what her life in New York had been like.

He said, "I think I'd like them."

"I'm sure they'd like you," she said. "If you return to New York before I do, please look them up. I'll give you their telephone number and address."

His eyes fixed on her. "Were they satisfied to have you marry the count and leave the country?"

"They were heartbroken," she said truthfully.

"Yet you went ahead."

"You do cruel things when you're in love," she said.

"So you do," he agreed quietly, glancing down at his partly finished drink.

"You sound as if you speak from experience."

"I do."

"Care to tell me?" she asked.

"Not especially," he said. "But I will. My previous assignment overseas was in Spain. I fell in love with the daughter of a fine family and, against all my colleagues' advice, courted her."

"And?"

100

He continued to study the table grimly. "I was younger than I am now—and bolder."

"You seem very young."

"Not really," he said. "I went directly to her parents. Again against the advice of the older journalist in our bureau. I told them their daughter was in love with me, and I wished to marry her."

"What was their reaction?"

"Violent," he said bitterly. "They politely refused and asked me to leave."

"And?"

"I was to see their daughter that night. We had a secret meeting place. I went there. She did not come."

"What happened?"

"A male cousin of hers appeared and warned me that I must not see her again. That her parents had taken her to a country estate far from Madrid and would keep her there until I left the country. He said our romance was not possible by their family standards. I was not of the nobility, and I was not of the Catholic religion."

"I married Alex in the face of both those things," she said.

"My darling wasn't given the opportunity," Ralph said. "I tried to locate her, but without avail. It was no mere threat on her parents' part. They had managed to remove her from my life."

"Didn't you persevere?"

"I had a rush order to go to Turkey and left Spain with every intention of coming back. I had no way of getting in touch with the girl I loved or letting her know I would return."

"What then?" Elsie asked.

"I was gone several months," the young newspaperman said. "When I returned to Madrid, my older colleague approached me with a look of infinite sadness on his face. I knew something awful had happened."

Elsie said, "What was his news?"

"My beloved had killed herself. Her parents had taunted her with my leaving the country. Telling her it was what would have happened in any case. That my love was not true for her. So she felt she had no reason to go on living

101

and threw herself to her death from a high balcony in the country house where she had been held captive."

Elsie was shocked by the account. After a long moment of silence, she said, "I'm truly sorry."

"Thank you," he said. "I thought you would be, or I wouldn't have told you. I don't dare think of it much, and I never discuss it. But I've made an exception with you, perhaps to let you realize that these foreign matrimonial alliances can be more difficult than one would expect."

"I'm beginning to find that out," she said soberly.

"What was the count's excuse about last night?"

"He offered none."

"He is asking a lot of you," the young man said.

"Yes."

"He also seemed anxious to be off on his own again to-day. I rather think he enjoyed my asking you to be my shuffleboard partner."

"I had the same impression," she said. "Not too flattering to me."

Ralph eyed her earnestly. "I don't think it is any reflection of his love for you. That may be sincere. I think it may be something else."

"What?"

"In the struggle which is going on in Russia now, there are all sorts of secret societies and secret agents. I have an idea he may be mixed up in one of the secret societies."

"Why?" she asked anxiously.

"Because I'm sure his murdered brother Basil was."

☙ Chapter 9 ❧

ELSIE WAS SEATED in the living-room of their suite at the Savoy Hotel reading the *London Times*. It was late afternoon of her second day in the great city, and Alex was out somewhere. As usual, he had been mysterious about his need to go off on some errand and had said he would be back in time for dinner.

She had reached the countess's room and found that she was also out. It seemed that she, too, had her concerns and didn't care whether Elsie saw the city.

Suddenly, there was a soft rap on the door of the suite. Elsie opened the door to a startling looking man standing in the shadowed corridor. The visitor was not much taller than herself, but grossly fat, with a moon face and double chins. His eyes were small and sunken in the folds of his fat face, with a wild, bright gleam about them. The man's black hair was unkempt and straggled down on his forehead, and he wore a brown shapeless suit and carried a battered soft hat in his hand.

"Yes?" said Elsie.

"May I see the count?" the man asked.

"He is not here," she said, wondering who this visitor might be and whether he were a madman. He looked like one.

"You are sure?" asked the man as his eyes searched the living room beyond her. It seemed he might force his way in.

"Of course I'm sure."

"He was to meet me."

"He is out. That is all I can tell you."

"Tell him that Litvinov was here."

"Litvinov," she repeated.

"He will know me," the fat man promised. "You can

103

tell him I'm staying at the usual place. I shall be in my room after midnight."

"Very well," she said in a small voice.

The fat man bowed and turned and waddled off down the dark corridor. His fat was of a soft, repulsive type, and his clothes were so ragged and old that she had been assailed by the stench of them. She shut the door with a feeling of relief to have him gone. What a strange person for Alex to know!

But then he consorted with many odd people. She recalled the conversation she'd had on the ship with her young journalist friend. The young man had assured her that he believed Alex was acting as a kind of liaison between the nobles and the anarchists. Ralph thought the count's brother Basil had been involved with the anarchists and in so doing had turned against his class. The chances were, the journalist had warned her, that Alex was also engaged in the same sort of activity.

This had been a shocking revelation for Elsie. And Ralph warned her not to face her husband with the charge that he was engaged in some sort of political plotting. He said Alex would only deny it, and it would do no good to inquire. Yet Basil had lost his life in the same sort of activity, and Elsie worried that the sad business would end with Alex also being a martyr to a lost cause.

She returned to her chair and the *London Times*, but was unable to concentrate on her reading. She stared ahead of her and thought of the recent events of these fast-moving days. The great liner had docked at Southhampton the day before, and they had all taken the boat train to London. As she had only been in the great English city once before, she had looked forward to her husband giving her a tour of the city.

But Alexander had been unwilling to take the time to do so, saying, "I have so few days here, I must make the best of every moment. Much of our investment money is here in London. I need to keep a sharp check on my broker."

So Elsie had called on Olga in her room and found her dressed for the street. She asked her, "Couldn't we do some shopping together?"

Olga had seemed uneasy. "Perhaps later. I have some

friends I must visit today. I cannot take you, and I doubt if you'd enjoy them. I'm sorry."

"It's all right," she had said, with a sigh. "It's just that Alex is also too busy to give me any time."

"Why not go out on your own? Many women prefer to be alone when they shop," her sister-in-law suggested.

"I'll think about it," she said. "I don't know London very well."

"Have a hansom cab take you to Selfridge's and wait for you," Countess Olga suggested. "They're very dependable." And she had gone on out.

So Elsie remained at the Savoy on her own. She wrote letters to her aunt and uncle and to Marjorie. She stayed away from the troublesome things now bothering her and told them about life aboard the great ship and the people she'd met. She promised to send postcards from Paris and write long letters when she finally reached Moscow.

Yet she did not dare tell them what she was gradually learning: that her husband turned to his sister before he did to her. That Olga and Alex shared secrets from which she was barred. That the chances were he had involved himself in some political game, which could find its end in his being assassinated in the same fashion as Basil and his uncle. The thoughts terrified her.

At five o'clock the telephone rang. It was Ralph. His voice was friendly. "I didn't expect to reach you. I only phoned by chance. Did you just return to your room?"

"No," she said. "I'm sorry to tell you I've been here all the afternoon."

"Where's your husband?"

"Out."

"Where?"

"He wouldn't tell me."

"Damn!"

"Don't worry about it," she said.

"It's not fair!"

"What about you?" she asked, changing the subject and trying for some brightness in her own tone. "What have you been doing?"

"Reported to the local office and been given a briefing on what is to be expected of me," he said.

"They haven't changed your assignment?" she asked anxiously. "You're still going to Moscow."

"I am going to Moscow," he assured her. "I leave in about three days."

"I don't know when we're leaving."

"I'd ask you to dinner, but I expect your errant count will at least return to dine with you."

"He promised he would. But just a while ago there was a strange, fat man here to see him. He said he'd be in his room after midnight. He was grossly fat and had a mad look in his eyes."

"Oh?" Ralph sounded interested. "He was looking for Alex?"

"Yes."

"Did he give his name?"

"Yes," she said. "He said to tell the count that Litvinov had called."

There was a low exclamation of shock from the other end of the line and Ralph said, "That fits."

"What fits?"

"You wouldn't understand," he told her. "I'll explain when I see you."

"Why must you all be so mysterious?" she complained. "I must say I didn't like either the look or smell of that Litvinov."

"I can well believe that," he said. "Suppose I take you on a walking tour of the center of London tomorrow, the theater district, and some of the art galleries?"

"And maybe some of the shops?"

"We can do that the next day if the count gives his permission," Ralph said.

"Don't worry about that," she said. "My guess is he'll be delighted to have you take me off his hands."

"Well, you discuss it with him," Ralph said. "I'll phone you again in the morning."

"When we meet will you tell me about Litvinov?"

"Maybe," he said. "I'm going to ask some questions in the meanwhile."

Alex returned to the suite shortly before six. He looked weary, slumped down in a chair, and had her bring him a glass of whisky. He took a gulp of the strong liquid and sighed.

106

"At home I drink vodka. It is the national drink. They do not have any taste for it here."

Standing by him, she said, "I have never tasted it."

"You will in Moscow," he promised. "I'm sorry to be so late, but I had an exhausting day. What about you?"

"I remained here and did nothing. Olga had a visit to make and couldn't take me. I had a visitor and a phone call."

"Sit on my knee," he told her and placed an arm around her. "Who phoned?"

"The young American from the ship. He wants to take me on a walking tour of the city tomorrow afternoon."

Her husband frowned. "What did you tell him?"

She was seated on his lap, with her left arm around his shoulders. She smiled into his weary, handsome face. "I said that I've have to ask your permission first."

"Why not?" her husband said. "It's likely I'll have another busy day tomorrow. You may as well get some enjoyment as sit alone here."

"You're certain?"

"Yes," he said. Then he gave her a warning glance. "There is just one thing. Do not discuss any of our affairs with him. Don't talk about either me or Olga. I don't want my doings to get into the press, and you cannot completely trust these journalists. Especially not the Hearst outfit. They are very enterprising."

She said, "You don't trust him?"

"I trust him as much as I trust any newspaperman, which isn't all that far."

"I'm sure he means us no harm."

"Sometimes a simple, harmless story can have shattering reverberations. See your friend, but tell him nothing about us. Do you understand?"

"Yes," she said, not at all sure she could keep to her promise.

Alex smiled, "Tonight, we shall have dinner and go to the music hall. It is a special sort of British theater that you must see."

"I'd like that," she enthused. Then she remembered, "I didn't tell you about your caller. He said his name was Litvinov and that you knew where he'd be and he'd be there after midnight."

"Litvinov, here in London," he said, his body going taut.

"Yes. He's a very odd person. Terribly fat."

Her husband lifted her off his lap and stood up in a state of concern. "You should have mentioned his coming, first."

Let down, she said, "I didn't know it was all that important."

Alexander's face had paled. "Litvinov is here from Moscow. I must see him. He told you after midnight?"

"Yes," she said. "He seemed a dirty, awful person. And he had mad eyes. Why do you have to meet him?"

Alex was pacing restlessly. "It has to do with my brother's murder. He may have a message for me. I cannot ignore his message."

She stood there in despair. "I don't want you mixed up in some political troubles. I don't want to have you murdered as Basil was."

He gave her an impatient look. "I won't be."

"Will we be having dinner and going out, then?"

"Yes," he said, hardly listening to her. "I've already told Olga we'd be meeting her at seven."

"Must Olga join us? She left me alone all day."

Alex frowned. "You mustn't be childish about these things. She is my sister. I can't neglect her."

Elsie was about to burst out that he didn't worry about his neglecting her, but decided against it. She knew it could mean his becoming angry and refusing to go to dinner or the music hall at all.

Dinner at the Savoy was a most fashionable ritual. The diners were more elegantly dressed than any she had seen at similar places in New York. The service was first class and contrary to the usual stories about English food, the meal was a delight in every course. About midway through the dinner, a small, smartly dressed man with black hair and a mustache passed their table with a slender, younger man beside him.

Seeing Alex, the man showed a look of pleasant surprise on his aristocratic face and stopped to speak. He extended a hand as Alex rose.

"My dear count," he said in a voice with a slight stutter, "I did not know you were in London."

"Just for a few days," Alexander said. "You remember my sister?"

"But of course. We met at the ballet in St. Petersburg."

"And this is my wife," Alexander went on.

"Your wife!" the little man said. "What a charming creature." He gave Alex a challenging look. "This must have been recent. I didn't know you had married."

"A few weeks ago in New York," Alex told him. "And I hear you also have taken a wife."

"We are all become benedicts," the dapper man said with a glance of appeal to the gods. "What an amusing situation. Enjoy London!" And he moved on.

"Who was that?" Elsie asked.

"Somerset Maugham, he's a former doctor who has become a novelist. They say he's planning to do some plays that may rival Shaw."

Countess Olga spoke up, "He'll never rival Shaw. Never."

Elsie was surprised, for Olga had said little all evening. "I had no idea you were such an admirer of Shaw."

"He is England's finest playwright," Countess Olga said. "And he is a socialist."

Alex gave her a warning look. "Spare us a discussion of his politics. Tonight we are going to the music hall, and we shall forget all our troubles enjoying that wonderful British institution."

Countess Olga grimaced. "Music hall is the best these island people can produce. Wait until you reach Moscow. There you will truly see art. Our ballet with Nijinsky and Karsavina. London has never seen anything like them. That is true entertainment and beauty."

Alex told her, "There is talk of our ballet coming here. So the English may soon see our fine talents. I still insist that music hall is also a kind of art."

London by night was as crowded and as colorful as New York. They took a hansom cab at the Savoy and rode over the narrow cobblestoned streets until they reached the busy theater district and the Palace Variety Theatre, which was modestly calling itself the greatest music hall in all the world. And as Elsie sat with the count and countess in a box of the great theater, she began to believe this was true.

The theater was filled from the fashionable boxes and dress circle to the gallery high up in the shadows. The large orchestra played a lively overture to introduce the performance. Then the curtain rose on a lively group of acrobats. Harry Tate came on to do his "Golfing Sketch" followed by a young woman of American origin known simply as Louisa. The woman sang a medley of sentimental ballads, finally being joined by a chorus of men in flat straw hats, the sort known as boaters.

The next was an animal act of donkeys, dogs and monkeys. Alex laughed at this until his eyes filled with tears and she and he held hands. She had a sudden moment of sentiment with the realization of how much of the little boy there was about this often sullen and moody young man. The Countess Olga caught this moment of intimacy between them and with a haughty expression raised her pert chin and looked back at the stage again.

The featured act on the bill was Vesta Tilley, who in a man's top hat and evening dress, complete with white tie, did her songs. The performance went on with another comedian named George Robey who did Yorkshire comedy and was excellent. A bear act followed. The show concluded with a mixed chorus line of men and women led by Vesta Tilley. The crowd applauded long and loudly when the curtain finally fell.

They left the giant theater to the strains of the orchestra playing lively tunes of the day. Alex proved himself adept at summoning a cab, and they were soon on their way back to the Savoy.

"Did you enjoy it?" he asked her.

"Very much," she said.

"And you?" he inquired of his sister.

She shrugged. "I miss a lot of the English humor."

Elsie knew that Olga was seldom pleased with anything. But she was content with the evening. However, when they reached the Savoy and entered the lobby of the famous hotel there was a shock waiting for her. From the sidelines in the busy lobby, Litvinov appeared. He raised a plump hand to signal Alex, and her young husband paled.

He said, "Please excuse me for a moment." And he went to speak with the fat man.

Elsie said, "I'm surprised they allowed such a scruffy person in the lobby."

Olga gave her a sharp glance. "You ought not to judge by appearances. Litvinov was once a very important man in Russia. He had a thriving business. Lately, he has fallen on evil times here; but I'm sure he will return to his proper station in life."

"He is so odd in appearance and manner," she said.

Olga chose to ignore her. Then Alex came back to them and with a frown, he said, "I have an urgent message to see someone. A matter of some importance. You two can see each other to your rooms. It will save me time."

Before Elsie could voice any objection to this, he had gone back to the fat man, and they were on their way out of the lobby. She knew it would be useless to complain to her sister-in-law who seemed to enjoy siding against her. So wordlessly, the two took the elevator to their floor, bade each other good night and went to their respective rooms.

Elsie was unable to sleep. This abrupt and odd end to the evening had spoiled all that had gone on before for her. She lay awake staring up into the darkness, fearful for her husband. Olga had said that Litvinov had been a successful businessman in Russia, but she could not believe that such a man had ever filled such a role. She was more inclined to think Ralph had told her the truth about the fat man.

The journalist had mentioned that Litvinov was mixed up in politics in some way. And this seemed more likely. She had an idea she would have to depend on the young American for whatever she learned about her husband's mysterious activities, since neither he nor his sister seemed willing to be truthful with her.

Had Litvinov been mixed up in the murder of Basil in some way? Or was he attempting to give Alex the information he wanted about who had committed the murder? It could be either. In any case, she was certain of one thing: She did not like the appearance of Litvinov and would not trust him.

It was nearly three in the morning when Alex returned. He turned on a light, and Elsie glimpsed his pale, tormented face. He looked like a shell of the man who had left her in the lobby a few hours later—a worn shell.

Raising herself on an elbow, Elsie studied him with anxious eyes and asked, "What are you doing to yourself? You look awful. Where did you go with that awful man?"

He removed his coat. "No questions, please," he begged of her.

She got out of bed and went to him. She was still shocked by his altered appearance. "You look ill."

He waved her concern aside. "I will be all right," he said. "It's just that I need rest. I attended a long meeting."

"What sort of meeting?"

"Nothing we can talk about now," he said in a tired voice. He kissed her gently. "Let us hurry to bed as quickly as we can. I desperately need rest, and I have a long day again tomorrow."

She looked at him with frightened eyes. "You're not going to see that awful man again, are you?"

"No," he said, although she was by no means sure he meant it. "There are many other things to attend to before I leave London."

After they were both in bed, Elsie lay awake for at least an hour worrying about him. Then exhaustion overruled her concern, and she slept. The next morning was gray and foggy; by the time Elsie awakened, Alexander was already gone. A note on his pillow said, "Dearest, Have a good afternoon with Manning. I shall see you at dinner. Love, Alex."

Depressed, she had her breakfast alone in her room. She tried to telephone Olga, but could not. So she waited until Ralph came to take her to lunch.

The young journalist arrived promptly at twelve-thirty, wearing a bowler hat, a brown suit, and a raincoat. Ralph Manning looked very manly and attractive, Elsie thought.

He said, "I'm going to take you to a restaurant in the Strand that was a favorite of Dickens's years ago."

It was a combined pub and restaurant and had an almost purely male clientele for lunch. But Elsie liked it, especially the privacy offered by the booths with their rich walnut wood and leather seats and backs in red. An elderly waiter served them drinks and announced that the specialty of the day was, "Beefsteak and kidney pie, Guv'nor!" Both ordered it.

He said, "Have you seen Litvinov since you talked with me?"

"Yes," she said worriedly. And she told him about the fat man turning up in the Savoy lobby and Alex going off with him. She also told him about what followed. The sad state in which her husband had returned and that he had left again this morning before she was awake.

Ralph gave her a questioning look. "Was he drunk when he returned last night?"

"I don't think so," she worried. "Yet, I do feel there was something strange about him. Now that I think of it, his eyes were not as they should be. The pupils seemed so large."

The young man opposite her nodded. "That is what I would expect if he spent the night with Litvinov and his friends. I'd say your husband had been using some sort of drug."

"Oh, no." She hadn't thought of this before.

"It's not all that rare," he explained. "There are certain Russian secret societies that use drugs as part of their meetings. Litvinov is a member of one of those societies. Have you ever heard of the Skoptsi?"

She shook her head. "No."

"You're certain? You never heard your husband or his sister mention them?"

"The name is new to me."

Ralph waited for their drinks to be served, then resumed talking, "The Skoptsi is one of the most dangerous underground groups in Russia. And their thirst for power goes beyond Russia; they dream of one day controlling the world by enlisting its leaders in their membership."

Elsie frowned. "You seem to know a lot about them. Do you think Alex is mixed up with them?"

"I very much fear it," was the reply. "I will not dwell on the nature of the movement, except to say it is repulsive to any normal individual. They are fanatics and their zeal borders on madness. Once completely in their power, there is no returning."

Her eyes widened. "You terrify me."

"I don't think Alex is deeply involved with them yet," he said. "But Basil was. And it was through his association with the Skoptsi that he was murdered."

"And Alex is likely trying to find his murderer and avenge him," she suggested.

Ralph sipped his drink. "I hope that is it."

"What else could it be?"

"Alex may be following along the same path of politics as his late brother. If so, it is dangerous. You see one of the chief high priests of Skoptsi is Rasputin. And he is an avowed enemy of the nobles."

She nodded. "And when I mentioned Rasputin, I was shocked that Alex defended him. It was something I didn't expect."

"You mustn't panic," Ralph said. "But it sounds more and more as if your husband is being wooed by this group. He could be a great help to them. They have few counts among their ranks."

"Litvinov's physical appearance alone disgusted me!" she said with a shudder.

"I will follow this up," Ralph promised. "It may take a long while to learn what is actually happening. Rasputin was discredited, but he managed to wriggle out of his predicament and win the favor of the royal family again. The tsarina and the tsar are completely under his influence and refuse to see, or entertain, any of the aristocracy. Rasputin has interfered with the government, which was corrupt enough in any event, and now he names those whom the tsar should appoint."

She was stunned by this. "Rasputin must be a vile person."

"The tsarevich is a hemophiliac, a bleeder! He inherited the disease from his mother. The tsarina can think only of his cure. Rasputin was a monk in the country (in Russia, the religious are divided between monks and priests; priests may marry, but not monks). It makes no difference in Rasputin's case. He is a wild peasant of great stature with hypnotic eyes which can make others do his will."

"And he has pretended to cure the young tsarevich?"

"Yes," Ralph said. "Now he is prominent at court. He has exchanged his rough linen shirts for blouses of silk in a rainbow of colors. He no longer stamps around in coarse boots. He wears black velvet trousers stuffed inside boots of soft kid leather. The plain belt about his waist is now a silken cord with tassels. And he wears a handsome gold cross hung at his throat. A gift of the tsarina."

"How can they accept him?"

"He is a magnificent charlatan. The peasants in the country areas think of him as God's personal emissary. And he is still a moujik, one of them, despite his fine trappings. He likes to describe the sexual activities of horses at state dinners and then reach out to some lovely member of the aristocracy and say, 'Come to me, my mare!' If the tsarina reproves him, he tells her they are all too much pampered. His table manners are those of the lowest peasant, but he is a diversion for a decadent society."

"You mean others tolerate him beyond the royal family?"

"He has an apartment and many women of the aristocracy pay secret visits to him—to ask his prayers, they claim. But I have serious doubts about Monk Rasputin."

"Does he spend most of his time at the royal palace?"

"No, his headquarters are really in St. Petersburg. It is there that he reigns over the Skoptsi."

"And where my husband's brother was murdered."

"Yes," Ralph Manning said. "As soon as I return to Moscow, I will look up the file on Count Basil Martynov. It may take a little while, but I promise to dig deeply into it. I don't think it was done before. He wasn't that important in the plan of things."

"What makes him more important now?" she asked.

The eyes of the young reporter met hers. "You," he said with deep sincerity. "I'm gravely worried about you and your safety."

"I feel you are the only friend I have at the moment."

Ralph's face took on a pained look. "You must have guessed I've fallen in love with you, Elsie. I worry about your going to Moscow. Why not give it up now? I will look after getting you back to New York."

She reached out and touched her hand on his. "I'm fond of you, Ralph. But I have made vows. And I do care for Alex. I cannot desert him now, not in this crisis."

115

❦ Chapter 10 ❧

DESPITE BEING TOUCHED by Ralph's telling of his feelings for her, Elsie felt she must do all she could to make her new marriage work and save Alex from whatever dark circumstances he had become involved in.

For a while, Elsie and Ralph ate in silence. Each needed time to resolve his thoughts. Elsie felt she could still keep Ralph as a friend. He seemed decent enough to understand how she would want to try to make her marriage work. Also, he had known personal pain and sorrow; so he could understand this love she had for Alex, which mightn't make sense to many others.

When the two finished their tea, Ralph smiled at her across the table and said, "Now shall we take our promised walk about the West End?"

"I've been looking forward to it. Next to home this is my favorite city," Elsie said.

"It is mine," he observed. "I only wish we had more time here."

"So do I."

"You won't be staying long in Paris?"

She shook her head. "Not according to what I've heard from Alex. We'll go directly to the railway station from the boat train and shift to another train immediately for the start of our trip to Moscow. There will only be an hour or so wait."

"I'll be taking the same train," he agreed.

They left the restaurant and strolled through several side streets. Then they spent considerable time in an art gallery, where Ralph showed his knowledge of English artists by giving her a helpful lecture on Constable as they viewed some of his paintings.

They had barely left the art gallery and were walking

116

toward Piccadilly Circus when they both became aware that something unusual was going on. A large group of people were milling around Piccadilly Circus and shouts were raised in the air.

"It's a riot of some sort," Ralph said, his arm at once protectively around her.

"It looks like a lot of women to me," Elsie said, as she studied the scene.

"I know," Ralph suddenly explained. "It was in all the newspapers this morning. It's the new march by the suffragettes. Mrs. Pankhurst said it would happen, and it has."

Elsie pressed close to him as the paraders drew near. "All this violence! And she's such a pretty, mild-looking woman."

"Not where womens' rights are concerned," Ralph shouted and quickly headed her for the doorway of a boot repairing establishment where they might escape injury.

The battalion of angry women advanced up the street like a rising tide. They held hammers and other weapons; and as they advanced, they smashed windows of any shop along the way. There was also some stone throwing at windows at the upper levels. The din of their angry cries filled the air!

Elsie didn't attempt to talk above the hubbub. She saw Mrs. Pankhurst near the head of the group with a girl beside her. She decided this was probably her daughter, Christabel, who was active in the organization.

Shouts of "Stop torturing women in prison!" filled the air.

Other's cried, "Vote against the government!"

A girl came up to them with a folder and thrust it at them, "Asquith is dishon'able!" she cried and then moved on.

Another young woman shouted, "Vote against the liberals."

The women moved on with a few embarrassed, tired-looking policemen trailing them. They seemed to be doing little better than take stock of the damage done. Angry shopmen came out to curse the women and shake their fists at the police.

The danger over, Ralph and Elsie stepped out onto the

sidewalk. Ralph gave her an amused look. "At least we selected a lively day to see London."

She marveled, "I had no idea the suffragettes were so well organized or so violent."

"Mrs. Pankhurst has decided violence is the only way," the young journalist said. "I'll have to get this story on the wire for America."

"I might have known our afternoon would be ruined," she said with a teasing smile.

"It won't take me too long," he said. "Some of the others will get the rest of the story, and we'll piece it together. We often cooperate that way."

"Do you want to go straight to your office now?" she asked.

"I should," he admitted. "But I promised to give you the rest of the afternoon."

"It doesn't matter," she protested. "Find a hansom cab and drop me at the hotel on your way to the office."

"I could do that," he said, thinking aloud. Then he glanced at her, "And if your husband hasn't anything planned for you tonight, I'll take you to the theater."

She smiled. "I sincerely hope he has some plans. It is to be our last night in London."

"There's a cab," he said, sighting one near the Piccadilly Circus and waving to it. The carriage slowly rumbled their way.

It took them only about ten minutes to reach the Savoy. He helped her out and saw her to the lobby with the promise that he would call her at dinnertime. She took the elevator and went upstairs. On the chance that Olga might be in she stopped by her room.

Surprisingly, the dark girl had returned. She opened the door and said, "Oh, it's you!"

"Are you expecting someone else?" she asked, hesitating in the hallway.

"No," Olga said. "Only I thought it might be Alex. But do come in."

"I was out for lunch, and I had an unusual experience," she said and went on to tell about the suffragettes' rebellious march.

Olga stood listening with concern. "It's frightening to

think of such violent action here in London. I don't think
it at all necessary."

"Mrs. Pankhurst seems to think it is the only way they
will be listened to and have their wrongs righted."

Still standing, Olga said, "I think it will only hurt their
cause."

"Time will tell," she said. "Are you expecting Alex
soon?"

"I have no idea when he will be here," Olga said. She
indicated a chair. "Won't you sit down for a moment. I
did some shopping. I'll show you what I found."

For the next twenty minutes Elsie was treated to a dis-
play of a group of gowns Olga had purchased from an
exclusive ladies' shop in the West End. It was evident by
the quality of the dresses and their price tags that money
was no concern of the young countess.

Olga put her clothes back in the closet after showing
them and said, "That demonstration you saw today is just
a sample of what goes on in Russia a lot of the time. We
have students' rebellions, factory workers' rebellions, and
just plain rebellions of the people. One gets very sick of
them since they accomplish nothing."

"But there must be wrongs to motivate such demonstrations," she said mildly.

Olga lit a long cigaret and took a deep puff on it as she
slumped down in an easy chair opposite Elsie. She said,
"Russia is mired down with wrongs."

"So you have rebellions! That's a healthy reaction."

"Not when we have such a large underground. No one
knows how many. But when they call a revolution, it will
be the end of us." The dark girl symbolically ran a line
across her throat with a forefinger.

Solemnly, she said, "You think there will be a revolution. That it will really happen?"

"It must. It is only a matter of time."

"Then why do you and Alex return to Russia?"

The dark girl gave a small gesture with her right hand.
"It is our home, Mother Russia! Where else can we go?"

"Leave the country while you have money. Live in
France, Germany, or England. You could even go to the
United States?"

119

"Alex will never hear of it," Olga told her. "And I have not the courage to do it alone."

"So you return?"

"Yes."

"Whatever the risk for Alex," she said. "Don't you worry about him at all?"

"He is in the hands of the fates."

"That is no answer at all as far as I'm concerned," Elsie said disdainfully. "You know much more about all this than I do. What about Litvinov?"

The dark girl showed unease. She said, "Alex merely has tried to help Litvinov."

"Don't lie to me," Elsie said. "I know better. I know Litvinov is a member of a dread secret society—a society with Rasputin as its high priest!"

Olga's mouth gaped open. "Where did you hear that?"

"I heard it," she said.

"That newspaper man. He doesn't know what he is talking about."

"The Hearst people must think differently. They are paying him well to head their office in Moscow."

Olga paled. "It is something I prefer not to argue about."

Elsie said, "What about Basil? Wasn't he a member of that secret organization?"

Olga shot her a warning look. "You will do well to learn that in Russia we do not talk about such things."

"You may not admit them openly, yet they exist," she said.

"For the sake of your husband, you should be silent."

Elsie rose. "I do not want to endanger Alex in any way. But I still maintain he is in the most danger returning to his native land."

"There is no other way," Olga said in an unhappy tone.

"I at least can challenge him on that," she said.

"He will tell you the same thing," the countess said.

"Is it all this conspiring with this secret society which is taking so much of his time here in London?"

Olga said, "My brother has many things to look after here. I do not know what occupies his time."

"But we are leaving tomorrow," Elsie said. "That, at least, is definite."

120

"Yes," Olga said.

Elsie left the dark-haired girl and went on to her own room to wait for her husband. As the afternoon waned, Alex did not arrive and Elsie began to feel a grim concern once more. The telephone interrupted her thoughts. Alex was on the line.

He said, "I will not be able to join you for dinner. You and Olga can dine together in the hotel. I will be home as early as I can. Be sure to start packing as we leave tomorrow."

She said, "Surely you can manage to join me for a late dinner on our last night in London."

"Impossible," he said at the other end of the line.

"Who is keeping you away? Litvinov?"

There was a moment of silence and then he said, "You must not mention that name. Ever."

"I think your behavior since we've been here has been completely mad," she said bitterly. "And I blame this gross man who seems to have haunted you."

"I will see you later," Alex said firmly and hung up.

Elsie put the telephone down with a feeling of despair. Whatever the hold this Litvinov had on her husband, it appeared to be stronger than his loyalty to her. It was a shattering thing to accept. She debated what she should do about dinner and then called Olga.

Elsie told her husband's sister, "Alex will not be able to meet us for dinner. He suggests that we dine downstairs."

"I am having something brought to my room," Olga said. "I have a headache."

Elsie said, "That is too bad. I hope you feel better for our journey in the morning."

"I'm certain I shall," Olga said.

Once again Elsie was faced with a decision. She did not feel like dining alone in the hotel, and it upset her to think of having a solitary meal in her room. Her choice was made when Ralph called.

He said, "I've called on the chance you're still on your own."

Elsie's pleasure at hearing the young journalist's voice at once gave her pangs of guilt. She was a married woman playing a dangerous game. Ralph had already admitted his love for her, and she liked him much more than she cared to admit. Dare she go on seeing him?

Yet in her present plight, could she afford not to keep his friendship? Too clearly, Elsie knew she needed Ralph's support now and might need it even more in Moscow. It was her husband who had placed her in this precariously involved position, and she would tell him so if he made any complaint. Oddly enough, at this point, he had actually encouraged her friendship with Ralph.

She said wearily, "Alex is still occupied with his own affairs. Olga is having dinner alone in her room. I am truly on my own."

"Great!" Ralph said enthusiastically. "If we hurry we can have dinner together, and I have tickets for Robert Loraine in George Bernard Shaw's 'Man and Superman.' I'm sure you'd like it."

"We can dine here in the hotel," she said. "That would save time."

"I shall be there within the half-hour," he promised.

Elsie wore a lovely yellow evening gown, which she had purchased especially for her honeymoon. She thought wryly what a strange honeymoon it had become. She had spent the major London part of it with the young journalist.

He said, "I presume the count called."

"Yes, with the usual excuses. I am almost at the point of suspecting there is another woman. But I know it is Litvinov."

Ralph nodded to her across the dinner table. "I'm sure it is Litvinov and his associates."

"I mentioned Litvinov's name and Alex ended the phone conversation at once," she said.

"He appears to fear him."

"I'm sure he does," she agreed. "So does Olga. She warned me never to speak of Litvinov for the good of Alex."

The young journalist frowned. "There is no question that Litvinov has some direct link with Rasputin. And Rasputin is controlling the affairs of Russia today. He is the leader of a large, degenerate underground."

They finished dinner and went on to the theater. Once again, Elsie temporarily forgot her concerns in the enjoyment of the Shaw play. The audience was smartly dressed, the play intellectual. It was an exhilarating evening. When it was over, Ralph escorted her out into the gas-lit street and suggested they go somewhere for a late supper.

She shook her head. "No, I must go home. I'm sure Alex will be there now."

Ralph looked unconvinced. "You can't tell about him."

"He said he would get home as early as he could," she told the journalist. "I've enjoyed the evening so much I don't want to spoil it."

"You are the judge," he said with a rueful smile and then hailed a cab to take them to the Savoy.

They sat close together in the cab; and as they came up to the hotel, he kissed her gently on the temple. "You must forgive me," he said. "I'm very concerned about you."

"I know," she told him, studying him with a grave smile.

He held her hands in his. "I will be in touch with you as soon as we reach Moscow."

"I count on that," Elsie said.

The cabman opened the door for them, and Ralph helped her out. He saw her into the lobby and was going to go up in the elevator with her, but she refused this offer.

"I will be perfectly safe now," she told him by the elevator. "And it looks more seemly if we part here."

He smiled. "You astonish me with your deference to appearances."

"I'm thinking what is best for the future," she said. "A wrong move now, and my husband might feel constrained to oppose our seeing each other in Moscow."

He appeared to see the good sense of her statement and didn't argue the point. Instead, he bid her good night and wished her a pleasant journey. She thanked him for the wonderful evening and entered the elevator.

It was not until she was in the elevator that she began to worry and feel tense. What if her husband still had not returned? Would he arrive in the middle of the morning and in the same condition as he had before? She was sure that he was under the influence of some drug when he had arrived home last evening.

The elevator halted at her floor, and she was the lone passenger to get out. She made her way along the silent, shadowed corridor in the calm conviction that she was in no danger; the hotel corridors were patrolled at night by security men. She passed the door of Olga's room without pausing, thinking her sister-in-law would be asleep by now. Then she came to her door and hesitated.

The door was a few inches ajar!

At first it gave her a start. And then she suddenly felt relieved, thinking that Alex must have returned and, in his desire to see her, had neglected to completely close the door. She had left a note for him on the desk in the living room of the suite.

Quickly entering she closed the door after her and removed her gloves and hat. With her hat in one hand and her gloves and hatpin in the other, she moved further into the silent room. The lights she had left on still burned and the note on the desk had been removed! So Alex had found it and read it!

"Alex!" she called out, waiting for him to appear from the doorway of the bedroom.

But no one appeared. Then she began to worry that he was angry at her for going out with the young newspaperman. She headed toward the bedroom, saying, "Alex, please answer me. You can't be angry. You didn't want me to spend the evening alone."

She stepped into the bedroom with the small single light on the bedside table and still no reply. It was then that she felt real fear. She suddenly became taut with the sense of danger close by.

"Alex!" she said in a faint voice, glancing around.

It was then that the door of the bedroom was slammed shut and she saw the gross, malevolent Litvinov hiding behind it. The fat man had his arm upraised and a knife gleamed from it. The gleam of the knife was no match for the mad hatred in his small, deep-set eyes. He lunged at her with the knife.

Elsie staggered back with a scream as he missed her. But he came after her again, his breathing labored and the grim madness in his eyes showing that he had no intention of giving up his attack on her.

"Please!" she sobbed and dodged around the big double

bed. Her only weapon was her agility as opposed to his slow movement because of his gross weight.

He came close again, and it was then she remembered the long hatpin still in her left hand. As she dodged away, she stabbed at him with the hatpin; and it found its mark in his lower arm. He winced with pain and faltered. This gave her time to reach the door to the living room and throw it open.

The fat Litvinov came lumbering after her, the knife ready for the attack as she ran toward the corridor door. She feared she would not make it in time, but just as she was within a foot of it the door was flung open and a white-faced Alex stood there!

She ran to him. "Alex save me."

Alex said nothing, but shoved her behind him and then went on inside to confront Litvinov. He cried out a torrent in Russian in an angry fashion. The stout Litvinov cowered before her husband's wrath. He stood there abjectly with the double chins of his moon-face quivering.

Alex wrenched the knife from the fat man's hand and spat out other words in Russian. Litvinov mumbled a reply in Russian and then slowly made his way out to the corridor. As he came by her, she could smell the stench of him; and his gaze at her was filled with hatred. Then he moved slowly on toward the elevator.

Alex came out and took her into the suite and shut the door. Holding her in his arms, he said, "I'm sorry."

She looked up at him in a stunned fashion. "The police? Aren't you going to turn him over to the police."

Alex shook his head. "No."

"Why?"

"I cannot," he said wearily, and she saw that again his eyes were strangely dilated.

"You've been taking some drug," she accused him. "Your eyes are strange."

"No," he protested feebly.

"That horrible man tried to murder me, and you let him go free! Why?"

"I cannot explain."

"Why do you fear him?"

"There is nothing I can tell you," he said. "He will not threaten you again. I can promise you that."

125

"I don't believe it," she said unhappily. "He has some power over you. What is it?"

"It has to do with things in Russia," Alex said. "It is neither anything you would understand nor something I can discuss with you. We will be leaving London and Litvinov behind tomorrow."

She shook her head. "Litvinov wanted to kill me. He will follow us."

"Now you are being childish," her husband said wearily. "I love you more than anything in life. If I thought he would be any danger to you, I would not have let him go free."

"How can you be sure what he will do?"

"I am reasonably sure," Alex said. "He is my country-man here in a foreign land. I could not turn him over to the authorities. In his own way, however misguided his acts may sometime be, he is working to save Russia."

Elsie's tone was bitter. "I will be haunted by his look of hatred."

Alex held her close to him. "You are safe with me. Never have fears about that."

Once again their lovemaking was eager, almost frantic. The dangerous moment had left them both in a highly strung state. Alex was never more ardent and she never more receptive to his passionate attentions. When at last they lay back ready for sleep, she had no doubts of his physical passion for her. But in her mind lingered a fear that even before she had met Alex he was lost to her in other ways.

The question of Alex's having an incestuous relationship with Olga seemed much less likely now, although there was yet a small hint of this. But Elsie felt now her husband was engrossed in the doings of some secret society dedicated to the domination of Russia and the world. An obsession with this cult had resulted in the death of his younger brother Basil, and now Alex was following in the same dangerous pattern as his brother. It terrified her to think that both his life and hers could well be in danger. Why had Litvinov wanted to kill her?

Elsie remained awake long after Alex slept. And so she was able to observe his tormented turning and twisting in the bed beside her. And when he began to murmur in his sleep in a tortured fashion, she was able to make out a few of the words he said.

"Basil!" he repeated, again and again. "The cause," also came from his feverishly moving lips before he finally sank into a deep sleep and lay still.

She heard his murmurings with a new fear building within her. She knew that her husband's strange behavior had to be related to his brother's murder. And it seemed to her if he gave up his quest for vengeance all would be well.

Next morning as they shared an early breakfast in their room, she told him, "You talked a great deal in your sleep last night."

"What did I say?" he asked, concerned.

"Many things."

Angrily, he said, "You should not eavesdrop on me when I sleep. I'm sure I wouldn't do such a thing to you."

She said, "You spoke of Basil. Repeated his name many times."

He frowned. "Did I?"

"Yes," she said. "And then you mentioned the cause."

"I was having a nightmare," he said casually, sipping his tea. "You are silly to make so much of words spoken in a nightmare."

"I think in your sleep you revealed the truth. All your mysterious absences in London have been dedicated to trying to discover your brother's killer, or killers."

Almost impatiently, he said, "Think what you like."

"I know it has to be that," she went on. "And I beg you to give up your desire for vengeance."

He stared at her. "You ask that?"

"I do. I think you are wrong to be mixed up with people like Litvinov, and I say you should have turned him over to the police. But aside from that, I think you should avoid these people who had something to do with Basil's murder."

Alex eyed her grimly. "You do not know what you are saying."

"I think I do," she told him. "It is only because I love you that I don't break up our marriage now and return to New York. All good judgment would indicate that I should. But I elect to go to Moscow with you."

He reached out and took her hand. "Have faith in me."

"I'm trying," she said. "But you are not making it easy."

After breakfast there was the flurry of last minute packing. Then they joined Olga and took a carriage to the railway station. It was a dreary, sooty morning with gray clouds hanging over London. Elsie hoped their journey would take them to better weather.

The Dover boat train was a new experience for Elsie. And since the channel was rough that day, she did not leave her compartment. Alex roamed the train, but Olga remained with her. They were happy to touch French soil and resume the railway journey to Paris.

At the Paris railway station, they ate in a good restaurant catering to travelers like themselves, and she kept an eye open for Ralph Manning as Alex and Olga talked earnestly to each other in their native Russian. It was a habit becoming more frequent with them lately; and of course, she could not understand what they were saying. It made her feel uneasy, but she did not want to make a formal complaint now.

Alex finally turned from his sister to her and asked in English, "What about your newspaper man?"

"Ralph Manning," she said. "He is also on his way to Moscow."

"It is a wonder we haven't seen him," her husband said.

"He may have been delayed."

"Likely," he said. "We must entertain him when he arrives in Moscow."

"Yes," she said. "He was very kind to me in London."

Alex gave her a cynical smile. "Why not? It gave him the chance to escort a pretty young woman around."

She gave Alex a reproving look. "Not every man enjoys being courtier to another man's wife."

Alex looked slightly abashed. "I suppose not. Yet I think Manning did enjoy your company. At least this is the way I sized it up."

The announcement that their train was leaving made them hurry from the restaurant and seek out their compartment. This railway car would be changed from train to train until they reached Moscow. It would be their home all the way across Europe.

The Paris railway station was all noise and confusion

128

with people, clutching their bags and other possessions, rushing about. Elsie clung to Alex, and Olga walked alongside them as they went down the long wooden platform to find the railway car to which they'd been assigned. At last they found it and were about to get in it when Elsie suddenly spotted what seemed a familiar figure ahead. A fat man mounted the steps into a forward car.

In a frightened voice, Elsie said, "Look, I see Litvinov boarding the train."

Alex shook his head. "Nonsense! Litvinov dares not leave England! You've seen another fat man! They all look alike."

She boarded the train with an uneasy feeling that her husband was not telling her the truth.

Chapter 11

THE TRAIN JOURNEY was confining, but less trying than Elsie had anticipated. She was almost constantly with Alex, and she thoroughly enjoyed this. Olga, also, seemed less arrogant and more friendly as she drew nearer the Russian border. It was plain that the dark girl was fond of her native land and getting home made her feel better.

Although Elsie went regularly to the dining car with her husband and sister-in-law and roamed to other parts of the fast-moving express train, she did not see Litvinov, or the man she might have mistaken for him, again. Eventually, she forgot the incident.

Visas were checked, and the train inspected by customs officials at the various borders. Elsie noted that her husband was always addressed respectfully by his title, and the border officials gave them little bother.

As the train moved into Russia, Alex began to talk more of his home and his family. It seemed that he wished to help prepare her for the meeting with them.

He said, "My Uncle Andre Martynov lives at the palace with his wife, the Countess Marie. They are both elderly. My uncle is interested in little but his collection of fine books, and my aunt attends endless teas and social engagements with women of her own age. They live in the past and have little social life together since the tsar has ceased having parties."

"I look forward to meeting them," she said.

"You will find them pleasant folk," he assured her. "They are not even dimly aware of the conflict that is tearing our country apart. Although they do bemoan the influence Rasputin holds over the royal family. This is a common plaint among the aristocracy."

She glanced at him as they sat beside each other in the

130

train compartment. "And you do not agree." They were alone as Olga had left the compartment for a little.

He said, "I see Rasputin differently from most of the others, but I do not make an issue of it. My Aunt Marie is frail and she has a companion, the youngest daughter of a minor nobleman who fell on bad times through gambling. The girl, Sophie Zemski, could accept the position of companion without losing social position."

"Is she also elderly, this Sophie Zemski?"

Her husband smiled tolerantly. "No, she is young, not much more than your age. A lovely, blonde girl with an excellent disposition. My Aunt Marie has been trying to make a match between this girl and her adopted son, Timofei. But neither of the young people is interested."

"You have an adopted cousin, Timofei."

"Yes. Count Andre and Countess Marie adopted him as a child. He has grown into a confident, if somewhat melancholy, young man with a talent for art. He has ambitions of becoming a fine portrait painter."

"He sounds interesting," Elsie said.

"You will find him so," Alex assured her. "But be wary of him, he can be deceitful. And he is fond of women."

"And he does not care for Sophie?"

"I have an idea it is she who will not have anything to do with him," he said. "Sophie is a proud, intelligent girl who may not think Timofei her equal, despite his artistic ability."

She smiled, "You are giving me such an excellent picture of them I feel I already know them."

"I think you should have some preparation," he said. "The servants are all veterans in our employ. Frederick, our butler, is in charge of all the others. We deal mainly with him."

She said, "I trust Olga will continue to take an active part in the management of the palace."

"I'm sure she will," her husband said. "Gradually, you can take over. I have discussed this with her. There is also the summer house outside Moscow, but we need not concern ourselves about that yet."

"What will the weather be like when we reach Moscow?" she asked.

"Spring weather, which means snow and fog, as the

melting process begins," he said. "We live on the bank of the Moskva River, and at this season of the year our estate is often swathed in the mists that rise from the great river. It most frequently happens in the night and mornings. During the day we get a glimpse of the sun. Then spring gives way to summer, and it all changes to a fresh beauty."

"I expect to find the mansion overwhelming," she said. "I lived in a small house in New York."

He idly glanced out the train window at the snow-mantled evergreens lining the countryside through which the fast express was passing. He said, "You will become used to it. We only occupy one apartment of the palace; my Aunt Marie and Uncle Andre have another section with Timofei; Olga has still another area for herself; then there are the main gathering rooms and the servant's quarters. We use every inch of the place."

She smiled at him again. "And you have a family ghost, the late Count Nicholas, murderer of his three wives. Does he roam the house at will?"

Alex looked annoyed. "Olga should not have filled you with that nonsense. It is an old wives' tale whispered about in the servants' quarters, but never above the stairs. You would do well to forget about it."

Her eyebrows raised. "You do not think I will see the ghost?"

"No, I do not."

"I shall feel cheated."

"Don't talk nonsense," he protested. "We will have enough real problems. One of them being to have Timofei accept you. He is not always pleasant to newcomers. But I have an idea you will win him over."

"I'll try," she said. "What are his political views?"

"Hard to say," her husband mused. "He is a great lover of the ballet and has done some sketches of Mathilde Kschessinska."

"Who is she?" Elsie asked.

"You have not heard the story?" His handsome face showed his surprise.

"No."

"It is most familiar in Russia," her husband said. "Not only is Kschessinska one of our greatest ballet stars, she was also the tsar's mistress for some time. It was a truly romantic story."

Elsie's eyebrows raised. "I have always thought of Tsar Nicholas as a meek, family man dominated by his wife, much in the same way as his cousin King George V of England seems to be dominated by Queen Mary. And both men look so much alike."

"They do," he agreed. "I understand they have been mistaken for each other at royal functions they both attended. I do not know much about England's George, but I can tell you that Russia's Nicholas was not all that meek as a young man."

"Really?"

"He met Kschessinska when he was a young army officer and she danced for an entertainment for his company. It was love at first sight for both of them. Soon all Russia was whispering about the royal romance with a commoner. It has been the custom of the aristocracy to have mistresses in the ballet; but when the heir to the throne is involved, it is a little different."

"I can imagine."

Alex appeared to be enjoying himself as he went on, "The two saw each other constantly, except for the time Nicholas was out of the country on tour. When he returned, he gave her a bracelet of gold, studded with diamonds and a huge sapphire. The story is that after her ballet performances, she and he went for long horseback rides under the moonlight. And after these excursions, Nicholas sometimes remained with her until dawn."

"Of course it could not last," Elsie said. "He could not marry her."

"Kschessinska's father was well aware of that and pointed it out to his daughter. But by this time she was too much in love with Nicholas to care. She was willing to accept the happiness offered by the moment. A house which belonged to Rimsky-Korsakov, the composer, was available for rent and she took it."

"And the romance continued?"

"Nicholas came there often. They held parties and used a gold vodka service which he presented to her. There was dancing and music and all was gaiety."

"And?"

"Nicholas left Russia again and Mathilde Kschessinska's career continued to prosper. She appeared in the 'Sleeping Beauty' by Tschaikovsky, dancing the star role of Princess Aurora and in his 'Nutcracker' in which she appeared as the Sugar Plum Fairy. But the romance between her and Nicholas began to fade."

"He had met the princess who was to become the empress," Elsie said.

"Yes," Alex agreed. "According to my information— and I think it valid—Nicholas had never tried to hide his interest in Princess Alix from Kschessinska. The legend is they parted at a final rendezvous before his marriage. He on horseback and the petite ballet dancer in a coach. When he rode off, she was left sobbing. For months she did nothing but mourn for her lost Nicholas."

"A sad ending to the story."

Alex smiled. "Kschessinska has survived. She returned to the ballet theater under the guidance of the famed ballet master, Marius Petipa. Soon after, the younger Grand Duke Serge became her patron. He bought her a dacha near the ocean with a lovely garden. She is now at the height of her success as a ballet star."

"Do you think Nicholas is happy?"

Her husband shrugged. "I think royalty is almost never happy. Their responsibilities outweigh their benefits; and for Nicholas and Alexandra, the future looks dark. What will happen if revolution comes?"

"They would be deposed and likely escape with plenty of money to keep them," she suggested.

"I hope so. He is a mild, if not too intelligent man; and I'm sure she means well. But she is confused now about her little son's illness. She thinks Rasputin holds the only key to his continued life."

"And you?"

"I think of Rasputin as more of a political force than as a healer," he said, his handsome face shadowing. "I do not believe in faith healers. But the empress does, and perhaps it may all work out for the best."

She said, "Rasputin has become a powerful man."

Alex nodded. "At the moment he is perhaps the most powerful person in all Russia. But many forces are at work. Some of the nobles despise him and have threat-

134

ened to murder him. He was attacked once, but escaped."

"And where do you find yourself in all this?"

He hesitated. "I favor Rasputin, but only to a degree. He has some good ideas and some very bad ones."

"If that Litvinov is one of his cultists, I can't imagine my approving of your mad monk," she said.

"That is different," he was quick to say.

Countess Olga returned to the compartment at this time, and the discussion came to an end. The last hours before they reached Moscow were tedious ones. Elsie slept fitfully, sitting up; and when the train finally came to a lurching halt in the Moscow station, she wakened with a start.

"Have we arrived?" she asked.

"We have." Countess Olga said with a smile. "Home at last!"

Count Alex was on his feet to help the two women dress for the cold outside. They left the train and found themselves in a swirling crowd. The fur hats and the trousers of the men stuck inside felt boots were different from anything she'd seen at the Paris station. They walked over to a side exit, and a young man came to greet them. He wore a heavy green coat and tall fur hat. He smiled and said, "Welcome home, count! And to the new countess and Countess Olga. I have brought the droshky. It is snowing, but only a few flurries and most of the streets are bare."

"Very good, Joseph," he said. "Our luggage is being removed from the luggage car. Once you have arranged for the transportation of it, we wish to be driven directly to the palace."

"Yes, count, it shall be looked after at once." Joseph gave her a warm smile as he bowed to her husband and hurried off on the errand.

Within a few minutes the three were in the droshky, with Joseph at the reins, making their way through the narrow streets of this section of Moscow. It was getting dark, and the street lamps had come on, casting a magic yellow glow around them in which the falling snowflakes could be seen descending gracefully.

Then suddenly the eventide ringing of the innumerable church bells began filling the air with their sounds. Elsie was thrilled by everything she saw; it was the Moscow she expected. Alex did not try to speak above the clamor of the cathedral bells, but smiled at her and took her gloved hand in his.

When they reached the mansion of the Martynovs, Elsie found it huge, sprawling over several acres of grounds, standing by itself surrounded by tall, ancient trees. The River Moscow was in the background for a fitting setting. Most of the windows of the palace showed yellow light, and she guessed this was probably in celebration of their arrival.

Joseph halted the droshky with its two magnificent gray horses in front of the wide entrance to the graystone mansion. They descended, and the door was opened to them by a tall, stooped man with a mane of silver hair and a thin face with a prominent Roman nose. The old man's blue eyes twinkled beneath shaggy, gray brows as he embraced Alex, then Olga, and finally waited to be introduced to Elsie.

Alex showed pride as he said, "My new bride, Elsie; my dear uncle, Count Andre."

"A thousand welcomes," the thin old count said, embracing Elsie.

"I have heard many nice things about you," she said. "And I'm anxious to see your collection of rare books."

"You shall," the old man promised. "Forgive the Countess Marie for not being here to welcome you. She has not been feeling well, but she has promised to be down for the dinner tonight in your honor."

Alex asked sharply, "Where is Timofei?"

The old man's thin face showed embarrassment. "He has been absent for a few days. But a message has been sent. I feel certain he will be with us at dinner."

They moved on toward the curving stairway, which led from the entrance hall. As they did so Countess Olga gave her brother a meaningful look and said, "It seems nothing has changed."

Elsie noted the glances exchanged by the two and guessed their comment had to do with the missing Timofei. It appeared the adopted son of the elderly count and countess was the black sheep of the family.

Alex led her up the stairs saying, "I'm taking you directly to our apartment to rest and change for dinner.

136

You will have plenty of time to make a tour of the house later."

"Of course," she said.

Count Olga walked up the stairway ahead of them. At the first landing, she parted with a small smile and said, "Until dinner."

"Until dinner," Alex agreed. He and Elsie turned down another corridor that led to a huge oak door. He opened the door and a maid standing just inside curtsied. She was a small, dark girl with a plain face but lively eyes.

"This is Elena," Alexander said. "She will be your personal maid. She has traveled with my Aunt Marie and speaks good English. Isn't that so, Elena?"

The maid curtsied again. "Yes, sir," she said in a low respectful voice.

The living room of the apartment was the epitome of elegance; from its crystal chandeliers to its light, wood-paneled walls, the room exuded richness and taste. The fine oil paintings on the walls, the heavy golden drapes at the windows and the exquisite period furnishings and art pieces decorating them, spoke of the family's wealth and high standards.

She stood in the purple of their bedroom and gasped at its beauty with its canopy bed and perfect decor. She turned to her new husband and embraced him. "I've never seen such a house. It's a dream castle."

Alex smiled and kissed her. Then he said, "I will now leave you to enjoy your dream castle and ready yourself for dinner. You have a good hour."

"That will be long enough if my luggage arrives," she said.

"It is on its way up at this very moment," he promised her.

She turned to the maid with a smile. "Then I shall have Elena draw me a nice, hot bath. I feel soot-covered after that long train ride."

She relaxed in the bathtub in the big room finished in gray marble and featuring gold fixtures. The tub itself was sunk deep in the center of the bathroom floor. While she took full enjoyment of the tub, the maid, Elena, unpacked her bags and put her things away.

Three-quarters of an hour later, Elsie sat before the mahogany dresser with its giant oval mirror and put on the earrings which had been a recent gift from her aunt and uncle. She tried to guess what their reaction to the palace would be when they made their promised visit to her and thought about how she'd describe it in her letter to them.

Elena hovered helpfully in the background. "You look most beautiful, countess," the maid volunteered.

"Thank you," she said, smiling into the mirror. "I think I am ready. I wonder where my husband is?"

"He is downstairs in the study conferring with Count Andre," the maid said. "There is much to be done when the young count returns."

"I suppose so," she said. "But surely he will want to freshen up after his long train journey."

Elena glanced across the room to a door on the left. She said, "His quarters are beyond that door. I think I heard him come in a few minutes ago. He will probably join you here when he is ready."

She showed surprise. "I had no idea he would have his own area of the apartment."

The maid nodded. "Yes. That was the part he used before his marriage."

"I see," she said. At least they would not be cramped for space. She went out to the living room of the apartment and admired the dark, oil paintings lining the walls.

She was standing admiring one very ancient study of a forest when someone tapped lightly on the door. Elena gave her a questioning glance and then went over to open the heavy oak door. A blonde young woman with an even perfection of features and golden hair entered. She moved straight across the room with her hand outstretched to Elsie, a gliding beauty in her low-cut pale blue gown.

The newcomer said, "I am Sophie Zemski; and I wanted to meet you before I went down with the countess. The poor old dear is so frail and nervous she takes all my attention and I would not have been able to greet you properly."

"So nice of you," Elsie said, taking her hand. "Alex has told me about you." She spied a large cameo brooch with a sixteenth-century scene of lovers seated on a bench and exclaimed, "What a lovely cameo!"

Sophie flashed a smile, showing perfect teeth to match

138

her perfect face. She said, "One of the few family treasures my father didn't gamble away!"

"You are like all the others. You speak English so well."

"My French is better. I have an accent when I say some things in English," she apologized.

"I say you speak very well. I doubt if I shall ever master Russian."

"Of course you will," Sophie said. "I'll be happy to help you. In the mornings and late afternoons the old lady sleeps a lot and I get some time. And then there are the evenings. She goes to bed early."

"I count on your help," Elsie said.

Sophie studied her for a long moment with blue eyes under long black lashes. "You're lovely! But then so many American girls are beautiful. I hope you and Alexander are very happy."

"Thank you," she said, somewhat embarrassed by the hard scrutiny of the blonde girl. "I suppose you have known him a long while."

"Since childhood," Sophie said. "You see, I am a very distant cousin—so distant it hardly counts—whose family fell into hard times. So the post of companion to the Countess Marie has been a blessing."

"Are you also a countess?" Elsie asked.

"I have abandoned any claim to a title," the blonde said with a wry expression. "I like to think my father lost our title at the gaming tables, along with everything else."

"I'm so sorry," she said.

"Don't be," Sophie replied. "My misfortune has made me a useful human being. Russia has too many noble families and not enough noble hearts among them. I have learned a thing or two about life."

"I'm sure of that. I hope we can be friends."

"If you can get along with Countess Olga, you will have no trouble with me," the blonde girl said, insinuating that Countess Olga was not the easiest person to get along with.

"I'm looking forward to meeting Countess Marie," she said.

"She is anticipating you," Sophie said. "She is sure you are very rich as all Americans have to be and that you will be dripping in diamonds. Your modesty will disappoint her. Also she is terribly deaf."

Elsie smiled. "I haven't enough diamonds to dazzle her; and I didn't plan to wear any tonight, aside from the ring which Alex gave me. But I shall remember to speak loudly to her."

"The important thing," Sophie said with approval. "It will save me doing a lot of repeating for her benefit."

"What about Timofei?"

Sophie's blue eyes twinkled with grim amusement. "Let me tell you confidentially he has been absent on a drunken binge for days. The privilege of an artist of his talents and great temperament, so he seems to think. Count Andre, who must kneel before lighted candles to ask succor for the error of adopting him, sent an urgent message to the house of one his cronies. He may or may not appear."

"He sounds a character."

"He is that," Sophie said. "The count and countess made a mistake in adopting him; he has not grown up to the manner born. But *c'est la vie,* as our French friends say."

Elsie smiled. "I will see you downstairs."

"Yes," Sophie said. "Enough of my gossip for the moment. I'm glad you're here. I hope you're not crushed by it all."

Seconds after Sophie left, the door which the maid had indicated led to the quarters used by Alex opened, and Alex joined her, resplendent in white tie and tails.

"You managed that nicely," Elsie told him.

"I consider it a fitting occasion to celebrate," her husband said, admiring her. "And you never looked lovelier."

"I've just had a visitor."

"Who?"

"Sophie."

Her handsome husband looked wary. He said, "Really? She couldn't wait to meet you downstairs?"

"No," she said. "She came to see me first because of the Countess Marie's infirmity. She felt it would be impossible to cater to the countess and greet me properly."

Alex looked a trifle less uneasy. "I hadn't thought of that," he admitted. "She is probably right."

"I like her. She's very nice. She says you two grew up together."

His handsome face showed crimson. "Hardly that. We

are distantly related. Did she tell you that? So we did see a good deal of each other as children."

"So I gathered," she said. And she began to wonder if there mightn't have been a romance between Sophie and the handsome Alex at some time. Especially as Sophie had spoken somewhat derogatorily of her husband's sister, who also showed a great fondess for him. Could Olga and Sophie have been rivals?

Alex said, "Sophie is an impulsive, clever girl. Her beauty belies her brains. I think she will go far. I'd like to see her make a good marriage."

"Meaning a noble one?"

"The aristocracy would offer her the best prospects," he admitted.

"I wonder if she wants that? She didn't give me that idea."

"Did she not?" Alex said, trying to sound casual; but she felt his manner covered a tension he wished to keep concealed from her. "Well, you're on show now. Time to go below."

Drinks were served in the huge ground floor living room. Elsie was so nervous that she took in little of the detail of the huge room, except that it was even more elaborate than her own drawing room upstairs.

The tall Count Andre fetched her a drink in a silver goblet and then a trembling Countess Marie came into the room, leaning heavily on a radiant Sophie. The girl brought the old woman close to Elsie.

"My dear!" the Countess Marie said, stretching out her claw-like hands to embrace her. Elsie leaned close to the frail old body in the radiant green gown and touched her lips to the dry parchment of the older woman's cheek.

"I am happy to meet you, countess," she said, as she moved back from the embrace.

The old lady studied Elsie and said, "You are such a child." She turned to Alex and asked, "Why did you marry this American child?"

Alex smiled good-naturedly at his aunt. "I'm certain she is at least three years older than you were on your wedding day to Andre."

"That is true," Count Andre Martynov said, his hawk

face beaming. "And what a day that was. The celebration after. The tsar himself attended, you know!"

Countess Marie stared near-sightedly at Elsie again. "All people look so young these days. Is it the soap they use or the cosmetics?"

Sophie helped her to a chair. "It is neither," she said loudly. "You were every bit as young looking in your wedding portrait."

The old woman settled in her chair. "I was a lady-in-waiting to the tsarina at court. This is how the tsar came to attend the wedding. He was no special friend of Andre. In fact he told me once, he thought him too bookish."

The thin old Count Andre gave his seated wife an annoyed look. Then he raised his glass and said, "I offer a toast to the new Countess Martynov."

They all drank, including Olga, who had stood there quietly without a word. As the toast ended, someone entered the doorway of the room, and Elsie saw a mischievous smile cross Olga's face.

A hulking figure of a young man with an unruly mop of dull-colored brown hair came striding into the room. He was not in evening dress like the others, and the suit he wore was badly wrinkled as if he might have slept in it. But his big slab face was shaven, with a nick in one cheek. And his sleepy brown eyes met the gaze of the others with a hint of contempt. He turned to Elsie and with a sour smile extended a ham-like hand to her.

"I'm Timofei, and I welcome you, countess," he said.

She shook his hand, noting the tense quiet his entrance had brought to the room. "Thank you, Cousin Timofei," she said.

"Cousin Timofei! I like that!" the hulking young man said in a tone of pure mockery. "You are a nice American girl, and I hope you have better luck than the last bride who came here."

Alex was crimson with anger. He said, "Timofei!"

The big man waved his hand. "No offense meant, Cousin Alexander. But I couldn't help remembering the night the late Basil brought his bride here. And it wasn't too long afterward she hung herself in this very house."

142

❧ Chapter 12 ❧

EVERYBODY REACTED TO Timofei's statement. An enraged Alex led the big man apart from the others and began to give him a lecture in a loud voice.

Elderly Countess Marie from her chair demanded, "What did the boy say?"

Sophie bent to her and replied, "It doesn't bear repeating at this moment."

Count Andre's hand trembled as he took Elsie's glass from her and said, "Allow me to get you another drink."

Countess Olga shrugged, came over to her, and said, "I don't know why they are making such a fuss. You were bound to find out sooner or later."

"About the suicide?" Elsie said.

"Yes. The bride they are speaking of was Katrin, Basil's wife. And she did hang herself in one of the upstairs bedrooms after she heard of his murder.

"Katrin was a soft-hearted girl, a sentimentalist. She didn't seem to understand the cruel business Basil was mixing in. I don't think she ever tried to restrain him. And when she found out that he'd been murdered in St. Petersburg, she took it badly. She killed herself before the body was brought back."

"Alex didn't tell me," Elsie said.

"We prefer not to mention it," Olga said. "At least everyone but Timofei. You will soon get used to him. He tries to scandalize the rest of us. You will do well to avoid him as much as possible," Olga advised.

"I see."

"He likes to cause trouble," Olga said darkly.

Count Andre returned with another drink for Elsie. As he gave her the silver goblet, he cleared his throat nervously and said, "I fear my son has given you a bad impression of us."

"No," she replied.

"What he said is true," the thin old man went on carefully. "But he neither presented his facts at the proper time nor in the proper manner. Katrin was a dove-like creature, unable to withstand the cruelties of life. The loss of a beloved husband was more than her poor heart could bear."

"Katrin?" the old Countess Marie asked from her chair. "How could she have known Katrin? Was Katrin ever in America?"

Sophie gave Elsie a resigned look and then spoke loudly to the old lady, "She did not know Katrin. She is just hearing about her now."

"A sorry story!" the old woman nodded. "Crushed like some poor little sparrow!"

Count Andre smiled bleakly. "My poor wife is rather deaf. She is also a trifle sentimental."

"A good fault," Elsie suggested politely.

Count Andre nodded. "You are from New York?"

"Yes," she said.

"I was in New York years ago," he said. "It was during the Spanish-American War—your Teddy Roosevelt and all those rough rider chaps."

She smiled. "He was world famous. And he's still around. There is a rumor that he may run for office again."

"President Theodore Roosevelt," Count Andre said with a smile at his remembering the exact name. "Yes, I liked your New York. I would enjoy seeing it again one day."

"My Aunt and Uncle Cooper would welcome you, although we have a modest home compared to this," she said.

"Exciting idea," the old man said, his eyes sparkling. Then he looked at the old woman crouched over her silver goblet in the easy chair, "If only the countess were in better health. And I dare not leave her. She is very dependent on me."

Alex had returned from lecturing Timofei, and now he said sternly, "I think it is time we went in to the table."

"Past time," the Countess Olga said with another of her looks full of sisterly meaning.

Alex took Elsie's on his arm as the group began to move to the dining room. In a low voice, he said, "I'm sorry about what Timofei said."

"It doesn't matter," she told him.

"Worse than that, you'll be sitting to the right of the oaf at dinner. You'll be between my Uncle Andre and Timofei. Ignore Timofei as much as possible."

"I daren't be rude."

"And he isn't to be encouraged," her husband warned her as they entered the long, narrow dining room, which had a huge table set with a gleaming white cloth and dishes of gold.

Count Andre Martynov was seated at the head of the table with his ancient wife at the other end. Alex and Sophie sat on one side of the table, while Elsie, Timofei, and Olga sat opposite them. As Alex had warned her, Count Andre was on her left and Timofei on her right, Timofei nearer her.

Candles flamed in silver holders and there was a cluster of roses in the center of the table. Waiters in colorful silken blouses with high necks and sashes tied around their waists served the courses quietly and with the skill of long training. A wine steward presented a sampling of a bottle for the thin, old Count Andre to approve. The old man nodded and the wine was served.

Conversation at the table was lively enough with an occasional toast offered. Timofei drank heartily and soon turned to her in drunken good humor.

"What made you decide to come to Russia, little innocent?" he wanted to know.

She smiled. "That is not a mystery. I fell in love with your cousin."

"That is," Timofei said promptly. "You have made a most unfortunate choice. The male line of the Martynovs has not been impressive for their laudable qualities in the last few generations. I do not qualify as I happen to be a mongrel chosen from a score of cots in an orphanage."

Elsie was embarrassed. "I'm sure you are joking."

"Not at all," he insisted. "Take my foster father, Count

Andre. Did you know he was once a captain in the Russian navy?"

Elsie glanced at Count Andre, who was having an earnest conversation with Alex. She looked back at Timofei and said, "Surely being a captain in the navy is commendable."

"It would have been," Timofei said, "if he hadn't had his ship sunk from under him the first day of battle."

"Oh!"

Timofei grinned. "The Russian navy sailed halfway around the world to meet the Japanese fleet, and in a few hours the war was settled. The cream of the Russian fleet was sinking to the bottom of the ocean. And we had goaded the Japanese into fighting the war. That's a historical fact."

"I know little about it," she said.

"You must study the facts, "Timofei told her. "Now let us deal with the late lamented Basil, a handsome fellow. You will find his portrait on the living room wall, and it is a good likeness."

"He was murdered in St. Petersburg."

"Because he became a turncoat to his class. He became one of a most undesirable group and paid the price for it, as did the poor girl unfortunate enough to marry him. Katrin was a find girl. She deserved better."

"It is all very sad," she said, touching her napkin to her lips.

"And not over yet," Timofei said with drunken triumph. "Here we have Alexander, the pride of the family. He brings us back a bride from America. And yet he is following in the same footsteps as his late brother. He treads dangerous ground."

In an effort to change the subject, she said, "You are an artist. I hear you wish to be a portrait artist."

"No," he scoffed. "That is all behind me. What is the future of portrait painting in this country?"

"It should be good. You have many noble families with wealth."

"Ah! But it will not remain that way long. We are on our way to a revolution, the like of which the world has never known before. And with the tide of revolution the wealthy and noble will be swept away."

"You believe that all this grandeur will vanish?"

"You are here to witness its death," the big man said gravely. "I have one interest now. That is, aside from being the marathon drinker of all Moscow. I want to paint a fine icon."

"An icon?"

"Do you know what an icon is?"

"I'm not certain," she said.

"I will explain," he went on with drunken gravity. "An icon is a religious painting, or object of art. Our cathedrals are filled with them. And you may even find some good examples in the most out-of-the-way rural church."

She said, "So you wish to do a fine church painting."

He shook his head. "No, I want to produce an icon of true splendor. But I don't intend to paint it for a church or cathedral. I want to do it on the wall of a drinking place, a spot where the vodka sodden can gaze on it and gain hope from it's beauty."

She laughed. "You are making fun of me."

"I am serious," he said. "You will see. I will paint my icon, and it will be on the wall of one of Moscow's most notorious dives. That is where it has to be."

Alex addressed her from across the table. "You must not pay too much attention to anything he tells you."

Elsie said, "We are having an interesting discussion about icons."

"Fault that, Count Martynov," Timofei said taunting him. "I'm educating the girl in our Russian art forms."

"Very generous of you," Alex said grimly.

Dinner ended, and everyone returned to the living room. The ladies had coffee; the males, brandy and cigars. Elsie slowly made the rounds of the fine oil paintings on the walls of the big room. She finally came to one of a young man who so resembled Alex that she knew it was the dead Basil.

Countess Olga came up beside her. "You found his portrait."

She studied the resolute, handsome face of the slim young man. "Yes, he could almost be a twin of Alex. It is a study of Basil, isn't it?"

Olga nodded. "Yes, done a year before he was murdered."

"Sad," she said. "And equally sad that his Katrin should have felt that life was not worthwhile without him."

The dark girl sighed, "She was a gentle girl, too gentle for her own good. We are not an easy family to live with. You are soon finding that out." She indicated Timofei, now standing and talking with Sophie.

"He doesn't bother me," she said.

"Give him time enough, and he will. You'll find yourself feeling like the rest of us," Olga promised her.

They moved back to the others, and Elsie addressed herself to the ancient Count Andre, saying, "I hear you are a naval veteran of the Russian-Japanese War."

The thin face of the old man showed angry emotion. "We were tricked into a trap. The whole fleet was lost. I could have been drowned. My ship sank under me."

"You were fortunate," she said.

The thin old face was torn with mixed emotions as he said, "There are times when I wonder. Perhaps it is better to die in battle rather than wither away with age. I think that is why men of all centuries have been willing to go into battle, despite the lessons of history."

She smiled, "I can see that you are a romantic."

The old man looked pleased. "In my youth I was considered one of the most dashing young men around the court. And my dear Marie was a reigning beauty." He sighed. "You see what age has done to us."

Timofei came across to them, a glass of some amber liquor in his hand. "Did I tell you about the family ghost?" he asked.

His foster father lifted a thin old hand in protest. "I say we can spare her that."

"No, she should be told," the slab-faced young man said. "His name is Nicholas, Count Nicholas. Lived here ages ago. Built this place. Murdered three wives and hung himself when it was found out."

"A legend," Count Andre said placatingly. "We give small attention to it."

Timofei would not be put off. "Wrong," he said. "I have seen the ghost. So have others. And you can be sure that sooner or later he'll be bound to present himself to a new bride in the house. The occasion calls for it."

"I've heard about the phantom," she said quietly.

Timofei went off, repeating, "The occasion calls for it."

When he had gone from the living room, Count Andre apologized for him: "Timofei can be a most interesting young man when he is not in his cups."

"He talked well at dinner," she agreed. "He told me he wants to paint an inspirational icon."

Count Andre's thin face showed amazement and pleasure at this bit of news. He said, "I'll vow he's never mentioned it to anyone before. I hope he means to go through with it."

"I'm convinced he does," she said. But she didn't explain that he planned to paint his icon in some low drinking place.

After a little, Alex came to her and said, "You must be weary."

"I am," she admitted.

"Then we should retire to our apartment," he told her. "Everyone knows we've just completed a long journey."

Alex and Elsie said their good nights to everyone but Timofei, who had vanished somewhere. Then they went upstairs to their private apartment. The maid had turned down the bed and Elsie's night things were neatly set out.

She asked her husband, "What about your things?"

"In my room," he said. "I'll bring them here."

She gave him a teasing smile. "I'm glad to hear that. I was afraid you were going to leave me alone on our first night in our own home."

"Hardly," he said, taking her in his arms. "How do you feel about them?"

"What do you mean?"

He frowned. "About the sort of people they are. Do you think you'll be able to get along with them?"

"Surely," she said. "Even with Timofei."

"He doesn't count," Alex said angrily. "I don't know how much longer my aunt and uncle will tolerate him. But I'm about at the breaking point. He resents all of us because he knows he is not one of us."

"Yet I think he must have talent," she said.

"He does," Alex agreed. "But it will do him no good. He is too bitter and erratic. It's a shame, but he seems to have decided to drink himself to death and cause us as much disgrace as possible along the way."

"Perhaps if you talked with him, treated him in a more friendly fashion?"

"It wouldn't help," her husband said with disgust. "We have done our best and failed."

"He talks about a coming revolution as if he is sure it will happen," she said.

"Because he wants it to happen."

"I wonder," she said. "Or is he truly frightened and this is his way of coping with it."

Alex eyed her with humorous cynicism. "You think you understand him?"

"He seems to like me. Maybe if I talked to him he would listen."

Alex shook his head. "Don't count on it! He tried the same game with poor Katrin when she first came here. He won her sympathy and then made fun of her."

She was shocked. "He can be that cruel?"

"Even worse," her husband said. "I'll go to my room and gather up my pajamas and some of my other things. I won't be more than a few minutes."

He left her, and she went to the window to gaze out at the wide river, still covered with a thin coating of ice. In the distance, she heard the wailing howl of a dog or perhaps a wolf. There was a bright moon and the snow flurries had ended. She gazed down at the river bank directly behind the mansion.

Crossing along the bank was a familiar figure whom she could recognize even though she was now wearing a shawl. Countess Olga was moving about nervously down there, apparently waiting for someone. As she watched, Olga moved further down the river bank and was hidden by the shadow of some tall trees.

She left the window to change into her night clothes and wash. While she busied herself, she wondered about what she had just seen. What had Olga been doing out there? It was all too likely that she was there to meet someone. That she didn't want the others in the house to know about it. But who and why?

The Martynov family were a complex lot. She was forever finding herself faced with puzzles, and the answers were by no means apparent. She no longer thought it strange that Alex was so moody. He was one of a temperamental family. Even the adopted Timofei had become a neurotic. And Basil's wife had hung herself somewhere in the house, perhaps on this same floor. She didn't like to dwell on it.

She had listened to Timofei say that Alex was following in Basil's footsteps and from what had happened in London, she knew all too well this was true. She now must see to it that Alex kept away from Litvinov and the cultists with whom he fraternized. She hoped that she would soon hear from Ralph Manning and that he would have more information to offer her concerning Litvinov and the Skoptsi cult, which had been reputedly organized under the leadership of the venal Rasputin.

Thinking of Ralph made her realize how different her surroundings were from what she had been used to. It was as much different as being on another planet. She had been so at ease in New York and now she was faced with a change of language, customs, and setting. She would need all her courage to meet the challenge. And she would if only Alex did not falter and let her down.

She was standing in the shadowed light of the room debating these many things when the side door opened, and Alex came back into the room, resplendent in a brown silk dressing gown and pajamas in a matching shade. He smiled at her.

"I decided to change in my own room," he said.

She went to him, conscious that her svelte figure was clearly visible to him beneath her diaphanous pink nightgown, and enjoying the moment. It thrilled her to reach out to the male in him.

He took her in his arms and studied her with adoring eyes. "You are lovely."

"I want to be for you," she whispered.

He kissed her passionately and then lifted her in his arms and carried her to the canopied bed. Their lovemaking on this first night in the Moscow palace was more fervent and prolonged than ever before. The total abandon of their perfect union left them pleasantly weary. They slept side by side like the lovers they were.

Things had begun so well that for a brief time Elsie allowed herself to hope that all their problems had been left behind. That in this house on the banks of the Moscow River they were destined to know true happiness.

When Elsie awoke the next morning, Alexander had already left her. She knew he had many affairs to look after, but wished he had wakened her before he left. But this was not Alexander's way. She had come to know that.

The maid, Elena, came with her breakfast tray and remained to help her with her morning ablutions and to tidy up the room. Elsie found the breakfast satisfying and interesting. She had the tray placed on a table near the window and sat with a view of the river as she ate.

She recalled seeing the Countess Olga lingering out there on the river bank the night before and wondered what it had meant. She was certain it had been Olga, and she must have had a rendezvous with someone.

Elsie looked up from her plate of bacon and eggs to ask the maid, "Is the river still frozen over?"

Elena hesitated in her making up of the bed. The petite girl said, "There is a thin layer of ice, but it is no longer safe for the sleighs. It should break clear within a week or two."

"The river is used for transportation during the cold months?"

"Yes, countess," Elena said. "Many people prefer the even surface of the river to the rough roads for getting about. And then there are races on some occasions. And the cossacks do special drills out there when the tsar is in Moscow."

"I have only had a glimpse of the city," Elsie said. "I want to see more of it."

"It is a huge city," Elena said. "But I have seen both Paris and London. And I like Paris best of all. My mistress used to spend months at a time there when the weather was severe here."

"And now you are in the service of the Martynovs. Have you traveled any since you came to this house?"

The maid's face shadowed. "I made one visit to Paris with Countess Katrin and Count Basil."

Elsie's eyebrows raised. "Then you must have known them well."

"As well as a servant may know her employers," the maid said respectfully.

"What was she like, the Countess Katrin?"

"Beautiful, like a golden-haired doll, but very fragile in health," Elena said. "She had a baby girl, and it died a month after its birth. This brought both her and Count Basil much sadness."

"I can understand," she said, sipping her tea.

The maid sighed. "But she got over that. She and the count were very happy in Paris. It was after they came back that the count began to change, and she began to fret."

"Count Basil changed? In what way?"

The maid showed embarrassment. "It is not a matter I should discuss."

"You may speak plainly to me," she said. "I will repeat it to no one. I'm new here, and I must somehow find out what has gone on here."

Looking uneasy, the maid said, "I know little of it, except that Count Basil began going to St. Petersburg and remaining there for days at a time."

"What was his excuse?"

"He was supposed to be looking after family business. But I overheard an argument between him and his wife, and she told him that Count Alexander had assured her there was no family business which required those long absences."

"Could it have been another woman?" Elsie ventured.

"I'm sure Countess Katrin thought so," the maid said. "I know she spent a great deal of time alone, and she cried a lot."

"And then what?"

"Count Basil would come home in a drunken state and not even stop by her room to see her. He slept in another area of the house."

"So things became worse. They drew further apart."

The maid nodded. "At the end, he was barely ever sober. But the morning before he went away, he came to her and stayed with her for a long while. I know by the way she behaved afterward that he must have begged her forgiveness and told her that he loved her despite all his bad actions. She was fairly happy for a few days. Then the word came."

Elsie said, "That he had been murdered."

"Yes."

"How did it actually happen?"

"We did not hear much about it," Elena said. "We think he was a member of one of the revolutionary groups and that he was killed in a bomb explosion. These things happen here all the time. Countess Katrin fainted when she heard the news, and Count Alexander at once left for St. Petersburg to bring the body home."

"And before the body arrived Countess Katrin took her own life," Elsie said.

The girl looked frightened. "She hung herself in a closet off her bedroom. Frederick found her and cut her poor body down."

"What room did it happen in?" she asked, getting up from her chair.

Elena took on a pale, trapped expression. "I'd rather not say, countess."

"Go on!" she urged the girl. "You need not be afraid to tell me."

Elena swallowed hard. "This room!"

"This room?" Elsie repeated.

"Yes, countess," the girl said. "Count Basil and his wife occupied this apartment when they were alive. Count Alexander moved in after their deaths."

"No one told me," she said in a hushed voice. "Which closet did they find her body in?"

"That one," Elena said, indicating a door on the wall where the head of the bed was, a door to the left of the bed. It was where Elsie had most of her good dresses hanging. The news gave her a strange feeling. But she knew she had forced the information from the girl, and so it would be stupid of her to complain. Yet it seemed to her that Alex might have been more considerate if he had chosen another apartment for them. Perhaps there was no other suitable one in the palace.

She tried to hide any nervousness she felt, saying, "Well, at least now I know."

"I'm sorry," Elena said. "I oughtn't to have told you."

"I asked you directly."

The maid was sympathetic. "You need have no fear of ghosts, countess. Countess Katrin was a lovely person who would harm no one."

154

"I'm sure that must be so," she agreed.

"And Count Basil was seldom in this room."

"I see," she said. "I presume he had his own quarters where my husband does."

"Yes, countess," Elena said. The bed finished, she stood awkwardly. "They had a double funeral for them, sad business. The countess looked lovely in her casket, but Count Basil had been so badly injured they did not open his casket. It was a heavy blow for Countess Marie. She has not been well since."

"I noticed that she is feeble," Elsie said.

"Much worse than before, but now that you are here she may brighten up again. She has talked about plans for the wedding with Frederick. He is the head of all us servants."

"The wedding," she remembered. "I'd almost forgot about that. You see the count and I were married in America."

Elena said, "But there is to be a wedding here as well. At least that is what I've heard."

Elsie managed a smile. "I've been here only such a short time and I haven't had time to think about it."

"I'm sure Count Andre will be discussing it with you," the maid said. She gathered up the linen from the bed and added, "I'll take these downstairs and come back with fresh towels later."

Elsie thanked her and then began to dress. She had received a good fund of information from the maid, some of which she could have done without. Every time she approached the death closet, she had a feeling of apprehension.

When she finished dressing, she left the apartment and went down the broad, curving stairway. At the bottom of it was Count Andre, who had just emerged from the living room.

The count's thin face lit up as soon as he saw her. "I'm glad we met this way," he said. "I have something important to discuss with you. There has been a change in the plans for your wedding here."

Chapter 13

ELSIE WAS SURPRISED to have the matter of her wedding brought up so soon after her discussion of it with the maid. She told Count Andre, "Alex and I have not had any time to discuss the matter."

"I realize that," the count said. "Alex and I talked about it this morning. It was his idea that I speak to you."

"I see," she said, wondering why Alex had done this rather than approach her about it personally.

The gray-haired man said, "You have not seen our private chapel?"

"No," she said.

"Come with me," Count Andre said, taking her gently by the arm and leading her along a corridor toward the rear of the great house. Part way along the shadowed corridor they turned and took a second, narrow passage on the right. This led to closed doors with intricate carved panels of light oak. The old man made the sign of the cross and opened the doors to reveal a fair-sized chapel, complete with windows of stained glass and an ornate altar. The floor of the chapel was done in mosaic and represented religious patterns.

"How beautiful," Elsie said, entranced. The vaulted ceiling rose high to be lost in shadows, and the daylight, which seeped in through the picturesque windows of stained-glass, lent a suitably restrained atmosphere to it all. She saw an organ at the rear by the altar; down front was a stone baptismal font in soft gray, which boasted a continual fountain of water.

"The chapel is as old as the house," Count Andre said, a smile on his wrinkled, thin face. "Our ancestor who built it may have been a three-time wife murderer, but he had a keen appreciation of religion at the same time. It was too

156

bad he took his own life, the church was not able to give him absolution."

"At least he left you this beautiful legacy," she said.

"It has served the Martynovs through the centuries," he went on. "You will see that it is empty of seats of any kind. Most of our churches and cathedrals are. The ailing and very feeble bring their chairs, or come with wheelchairs. This chapel has been the scene of christenings, funerals, and weddings for all the Martynovs. And when Marie and I die, we will be buried from here."

She glanced about her and on one wall she saw a fine painting of the "Virgin and Child" and on the opposite one a large head of the Savior. She also noted the brass candle holders and incense burners near the altar. She said, "The icons are beautiful."

"Every holy place in Russia has some of them." The old man smiled.

She remembered Timofei's talk of icons and his desire to do a major one. He had claimed it was his major ambition as an artist. "I'm just becoming familiar with them," she said.

"The one on the right is 'The Virgin of Compassion' and dates to the construction of the house in the late seventeenth century. Of course, the other is the 'Holy Image of the Savior' not made with hands."

"What does that mean?"

He stepped closer to the icon on the right wall so they were just below it. He said, "The saviour not made with hands is a popular subject for the icon painter. It goes back to a legend which relates that when Christ was carrying his cross to Golgotha, a woman handed him a cloth, or veil, to wipe the sweat off his face. He did so, and the veil became imprinted with his image as we see it up there."

She gazed at the painting in awe. "I see; it depicts the head of Christ with the veil as a background. The hands and shoulders aren't there, because they weren't on the veil. But the strands of hair falling to His shoulders on either side cover this missing detail." She turned to the old man. "The eyes are the most striking feature, so much expression in them!"

He nodded. "We are proud of our chapel and the icons in it."

She said, "I'm glad you've shown it to me."

Count Andre moved a few steps nearer the altar. "We have everything here for a proper religious service. And this brings me to the discussion your husband and I had this morning. Our original plan was to have a wedding in the Cathedral of St. Gregory, where our family normally worship. We had set the date about a month hence."

"But now Alex has a different thought?"

"Yes," the old man said seriously. "He was at once aware of the sad state of health of the Countess Marie. She seems to fail almost daily. The major weight of the preparations would be on her shoulders for a fine public wedding."

"That would not be fair," Elsie said at once.

"Alex and I agree," the old man said. "Our thought now is to hold a simple service here with a few close friends and the immediate family in attendance. As you can see it is a lovely setting. Would you mind?"

"I'd be pleased," she said. "We have already gone through one public wedding in New York, and I would be relieved to escape another."

"My wife could attend without any strain on her," Count Andre went on. "And afterward, a fine feast of celebration with entertainment could be held here in the palace. If my wife became tired she would merely have to be helped to her room. It would be much simpler all around."

Elsie was relieved by the suggestion. "I think you are being very wise."

"Then that is how we shall proceed," the old man said. "Olga will be able to take the main burden of invitations and arrangements with my wife acting as adviser. Alex wants the wedding to be held in three weeks or so, and tomorrow morning a priest from St. Gregory's Cathedral will come to give you instruction in our branch of the Christian faith. He will come daily until you have a proper knowledge."

She said, "I don't think I'm prepared for conversion."

"That is not required," Count Andre said. "Although the tsarina did have to convert from Lutherism to Catholicism to become our empress. In the case of a noble marriage such as yours, only instruction is required and the promise that your children shall be raised in the Eastern Orthodox faith."

She said, "Alex explained that to me before our marriage, and I'm quite willing to abide by that rule."

"Excellent," the old man said as they stood facing each other in the silent, subdued atmosphere of the chapel. "I hope you have many healthy children. The late Count Basil had only one, and the child was sickly and died shortly after birth."

"I heard that. And also that the Countess Katrin was despondent about it."

"She was," he said, his wrinkled face a mask of sadness. "I think it helped upset her mind. And when her beloved husband was murdered, it was the final straw. She hanged herself."

"In the very room in which I am now," Elsie said dryly.

The old man showed embarrassment. "You were not meant to know that."

"It doesn't matter."

"Of course not," he agreed. "Many have lived and died in this house. If all their ghosts returned, it would be too crowded for we humans here now."

"But the ghost of Count Nicholas is said to haunt the palace and grounds."

His face shadowed. "They say so." And he made no attempt to explain further. It was evident by his manner the subject was distasteful to him.

They lingered in the chapel for a few minutes more. The count promised to place chairs in there for the priest and her, so she might receive her religious instruction in a proper setting.

Elsie parted from the old man in the foyer, where they had met. It was sunny outside, and she went up to her apartment and found a warm cloak and heavy shoes. Then she went back down the curving stairway to take a stroll outside.

Frederick, the butler, a wizened little man of seventy with a completely bald head, was there to open the front door for her and give her instructions as to where she might best enjoy the walk.

"There is a path around to the left, countess," he said. "By that route you avoid the stables and other outbuildings. And it leads to the tall trees that border on the river bank."

"Thank you," she said with a smile. And she went out.

The air was cool but refreshing. Although the palace was not far from the great city of Moscow, it seemed isolated. The ground was soggy and thick with wet leaves. The trees still had tufts of snow on them from the previous night's flurries, and the thin ice of the river gleamed under the sun.

She walked out to the place where she had seen Olga waiting the night before and saw that there was a path which led to adjoining woods. While she was standing there a great white Borzoi hound came bounding to greet her. She had seen an occasional Russian wolfhound with their aristocratic, slim bodies and delicately shaped heads, but never had one come up to her with such abandon. She stepped back timorously and then, when she saw it was friendly, patted its head. It remained at her side only a moment and then bounded on about its business.

The Borzoi had barely left her when Timofei came in sight. He was evidently on his way from the stables on the other side of the palace and came toward her with a slouching air. He wore a dark, peaked cap, a jacket of brown, and gray trousers stuffed into tall brown leather boots at the knee level. His face took on an amused expression as he came up to her.

"Having a constitutional, little innocent?"

She smiled. "Yes, it's a lovely day."

"Tonight mists will rise from the river," he said, turning to gaze at it. "And phantoms will move along this path where we are now."

"You have a strong imagination," she said.

Timofei turned to her again. "Unlike the Martynovs."

"You talk as if you hated them. I think you are fortunate to have been adopted by Count Andre and Countess Marie."

"No," the big man said, lifting a huge hand to emphasize the point. "You have it all wrong. They chose me, an innocent babe in an orphanage cot, and doomed me to become a member of the foul aristrocracy. I could well have been adopted by someone like Trotsky, Feodor Kerensky, or even Lenin. I might have become the son of a revolutionary; and it would be all beginning for me, not coming to an end as it surely is now."

"You need not remain here. You could go away on your own and be whatever you like," she said.

"A part-time revolutionary like the departed Basil," he said with disgust. "That could only end in one group or the other betraying me and putting an end to me. I prefer to live."

The cool spring wind brushed them in a melancholy fashion as they stood beneath the giant, leafless trees. She gazed up at him. "I think you are a fraud. You really like the Martynovs but enjoy pretending you don't."

Timofei studied her with new interest. "Do all American girls have your charm?"

"That is a nice compliment," she said. "I didn't suppose you capable of it."

The huge young man grinned. "I have only had my beginning supply of vodka for the day. I become more sharp-tongued as evening approaches."

"I must remember that. Do you come out here often?" she asked.

"Yes," he said. "I enjoy being alone. Do you?"

"Yes," she said. "I thought I saw Olga out here late last night. It was moonlight, if you remember. She seemed to be waiting for someone."

Timofei looked wise. "You want a word of advice?"

"If it will be helpful."

"Don't tell her you saw her."

"Why?"

"She wouldn't appreciate it."

"I don't understand."

"Countess Olga has irons in the fire that she prefers to attend solely by herself. She might get the idea you were spying on her."

"I see," she said. "Thanks. I had no idea it might be something she wouldn't want to discuss."

Timofei said, "All the Martynovs have that in common. They all have secrets they prefer not to discuss. Even your beloved Alex."

She blushed. "You don't like him, do you?"

Timofei chuckled. "If I liked him he would be the exception in the family. Shall we stroll down to the river. I want to see how near the ice is to melting."

Elsie held her blue coat tightly around her. Its dark fur collar was welcome on this coolish morning. She wanted to keep chatting with the young man, since she felt she might learn more about the Martynovs and especially about her husband.

She said, "Yes, I'll walk down the bank with you."

"Let me take your arm," he suggested. "The leaves and the mud may make it slippery even though the ground is still frozen."

"Thanks," she said, allowing him to take her by the arm.

"In the winter, I raced here on the river," he said. "I have a fine team of brown stallions. They won me a bundle of rubles, I can promise you."

She smiled up at him. "I'd say you enjoy life. And one day you will paint your great icon."

"Be sure of that," the big man told her. "And it will be in a bar, or a place of ill-repute. Never in a church."

"You're incorrigible," she laughed.

As she spoke, she slipped on some leaves and almost fell. They were close to the river's edge, and he quickly caught her. Then before she realized it, he brought her close to him and planted a kiss on her lips. Then he let her go and laughed.

She looked at him. "I can't say I wasn't warned against you!"

"So I had to live up to my reputation."

"It isn't necessary with me, Timofei," she reprimanded him. "I won't expect it to happen again."

"Most girls are grateful for my kisses."

"I'm married."

"Married women are often the most grateful of all," he teased her, bright eyes sparkling.

She said seriously, "I want us to be friends. Don't spoil it."

The big man reacted at once. "Very well, little innocent, it is friends we shall be. But let me ask you one personal question?"

"What?" she asked him warily.

"What sort of lover is Alex? Is he any good in bed?"

She gasped. "You just made me a promise! Why break it?"

"I'm serious," he told her. "There are things you don't know about your Alex. Things you should be warned about. For one, he and Sophie were lovers and not all that long before he went to America and met you."

Elsie listened without knowing whether to be shocked or grateful. From the first, she had suspected that her husband and Sophie had been closer than either seemed to admit.

"Why did he give her up?" Elsie asked.

"An interesting reason," Timofei said mysteriously. "And one that might concern you."

As distasteful as the conversation was, Elsie could not help continuing it. With one secret revealed, she thought she might probe to discover whether another of her concerns had any foundation. She said, "You are picturing my poor Alex as an unprincipled Casanova."

"I'm telling you truths you should know," the big man countered. "It is over with Sophie now. But you are better for having the knowledge of it."

She challenged him, saying, "Next you'll be telling me that he and his sister, Countess Olga were lovers."

Timofei showed amazement. "You outdo me in your imagination, little innocent. You are wrong there. Alex and Olga are devoted, but there is no incest. A Martynov would never commit such a sin."

Elsie felt a great weight slip from her. The frank talk had proved helpful in this at least. She need not have any further concern on this score. She asked, "Why do they go off together for mysterious talks?"

Timofei winked at her. "They have their secrets. And they are not for repeating, at least not now. I must hold something back. And you have not answered my question, whether Alex is an ardent lover."

"I do not have the experience to measure love," she said. "But he has been warm enough. The trouble is he has so often been distracted by matters I don't understand. In London he spent most of his time in the company of a villainous man named Litvinov."

Timofei whistled. "Litvinov! From St. Petersburg!"

"You know about him?"

"Enough not to want to know him better," Timofei said. "I'd say Basil might be alive, but for him. He is one of Rasputin's cult leaders."

"Why should my husband make a friend of him?" she worried.

The big man studied her seriously. "You do well to be upset. My seemingly impertinent question had a meaning beyond your understanding. Basil was once the most ardent of lovers and the best of husbands. In the end, under the influence of that scoundrel, Litvinov, he became a hater of women. He was a mad shell of himself when he last saw Katrin. And she knew it, for she came to me in tears about him."

She stared at the big man in dismay. "What is all this mystery surrounding Litvinov?"

"I do not dare discuss it," Timofei said. "And you should be careful. Mention it to no one but your husband. And do challenge him about it. That is my best advice to you."

Elsie said, "I have talked to you about things I have never discussed with anyone before. I have tolerated what I might ordinarily term vulgarity and insult. We have been completely frank with each other. I think that is good and that we may be friends."

He extended his huge hand to her, and they solemnly shook hands by the edge of the ice. He said, "Now I will see you safely up the bank, and if you should slip again, I shall behave as a proper brother."

Timofei was as good as his word. His behavior was that of a perfect gentleman. When they reached the path, he saw her to the corner of the house. Then he told her, "I shall continue my solitary walk in the woods."

"And I'll go inside; I'm getting chilled," she said.

"Wait until you have spent a winter here." He laughed in parting.

She made her way back to the front entrance of the palace. She was perhaps more confused than ever. She had learned a great deal from the rebellious Timofei in a short time. She no longer need have fears that her husband and Olga were lovers, but she must be wary of what she said to Sophie.

What worried Elsie now were Timofei's comments

about Alex as a lover. She knew that while he had been more than satisfactory at times, he had turned from her almost coldly at others. It was something that had bothered her, but which she had not thought of as important until now.

This, along with what Timofei had to say about Litvinov, produced a new anxiety in her. Timofei had almost openly declared that Basil had changed in character after coming under the influence of the cultists whom Litvinov represented and that this weird association with the fat man had brought about Basil's murder. And he insinuated that Alex might be following the same path to his being murdered.

Elsie entered the palace foyer with this most disconcerting conclusion in mind and was about to go upstairs when she saw Sophie.

"You have enjoyed a stroll?" Sophie asked.

"Yes," she said, trying not to appear awkward.

Sophie said, "I would find it too cool."

"It was cool. I didn't stay out long."

Sophie's blue eyes challenged her. "Long enough. I saw you from the window of the room occupied by the Countess Marie. It has a very good view of the river bank."

"Oh!"

"I thought you stayed down there a long while, in spite of the weather."

She said, "The time went by quickly, I guess."

Sophie offered a knowing smile. "Since you had interesting company."

Awkwardly, she said, "You mean Timofei."

"Who else? He was the one I saw with you."

"Yes." She desperately wanted to end the conversation and get away from the girl.

"He was sober?" Sophie asked.

"He seemed so."

"That is unusual for him, even in the morning."

"Oh?" she said, not wanting to continue any detrimental talk about the young man she felt was her friend.

"He talks a lot even when he is sober."

"I found his conversation interesting," she said. "He knows a lot about icons."

165

Sophie sneered. "He knows plenty about more than that."

"Really?"

"You mustn't pay too much attention to anything he tells you," the blonde girl went on. "He enjoys telling lies. The bigger they are, the more he enjoys them."

"He is a very different sort of person," she said, trying to be careful. She could imagine the feline Sophie repeating anything derogatory she might say to Timofei and enjoying it.

"He is a drunken degenerate," Sophie said. And in a more confident tone, she said, "Count Andre would put him out of the house in a moment. It is the countess who protects him. She dotes on him, as if he were her own flesh and blood."

"She brought him up. I suppose he is like her own."

Sophie registered disgust. "She takes spells and prattles on about what a cute little boy he was. And I have to suffer her senilities."

"How is she, this morning?"

"Asleep," Sophie said. "She is at her best asleep."

"I hope she gets a good rest."

"She only cat naps," Sophie said viciously. "I will no sooner be settled down to reading a book than she will call for me." And she moved on.

Elsie hurried up the curving stairway, relieved to be free of Sophie. She had not realized in their brief meeting that there was more to Sophie. But now she understood why Sophie had sought her out so early: She had wanted to see and appraise the woman Alex had married.

Now Sophie had seen Elsie talking with Timofei and no doubt suspected that the big man had given the whole story away. Elsie was positive of this by the jabs Sophie had taken at him and by her insisting that he enjoyed telling lies, the more monstrous the better.

In her room, Elsie settled down to writing a letter to her aunt and uncle. It took her a few minutes to get into the proper mood and decide what she would write and what must be left out. So many things had happened, and she didn't want to hint anything which might make them worry.

She wrote mostly of the travel and her first impressions

of Moscow, of which she had yet seen little. And she gave a long description of the chapel in the old palace where her second marriage ceremony would take place. When she finished, she signed it, sealed the envelope, and addressed it.

As she rose from the task, someone knocked on her door. She went over and opened it to find Countess Olga. The pretty dark girl said, "I'm not bothering you."

"No," she told her. "Do come in. I've just finished writing a letter to my aunt and uncle."

"Of course, they will want to hear from you," Olga said, entering the room.

"Yes," she agreed.

"Do you like it? I mean, the apartment?"

"Yes," she said. "I have an excellent view of the river and its bank."

Olga, who had gone to gaze out the window, turned with an almost guilty expression on her fine-featured face. "It does, doesn't it."

She said, "I now know the history of the room."

Olga said, "You men about Katrin. Her suicide here?"

"Yes."

"Who told you?"

"I don't think I should say. The information was dropped innocently enough. I was a trifle bothered at first. But now I realize I shouldn't be."

Olga said bitterly, "This room isn't unique! It is a house of ghosts."

She ignored any special intent the other girl's words might have, saying, "All old houses have to be."

Olga said, "I came to ask you if you would like to go in to Moscow with me this afternoon. I have some shopping to do. You have seen only a small part of the city."

"I would enjoy it."

"Good," the other girl said. "We can leave after lunch."

"That will suit me. I don't expect Alex will be back until dinner time."

"Not likely."

Elsie said, "I would one day like to take some time visiting the inner city of the Kremlin."

"Better have Count Andre accompany you on that excursion," the other girl said. "He is the family expert on history, and the Kremlin was the original Moscow."

"A walled fortress city within a city," she said.

"Yes," Olga said. "The social life here is much more dull since the royal family have gone into retreat because of that villainous monk, Rasputin."

"I can imagine it has changed things."

"Moscow has become a city of fears and rumors," the dark girl observed with a sigh.

As soon as lunch was over, Elsie dressed for the shopping expedition. At Olga's warning, she had again put on her warm coat. This time a closed carriage awaited them, although the driver was the same boyish Joseph, as impressive looking as ever in his tall fur hat.

In the carriage Olga said, "I have just heard there is some sort of trouble in the city."

"Trouble?" she asked.

"Yes," Olga said. "We are always having some sort of demonstration these days. It may be the workers, or the students, or even the peasants. Someone is always parading about their griefs. After a time, one comes to look on it as an ordinary happening and live with it."

"The unrest Alex mentioned is very real then?"

"Too real," Olga said, gazing out the carriage window at the countryside. "But one goes on."

At the edge of the city, a cluster of carriages blocked one of the streets. Joseph reined the horses and with an angry oath descended to inquire from one of the other drivers what was causing the delay.

A few minutes later he came back to them and said, "There is a workers' demonstration going on a few blocks from here. There has been some rock throwing and all the rest. Does the countess wish to go on?"

◦§ Chapter 14 §◦

COUNTESS OLGA at once replied to the young man in a torrent of Russian, to which he replied in the same language. This left Elsie out of it, although she could see a slight movement ahead. Several of the droshkas and carriages had wheeled around and were heading out of the city, allowing those determined to go on the free passage to do so.

Joseph closed the carriage door and jumped up on the seat again. He shouted to the horses, and they went forward. Olga had decided not to turn around.

The dark girl turned to Elsie and apologized. "Forgive me for lapsing into Russian. It was easier to make Joseph understand. He speaks little English."

"I didn't mind," she said.

"I feel we should go on," Olga explained. "The shops I wish to visit are not in the area of the uprising, although we may have to drive close by the rioters on our way to them."

"You know best," she said.

The dark girl smiled grimly. "I wish I could assure you of that. The truth is, it is hard to tell. We could be taking a risk if the rioters move forward. But I dislike having my plans upset by anything."

She smiled at the dark girl. "I'm sure Joseph is equal to any situation we find ourselves in."

"We shall see," Olga said as they drove on over the rough cobblestones. She leaned forward, peering out the window anxiously.

The carriage rolled forward at a fairly fast rate now and they entered a wider street. And it was then that they first heard the sounds. The commotion was something new and foreign to Elsie's ears. She now leaned forward to be able to see out the window with Olga.

"We are nearing the section where the demonstration is going on," Olga said, without turning to her. The girl's voice was taut with excitement.

"Do these demonstrations ever become very violent?"

"People are sometimes killed," Olga said tensely, not ceasing to gaze out the window.

Now they came to an intersection, and Joseph brought the carriage to a quick halt. There was a ringing of voices in the air, combined with shouting that could be heard even inside the carriage. Other vehicles came abreast of them, and they also halted rather than dare cross the wide thoroughfare.

Joseph was fighting to keep the nervous horses reined, and they were champing at the bit and rearing a little so that the carriage was subjected to a drunken motion. The voices came nearer, and Elsie could clearly hear the singing of the "Marseillaise." It seemed strange to hear the French anthem being sung in Moscow. But she supposed it was associated in the workers' minds with the idea of revolution.

And now a great torrent of people came marching up from the left and filling the wide street ahead of them. She could not ever remember seeing so many marching people. And the clamor assailed her ears and at the same time made the horses more nervous. Joseph was fighting to control them.

The window of a carriage next to them was rolled down, and an aristocratic looking old man in fur hat and coat leaned out and raised a fist at the marchers who had impeded the progress of his vehicle. He directed curses at them and looked in a rage.

Elsie was fascinated by the faces of the marchers. They all wore the same inspired expression as they sang their marching songs. The sheepskin hats and the heavy winter coats were strange to her, as were the shawled heads of the women. There were marchers of every age, even old men and women and very young boys and girls.

Then suddenly the drama took a new turn. From the other side of the street, a band of shouting cossacks appeared in their typical regalia of fur hats and long coats.

Their sabers and whips held high, they rode their horses into the crowd.

Now the singing gave way to cries of fear and shouts of anger! The people marching cringed under the onslaught of the cossack's sabers and whips. And the highly trained soldiers of the tsar seemed to care little whether their weapons struck down the old or the young.

Elsie gasped as she saw an old man fall under the sting of a long whip and the cossack's mount seem to trample over his fallen body. Before she could fully realize this had happened, another soldier struck at a teen-age girl with his saber and she saw the blood spurt from the girl's cheek as she also fell.

Now the marchers were no longer an orderly procession. They were a seething mob of frightened human beings in a chaotic mess. They ran one way and then another in an effort to escape the avenging cossacks. The grim envoys of the tsar continued to ride among them wielding their weapons until the brave singing of the comrades had changed to moans and pleas for mercy.

A shot rang out. One of the cossacks toppled from his saddle and was dragged off in the stirrup by his frightened steed. This was the signal for the rest of the cossack platoon to open fire on the remainder of the marchers. A body fell and then others, and the street emptied rapidly. In the end, there were only the fallen bodies of the dead and injured stretched out in pools of their own blood and the cossacks rallying to make sure they had completed their task.

A man with blood streaming down his face came running between the carriages. He was hatless and seemingly blinded by the blood spurting from a gash in his forehead. He fell against the carriage in which the old man sat at the open window. The old man spat down at him and cursed him. The injured man staggered on, sobbing out his pain.

Now the cossack leader posted men to keep the intersection clear, and he waved for the traffic to go ahead. Joseph gave the horses free rein, and they trotted on quickly, as if even they could not stand the scene of horror. Elsie saw the face of the cossack officer as they drove by. He had a wide black mustache; and his face, although young, was set in a grim expression. The crisis over, she sank back against the horsehair seat of the carriage with a sigh.

Olga also seemed weak and ill from the ordeal. She, too, sat back and in a weary voice said, "Now you have seen how the tsar treats those who complain."

"It was dreadful!" she exclaimed. "Ralph and I saw a riot of the suffragettes in London, but it was nothing compared to this. And they threw rocks and did a lot of property damage."

Olga laughed bitterly. "What you saw had little to do with rock throwing! You must know that people died back there."

"Yes," she agreed in a stricken voice. "And some, like that man, were badly wounded."

"I did not think it would be so bad."

"This happens often?"

"Too often."

"How can it go on?" Elsie wanted to know.

Olga grimaced. "Not much longer. Mother Russia has borne about all the human suffering she can stand. It will soon come to Judgment Day."

"You believe that?"

"Don't you, after what you've just seen?" her husband's sister asked.

Elsie could not offer any reply. The answer was all too clear. There were strikes in New York. She had read of them. Sometimes a few people and policemen trying to suppress the rioters were injured. But this was different. This was like a kind of warfare.

The afternoon's shopping was an anti-climax after what they had gone through. Olga took her to several fine stores, where the gentry were the only clientele. The shopowners and clerks fawned on the Countess Olga and on Elsie as the new Countess Martynov, but she could only think of those injured and dying in the streets. The memory sickened her; so she paid little attention to what the various clerks showed her. She wound up the afternoon by buying only a brooch of an interesting design. Olga claimed it was an antique item of excellent value. It depicted an angry looking eagle.

Olga purchased a new gown of blue with a great deal of lace trim in the same shade. When they returned to the carriage for the journey home, the streets were oddly quiet.

Elsie commented on this. "No one seems to be in the streets now."

"They empty after a storm like that," Olga said. "But you can depend on it that many of those marchers are gathered in hidden cellars now planning against the regime."

"You think so?"

"I know it," she said. "They break up into small groups. The cossacks will ferret some of them out, and there will be more violence. But the people will not be conquered; others will continue to plot revolutions."

Elsie gave Olga a surprised glance. "I have always felt you to be a dedicated aristocrat. Now you sound as if you sympathize with these revolutionaries."

Olga said, "I have pity for the human being. I cannot help that. But you are right. It is difficult for me to play traitor to my own class. We are in the minority, and if we do not stay loyal and use our power—well, Heaven only help us!"

They had left the central part of Moscow behind them and were riding in the countryside now. It seemed strangely quiet. Elsie said, "Your brother Basil became a traitor to his own class, and it cost him his life."

"You do not understand," Olga said. "Basil's case was different."

"Because he became a follower of Rasputin?"

"Partly," the girl said. "It is not anything I wish to discuss. Basil is dead. Katrin is dead. They cannot be brought back no matter how much we lament them."

"No one seems to want to talk about Basil," she said.

"You are right," Olga said. "I feel most sorry for my Aunt Marie and Uncle Andre. I wish they would leave the country now while they can. If they remain too long, they will be caught in the tidal wave. But they love Russia and are so old and weak. It is hard for them to make a choice."

"I know that," she said. "We are being married in the chapel at the palace because Countess Marie is so ill."

Olga said, "So you have been told."

"Yes. The priest comes to offer me instruction tomorrow."

"The church is also lost." Olga said bitterly. "When they cannot control a Rasputin they are in a bad way. Bishop Hernogen of Saratov is the only one who dares to stand up to him. He refused him forgiveness for his sins."

"Yes, Rasputin has the confidence of the tsar."

"Through trickery! And the church is too weak to join in condemning him." She gave Elsie a troubled glance. "If I were you I would refuse to be a party to a second marriage. It is a farce."

They had reached the entrance of the palace, and the carriage had come to a halt. Elsie said, "I will do it for the sake of the old people. I'm sure it means a lot to Count Andre and the Countess Marie."

"It is your choice," Olga said in a toneless voice as Joseph opened the carriage door and helped them out.

The main topic of conversation at dinner was the riot in the city. And as Timofei had not returned home for dinner, the feeble Countess Marie did nothing but worry about him.

"I do hope our son was not somehow caught up in the violence," she said for perhaps the fourth time.

Alex, who had returned home early, told her in a loud voice, "You can be sure he was in some dive soaking up vodka when it happened. He will be all right."

Count Andre at the head of the table showed annoyance on his thin face. "Timofei is an artist. He drinks because he is of a sensitive nature. He is not, as you suggest, a drunkard."

"I am sorry, sir," Alex said with grim politeness.

Elsie managed to keep fairly silent during dinner; afterward, she and Alex went up to their apartment. They sat on the divan in the drawing room and had their after-dinner brandy in privacy.

Alex's face showed his annoyance. "I could not stay down there any longer and hear that poor old woman bleating about her lost sheep."

She studied him over her brandy glass. "Timofei is her adopted son. She loves him dearly."

He took a gulp of the brandy. "I try to make myself remember that."

"I do not think he is so bad."

Alex eyed her with surprise. "You can't mean that? He has nothing but hatred for the family."

"That is understandable," she said. "He is a kind of lost soul. He has no idea who his parents were. And because he was adopted by your aunt and uncle, he has grown up to be a member of the aristocracy."

"For which he should be grateful."

"I wonder," she said, staring at her glass. "After what I saw this afternoon, I'm not all that certain it is an honor to be of the privileged class in this country."

Alex raised his eyebrows. "You surprise me."

"I'm sorry," she said. "What I saw today was cruel and obscene."

"Violence must be met with violence."

"But these people weren't violent. They were merely parading to have their opinions heard," she argued.

Alex rose and began to pace slowly before her. "You were unfortunate enough to happen on an ugly moment. It isn't all like that."

"Olga says there is a lot of it," she said.

Alex frowned. "You must not allow Olga's opinions to have too much influence on you."

"Why not? I think her fair."

He paused in his pacing to stare at her. "You two have suddenly become friends?"

"Yes."

"You resented her in New York."

"I didn't understand her then."

Alex considered this and asked her, "Why are you so sure you understand her now?"

"Because I know her better. I would trust her before I would Sophie, whom I think has a vicious tongue."

Alex's reaction was to crimson. "Sophie is not all that bad."

"I wouldn't expect you to think so. She is very lovely in appearance and that is what men go by most."

"She is my cousin," he protested.

"So far removed."

"Still, my cousin," he said. "I would prefer you not speak ill of her."

"Very well, I won't; but my opinion of her remains the same," she said.

Alex came to sit with her again and in a confidential tone said, "I am going to tell you something, one of the family secrets. And you must not repeat it."

She was all attention, thinking he might be going to reveal some of the mystery surrounding Basil's murder and the evil Litvinov. She said, "I can be discreet."

"I know that," he said. "And what I tell you must not be repeated, not even to Olga."

"Very well," she agreed.

He paused for a moment and finished the rest of the brandy in his glass. Then he set it down and said gravely, "Olga has a lover."

"I wondered," she said.

"Oh?"

"Yes, I saw her last night when I was standing by the window looking out at the river. It was moonlight, and I saw her on the riverbank. She seemed to be waiting for someone."

"Did anyone turn up?"

"I don't know," she said. "She vanished in the shadows, and I lost sight of her."

"She was indeed out there to meet someone," her husband said. "The affair has been going on for some time. I feel it is coming to a climax. And I fear what the shock of it will do to our aunt and uncle."

"Who is the man?"

"A college student who is also the leader of a revolutionary cell," he said.

She was stunned. "Olga is in love with one of the leaders of the revolution?"

"Yes," he said gravely. "I'm the only other one in the family who knows about it."

"And that is why you two had all those secret talks?"

"Yes, some of his fellow revolutionists were in New York when we were there and in London."

"Why didn't you tell me?"

"I thought you disliked Olga. That the time wasn't right."

Elsie smiled, "I disliked her mainly because of the

secrecy between you two. So often you shut me out. I now understand."

"You will tell no one," he counseled her.

"I will say nothing. But I'd be willing to bet there is someone else who knows."

Alex frowned. "Who?"

"Timofei."

"What makes you think that?"

"He seems to know everything."

"That's true enough," Alex said grimly. "Did he say anything to you?"

"Not about Olga. But I'd be willing to bet he is aware of her romance and on her side."

"I wouldn't count on that," Alex said grimly. "With Timofei you never know."

She said, "I still like him."

Alex eyed her uneasily. "You won't get a very good report on him from Sophie. Aunt Marie wanted Sophie and Timofei to marry, but she detests him and refused."

"Perhaps he doesn't care for her either," Elsie said in his defense.

"What right has he to be particular? Who is he?" Alex demanded.

"I believe he is a Martynov, if only by adoption," she said quietly. "I did not think you were such a noble snob, dear Alex. In America that wouldn't go down well."

"Sorry," her husband said. "That was bad on my part." And as an act of contrition, he leaned forward and kissed her gently.

"You can be so marvelous as a lover," she said, touching his face softly with her fingers, tracing the strong features as if to engrave them on her mind.

He said, "Uncle Andre told you about the wedding plans."

"Yes."

"You are satisfied?"

She smiled at him with a gentle light in her eyes. "I'm pleased. I do not want another big church wedding."

"I was worried that you might be upset because of our change of plans," he said. "But in view of my aunt's health, nothing else is practical."

"I fully agree."

"One other thing," he said. "Tomorrow I will have to go to St. Petersburg. I may be away several days, even a week."

She was at once afraid. "Alex!"

He stood up and moved a distance away from her. "I knew you would not like the idea, but I have no choice."

"Why?" she said, also rising.

He turned to her, his handsome face troubled. "What do you mean, why? I say I have to go. That should be enough."

"No!" she said, ready to cry.

He came to her quickly. "There's no need for all this fuss. I have grave responsibilities. I cannot shirk them."

She challenged him, "Does it have to do with Litvinov?"

"We won't talk about it," he said angrily.

"Take me to St. Petersburg with you."

"I can't."

"Because Litvinov and his friends wouldn't approve?"

He shook his head in a weary gesture. "You are arguing about things about which you know nothing."

"I know that I love you and that something is taking you from me," she accused him. "A cause, some crazy belief, which you place before us. Do you want to end up murdered like Basil?"

"Leave my brother out of this," he said.

"How can I?" she sobbed.

He stared at her, his handsome face crimson. Then he gave a resigned shrug. "I cannot argue with a hysterical female." And with that he strode out of the drawing room and into his own quarters, slamming the door after him.

She stood watching after him in disbelief for a moment before collapsing on the divan sobbing. She remained there enduring her pain for what seemed like a long while. Then, her tears exhausted, emotionally drained, she sat back to try and think what she was going to do.

Alex was behaving just as he had in London. The old restlessness had come back. And whatever it was that was bothering him seemed to exert a more powerful pressure on him than his love for her or their marriage.

She was beginning to realize how little she knew of the people with whom she found herself in this great palace. All of them seemed to be living with grim secrets. None of them could be taken at their face value, not even the patriotic old Count Andre who had been a dismal failure and coward in naval action. His failure as a captain haunted him down through the years.

Olga, the epitome of an arrogant aristocrat, had given her heart to a young revolutionary. Sophie had carried on a romance with Alex under the eyes of the family. Timofei was a romantic drunkard who resented his having been an orphan. And no doubt even poor old feeble Countess Marie would have some dark secret. She had been a lady in waiting to the former tsarina, perhaps she had once had a prince as a lover. Anything was possible.

No sound came from the other side of the door to her husband's rooms. Elsie could not tell whether he was there. But she knew they had just had their first real quarrel since arriving in Moscow and at a time when she had been thinking all their differences had been resolved.

She tried to recall what Timofei had said about him when they'd had their talk earlier by the river bank, and she couldn't clearly remember it all. But she was sure the young artist had warned her that she was in danger of losing Alex. This was why he had tried to fathom their physical relationship and she did not think it had been vulgar curiosity on his part.

But had she been truthful in saying to Timofei that she and Alex had a good love life? She worried now that her reply had been deceptive. Something was coming between her husband and herself. Their passionate interludes were becoming more scattered. Something was drawing him away from her, something evil that she did not understand. And Litvinov was part of it, Litvinov who had his headquarters in St. Petersburg.

Elsie now was sure the evil fat man had been the one she had seen taking the Paris-Moscow Express. Alex had denied it, but he had lied. And now Alex was keeping another meeting with this man who had tried to murder her. Why?

With a sigh, Elsie rose from the divan. She felt she could not remain alone in the apartment. And she didn't want to give in to Alex by going and knocking on his door. This would be a suppliant act, and she couldn't bring herself to it. So she slowly made her way to the door leading to the corridor and went out.

The corridor was dark; when she reached the landing, she met Sophie coming down the opposite corridor. The blonde girl gave her a wry look.

"The old crow has just gone to sleep," she said with disgust. "Staying awake all this while worrying about Timofei."

"The poor old woman loves him," Elsie sympathized.

"That drunken creature."

"She does not see him that way."

"I can't stand much more of it," Sophie said grimly. She gave her a curious look. "What ever made you come to this country? To a house like this?"

Elsie thought the question somewhat shocking. And she hoped no betraying sign of her tears showed on her face. She had not expected to meet Sophie.

She said, "I fell in love."

Sophie spoke with sarcasm. "And you think that is the answer to everything?"

"It is for me," she said quietly.

The blonde girl moved nearer her and said in a low voice, "Would you mind if I told you I think you've made a colossal mistake."

She shrugged. "I can't stop you saying anything."

"A warning," Sophie said. "You will not hold Alex. No one ever will."

Elsie was angry enough to ask the girl if she were speaking from experience; instead she curbed her wrath enough to say, "What is your authority to tell me that?"

Sophie smiled. "Alex is a torn man! He is a victim of what is happening to this country. And you saw something of that today."

Elsie said, "You aren't making yourself very clear."

"I will tell you something," the blonde girl said. "You were mad to leave America and place yourself in this boiling mess. I pray that I may somehow escape."

"You want to leave Russia?"

"Yes! If I had the money I'd go to Paris, or New York tomorrow! I'd go to Denmark! Anywhere to get away from here and all that is happening here!"

Elsie said, "Surely you can get away if you want to go."

"How?" Sophie asked bitterly. "I am trained only to be a lady, or a lady's companion. Now I am tied to this dying old woman, so that I have no time to myself. I have no private means and no friends in high places. I feel as the passengers must have felt in the *Titanic*. I'm sinking into an unknown without hope."

"I'm sorry," she said. "We can talk about it later. I may be able to help you."

Sophie looked bitter. "You help me? When you left paradise of your own accord!" And she passed her and went on down the curving stairway.

Elsie hesitated there for a moment and then made up her mind that she preferred the solitude of her room to more of this bitter exchange with Sophie.

Feeling in a battered mood, Elsie opened the door to her apartment and went inside. Alex was there in his pajamas, looking contrite. He advanced to her and took her in his arms, showering her with ardent kisses before he spoke.

"You know how much I love you," he said.

"I want to think you do," she said, gazing up at him sadly.

"We must not quarrel again."

"I know," she said in a small voice as he lifted her and carried her over to the bed.

It seemed that each time they had a quarrel, the lovemaking that followed was of a fierce intensity. Tonight was no exception. Alex seemed maddened with passion. She was lifted to new heights by the overwhelming passion he revealed. But tonight something was different: All during the lovemaking, a small area of pain remained within Elsie to spoil the perfect moments.

When they lay together for sleep, Alex first dropped off into the velvet depths of slumber, while Elsie remained awake and tormented by the knowledge that he would leave her in the morning. She knew how stubborn he was and that he would go to St. Petersburg as he had said. And when he began to toss in a tormented dream and spoke the name of Litvinov aloud several times, her terror for their future increased.

◆§ Chapter 15 ﾇ◆

OF COURSE ALEX WAS GONE when Elsie awoke and there was no note saying when he would return.

Elena arrived with breakfast, setting it on the table by the window as usual. The maid told her, "The air is milder today and with the strong sun the ice will be melting fast. Do you wish the window opened a little?"

"Please," she said. And then she asked, "Do you know what time Count Alexander left this morning?"

"I think it must have been early, countess," the girl said. "Joseph brought the droshka around soon after I left my room. I saw Frederick carrying out the master's bags, and the cook said that Count Alexander was catching the early train to St. Petersburg."

She sat down to her breakfast, but was not hungry. She asked Elena, "Do you know St. Petersburg?"

Elena halted in her work. "I was there as a girl, countess."

"What is it like?"

"I have heard Count Andre call it the Venice of the North; it is the capital of Russia now. The tsar rules from there. It was not always so."

"So it must really be the political center of the country," she said, thinking of the reasons Alex might be there.

"Yes, countess," the girl agreed. "It has a look of Italy. And they say the Cathedral of Our Lady of Kazan is an exact copy of St. Peter's Basilica in Rome."

"I must visit St. Petersburg," she said.

"You should, mistress," the girl agreed. "In the winter, the nights there begin in early afternoon darkness and last until the middle of the following morning. It is very strange. One must wear many layers of clothing during the

182

cold weather. Summer is the opposite, terribly hot and as light as the winters are dark."

"Is there much social life there?" she asked.

"A lot, countess," the girl said. "There are great opera and ballet companies, and there used to be parties every night. But not so much now that the royal family has ceased to entertain. The best time for parties was from New Year's Day to the beginning of Lent."

Elsie said, "The troubles have changed all that."

"It is no longer the same," the girl agreed. "The noble families live in fear, and the common people live in terror. No one is happy in Russia today."

"The tsar still has a palace in Moscow?"

"Oh, yes, countess," the girl said. "But lately the visits of the royal family here have been fewer. It is that Rasputin; he has his headquarters in St. Petersburg. He has taken control of the royal family and insists that they remain there much of the time."

Elsie drank some of her morning tea as the maid went about making up the bed. She said, "I suppose I shall never truly understand Russia until I learn the language."

The maid paused. "I just remembered, mistress. Count Andre told me the priest will be here to talk to you at ten this morning."

"Ah, yes," she said. "We are to meet in the chapel."

After breakfast, Elsie dressed in a simple brown gown and went downstairs, directly along the several corridors to the chapel. There she found the priest waiting for her. He was younger than she'd expected, probably in his middle thirties, with a majestic black beard to give him an appearance of authority. He wore black robes, the traditional Orthodox cap and a silver cross hung at his neck from a long chain.

He greeted her with a smile. "You are Countess Elsie. I am Father Peter," he said, offering her his hand.

She smiled. "I have been looking forward to meeting you, Father."

He waved her to one of the two armchairs provided for them and then sat opposite her, his Bible in hand. He said, "I have been chosen as your tutor, not because of my vast wisdom or great saintliness, but because I can speak English. So you must not expect too much."

Elsie liked him immediately. "You speak with a pronounced British accent, far more pleasant than my unadorned English."

Father Peter said, "I like your accent; it is fresh and disarming. Are you finding our Russia a maze of complexities?"

"Life here is not simple," she said. "At least not for anyone but the moujiks."

"Nor for the moujiks," Father Peter said seriously. "I have lived and worked among them. When I first returned from my studies at Oxford in England, my bishop thought it seemly to send me to the most distant and poorest of districts. I learned the life of the peasants there. They suffer in silence, wrapping themselves in more rags when the weather gets colder. They slave for the landowners and curse them readily. But they have strong loyalty for the tsar. They see him as next to God. The peasants are all devotedly religious people."

"I am very ignorant of it all."

"That is forgiveable in you, not in our ruling classes," Father Peter said with a sad look on his bearded face.

"What about Rasputin?"

The young priest showed anger. "That vile monk is one of those shattering the pillars of our nation. When all crashes down, he will be foremost among those to blame."

"Can't the church control him?"

"We have tried. It seems to do no good. He has become too powerful."

She glanced around. "I love this chapel. It seems a truly holy place. And the two icons are beautiful."

He followed her glance. "You are right. But sadly the chapel is no longer the center of family living as it once was. Now it is used for the formal occasions of baptism, confirmation, weddings, and funerals."

Elsie smiled. "I know little about your church."

Father Peter said, "I have been told you are what is known in England as an Anglican, a member of the Church of England."

"In the United States we are called Episcopalians."

"Both an offshoot of Rome, if we examine back to the time of the Eighth Henry," Father Peter said. "Our Orthodox church is also an offshot of Rome, and we also deny the authority of the pope. We are headed by a patriarch, and have the usual systems of districts ruled by bishops and so forth. So you see we are not that far apart in views."

She said, "You are Catholic, and I am not."

He corrected her, "You are Catholic and not Roman Catholic. We also call ourselves Catholic by turn, but the other name for us is Orthodox. We sing the liturgy; we do not place stress on the confession, and we administer last rites to the ill rather than only to the dying."

Elsie smiled, "At least you make it all easily understood."

"Then I'm doing well," the bearded young priest said with good humor. "For there is much I still need to learn for myself."

"You are a good teacher."

"Thank you," he said. "All religions, including those outside the Christian faith have much in common. The ethics of mankind must of necessity be much the same. I approve of the Martynovs not asking you to change your religion. And I shall look forward to assisting at your marriage."

"You're very kind," she said. "You know my husband?"

"Yes. I know all the family. I am what might be termed the family priest. I was close to Count Basil until he went beyond my reach."

She could not help but notice the sadness now in the priest's voice and his facial expression changed as he spoke of Basil. She said, "His was a tragic case, as was that of his wife."

"Needless tragedy."

"Why do you say that?"

"Basil allowed fanaticism to take hold of him. He was a young man of genius, but the line between genius and madness is commonly said to be a fine one. It was in his case. He veered to madness."

"What brought about his murder?"

"He became obsessed with a cult that is said to be led by Rasputin," Father Peter said. "It drove Basil to madness and death."

Thinking of Alex, Elsie asked, "What sort of cult is it?"

"Very secret," the young priest said. "It's object is world

185

control. I hear there are several stages of priesthood within its ranks. Women are members of the lower orders, and the men and women are said to indulge in orgies. You can be sure this would appeal to the immoral Rasputin. At the top level, the aim is world domination and complete asceticism. This is all I have been able to find out."

"Then it is semireligious in nature," she said, recalling that Alex had defended Rasputin as a misunderstood martyr. All she was hearing now disputed this.

"It is religion distorted into the most sinful of mystic orders," Father Peter said severely. "It is close to black magic. But we are not here to discuss such sordid things." And he went on to instruct her in the tenets of the Eastern Orthodox faith.

When the session ended, Elsie saw the priest out. He paused to say, "I do not think it necessary for me to come every day."

"Whatever you think," she said.

"Let us make it every other day and skip the Sabbath," he suggested. "The main thing is that you know the history and customs of the church so you may be able to discuss them with some intelligence."

She smiled at him. "You are making that easy for me, Father Peter."

"I hope so," he said. "The other thing is to have you aware of the proper responses and movements at the wedding ceremony. This is merely a matter of memorizing the ritual."

"I'll do that, Father," she promised. And then she said, "I understand you are allowed to marry in the Orthodox priesthood. Are you married?"

"No," he said with a smile. "I hope to be one day. I would like to marry a nurse, or perhaps a young woman with a medical degree. There is more need of good medical techniques in the barren rural areas than of priests."

"You would like to go to some small village and establish a medical clinic along with a church?" she suggested.

"I would," he said, pleased that she understood.

"In the United States we call doing that medical missionary work," she said. "My Uncle Gordon thinks of himself as an avowed atheist, but medical missionary work is one thing he approves of and supports financially."

186

Father Peter's eyes twinkled again. "Your Uncle Gordon sounds like a wise man."

After she had seen the priest out, the butler, Frederick, came to her and said, "Countess Marie wishes to see you."

"Very well," Elsie said. "Is she in her apartment?"

"Yes, let me show you the most direct way up there," he said.

She followed him down a short hall and up a flight of stairs which were new to her. The house was a maze of corridors and stairways, Elsie thought. To Frederick she said, "I would think that even the ghosts might get lost here."

In a sober voice and with an expressionless face, the manservant said, "The ghost of Count Nicholas has no difficulty. It was he who built the house and knows its every corner. I have seen him on those stairs which we just climbed."

"Are you sure it was he?" Elsie asked, slightly chilled at the thought.

"Most sure. I have seen him many times in my long years of service here," Frederick said. "He looks exactly as he does in his portrait; you should study it, so you will recognize him; but at close glance he is somewhat transparent."

"I shall be on the lookout for him," Elsie said, half in jest, half in earnest.

Frederick halted by a wide door of rich, paneled walnut and knocked. After a moment, Sophie opened the door. Frederick bowed and said, "Countess Martynov."

"Come in," Sophie said. "Countess Marie wishes to talk with you before she has her nap."

"Of course," she said and went in.

"I'll take care of a telephone call while you are with her," Sophie said. "I haven't had a second to myself all morning." And she left as Elsie headed for the adjoining bedroom of the older couples' living quarters.

The sun was streaming through a partly opened French window in the large bedroom and the countess was propped up on several pillows.

The countess offered and stretched out a frail hand. "How kind of you to take the time to come to me."

Elsie kissed the older woman and seated herself by the

bed. "I would visit you more often, but I worry about intruding on you and tiring you."

"Not at all. Come when you like. You are alone today?"

"Yes, Alex is away."

"St. Petersburg?" the old woman said unhappily.

"Yes."

"I wish there were no St. Petersburg. Basil kept going there until he finally was caught up in the trouble that took his life."

"I know," she said.

The old woman said, "You are a fine, healthy child. You and Alex will carry on the Martynov line. It is your duty. Our family must not ravel out. You have only seen the palace. We own vast acres of land and a fine summer place. We are enormously rich, and each year the estate brings in more."

Elsie said, "There seems to be a distinct division in this country. I mean between the rich like us and the cruelly poor."

Countess Marie glanced at her. "You must not listen to all this talk of injustice. There will always be injustice. The rulers and the ruled. Be content that you find yourself among the rulers and be proud to contribute new leaders for the generations to come."

"I suppose that is one way of viewing it," Elsie said, trying to hide her distaste of the idea.

"The only way," the old woman said. "You have spent your first instruction period with Father Peter?"

"Yes."

"He has explained the faith to you?"

"He has started to."

"It is a good faith," the old woman said in her thin voice. "I hope that one day you will follow the example of our empress and embrace it."

"I have not considered that," she said frankly. "I am content for the moment to understand it."

"Father Peter is a good young man," the old woman went on.

"He said he was the Martynov family priest."

"Yes," Countess Marie said. "And since that only takes part of his time, he spends the rest of it helping the poor in the slums of Moscow. Have you seen our slums?"

"No, only the main streets and the shops."

"They try to hide them, but they are there," the old woman said. "So many poor! It is hopeless! I wonder that Father Peter doesn't give it up as a poor job. But he is young, and the young believe anything possible."

"Isn't that a good thing?" Elsie suggested.

"They come to know better in time," the old woman said wearily. Then she brightened and said, "Timofei has talked to me about you."

"Has he?"

"Yes. He likes you."

"I'm glad. It happens that I also like him."

Countess Marie smiled. "Good girl! The rest of the family despise him. Even Sophie, who would have made a good match for herself if she'd consented to marry him."

"I don't think them suited."

"Timofei says not. He is still my dear son; he was a lovely little boy." The old woman's voice trailed off. "He drinks too much you know."

"Perhaps for a reason. One day the reason will vanish, and he will change."

Countess Marie eyed her hopefully. "You think that may happen?"

"Yes," Elsie said. "He has a fine mind and great talent. He wants to paint a famous icon."

"He told you that?"

"Yes."

"Heaven be praised! You think he was sincere?"

"I'm sure he was," Elsie said, but again not revealing where Timofei intended to paint the icon.

"Be kind to him; so few are," the old woman said softly and closed her eyes. She said no more; she had fallen into a state of sleep.

Elsie rose quietly from the chair by the bedside and left the room. She made her way out to the corridor and down the same flight of stairs Frederick had shown to her.

In the main foyer, she met Count Andre and told him, "I have just left Countess Marie. She is asleep."

"Good," the thin old man said. "She needs more rest these days."

"Do you think she is much weaker?"

189

"You would not notice," he said. "But compared to a year or two ago yes. Dr. Orlov is coming this afternoon."

"I hope his prognosis is a good one."

Count Andre said, "He keeps a close watch on her. Of course, she worries a lot about Timofei."

"It's too bad."

"Tragic," the tall old man said. "I haven't seen either him or Olga this morning? Have you talked with either of them?"

"No," she said. "I spent most of the morning with Father Peter."

Count Andre registered approval with a nod of his white head. "He is a fine person."

"I agree."

"Did he help you?"

"Yes. He feels he will only have to give me an hour every other day or so."

"He shall be the judge," Count Andre said. "Olga has already begun preparations for the wedding with my help. It will be on a Friday night, in three weeks."

"Has Alexander approved the date?"

"Yes," Count Andre said. "I was careful to take the matter up with him before he left for St. Petersburg."

"I would like to see the city. I'm sorry he didn't take me with him."

"That is a pity," the old man agreed. "But perhaps he felt you ought to get to know the palace and Moscow better before you do any traveling."

"Perhaps," she said. "Is he in St. Petersburg on family business?"

The thin face of Count Andre shadowed. "No, it is a personal matter of which I know nothing."

"I see," she said.

They parted and she read for a short time from a booklet in English Father Peter had left her. It was an involved history of the early church. Then Sophie came in and suggested they lunch in one of the glassed-in patios together.

"Everyone else seems to be busy somewhere," she said.

A few minutes later, Elsie and Sophie went to the small table set out for them in the conservatory, which was filled with plants and flowers. It was almost like an inside garden. There was a wide open space with a floor of tile in the center of the observatory, where they had a light luncheon of salad and fruit and tea.

Sophie smiled and asked, "What did the old woman want?"

"Countess Marie?"

"Who else?"

"She asked me about my religious instruction and whether I liked Father Peter."

"These old crones live by the priests," Sophie said with a look of annoyance. "There is no true religion in Russia today."

"I cannot think that," she said. "Father Peter seems a very serious, dedicated young man."

The blonde girl gave her a leering look. "They all can put on that front. I've ceased to believe in any of them. I had a priest try to strip me once and then he claimed it was in a fit of holy ecstasy."

"Sophie!" she said in reproval.

The blonde girl leaned closer and in a low voice said, "You know the monk Rasputin has a secret society in which he leads both men and women in orgies. They say he is insatiable, with a liking for men as well as women."

"But Rasputin is not any ordinary monk," she protested. "He is apparently a man of hypnotic talents who has put them to evil use."

Sophie looked around cautiously to be sure no servants were within earshot, then in a low voice, said, "Do you know what the newspaper *Golos Moskvy* calls Rasputin, 'That cunning conspirator against our Holy Church as well as the fornicator of human souls and bodies.' What does that tell about your Gregory Rasputin, mad monk!"

Elsie thought of the weird devotion Alex had shown to the corrupt monk in his talk of him. More and more, she was beginning to think he sided with Rasputin because he was one of those reveling in his orgies. Perhaps the orgies were what had taken him to St. Petersburg, away from her. She could not compete with such a power of evil.

She said limply, "Some of it must be exaggerated. He stays in power with the royal family."

"The newspaper is taking a chance saying such things. The highest dignitaries of the church have been criminally tolerant of Rasputin. And I will tell you why. The tsar has issued an order banning any mention of Rasputin in the press on the pain of a fine."

"The tsar must still believe in him."

"The tsarina! That German bitch, Alexandra! She pulls the strings, and the tsar is her puppet."

"You honestly think that?"

"You know the stories that are told," Sophie said, pausing with her salad and lowering her voice still further. "The stories the papers dare not print."

"What stories?"

"The empress and that slut Anna Vyruboa are said to share the peasant monk's bed."

Elsie shook her head. "It must be wicked gossip."

"Perhaps," Sophie said, taking more of her salad. "But they tell that Rasputin ordered the tsar to pull off his boots and wash his feet as the disciples washed the feet of Christ. And when the tsar had obeyed him, he drunkenly shoved him out of the room and had sexual intercourse with the tsarina in the royal bed."

"We call such stories as that items from the yellow press at home," Elsie said with disgust.

"You do not know what a peasant hog this mad monk is," the blonde confided lewdly. "Royal servants have whispered that he has raped all the grand duchesses and made the nurseries a haram. They say the daughters of the tsar vie for his loving like bawds in a brothel."

"There must be some responsible men in government to give the tsar advice," she said. "Someone should warn the royal family and have them turn this Rasputin out."

"Rasputin controls most of the political appointments through the empress."

"Is there no one?"

"The Duma."

"Which would be like our Senate and House?"

"Or the British Houses of Parliament, but they do not have proper leadership. There is some hope in Prime Minister Kokovtsow, but the gossip is that Rasputin will topple him from his position. Then the revolution will really come."

"You seem sure of that."

"This is why I must escape. I despise this country."

Elsie said, "While I am new here and find many things to admire in spite of the many inequalities and cruelties."

"You have heard of Siberia?"

"Yes, it is very far North."

Sophie nodded. "The land of exiles and criminals. This is where our political prisoners go. Those who try to fight against the tsar and what he represents. They leave Moscow by the trainload and only a few ever return—and they as broken men and women."

"It is a cruel climate of course," Elsie said.

"And the prison commandants and guards are no less cruel. Prisoners are not sent to Siberia to be reformed, but to be destroyed. They die in the cold blockhouses and in the icy forests. And no one cares, because things are so bad right here in Moscow."

Elsie finished her tea and sat back. "There seems a rule of life that things can only get so bad and then they change. Perhaps it will be so in this case. Perhaps Russia will soon take a turn for the better."

"I would not bet a single ruble on it," was Sophie's grim reply. "By the way, part of my position here is to teach you Russian. Have your forgot?"

"No."

"When do you wish to begin?"

"Why not tomorrow?" she suggested. "In the morning. I can use the same time I give to Father Peter on the alternate day."

"So I shall share you with the priest," Sophie said in her cynical way. "Why not? Many Russian ladies offer the same arrangement to their husbands."

She blushed at this lewd comment, knowing that Sophie was deliberately taunting her. She could not get over having once been mistress to Alex and losing him. Elsie said, "I will ask the privilege of paying you personally for my lessons."

"There is no need," Sophie said, without too much protest in her tone.

"I want to."

"As you wish," the other girl said as they rose from the table. "It is settled; we shall begin in the morning. It will get me away from the old crow for a little."

Elsie could not feel easy at these derogatory comments

about her husband's Aunt Marie. She thought the old woman was a true lady, despite her growing infirmity, and deserved more respect.

Back in her own apartment, Elsie paced back and forth in troubled thought for a time. The things Sophie had revealed about Rasputin had been more shocking than anything she had heard to date. If these things were true, the royal palace had become a shambles and the people would soon lose all respect for the royal family.

The orgies Sophie described must be part of the every day gossip of Moscow. And since fire rarely appeared without there first being smoke, there must be some basis for the lewd stories. It stunned her to think that her own Alex might be one of Rasputin's band of degenerates.

She was debating all this when Elena came and summoned her to the telephone extension in the upper hall. She picked up the receiver and heard the warm voice of Ralph Manning say, "So I've caught up with you at last."

Chapter 16

A RUSH OF WARMTH went through Elsie at the sound of the friendly voice. She exclaimed, "You don't know how glad I am to hear from you!"

"I've only just got things set up here," he said. "You arrived safely?"

"Yes."

"How do you like the palace?"

"It is a different world."

"I'm sure of that," the young newspaperman said. "I have some ideas about showing you around."

"You mustn't burden yourself," she said.

"Don't worry about that," he joked. "Showing folks from home around is part of my job."

"I've been wondering what became of you."

"What about the count?" he asked.

She hesitated. "He left here this morning. He has gone to St. Petersburg for an indefinite stay."

"That's too bad," the reporter said. "I had some plans. Why did he leave you here? You should have gone with him."

"I was not invited."

"So that it how it is," he said.

"That is exactly how it is," she said grimly.

There was a slight moment of hesitation at the other end of the line, then Ralph said, "Is there any chance of you coming into Moscow and meeting me this afternoon?"

She debated it. "Is it important?"

"I'd say so," he replied soberly.

"What time?"

"Around three. I'll be finished with my overseas dispatches by then," he told her.

"Where will we meet?"

"The Metropole Hotel," he said. "This is where I have my rooms and headquarters. I'll wait for you at the entrance to the bar."

"All right," she said. "If anything happens to stop me coming, I'll send a message."

"I hope nothing does," he said. "I've been worried about you."

"I'll try to be there," she promised.

When she put down the telephone, she felt a lot better. The prospect of being free of the great mansion for a little and being able to talk with one of her own countrymen was pleasing. But she didn't know whether Count Andre would allow her to go alone. Perhaps she could get Olga to go in town with her. She could order the carriage, and everyone would think that they were off on another shopping trip.

She went to Olga's apartment and knocked on the door. There was no reply. She was standing there waiting when Elena came by.

"You want Countess Olga?" she asked.

"Yes."

"She has gone out," the girl said. "She left early this morning to visit friends and hasn't come back."

"I see," Elsie said, seeing that her plan was wrecked.

She went down the broad curving stairway to seek out Count Andre and confront him with her request for a carriage. As she made her way down the stairs, she overheard Timofei talking with Frederick. Timofei was ordering Frederick to have a carriage sent around for him. Elsie waited until the butler had left, then went the rest of the way down the stairs to greet Timofei.

"Hello, little innocent," he said.

"Must you always call me that?" she smiled.

"I like it, and I think it suits you," he said.

"I'm not so sure."

The big man's manner was friendly. "I missed you in the woods this morning. Why didn't you walk along the riverbank? It is lovely out today. Spring is slowly coming."

She smiled, "I had to spend the morning taking instruction from Father Peter."

"Beware of those priests," the big man admonished. "They will instruct you straight to the devil."

"Not Father Peter!"

Timofei nodded. "He isn't so bad. He is kind to my foster mother. I'll give him a good many stars for that."

"I think he's a fine man. The family is fortunate to be able to have his religious advice," she said.

Timofei laughed. "The Martynovs are fortunate to have any religious advice; we're a bad lot!"

"Not as bad as you like to pretend," she said. "And you are far from the worst of them."

"That is not so," he said. "I'm the dedicated servant of Satan. It's a well-known fact."

She laughed, "You boast too much to be really wicked. I want to ask a favor of you."

"I refuse to be best man at the wedding. Alex has many friends more suitable."

"Not that," she said.

"Fine! I'll do anything else for you."

"I want transportation to Moscow and back. I just heard you ordering the carriage. May I accompany you."

Timofei raised his eyebrows. "Are you so soon running away from us?"

"No!"

"What then?"

"I have a friend at the Metropole Hotel I've promised to meet. He's also a friend of Alex. I don't want to disappoint him, and I hate to ask Count Andre for a vehicle for myself."

Timofei smiled at her. "You are welcome to go in with me. But you will have to make your own arrangements with Joseph about getting back. I do not propose to return until after midnight, and I shall find my own transportation."

"I wouldn't ask the carriage to wait for me longer than an hour," she said. "I'm certain I'd be ready to return by then."

"Then hurry upstairs and get ready," the young artist said. "I'm thirsty and do not want to be kept waiting."

She knew he meant this. That he was impatient to get to whatever drinking place he and his cronies frequented and begin the serious drinking of the day. For her own part, she was almost as equally anxious to see and talk with Ralph again.

197

Clarissa Ross

Apart from her husband, Ralph was the man she most trusted and admired. She felt she could depend on Ralph. Her admiration for Timofei was of a different quality; she sympathized with him in his alcoholism and she liked him. But it was the sort of fondness one feels for a brother.

She put on a suitable silk dress, her best coat, and a wide-brimmed blue hat with a veil to cover her face. Then she rushed down to join Timofei.

He stared at her in admiration. "You are transformed! Transformed in beauty! I think I shall skip my meeting with my other girl and give myself wholly to you!"

"Don't!" she said. "You'd be disappointed."

"I refuse to believe that," he said, touching his hand under her chin. "You look saucy and intriguing. I like saucy young women."

"Aren't you in a hurry?"

"I am. And the carriage is outside waiting."

On the drive in to Moscow, he said, "So Alex has deserted you again."

"Only for a few days."

"He's a fool."

"He doesn't seem to think so," she replied.

Timofei said, "No fool does! If I had a wife like you, I wouldn't leave her alone."

"I'm sure you would!"

"Never. I'd desert the vodka for a wife like you."

"You say that because you know I'm already married," she said, smiling at him as they rode along in the carriage.

"I mean it," he said seriously.

"There are many other girls in the world, many more clever and attractive than I," she said.

"None for me," he said with a sigh. "It is too late. My bride is vodka, and she is a jealous one. But for you, it would be different."

"You're good for my self-confidence," she said. And more wistfully, she added, "And just now I need all I can get."

He eyed her sharply. "Doesn't that idiot Alex tell you how lovely you are? How special?"

"Yes."

"And does he not embrace you with passion?"

198

"All right," she said. "You only want to make me blush."

"And then?"

"Then he leaves me without even a message. We had a quarrel about his going last night. I thought he might change his mind. But when I woke this morning, he was gone."

"I'm sorry," Timofei said with some sincerity.

"Nice of you."

"I mean it. You deserve better. You mustn't be another Katrin. But then you're not. You have an appointment at the Hotel Metropole."

Elsie gave him a hurried, plaintive look. "Please don't make it sound like an assignation."

"Why not?" Timofei asked. "I can promise you that many take place there."

"Not so, in my case."

"I wouldn't blame you."

"I would hate myself."

Timofei spread his hands. "Would you be so wrong? Alex has left you for his certain, questionable pursuits in St. Petersburg. Why shouldn't you play your own game here?"

"I find such games distasteful."

"You turn your back on passion?"

"Not with the man I love and to whom I'm married." she said almost angrily. "You should understand me by now."

He lifted a protesting hand as the carriage lurched on. "Please, little innocent, I don't want to anger you. I'm trying to be a philosopher in my simple way."

"I dislike your philosophy."

"Then I'd better stick to painting my icon," he said.

"Yes, even in a bar, that would be better."

He gave her a teasing look. "Yet you are meeting a man?"

"So?"

"Many people would believe the worst."

"There are people who might suggest that about us; yet we are nothing more than relatives and good friends."

"You express it exactly, and I shall bother you no more," he said.

She said, "I make no secret of whom I'm meeting. He is a friend of Alex as well."

"Then he should warn Alex about St. Petersburg. You can only play with fire a little before you're singed."

"He has tried to warn him. My friend's name is Ralph Manning. You may have heard of him?"

"I fear my circles are less lofty than those of the Hotel Metropole."

"He travels about the city in search of news. He's a reporter for the American Hearst newspaper chain. So it is possible you may meet him."

Timofei said pleasantly, "If he descends to the lower depths, he'll eventually find me."

"He is very nice, and I'll be perfectly safe with him. Joseph can drive me back in an hour."

"Little innocent, I believe it all, chiefly because you are a little innocent," the artist said. "We shall shortly be at the entrance to the Metropole. You give your instructions to Joseph as he helps you out. Meanwhile, I shall sit here and dream of the low establishment to which I'm bound."

She leaned close to him and kissed him on the cheek. "You are a devil!"

"At last you recognize me," he said with pleasure.

When the carriage halted, he did not wait for Joseph to assist her, but did so himself. He saw her safely to the street and escorted her inside. Then he told her, "I shall give your instructions to Joseph. Good luck, little innocent."

"Thank you, Timofei," she said gratefully. He put on his fur hat and strode out.

Almost at the same instant that Timofei vanished, Ralph crossed the lobby to greet her. He said, "Who was that impressive looking young man?"

She smiled, "That was Timofei. The adopted son of Count Andre and so sort of a cousin to Alex."

"He's big and strong looking. Typical country squire."

"The strange thing is he hates the country, except for his painting. He's an artist."

Ralph showed amazement. "He doesn't look it."

"He's very sensitive and does good work. But not often. He drinks too much."

"Too bad," Ralph said. "Dare I invite you into the bar?"

"Yes," she said. "I need a drink. And I need a talk with someone from home worse."

The bar was discreetly dark, and they found a table in a deserted corner. He ordered for them and then studied her across the table.

"You're beautiful," he said. "But I must be truthful and say you look a trifle weary."

"I'm sure I do."

"Want to tell me about it?" he asked quietly.

"As long as you don't quote me in papers all over the world," she said with a wistful smile.

"Depend on me," he assured her as their drinks were served.

She sampled her drink before she began. Then she told him everything that had happened since their parting. She ended with her being upset at Alex deserting her to go to St. Petersburg. "He's still behaving strangely," she complained.

Ralph asked her, "Aren't the rest of the family concerned? Especially after what happened to Basil? And the effect it had on his wife?"

"They're concerned in a way," she said. "But they are all so wrapped up in their own problems. Believe me, I've learned that even the people living in a palace can have grim troubles."

He smiled wryly, "You should know that. Grimm's fairy tales are full of such situations."

"It's not funny."

"I know."

"I'm frightened," she said. "Preparations are being made for a second wedding, and I'm not sure Alex is honoring the vows he made at the first one."

"Have you been threatened in any way since the Litvinov thing in London?" Ralph asked.

"No, but that could come as well. I live in a house where violence is fairly common—a place where the ghost of a three-time murderer is seen regularly."

Ralph said, "You did need a drink. I see it's gone. I'll order another round." And he did.

Her eyes were wide with her fear. "How can I fight it? Fight an evil I don't even know! What can I do? That fat man hates me and wants to see me dead!"

"Litvinov."

"Yes, and I'm sure he was on the Paris-Moscow Express."

"You're right," Ralph said evenly. "I've been doing some investigation into it all. At this very moment, Litvinov is at his monastery in St. Petersburg—if you can call the place a monastery."

She leaned forward anxiously. "Then you have learned some new facts about him?"

"I've studied the files here," he said. "And I spent a few days in St. Petersburg. This is why I was so tardy in calling you."

"No matter," she said. "Just so long as you've learned something. Tell me!"

He stared at his glass with his brow furrowed. "To begin with, the organization of which I spoke to you, the Skoptsi, does exist."

"And?"

"They have a monastery and what they call cells in both St. Petersburg and Moscow; they have also spread out to other cities, even as far as London and New York."

She gasped, "That could explain the weird attacks on me in New York. They weren't just coincidences, but meant to eliminate me from Alex's life."

The young newspaperman said, "That is unhappily possible. It seems they have marked Alex to follow in his late brother's footsteps. They are building a dedicated group of terrorists and spies with a plan to take over the leadership of Russia and later all the world."

"And Rasputin is the leader?"

"There is every indication," he agreed. "To enlist their members they offer licentiousness, liquor, and drugs. There are orgies in which drugs play a big role and men and women indulge in group sex with complete abandon. But this is only the first level."

"Go on," she said, tautly remembering the strange change in her husband's eyes several times when he'd come back to her. This transformation had been presumably from some drug he'd taken.

Ralph gave her a cautioning look. "I must warn you that some of this is from hearsay. Later on, I hope to manage to see one of the gatherings. But I haven't yet."

"Wouldn't it be risky?"

"It could be, but my profession calls for risk; and I have a personal stake in this because of you. Besides, if I break the story about the cult, it might destroy Rasputin; and it would be a headline yarn all over the world."

"Alex seems to be gradually slipping under their power," she worried. "When I argue with him about it, he becomes angry."

"I would expect so," Ralph said. "After novices pass this first level of degeneracy, they move on to a much different style of ritual. This begins when they are satiated with the mixed sex orgies—when they become weary and are seeking a new thrill. The drug dosages are increased, and they join in wild demonstrations of asceticism. I will not say more about this at the moment. The final level calls for them to cut themselves off from wife, family, and all worldly associations and give themselves entirely to the cause! At this point, there is nothing else but a wild fanatical devotion to terrorism. Your gross, fat Litvinov is an example of one such devotee. These disciples stop at nothing to serve the dark order of which they have become members. And if nothing halts him, Alex, like his brother Basil, will work his way to this level."

"And carry out his role of terrorist until a bomb or a violent death of some sort ends it," she suggested bitterly.

"That is about it," he said.

"What can I do?"

"I don't know. You might beg your husband to consider you and his family above this evil association, but he may already be too deeply steeped in the wickedness to turn back. I have an idea the drugs they give their members are strongly addictive."

"When he has taken the drug he is not himself," she agreed. "He is like a madman."

"The Skoptsi are all madmen! Dangerous madmen! The best hope is that I may expose their movement and bring them down, Rasputin along with them."

"I pray that you do," was her earnest reply.

He sighed. "Meanwhile, life must go on. I had planned to ask you and Alex to join me at the ballet tonight. It is a special performance and Kschessinska is appearing in

Tschaikovsky's "Swan Lake." One does not see her too often these days. And later, after the performance, a ballet dancer friend of mine, Jacob Bogrov, and his wife are giving a party at their apartment. Bogrov is a fine dancer who married a wealthy man's daughter, so they live a lavish life."

"I would love to go," she sighed. "But with Alex away it wouldn't do."

"Surely they would not mind you attending the ballet with a friend from home?"

"It would cause talk," she said. "Gossip is a major sport here. I wouldn't want to embarrass the family."

"It's too bad," Ralph said with disappointment. "This will be an outstanding evening of ballet."

She suddenly had a thought. "There is one chance!"

"Good!"

"I might be able to get the Countess Olga to come along with me. Would you mind?"

"Not at all. So long as it would mean you might be able to attend."

"And if Olga is not interested—you can never be sure with her; she is given to moods—there is someone else, an attractive blonde young woman named Sophie Zemski. She is of noble blood and a distant relation of the Martynovs, but because her father gambled away her inheritance, she works as companion to Countess Marie. If the old woman would allow it, I'm sure Sophie would be happy to have an evening out."

Ralph smiled, "She sounds interesting. I leave it to you to arrange it."

"I'll do my best."

"And I shall reserve a table for three here at the hotel restaurant," she said. "We can meet at six-thirty and leave promptly in time for the ballet. They close the doors as soon as the performance begins and latecomers are left out."

She gave a deep sigh. "Just seeing you again gives me new courage, although the news you have of the Skoptsi frightens me."

"Try not to think about it," Ralph told her. "Let me do

what I can. Carry on at the palace and be careful. You know you have had some close calls before."

"I know," she said, gathering up her scarf and pocketbook. "Now I must get back. The coachman will be outside waiting for me."

The afternoon meeting with the young journalist had left Elsie with mixed feelings. She had enjoyed seeing him again, but was shocked about what he'd revealed concerning the secret society in St. Peterburg. Her great fear was that Alex had become so addicted to the drugs the group were giving him and the wild sexual orgies they offered that he was fast drifting from normalcy to become a willing victim to their way of life.

Her hope was that Ralph would be successful in exposing the secret group and destroying it. Meanwhile, her immediate problem was whether she would be able to attend the ballet.

When Elsie reached the palace, she at once sought out Olga, who was seated in the living room playing the piano. She went to the dark girl and told her of the invitation to dinner, the ballet and the party afterward.

She said, "You remember Ralph Manning. He would like to have you as his guest."

Olga gazed up at her nervously. "I'm sorry. I would like to go. But it would be impossible tonight. Tell him some other time."

"I will," she said. "That also means I can't go."

"I'm truly sorry," Olga said. "I have something I must do."

"I'll call Ralph," she said. "The only other possibility would be if I could get permission to take Sophie with me."

"Of course!" Olga said at once. "Mention it to Sophie; and if she likes the idea, you could present the request to Aunt Marie. The old lady is fond of you, and I'm almost sure she'd allow Sophie to accompany you."

"I'll try," she said, with new determination.

She located Sophie in the corridor outside Countess Marie's room and explained it all to her. "Would you like to go?" she asked.

The pretty blonde girl's eyes widened with excitement. "You know I would!"

"Then I'll ask the Countess Marie," she said.

Sophie at once looked glum. "I don't think she'll allow it. She can be strict."

But Sophie was wrong. Countess Marie quickly gave her permission, and she talked at length of the many times she had seen the famous Kschessinska. "It would be a pity to miss her," the old woman said. "And in the morning you must tell me all about it."

Frederick arranged a carriage for them, and the two young women, dressed in their finest evening gowns, drove in to Moscow to have dinner at the Metropole Hotel. Ralph was at once taken with Sophie. The young newspaperman declared, "I have the two loveliest girls in all Moscow as my companions for the evening. Who could be luckier?"

The dining room was filled with men and women in evening dress. Most of the patrons were going to the ballet, and there was a carnival air of enjoyment in the glittering splendor of Moscow's most noted dining place.

When they moved on to the ballet theater, it was the same. Elsie glanced around her before the curtain rose and felt that no other city in the world could gather such an elegant group for a night in the theater. She sat on one side of Ralph, with Sophie on the other. Sophie was all animation, and she and Ralph talked a great deal. It was obvious he found the lovely Russian girl fascinating

Many of the military officers were in their colorful uniforms with scarlet tunics and rows of gleaming gold and silver medals dangling from multicolored ribbons on their chests. Some ladies wore tiaras sparkling with diamonds and elaborate hairdos with jeweled bands and a tall feather to cap the decoration.

The lighting from the theater chandeliers faded, and the lights by the curtain blazed. The orchestra began the overture. The tension around her could be felt. Everyone was filled with excitement as the curtain rose and the beautiful set was revealed. Then the ballet began.

When Kschessinska danced her solos, she commanded everyone's attention. And the famous star was in truth one of the finest ballet talents Elsie had ever seen. The evening sped by.

Sophie leaned close to her as they strolled along the

promenade at intermission time and whispered, "How kind of you to bring me here. Ralph is such a charming man."

"I'm glad you like him," she said. "Did you notice Bogrov in the ballet?"

"Yes. He's very good and handsome," Sophie added in her mischievous way. "I noticed that also."

Elsie said, "He and Madame Bogrov, whom I understand is very wealthy, are holding a party in honor of Kschessinska after the ballet. We are invited."

"I can hardly wait!" Sophie said, her eyes bright.

The second half of "Swan Lake" seemed even more impressive than the first. When it ended, the elegantly dressed and bejeweled audience was on its feet applauding, Elsie along with them.

Later, as they waited for Joseph to arrive in the carriage line, Ralph smiled at the girls and said, "Where else in the world could you match a night like this? Russia leads in its splendor just as it leads in its squalor!"

Sophie gave him one of her cynical smiles. "This is the dying burst of energy of a society already near the end. I would trade Moscow for Paris any day!"

Ralph smiled at her. "That's another contradiction in you Russians—you are both romantics and realists at the same time. It has to be the climate."

Joseph drove up, and Ralph gave him the address of the Bogrov house. The three of them settled in the darkness of the carriage for the short ride. And Elsie noticed that Sophie was taking advantage of the moment to press close to Ralph and utter small flatteries as to his gifts as a host.

The Bogrov house was large and in a fashionable district of the great city. It was surrounded by other square, three-story buildings of the same size. Carriages were arriving and guests poured out of them and into the lighted entrance of the dancer's house. They followed in the line.

Jacob Bogrov was a handsome man with classic features, but shorter offstage than he had seemed on. His hair was black and receding a trifle at the forehead. His wife was slightly overweight, with large, gray eyes, and brown hair with streaks of gray in it. Her kindly smile and sympathetic eyes were her best features. The two greeted them, along with the other guests.

Sophie hesitated a moment longer than most to tell Bogrov, "I was thrilled by your dancing."

He glowed with pleasure and bowed. "We must discuss the performance later."

And later Elsie saw Sophie and the dancer engaged in what seemed a serious discussion of the ballet. She was glad that Sophie was enjoying this rare evening out.

⟨§ *Chapter 17* §⟩

JACOB BOGROV'S STOUT, graying wife wore a sparkling dress of an emerald shade and appeared to be everywhere at the party. Food and drink were served in a lavish manner, and the guests were scattered in every room of the fine house. Ralph told Elsie that most of the furnishings had been purchased in Paris and also pointed out that French was being spoken by the gentry at the party more than their native Russian.

She asked him, "How do you like Sophie?"

"An interesting girl," Ralph said. "And lovely. But bitter. Too bad her family lost their money, it has left its mark on her."

"She seems to hate Russia."

"I know, but then many of the noble families are like that. It is one of the grave signs that the country is in bad trouble."

She sighed. "I'm glad she came tonight. I wish she would meet someone and make a wealthy marriage. Then she might be happier."

"She seems to be a favorite with our host," Ralph said, nodding toward the other room, where Sophie still stood with Bogrov."

"He may introduce her to someone," she said.

"Which reminds me, you haven't yet met Kschessinska," Ralph said. "Come along." He led her by the hand through the various groups to the other end of the drawing room, where a petite, smiling woman was holding court. He awaited his turn and presented Elsie to the star.

Kschessinska was charming to her and in an accented voice, said, "American!"

"Yes," she nodded. "New York."

209

The petite star smiled with delight. "I have been! So exciting! So special!"

"We have no ballet such as I saw here tonight," she said.

Kschessinska shrugged. "You have so much else. Where is Count Martynov?"

"In St. Petersburg," she said.

"St. Petersburg," the star replied. "I dance there next month. "With the Imperial Ballet at the Maryinsky Theatre. Bogrov also comes along. He is a great artist, do you not agree?"

"Yes," Elsie said. "I had never seen him before."

"Special!" the star said with a wise look for her before she turned to receive the next guest waiting to be presented.

Ralph led Elsie away. "Well, do you think the tsar showed good taste?"

"How could he have missed her," Elsie said. "She is so vibrant! She radiates charm! And more than charm, I suspect in spite of her tiny body she is very strong."

"She is," Ralph said. "There are legends about her ability to work long hours and remain up all night."

"I don't think I can imitate her in that," Elsie laughed. "I think we should find Sophie and that she and I ought to go back to the palace."

Ralph gave her a serious look. "It has been a special evening for me. You don't know how good it is to see you again."

"It is my first glamorous experience of Moscow night life," she said. "I'm indebted to you. And I'm sure Sophie will agree."

They joined the blonde girl and Jacob Bogrov who seemed to be thoroughly enjoying her company. He told Ralph, "This young woman is an interesting discovery."

"Elsie found her," Ralph smiled.

Bogrov bowed to her. "I am grateful."

Sophie told Elsie, "I like listening to Jacob's stories of the ballet. He has visited almost every large city in the world. And he is soon to go on another tour."

"Away from troubled Russia," Jacob Bogrov said with a grim humor in his tone. "How are you interpreting us to the world through your Hearst press?"

"I'm doing my best," Ralph told him. "It is not always easy."

Bogrov's handsome face showed disgust. "One thousand large landowners own as much land as two million peasants. The tsar's family alone own seven million desyatins, and the peasantry are perishing with hunger. They can't feed their families on the small patches of land that come to their ownership after they have paid out big sums of redemption."

Sophie said, "Didn't someone write that the average poor peasant hasn't room on his land to turn a chicken out to feed?"

Bogrov gave her an interested reaction. He said quietly, "Yes. And I happen to know the man who wrote that. Would you believe that in 1900 there were roughly six million peasant farms that had no horse to help till the soil, or at best one horse. And this year the number of farms with no horse or perhaps one has increased to nearly nine million. People are starving and so become easy victims of typhus and scurvy. Our mortality rate is twice that of England."

Elsie said, "Yet you would not guess that from the splendor of this evening."

The dancer said, "This is the ornamentation on the cake. It means nothing. But I am one of those living in the charmed circle, so why should I complain."

Ralph said, "These contrasts are what makes it so hard to interpret Russia to the readers in the outside world. There are many Russias."

Jacob Bogrov gave him a meaningful look as he said, "I think there will come a day when there will be only one."

They said their good nights to the dancer and his matronly wife and then Ralph sought out their carriage and kissed them both good night in brotherly fashion. Joseph urged the horses on, and they began the journey home. It was a mild night, and the air was thick with mist so that it was difficult to see any distance. As a result he drove slowly.

Sophie leaned back with a happy sigh and said, "I feel like Cinderella. It was too much."

"I'm glad you enjoyed yourself. Everyone liked you."

"Did Ralph like me?"

Elsie said, "Of course!"

"I mean, did he like me very much. I wouldn't mind running away from Russia with your young newspaper man."

Elsie gazed at her in surprise. "You like him that much?"

"I like him well enough. One does not have to be madly in love."

She could not prevent herself from turning to the other girl and saying in a somewhat accusing tone, "You're seeing him as a means of escape."

Sophie eyed her in the near darkness of the carriage interior. "Does that shock you?"

"I'm fond of Ralph."

"You're married to Alex."

"I mean, I like Ralph. He's probably my dearest friend."

"Oh?"

"I wouldn't want him hurt."

"And you think I'd hurt him?"

"You might if you became his wife simply to get out of Russia," she said.

Sophie spoke in a dull tone. "Naturally, you wouldn't understand my feelings. You married Alex and came here without a qualm."

"If you and Ralph truly fell in love, I'd be very happy for you both," she went on, wishing to be fair to the other girl and not wanting to spoil her evening.

Sophie sighed again and stared off into space. "Maybe we will! I have a feeling my luck is about to change, that tonight was an omen."

"I wish you well, Sophie," she said. "You know that."

Sophie gave her a smiling glance. "Of course you do. And I thank you for introducing me to your Ralph. I think Bogrov is also a striking man."

"Smaller than he looked onstage."

"But striking and a thinker. You heard him talking about the misery of the poor here. And he has a wealthy wife."

"Plus a successful career. The Imperial Ballet is well rewarded."

"Yes," Sophie agreed. "I think my talk with him was one of the high spots of the evening."

They reached the palace and got out. Sophie complained of weariness, but Elsie felt very wide awake. She hated to go inside at once and suggested to the other girl that they take a stroll.

"In this miserable mist?" Sophie said, standing by the entrance door.

"It is warm."

"But damp."

"I will sleep better with some fresh air," she said.

Sophie shrugged. "Then remain outside on your own and enjoy it all you like. I'm sorry, but I'm going straight up to bed."

They said good night and Elsie remained outside alone. She was not afraid, since she knew the palace was set off by itself and servants guarded the grounds day and night. The unrest in the country had made this necessary. She moved around to the rear of the mansion to the spot on the riverbank where she had seen Olga that other night.

The mist was rising from the river now and swathed the grounds in an eerie fashion. The bare branches of the trees reached out toward her from the night shadows like menacing hands. She thought about the evening just ended and worried a little about what Sophie had said. She must somehow tactfully warn Ralph that the girl was desperate to escape Russia and might pretend to be in love with him if she thought he would take her away with him.

She sympathized with Sophie's plight and would do anything she could to help her. But she was so fond of Ralph and did not want to see him injured by someone who might marry him and then be unfaithful to him if she saw a better chance. In the past, Sophie had not hesitated to use her lovely body to achieve her desires. She would not likely stop at doing so again.

Elsie didn't think she was suspicious of the blonde because she had been mistress to Alex once. That was all over and did not matter. But she must somehow warn Ralph, without turning him against Sophie. This was the problem.

She continued walking along the riverbank in the thick mist with her mind full of these thoughts. She was hardly aware of her surroundings. Then, suddenly, she heard a footstep crunch on the melting snow of the riverbank, and she looked in the direction from which the sound had come.

At first she saw nothing, just the mist. Then gradually a figure took shape. A gross, fat man shuffling toward her in the mist. She went rigid, frozen with fear at the sight of the apparition. She was unable to speak or move as the eerie creature continued to come closer to her.

Then she somehow broke the spell of terror and let out an agonized scream. She turned to flee in the direction of the palace. But the fat man was already upon her. She felt her arm seized roughly, and she screamed again.

In the next instant, she was thrown to the ground and the fat man stood over her with a gleaming knife in his hand. Before he could bend to plunge the blade into her, there was a shout from the bushes. The fat man was at once alerted. He straightened and gazed fearfully in the direction of the bushes; and when a second cry came again, he turned and went shuffling off down the riverbank to vanish in the mist!

This series of events all took place within seconds. Elsie raised herself on an arm in the mixed snow and mud, still not knowing who her attacker had been and why she had been spared.

Then Olga came running over to kneel beside her, asking anxiously, "Are you hurt?"

"No! He ran off! Was it your cry which frightened him?"

"Yes," the dark girl said. And then she turned and spoke into the mist behind her, "It is all right, Feodor. You can show yourself."

As she said this, a young man in a fur hat and a short jacket with his trousers stuffed in peasant boots came into view and knelt beside Olga. He was young and had high cheekbones in a thin, intellectual's face.

He said, "The countess had a close call."

"I did," Elsie said, struggling to her feet with Olga's aid. "I was walking here lost in my thoughts. Then that figure came up from the riverbank."

"A fat man," Olga said.

214

"Yes, I was terrified. But it was too late. I couldn't escape him."

"We saw what was happening," Olga said. "I called out."

"He had a knife," she said, trembling now.

"And would have used it," the young man called Feodor said.

"It was silly of me to come this far alone," Elsie said.

"Not too wise," Olga agreed.

Elsie gave her a searching look. "But you are out here?"

"I only come here alone when I meet Feodor," she said. "This is Feodor Kurav, the man whom I plan to marry."

"I have heard about him."

"Oh? From Alex?" Olga said, nervously.

"Yes. He pledged me to silence. And I have kept my promise to him."

"Thank you," the girl said gratefully. "Feodor is very busy these days. He was in the route of marchers whom we saw."

Elsie smiled at him wanly. "The cossacks didn't leave their mark on you."

"No," the young man said grimly. "But many of my comrades did fall."

Olga told Elsie, "Feodor and I will marry as soon as the revolution comes."

"What will the family say?" Elsie asked.

"I don't care," Olga said, standing proudly by the young man. "I have had my fill of being a Martynov."

Feodor said, "I should have given chase to that villian with the knife, but I was afraid that in the melee, my presence here would be discovered. And that could have been bad for both Olga and me."

"You saved me. I can't ask more. Not likely you could have found him in this thick mist."

The three of them stood there talking in low voices in the misty night. Olga asked her, "Do you think it might have been Litvinov?"

"I'm not sure. He was grossly fat like Litvinov."

"And he moved fast enough when he heard us," Feodor said. "For all his weight I think he was a young man."

"Litvinov is supposed to be in St. Petersburg," Elsie said. "I have an idea that Alex went there to join him."

"Another Basil!" Olga said bitterly. "He could not keep away from St. Petersburg. And then one day he did not return."

"I know," she said, and glancing at Feodor asked him, "So you are a revolutionary?"

"Yes," the young man said.

"Does that mean you are also a follower of Rasputin?"

Feodor showed anger. "It does not! That mad monk is the reason things have become so much worse here. He is the evil one guiding the tsar."

Elsie said, "Alex is associating with Rasputin and his Skoptsi cult."

Feodor quickly made the sign of the cross. "Do not mix with them. It always means death."

Olga turned to him. "Stop! You are only scaring her worse. I'll take her inside. It is time you went on."

The young man said, "All right. I'll watch along the way for the fat one. If I find him, I'll deal with him."

Olga kissed him. "Be careful." Then she joined Elsie to see her into the house, and the young man waved and hurried off into the mist.

As Elsie and Olga neared the front door, Olga asked her, "Are you going to complain to Count Andre about this?"

"No," she decided. "I won't take the chance. It would have to involve you and Feodor. And you must be protected."

"At your own risk?"

"I will manage. I'll clean my things and keep it a secret until Alex returns, then I'll tell him," she said. "For he is to blame for exposing me to these monsters and leaving me alone."

"Thank you for keeping silent about Feodor," Olga said. "He is my whole life. And he takes so many chances. If anything should happen to him, I would not want to live."

"He is young and resourceful," Elsie encouraged her as they went inside.

Later, in her own apartment, she surveyed the damage to her shoes, gown, and coat. None of it was bad. She cleaned most of the dirt off at once.

But the evening's ending had confirmed one thing: The

216

struggle between the weird Skoptsi cult and herself for Alex was not over. Perhaps it was just beginning, and she was grimly resolved to save the man she loved even under threat of her life, as had happened tonight and earlier.

When she slept she had terrifying dreams of being stalked by a vicious fat man in a monk's cowl and black, flowing robe. The face of her stalker was never clear in her nightmares, but the pattern was always the same: the hulking form shuffling toward her and the gleaming knife raised over her in threat.

Sophie was radiantly happy the next morning. When she met Elsie in the sun room, she asked her, "Did you have a nice stroll, all by yourself?"

Elsie had already decided not to mention the near escape she'd had from the knife of the fat man in black, so she said, "The air did me good. I slept well."

"I'm glad," the blonde said with a mocking smile. "I slept perfectly myself and dreamt of Ralph."

"Then you had a pleasant dream," Elsie said politely.

"Countess Marie is asking for you," Sophie told her. "She wants to hear all about the ballet and the party. And she's not satisfied to hear it from me."

So Elsie went up to the apartment of the old couple and found that Count Andre had wheeled his wife out on the small balcony off her bedroom to get the air. She sat there in her wheelchair bundled up and looking pleased.

Count Andre greeted Elsie as he stood by his wife's chair. "It is lovely out here today! Soon you will see Moscow in summer! And then we'll go on to our summer place."

"But first we shall have the wedding," Countess Marie said with a warm smile on her thin, wrinkled face.

"I must go back down soon," Elsie said. "Father Peter will be here."

"He always spends a moment with me also," Countess Marie said. "Now tell me about Kschessinska and the party."

Elsie gave her an account of the evening, stressing how much Sophie enjoyed it and thanking the old woman for her kindness in allowing Sophie to go.

A perplexed looked shadowed the old woman's face.

"We wish to treat the girl like our own. But there are times when she is so resentful and so hateful to Timofei."

Count Andre cleared his throat. "To be truthful, my dear, Timofei sometimes encourages her grim attitude toward him. He likes to taunt her."

The Countess Marie gazed out at the river and sighed, "These young people!"

Elsie left the old couple and went downstairs to the chapel where she found Father Peter waiting to give her additional instruction in the Orthodox religion.

The bearded young priest smiled at her and said, "I think my task is nearly completed."

She sank in one of the chairs provided for them and said, "My wedding day grows near and my groom is in St. Petersburg."

Father Peter said, "That disturbs you?"

"Yes. I do not think it is business that has taken him there, Father."

"I see," the young man with the black beard said gravely. "You know about his brother, Basil?"

"Yes."

"And his young bride, Katrin? And what happened to her?"

"A dreadful tragedy."

She looked at the young man directly. "I have heard that Basil courted his own death, that he was a follower of some cult organized by Rasputin. I fear that Alex may also be taking the same direction."

Father Peter looked shocked. "Heaven forbid!"

"I know your church is not strong on confession," she said. "But I felt I must speak to you of these things. You will be one of the priests officiating at the marriage."

"You are suggesting it might be an evil marriage?"

"I'm worrying that I may not be Alexander's real bride. That he may be wed to this wicked cult whose monastery is in St. Petersburg."

"I shall pray that this is not true," Father Peter said.

"I pray it every day. But my hold on the count seems to grow weaker."

The young priest looked uneasy. He said, "I have no more to offer you by way of instruction. You have my blessings. I shall go up and see the Countess Marie for a little now. My visits seem to have a cheering effect on her."

"They do," she said. "By all means go to her. You can offer her much more help than you can me."

The young Father Peter gave her a regretful look and seemed about to say something; then he apparently changed his mind, for he walked out of the chapel without any further parting words. She stood there entirely alone, staring up at the icon of the Savior without Hands.

Ralph called her from his office shortly after lunch. The line was noisy, but they managed to hold a conversation. He asked her if she arrived home safely and she had to be careful in her reply.

"We reached here safely," she said. "But there are some things which happened later that I will want to tell you."

"Something important?" His tone was tense.

"I think so," she said.

"I'll be out by the palace early this evening," he told her. "Would it cause any trouble if I came by for a moment?"

"No," she said. "I'll be glad to talk with you, and Sophie will enjoy seeing you again. She wanted me to tell you she had a wonderful time at the party."

"Indeed?" Ralph said, pleased. "She made a good impression on Jacob Bogrov."

"I'm glad."

"He thinks her smart as well as pretty."

"She is."

Ralph spoke cautiously, "Do you know who she quoted to him last night?"

"No."

"Lenin."

She said, "I'm afraid the man is not familiar to me."

"The name is to many Russians, you may be sure. But not a popular one with people like the Martynovs, or the guests at the party last night. He is in exile with a price on his head, I'd say. That is why it took some courage on Sophie's part to openly quote him last night."

"I must ask her about it."

"No," he said. "You might upset her. Let me do it quietly some time when I'm talking with her."

"Very well," she said. "If I don't hear from you further, I'll expect you later this evening."

As she put down the telephone on the stand in the lower hallway a mocking voice said from behind her, "Who may I ask are you expecting this evening?" It was Timofei.

She laughed. "A man, of course. Whom did you think?"

"My little innocent is trying to be a brazen hussy," the big man chuckled. "It doesn't suit you, my dear."

"An old friend," she said. "If you're at home, which needless to say you never are, I'll gladly introduce you to him."

Timofei said, "You may also have a chance to introduce him to Alex, as I understand he is expected back on the train from St. Petersburg this afternoon."

She raised her eyebrows. "His stay was short."

"Are you disappointed?" Timofei teased her. "He may have heard of your gallivanting off to Moscow parties and decided he should return."

"I hope he did hear," she said.

"Was Sophie a darling of the evening?" the artist wanted to know.

"Everyone liked her."

"Good for Sophie. She is a chameleon, you know. She can be whatever the occasion calls for. Myself, I prefer a simpler creature, one who is always the same."

"What about your icon?" she said.

He smiled. "You would tease me, little innocent. But I will surprise you. The icon is already underway. I will not tell you where, or what it is like. But when it is done, you shall see it."

"I want to," she said.

"It is a lovely day," he told her. "I'm taking out the droshka and driving myself. I'd enjoy a companion, and the tsarina is occupied with Rasputin. How about you coming along?"

She smiled. "I'd like to, if you promise to make no more bad jokes about Rasputin. I hate the sound of his name."

"I shall not mention him again," Timofei vowed. "And do hurry, little innocent. In Russia one does not waste the sunshine!"

She went upstairs and put on a cloak. She passed Sophie

220

in the hallway and told her about Ralph's coming by in the evening and that Alex was also expected home.

Sophie said, "About time Alex came back. He is neglecting you. I shall enjoy seeing Ralph again."

"He said Bogrov liked you."

"Bogrov is a genius of the dance," Sophie said. "Where are you going?"

"Timofei is taking me for a drive," she said on the top stair.

Sophie grimaced. "That one! I would rather sit at home in the damp cellar."

"I like him."

"If he's to your taste," Sophie said with bitter amusement. "I have been enlisted in helping Olga work on your invitation list this afternoon. So I shall be well occupied."

Elsie went out and joined Timofei in the droshka. He seemed completely sober and handled the horses well. They drove out into the country.

They chatted amiably about many things; then he suddenly pointed to massive gates guarding a broad roadway on their left and said, "There is one of the Yussoupov's estates. Twenty-nine-year-old Prince Phillip Yussoupov is the heir to this fine property and thirty-seven more estates scattered across Russia. His family is richer than the tsar's, and they say he has vowed to murder a man whose name you have made me vow not to mention."

She was interested and with a wan smile said, "You mean Rasputin?"

"You said the name," Timofei replied, allowing the horses to take the carriage along slowly. "He has not done it yet, but the story is that he promised he would. And a noble usually keeps his word."

"Where does his family money come from?" she asked.

"Coal, iron, oil, and the sweat of his factory workers," Timofei said. "He bleeds Mother Russia like a leech!"

"Tell me more about this Prince Phillip."

"He is handsome and a friend of the royal family, but he has come to distrust the mad monk and resent his domination over the tsarina. His wealth goes back centuries. There is one estate with a park, gardens, heated greenhouses. It also has a private zoo and a private theater. It is told that his grandfather had his own company of musi-

221

cians, actors, and ballet dancers. The old man had only to seat himself before the ballet company and wave his cane and all the dancers would, by a special lighting change, become completely naked."

"Fabulous!" she laughed.

"The old Prince was a credit to his sex," Timofei boasted. "They claim the gallery at the estate here contains portraits of his three hundred mistresses and when he died at eighty-one he was enjoying an affair with a girl of eighteen."

"The young prince enjoys a superb heritage."

"I hope he lives up to it," Timofei said. "Now your Alex had only one mistress in the palace, of whom I know. One doesn't count possible servant girls. And there is nary a portrait of her on our walls."

She said, "Timofei, you mustn't push a joke too far."

"Sorry," he said, looking straight ahead. "I've been thinking of you and Alex and remembering Basil and Katrin. It is all too much alike. I would not like to see you have Katrin's fate."

"It's not likely I shall," she said quietly.

Timofei gave her a sharp glance. "Did you know she had a narrow escape from death shortly before she hung herself? She was hysterical most of the time by then. And she told a strange story so nobody paid much attention to it. She had a bad fall on the stairs and she claimed a mysterious fat man came out of the shadows and pushed her!"

✺ Chapter 18 ✺

"A FAT MAN!" Elsie gasped.

"Yes," Timofei nodded, his eyes on the horses and the road ahead.

She was stunned by what he'd said and suspicious that he knew much more than he was letting on. Perhaps he had even seen the attack the fat man had made on her the night before. How much did he know?

She decided to play it warily. She said, "Are you telling me you think someone tried to take Katrin's life before her suicide?"

"That is what she said."

"This was after Basil had been murdered and brought back here for burial?"

"Yes. She was strange from then on. She talked wildly, and no one listened to her. I wish I had."

"Why?"

"I don't think she had a nervous breakdown," Timofei said, allowing the reins to hang idly in his hands as the horses moved on slowly in the sun.

"No?" She felt he was playing a cat and mouse game with her, but she intended to play it his way.

"I think she was telling us the truth and we wouldn't listen. She kept maintaining that someone wanted to kill her because she knew a secret."

Elsie frowned. "A secret?"

"That's what she said," Timofei replied with a trouble look on his face.

"Did she suggest what the secret was?"

"No," Timofei said. "Except to say that Basil had been killed for the same reason. She kept repeating that he had been destroyed to keep the secret."

223

"And no one thought her words worth taking seriously?" she asked.

"No one," the young man said. "Alex was one of the worst ones in that regard. He insisted she was demented and ought to be sent away to a hospital for treatment."

"Perhaps he was right."

"Dr. Orlov came and examined her and said there was not a thing wrong with her except the hysteria induced by her grieving after Basil's murder."

"Dr. Orlov is old and none to smart," she said. "At least that is what I've heard."

"You've heard right," Timofei said.

"So?"

"No one listened to her. And she kept getting more upset. When she fell down the stairs, it seemed a result of her confused state. And when she said a fat man had come out of the shadows and attacked her it was considered ludicrous."

Elsie said quietly, "Did they find it as humorous when she was found hanging in that closet?"

"Hardly," Timofei said. "Everyone was full of regrets then. But it was too late. And I wondered."

"Wondered what?"

"Katrin was a gentle girl. Crushed by the tragedy of her husband's death, not given to action."

"So?"

Timofei gave her another wise look. "I couldn't think how a girl like that could bring herself to deliberately hang herself."

"She may have reached the point of desperation."

"I agree," he said. "And yet it took careful planning, and she had to go about it calmly. Tie the cloth to a strong rafter, be sure she could kick the chair away. I don't know how that hysterical girl managed it."

She stared at him. "Are you hinting that she didn't do it? That someone else may have murdered her and made it seem a suicide."

He nodded. "I'm wondering if it might be that the fat man came again."

"That was hysterical nonsense!" she reminded him.

"We decided that. But was it?"

There was silence between them for a few moments

224

broken only by the creaking of the carriage wheels and the clopping of the horses' hooves on the dirt road. The sun seemed stronger than before, and yet she felt a chill surging through her.

She said, "Do you mean to terrify me?"

"Why do you ask that?"

"Because that is what you're doing!"

Timofei gave her a sad look. "I'm always too slow to act. That is my tragedy. I felt that Katrin might be telling the truth, and yet I didn't do anything about it. And I was fond of Katrin in my own way, as I am fond of you. I should have paid more attention to her. I didn't. And then it was too late. I don't want to be too late for you."

"Thanks," she said bitterly.

"I mean it."

"I know you do," she said. "But I don't know anything I can do about it."

Timofei gave her another of those knowing looks. "You might be careful to avoid fat men."

"If that's your suggestion, I will," she said.

"And you might tell Alex what I've said. If you have good luck he might stay away from St. Petersburg."

She stared at him. "Timofei, you're a very strange person."

"I know."

"You only tell a fraction of what you think," she accused him. "You're not fooling me."

He reined the horses and said, "I think it is time I turned the carriage around. We don't want to be too late getting back, especially when your dutiful husband is returning."

She watched him as he swung the carriage in the direction from which they had come. She said, "You hate Alex, don't you?"

"Hatred is a futile passion," he said. "Almost as bound to end in frustration as love. Let us use a milder term; say I distrust him."

"Why?"

"He is a Martynov. The Martynovs are the enemy."

"That's nonsense," she said, "You're drinking yourself to death to prove you're a rebel! Your foster mother and

225

father care for you deeply. They love you like their own son. And you cause them nothing but sorrow."

"I try to conform for them," he said. "Otherwise, I would have left the palace long ago. When my foster mother dies, I will go."

"You should remain," she entreated him. "You are the best of them."

"There is no future," he said. "The Martynovs will be lost in the flood of revolution when it comes. All the noble families will come down. Our best bet is Olga and her Feodor!"

"You know about him?"

He laughed dryly. "Of course. Do you think me stupid?"

"She thinks only Alex knows."

"I also know," Timofei said. "And I approve. She may survive as Feodor's sweetheart, never as the Countess Martynov."

She said, "I see things so differently now. Before I came here I didn't understand Olga. I thought she hated me for loving Alex."

"More likely she was frightened for you."

"Because of what happened to Katrin?"

"Because of many things," Timofei said. "You know, you needn't remain here and go through with the second marriage. You can still run away, take the train to Paris and a liner to New York. You'd have no trouble getting a divorce there. You could be free again!"

She shook her head. "I've thought of it. I can't. I think I would be deserting Alex at a time when he has great need of me."

Timofei told her, "I especially distrust people with a martyr complex."

"Sorry," she said. "That is the way I feel."

Timofei then lapsed into reveries of his own and said little for the rest of the drive back. But she did a lot of thinking. She was sure he had planned the drive to tell her that he suspected Katrin had been murdered rather than being a suicide. She did not know whether he had seen the fat man's attack on her the night before and that had prompted him to tell her of his suspicions, or whether it was purely from a desire to warn her.

When they reached the palace, she went inside and Count Andre was there to hand her some mail. "The mail has just arrived," he said, with a smile on his thin, old face. "I see you have some letters from America."

"Yes," she said, looking at them. "I'm glad to get them."

"Did you enjoy your drive?"

"Very much."

The old count gave an approving nod. "Timofei can be fine company when he is not in his cups."

"He is an interesting young man," she agreed.

"Alex ought to be here in time for dinner," Count Andre said.

"I'm so glad," Elsie said. "I'll go up and rest a little and read my letters."

She curled up on the bed in her room and read the thick letter from her Aunt Jane and Uncle Gordon. Each of them had written a few pages. And as usual their versions of things differed slightly. The gist of it was that they missed her grievously and that the news of Russia in the New York papers was ominous. They begged her to write them often and asked when the second wedding ceremony was to be held. They also wrote vaguely of making a trip to Moscow in the early autumn before the weather became too cold.

There was a letter from Marjorie in which her friend told her that she was at the point of becoming engaged to a young man from Boston whom Elsie had never met. To go by Marjorie's letter, he was a marvel of young manhood with excellent prospects as an engineer. He worked for a company with worldwide activity, and Marjorie was excited that he might one day be sent to Russia. They would have a reunion. She also told of the doings of other young men and women whom Elsie knew and said the new play with John Barrymore had taken New York by storm. It was by Galsworthy and was very serious.

Elsie finished reading the letters with tears of sheer homesickness in her eyes. She had never felt so lost. She had been careful in her letters home not to let them guess how troubled she was. And she would have to continue doing so. She was not yet desperate enough to admit that her love for the handsome Alex had led her into a trap.

She could not take Timofei's well meant advice and run off—not yet! But things had turned out much differently from what she'd expected. She now must hope that Alex would return from St. Petersburg in a repentant mood and that she would not be visited again by the vengeful fat man. She'd had enough of mystery and secret societies. She was at the point of being reluctantly willing to admit there was much of Russia she did not understand—or like.

She was dressed and seated at the dresser finishing her hair when Alex came into the bedroom. He came in from his own apartment, and she first saw him over her shoulder in the mirror. He stood there gazing at her with a kind of sadness, which touched her. She turned quickly with a smile and rose to throw herself in his arms.

"Alex!" she said happily.

"My darling!" He kissed her and held her close for a moment.

She gazed up at him. "You look so weary."

"And you are so lovely! A treat to return to," he said with his usual gallantry.

She was not trying to betray him, but she could not help taking particular notice of his eyes. And she was shocked and sickened. The pupils were greatly enlarged, just as they had looked other times when he'd been on that drug. She tried to hide her chagrin.

"You're home sooner than I expected," she said.

He crossed a hand over his forehead. "Yes. I completed the tasks I had to do. I found the train ride back wearying."

"No wonder," she said. "Promise me you won't go to St. Petersburg again until after the wedding."

"I don't expect to."

"And when you do go, take me along," she linked her arm in his.

He frowned. "Why would you want to go to St. Petersburg?"

"To be with you. And then I have never seen it."

"Moscow is much more interesting," he told her.

She fought her fear and went on making the pretense of trying to coyly coax him. "Come!" she said. "You will let me make my own comparison, won't you."

He was evasive. "When the time comes. Now I must go and hurry to dress for dinner."

She said, "Sophie and I attended the ballet last night with Ralph. We had a wonderful evening."

His handsome face showed interest. "So you do not sit at home by the fire when I am away."

"I was sure you wouldn't mind."

"No," he said, uneasily. "Of course not. So Ralph is finally here in Moscow."

"Yes. I think Sophie likes him. He is coming by tonight for a few minutes."

"Indeed!" Alex did not sound too pleased.

"He won't be staying long."

"It doesn't matter," he said irritably. "I'll come back for you as soon as I'm dressed."

He left her standing alone in the bedroom feeling despair. His eyes were strange; so was his manner. He was aloof and nervous compared to his regular self. But she had at least a half-promise that he would not go to St. Petersburg again before the wedding. She would work on that and gradually try to win him into not going there at all. He had to break away from the influence of Rasputin. It was the only hope!

Dinner was a strained meal. Countess Marie had a bad coughing attack and had to leave the table before she had her dessert. Count Andre looked worried at this example of his wife's failing health.

Timofei amused himself by tormenting Sophie and Olga alternately about their dresses and their hair styles. It was plain that he merely wanted to annoy them. Alex was oddly silent, so Elsie followed suit. They all adjourned to the elegant drawing room for brandy and coffee, and the Countess Marie recovered sufficiently to join them there.

Over her coffee, she asked Alex, "What is the latest word from St. Petersburg? Does it seem likely the tsar will hold any court parties this season?"

Brandy glass in hand, Alex stood opposite the old woman in her high-backed chair. "I was busy," he said. "I heard little gossip. To the best of my knowledge the royal family are not doing any entertaining."

Timofei chuckled over his brandy glass. "I hear Rasputin is entertaining them well enough."

229

Crimson showed in her husband's cheeks. He snapped back, "I don't think you have the knowledge, or ability, to criticize Rasputin!"

Timofei pretended amazement. "You hear him? He defends the holy man!"

Count Andre scowled at his foster son. "Timofei!" he said with reproach.

Sophie looked up from her chair and said, "Shouldn't your friend Mr. Manning be here by now?"

"Soon," Elsie said. "He suggested it would be a little after dinner."

Olga turned to Sophie and with an amused look, observed, "You have become so formal. I thought he was Ralph to you!"

It was Sophie's turn to blush. She said, "I prefer discretion in mentioning him before the family."

Timofei came up with a jeering comment at this. And Elsie suddenly noticed that her husband had left the circle and gone over to study his dead brother's portrait. He was standing before the colorful portrait of the young Basil who so much resembled him. She went over and joined him.

At his elbow, she said, "You miss him?"

Startled, he turned to her. "Yes. Naturally. We were close in the old days."

"You might have been twins."

"I'm two years older."

"Is he buried near here?"

Alex nodded. "In the Martynov private cemetery. A road behind the stables leads to a clearing in the woods. All the family and servants are buried there."

"I have never been there."

"I will take you one day," he said. "There is a fine view of the river. It is the custom to pick one's lot long before one dies."

She eyed him solemnly. "So one day we shall find our places there."

"Death is always a reality," he said.

She gave him a searching look. "What about Katrin?"

"She is there."

"I wasn't thinking about that," she said. "I was wondering about her suicide." She said it carefully, casually.

230

Even at that, he eyed her with a hint of suspicion. He asked, "What are you getting at?"

She went on the same pretended note of casualness. "From all I've heard about her, she doesn't strike me as the sort of person who would calmly plan a suicide and carry it out."

He showed upset. "You didn't know her."

"I have heard her talked about by nearly everyone. I feel as if I had known her."

Alex downed the rest of the brandy and said, "I find that quite different."

"You knew her. What do you think?"

"She was mad with grief. Her suicide was an act of insanity."

"I suppose Dr. Orlov decided that."

Alex frowned. "We all knew it!"

"I still think it strange," she said. "I hear she talked about a fat man wanting to kill her so she could not give away a secret." She gave her husband a meaningful look. "This gave me a shock after my nasty experience with your fat friend in London." She was not ready to mention the attack of the previous night until they were alone.

Her husband's handsome face was livid. "You are drawing very broad conclusions. Linking the ravings of an unfortunate mad woman with a misunderstanding in London. I will ask you never to bring up the Litvinov incident again. I took care of it, and it is finished."

"I hope so," she said.

It was hard to say where the sparring between them might have ended had not Frederick come to announce Ralph Manning at that moment. There were general greetings and introductions, and she and Alex gave up their conversation to join the group.

It was Timofei who asked Ralph, "And what are the news headlines this evening?"

"I thought you would have heard before this," the young journalist said. "There was a raid in St. Petersburg late last night. Some of Rasputin's friends were having an orgy when the police landed on them. The story is that Rasputin himself was there but literally hurled himself through a sealed-up back door to make his escape. Some

231

of the men and women were jailed, and some of them escaped through the rear exit with their leader."

There was a silence in the room until Count Andre said, "That confounded scoundrel again!"

Elsie was studying the expression on her husband's handsome face and felt it was one of guilt. He stood staring down at the rug and made no comment. So that was the reason for his arriving home days earlier than had been expected. She was sure Ralph had a suspicion of this, and that was why he had made his announcement so openly.

Timofei showed amusement. "The tsarina must have been upset to so nearly lose her darling."

Countess Marie gave him a dart of her sunken eyes, which still blazed authority. She said, "We will have no tarnishing of the name of the royal family while I am present."

"Sorry, mother," Timofei said at once. It was evident he had no wish to hurt her.

"I know it is the fashion to talk so," she went on. "But I was once a lady-in-waiting at a happy court. There was no scandal. And Nicky was a fine little fellow! How sad he has come to all this!"

Ralph said politely, "Both the tsar and the tsarina are nice looking people. So are the princesses and the ailing lad. It is too bad they do not command the same respect that the royal family does in England."

Count Andre nodded. "This villian Rasputin has caused all the gossip and trouble. Once he is removed, things will return to normal again."

After a few minutes the count suggested that it was time for his ailing wife to retire. He helped her rise, and they left the room after saying their good nights. Timofei wandered out soon after, as did Olga. This left only four in the big drawing room. Sophie and Ralph sat together on a divan talking earnestly, while Elsie and Alex made an awkward twosome before the fireplace.

She asked her husband, "Did you not hear of this raid before you left St. Petersburg?"

He shrugged. "There are so many stories going the rounds I pay little attention to them."

"This has to be true, since it apparently is in all the papers."

"I do not read scandal," he said. "And I have a bad headache. I wish you wouldn't discuss the matter any more. Please excuse me." And he left the room without looking Ralph's way.

Sophie rose from the divan saying, "Where is Alex?"

She said, "He has a bad headache. I think he went to take something for it. He should be back."

The blonde girl showed surprise. "I didn't see him go." Then she told Ralph, who was now also on his feet, "I must go up and see the Countess Marie safely in bed. I am an employee here, rather than a member of the family."

Elsie managed a smile. "You are both, and you know it. Ralph will excuse you until you return. I will entertain him for you."

"Wonderful," Sophie smiled teasingly. "I really won't be jealous." And she went on out.

Ralph turned to Elsie with a look of amusement. "She's a strange one."

Somewhat bitterly, she said, "They can all be strange when they like. Was she telling you how much she cares for you?"

"She was very pleasant and grateful."

"I'm sure she was being sincere."

"Talked a lot about Bogrov and his wife. She doesn't think they are well mated."

Elsie said, "I'm sure Bogrov thinks he has made a perfect match. His wife supplies him with all the luxuries a ballet dancer usually has to forego."

"He does well enough as a star. But you are right; it is Madame Bogrov who pays most of the bills."

She looked around to make sure there was no one to hear them, then in a low voice, she said, "You came at an interesting moment."

The young journalist looked interested. "I did?"

"Yes. Alex and I were close to a quarrel. You saved the situation."

"Good."

"Your announcement of the raid in St. Petersburg

shook him up a good deal. It was after that he had the headache."

Ralph nodded. "I wanted to test him on that."

"He failed to make the grade."

"It would almost seem so," the young reporter agreed. "Do you think he may have been there?"

"I'm almost sure of it."

"Bad business!"

"I know. If he comes in again take a good look at his eyes. They are still distorted from his using some sort of drugs."

"All the crowd in the cellar were on drugs. One of the girls died in hospital."

"Oh, no!" What had been merely distasteful now took on an aspect which was horrifying.

"Lives mean little to a man like Rasputin. He uses these people as puppets."

She moved close to him. "I have more to tell you before Alex or Sophie returns."

"What?"

"The fat man has appeared again. I was attacked out here last night after I came home." She gave him all the details.

"Do you think it was Litvinov again?"

"I can't be certain. I didn't see his face clearly. But it must have been!"

"I'll work on it," he promised. "And I don't even think you should remain here."

"I can't leave now."

"Why not? I can find you a room at the hotel until you decide what you are going to do."

She shook her head. "I'm sorry for him. Perhaps there is more concern than love now." She glanced over at the portrait of Basil on the opposite wall. "I want to try and save him from being murdered."

"If he has a death wish, what can you do about it?" Ralph demanded.

"I won't give up yet."

Ralph was tense. "You must keep in close contact with me."

"I will."

"I can make seeing Sophie an excuse for coming here," he said.

"Be fair with her."

Ralph said, "I'm sure she can take care of herself. I'm worried about you. More so since hearing about last night and this wild story about Katrin. Maybe the poor woman didn't kill herself after all. She may have been murdered by one of the Skoptsi group."

"I know," she said.

"Something may be revealed by the raid," Ralph said. "So I may get information within the next few hours. If Alex is implicated, I'll let you know."

"Do!" she said.

Sophie returned, and they could talk no more. Since Alex had not come back, she excused herself and went up to their apartment. The bedroom was empty so she judged he must be in the adjoining apartment. She went and knocked on the door.

After a moment, he came and opened it. He was in his pajamas and his dressing gown. He said, "Did your company leave?"

She said reprovingly, "He was your company as well. It wasn't very nice to just walk out as you did."

"He and Sophie were too busy talking to notice."

"I made excuses for you."

"Kind of you," he said.

"He's still down there with Sophie."

Alex smiled grimly. "That doesn't surprise me. Sophie is an opportunist. She is no doubt offering to sleep with him in return for his taking her to America."

She could not help replying, "You know her habits much better than I."

He reacted angrily. "What does that mean?"

She made a despairing gesture with her hand. "Nothing! Nothing at all! Do we have to do all this arguing on your first night back with me."

"You have been in a nasty mood since dinner," he replied.

"I'm sorry. My nerves are not the best. I have missed you and worried about you!"

"Touching," he said. "And when I return weary and

with a raging headache, you decide it is the ideal time to nag at me!"

"If I offended you, I'm sorry," she said.

"Thank you," was his cool reply. "I can't imagine how you managed to tear yourself away from your friend below."

"Please, Alex!" she said, reaching out to him.

"Good night," he said. "I am not at all well. I think it better if I stay in my own apartment for the night." And he made this decisive by shutting the door in her astonished face.

❧ Chapter 19 ❧

SHE STOOD THERE STARING at the door in disbelief. Tears
brimmed in her eyes and flowed down her cheeks. Then
she turned and ran across to the bed and threw herself on
it. Of course, he did not want to be with her after his extended orgy in St. Petersburg. She had known from the instant she'd seen the drugged pupils of his eyes that he was
not himself.

No doubt he was worn from the ordeal of the long scan-
dalous gathering in St. Petersburg and the strain of making his escape before the police closed in on him. He had
never looked more guilty than when Ralph had recounted
the story. Now he was pretending anger at her behavior when the truth was he was sexually satiated and had
used their argument as an excuse to keep away from her.

She lay there sobbing for a long while before she got up
and began preparing for bed. She felt she was at the brink
of making a decision. She must decide before the second
wedding ceremony took place. Perhaps Ralph was right.
She should pack her things and leave, admit failure! Her
marriage had been a calamitous mistake. Countess Olga
had tried to warn her in New York, and she had refused
to listen. Now she knew the dark girl had argued with
her for her own good.

She finally slept in spite of these distressing thoughts.
And tonight her dreams were not of the threatening fat
man, but of Alex. She had a series of nightmares in which
she was gazing down at her husband's dead body stretched
out in some dark place. She stood staring at him, knowing
he was dead, and that she could never do anything to
change it.

She opened her eyes with a start. It was morning and
Alex was standing by her bedside gazing down at her. She

237

waited, not knowing what to say, where to begin. He sat down on the side of the bed. He was dressed for the day. He took her hand in his.

"I had a bad night," he said.

"Did you?" she asked in a small voice.

"Yes."

"Your headache?"

"That and other things," he replied with a sigh. "I was hateful last night. I didn't mean to be. Can you forgive me?"

She stared at him. The pupils of his eyes were normal again. The effects of the drug had passed. He was the Alex whom she knew best and loved. Could you go on holding a grudge against him? Blaming him for the actions of that other man he became when drugged?

She said, "It's all right!"

"Elsie!" he said. And he bent down and kissed her tenderly.

She said, "You're not going away again."

"No."

Her gaze was earnest. "You owe more to me than anyone else."

"I promise," he said.

"You have my love and loyalty," she said. "But you must be fair to me. Last night I thought about leaving."

"Please, no!" he begged her.

"What about the fat man?"

A shadow she could only interpret as fear crossed his handsome face. He said, "You need have no worry about him."

She stared up at him wistfully, wondering if he truly meant it or if this was to be another of his moments of resolution soon forgot. But she knew she must give him the benefit of the doubt or turn her back on their marriage. And she still didn't want to do that.

Yet she knew there was a horror beyond what she understood shadowing this house. And she was certain most of the Martynovs, with the possible exception of the elderly Count Andre and the Countess Marie, knew at least something of what this menacing threat was. Several of them had warned her in different ways. But she had yet to learn the full truth. Perhaps it might be better if she never did.

Their reconciliation that morning marked the beginning of a new period of happiness for her and her titled husband. The preparations for the wedding were in full swing. The palace thrilled to the excitement of the coming event. The servants made preparations for the special feasting, and a noted group of musicians had been hired to play for the dancing in the great drawing room.

Alex spent much more time with her and was completely like his old self. The shadow of St. Petersburg and all it meant to her faded. Many afternoons and evenings they drove into Moscow. He told her fascinating tales of the old city as they moved about on foot, how it had evolved from a small twelfth-century village surrounded by a wooden stockade to become the holy city of Russia. It was there Ivan the Terrible had been crowned the first tsar of all Russia in 1547.

Elsie was enchanted by the city. The high green rooftops were surmounted by the blue-and-golden hued onion domes. There were avenues wider than any in New York on which were the imposing palaces of the nobility and the wealthy. And in the very heart of the city was the Kremlin with its massive red walls. It stood by the side of the Moscow River, a somber citadel of medieval power. It was a walled city within a city, a tribute to the past.

She also saw the other side of the city, the confusion of narrow streets with rows of two-story buildings all alike. There were also log cabins with primitive facilities that sheltered the poorly paid workers. Now that spring had arrived, these streets were thick with mud.

Elsie also watched the roving platoons of cossacks thunder along the avenues, these colorful representatives of the tsar's power. She would never forget the day she and Olga had witnessed the parade of the workers when the cossacks had appeared to wantonly strike them down. Olga's fiance, Feodor had been among the workers, but had managed somehow to escape any serious injury. The afternoon spectacle had shocked her.

In the evenings they attended the theater and ballet. Alex seemed to be known to almost everyone and have many friends. He enjoyed the colorful affairs, and she began to have confidence that she could hold him to this life. Sometimes they were joined by Ralph and either Olga or Sophie. But Ralph was doing a lot of traveling for his newspaper syndicate and frequently was not in Moscow.

They never encountered Timofei on any of these trips to the city. According to Alex, the young artist preferred to spend his time with the underworld characters of the great city in various of the riverfront dives. Places where ordinary people seldom dared to venture.

One night after the theater they went to a cabaret featuring a girl singer playing melancholy love songs on a balalaika. The place was intimate with the only light supplied by flickering candles and the atmosphere was delightfully romantic.

They held hands and Elsie told her handsome count, "This is what I expected Russia to be like."

"And you've been disappointed?"

"My eyes have been opened," she said. "There are many Russias. This surely is one of those I dreamt about most."

He said, "I'm only now beginning to realize how fortunate I was. To have you leave your country and come here with me."

"As long as I have your love, there will be no regrets," she told him, their eyes meeting above the table.

Almost as if he wished to change the subject, he said, "I had a long talk with Olga today."

"Oh?"

"Yes. She is very restless. She wants to run away with Feodor."

"But he is a revolutionary, wanted by the police."

"I know," Alex said with a sigh. "She does not seem to care about that. He is being sent elsewhere on a mission, and she wants to go with him."

Elsie worried, "It would be a devastating blow to the old people. Countess Marie is not well now."

"Only the excitement of the wedding is keeping her on her feet," he agreed. "And at that, she has to spend hours in bed and in her wheelchair."

"Olga is sure the young man truly loves her."

"Yes," Alex said with a grim smile. "His comrades hate

240

our class as much as we despise them. He is taking a chance of his life courting a countess. They could think him a traitor."

"And Olga will be lost to the ruling class once she goes with him."

He nodded. "The big question is how long will the present ruling class exist?"

She glanced around the cabaret filled with the wealthy and privileged. "It would seem a long while."

"Yet the girl singing and playing the balalaika is telling of the poverty of our people and the sadness of their plight."

"I don't know Russian well enough yet to follow her," she said.

Alex asked, "Is Sophie trying hard with your lessons?"

"She's doing her best."

"Her head seems to be in the clouds these days," Alex suggested.

"She does daydream a lot," Elsie said. "But don't all girls do that?"

"She is daydreaming about Ralph Manning," Alex said. "I'm sure she's in love with him."

"Perhaps it would make a good match," Elsie said, studying the reaction on her husband's face in the flickering flame of the candle on the table between them. He had never confessed to her that he and Sophie had been lovers and likely never would.

He hesitated. "Sophie is brilliant, but she is basically a cold person. She likes to use people, influence them for her best benefit. I worry that she is less in love with Ralph than wanting to use him as a ticket to America."

"She is anxious to leave Russia," Elsie agreed.

"Ralph should be warned."

She said, "I have tried to make it clear to him without actually offering him a warning about her. And don't forget he is a keen judge of people. He is not apt to be easily deceived."

"That is a good thing. I've told Olga that whatever she does, she must not leave before the wedding."

"Has she promised not to?"

"Yes. With a lot of persuasion on my part," he said.

"I'm glad. If she ran off, it would cast a shadow over everything."

"When the wedding is over I doubt if we'll be able to stop her. She's bound to vanish with Feodor."

"I can't think of the palace without her."

"Nor can I," he said. "We have always been close. But it is her life. I have talked to her, and it has led nowhere. Mistake or not, she has made up her mind."

The blissful days and the colorful nights eventually led to their wedding date. The invitations were out, the palace prepared, the gowns ordered and ready to don, the servants coached as to their duties in handling the nearly two hundred guests who would attend. Only less than a hundred could be fitted into the small chapel, and they would have to stand at that, the rest had been invited to the buffet and wedding dance which was to follow.

Elena and Olga helped Elsie into her gown of white. She did not see Alex until he appeared at her side in the chapel in his tunic of red trimmed with golden braid and epaulets, and his slim blue trousers, ending at the black, shiny shoes with the spurs of the cavalry brigade of which he was an officer.

The chapel was filled with illustrious guests, including young Prince Serge and his princess, representing the tsar. The Martynovs could not be ignored by the royal family. Elsie on the arm of old Count Andre, who was representing her uncle for the occasion, tried to search out Ralph amid the colorful uniforms of the males and the glittering costumes of the women in their furs and jewels. She knew that he was attending along with Jacob and Madame Bogrov, but she could not pick them out as she made her way down the aisle to the altar.

Count Alexander's handsome face wore a proud smile as he watched her come toward him. In the background, the organ was being played softly, and the perfume of incense filled the vaulted room.

Countess Marie crouched in her wheelchair, brilliant in her finery, her wizened old face alight with what might well be memories of her own wedding in this same chapel. Countess Olga was pale and elegant as maid of honor. Sophie and Timofei stood in the area reserved for family.

Father Peter stood in stately elegance in his ceremonial

garments, surrounded by two other older priests. The icons on the wall showed beautifully; there was a colorful high screen by the altar; Father Peter held a miter from which flashed rubies, diamonds, and emeralds. Elsie found herself dazed by the sights and smells—so much so that she remembered little of the ceremony.

It seemed to end only shortly after it had begun. Alex was kissing her; Father Peter, smiling, gave her his personal blessing; and dozens were crowding around them, congratulating them. She went to the Countess Marie in her wheelchair and knelt to kiss the old woman and be kissed by her dry lips. She felt that the countess was trembling and worried for her.

Count Andre embraced her and said, "You made a lovely bride! I shall see you at the party. Meanwhile, I think it best to take my wife upstairs; she is very weak. It has been a long trying period for her."

"You are right!" she whispered.

A moment later, Ralph was kissing her and showing a sober look which indicated he wasn't all that sure about the second wedding. The balding Jacob Bogrov and the matronly Madame Bogrov came forward to congratulate her. Then Alex took her to Prince Serge and his attractive princess.

"You must visit us at our palace in St. Petersburg," Prince Serge told her. "My wife and I will have a fine party for you."

"Thank you," she said. "I have not yet visited St. Petersburg."

The brown-mustached prince seemed amazed. "Not seen our capital yet. That is a grave omission on the part of Alex."

Looking embarrassed, Alex said, "One which I hope soon to correct, your highness."

"You must," the prince insisted. The princess congratulated her on her wedding dress, and Elsie moved on to the drawing room with her husband. She could hear the music already in progress.

Now she knew the full pressure of the two hundred guests. She and Alex went out to lead the waltz and then the others joined them on the floor until it was too crowded for any more dancing couples. The orchestra played wild folk tunes, as well as dance music; and as the night advanced, the party become more abandoned.

The buffet was in full swing in the next room with long white-clothed, candlelit tables groaning under the weight of fine foods of every kind. The bars were continually busy, and the celebration continued on without restraint.

Elsie danced with many of the guests, some of whom were strangers to her and to whom she was unable to converse because of the language barrier. But smiles and nods sufficed. She was grateful when Timofei swept her in his arms for a lively dance. The big man had been drinking hard and was ready to tease her.

"You did not run, little innocent. Now it is too late," he said.

"Had I fled I would have missed this party and dancing with you," she told him as they moved about the floor.

His large face held a mocking look. "And a lot more besides. But we will not talk of that now. It is a night for celebration!"

Next she danced with Jacob Bogrov of the Imperial Ballet. He told her, "I always feel awkward doing ballroom dancing. Our training is so much different."

She said, "But you dance beautifully."

"Thank you. You have restored my confidence."

"When do you go to Paris with the ballet?"

"In a few weeks," he said. "We are preparing the programs now at the same time we continue our schedule in Moscow."

After she danced with Bogrov it was Ralph's turn. He was perspiring and confided, "These Russian parties are too much. These people have consumed gallons of vodka and tons of food. And they are ready to dance the night through."

"We Americans haven't their stamina," she laughed.

His eyes met hers as the dance continued. "I'm glad that you are in a happy mood."

"What else on one's wedding night?" she said.

"Things are better?"

"Much."

"Let us hope they stay that way," Ralph said.

"One thing," Elsie told him.

"What?"

"About that raid in St. Petersburg? Did you ever find out if my husband was among the group?"

The young journalist gave her a bitter smile. "Surely this is not the night to discuss such things."

"You are right," she said. "Forgive me." But at once she had her answer. If the news had been good, he would have told her that Alex hadn't been caught with the others at the orgy. Since he refused to talk about it, there was no doubt in her mind that Alex had been there.

Their dance ended, and this time it was the courtly old Count Andre who came to take her as a partner. The spare, dignified old man was in a uniform of naval blue, and she thought he was quite handsome. He danced slowly, but most correctly.

"Are you satisfied with the party?" he asked.

"I couldn't dream of it being any better," she told him.

"I'm worried about the countess," he said with a slight shadow crossing his face. "She was very weak when we took her upstairs."

"Thank goodness this will see the end of the excitement," Elsie said.

"It is more than that," the old man said. "She is losing ground gradually. I cannot close my eyes to it."

Elsie was suddenly aware of a flurry at the other end of the drawing room, near the entrance from the main foyer. She looked over the old man's shoulder and saw that the group gathered there seemed to be opening a passage way, falling back to make way for someone to enter. There was a line at either wall and an open path between them.

The music stopped, and the murmur of voices filled the air. Old Count Andre glanced toward the door and placed a monocle in his right eye. "What is happening?" he wanted to know.

His question was immediately answered when a mountain of a man appeared in the doorway and then advanced down the open path into the drawing room. He had a bushy black beard and mustache and weird, hypnotic eyes! He gazed fiercely around him in an arrogant fashion. He wore a red silk blouse, with a silken cord of yellow with tassels tied around his waist. His trousers were of fine black velvet thrust into soft, leather boots. And at his throat on a golden chain there dangled a shining gold cross!

A hush had come over the room at the entrance of this formidable guest. The monocle dropped from old Count Andre's eye as he gasped, "Rasputin! Uninvited and unwanted!"

She whispered, "Someone must have invited him."

Her statement was underlined by a pale Alex moving out from the crowd and going to greet the giant of a man. Rasputin said something to Alex in a low voice.

Alex then turned to the orchestra and shouted, "Let there be music! Lively music! Some joyous folk tunes from the frozen country!"

The orchestra at once complied with his request. The head fiddler led his group in a tantalizing Gypsy tune. As they played, some of the guests began to do a rowdy folk dance. And the giant Rasputin came directly across the room to Elsie, those large, hypnotic eyes fixed on her and took her out to dance.

His dancing was abandoned, and he shouted to the orchestra, urging them to play at a faster tempo. Soon Elsie and the mad monk were the only ones left on the floor. The other guests had formed a kind of circle around them. The burly Rasputin had not attempted to say a word directly to her, but when he was not coaxing the musicians on to a new frenzy he stared at her sternly and executed wild and intricate steps!

She had been taken completely by surprise and did not know what to do or say. She simply followed his dancing lead, and as she neared exhaustion she hoped that someone might come forth and rescue her from the mad monk! Surely Alex would realize that it was a dance macabre and do something to save her.

Rasputin seemed tireless! Occasionally, he threw back his head and laughed hoarsely! Then he cried out something which she felt must be in poor taste as she saw the face of Prince Serge pale, and the young man turned away to leave the room. Others began to melt away from the onlookers.

It was Timofei who finally came to save her. He sprang out and made a gesture to Rasputin that it was time to change partners and then took her away from the glaring giant!

246

Timofei at once slowed the pace of the dance. "I couldn't stand by until you collapsed."

"Thank you! Alex should have come to my rescue instead of leaving it to you," she gasped, still breathless.

Timofei said, "I'm not afraid of Rasputin. I think your dear husband is. We will slow our steps now and dance to this corner and leave the floor before you faint in my arms." And that was what they did.

By this time, Alex and Rasputin had gone off to another room. Elsie watched them go with the corner of her eye and noticed that her husband, although a tall man, was a head shorter than Rasputin.

The orchestra paused for a little, and the excited murmuring that Rasputin's appearance had brought on was heard again. Some of the guests came to say good night to her, including Prince Serge and the princess. She was sure the majority had decided to leave because of the unexpected entrance of the mad monk.

Timofei remained by her side and between the departing guests managed to say, "I'll wager Rasputin and his cronies are in the banquet hall becoming uproariously drunk."

"I didn't know he came to Moscow," she said, upset by his appearance.

"He comes and goes as he likes," Timofei mocked. "And by the way he glared at me, he will surely call one of his old-fashioned curses down on my head!"

"You didn't look afraid of him!"

"I'm not," Timofei said cheerfully. "But you should be. They say he only has to stare hard at a woman for two minutes, and she becomes pregnant—and on your wedding night! He didn't take his eyes off you!"

She blushed and welcomed the opportunity of saying good night to some other wedding guests. The orchestra was playing again, but the guests were thinning. Alex was with Rasputin, leaving the task of bidding them good night to she and Timofei.

"Don't desert me," she told the big man under her breath. And then smiled a polite good night to an elderly couple.

Ralph presented himself next. He said, "How dare Alex desert you like this. It isn't even polite to his guests."

She said, "I imagine he has his hands full with Rasputin."

Ralph nodded grimly. "And if that monster gets circulating around, he'll be feeling down the fronts of the women's gowns. Or shouting vulgar insults, as he did when he was dancing with you!"

"I was sure he was saying something out of line," she said worriedly.

"You can't be blamed," the young newspaper man said. "But Alex must have invited him."

"I wonder," she said.

Timofei joined in, "He must have. No one else in the family would tell him. And he is very much here."

Elsie tried a rueful smile. "You should take advantage and interview him."

Ralph shook his head. "One does not interview a boar at a social event. I'm leaving with the Bogrovs. I'll phone you tomorrow."

"Have you said good night to Sophie?" she asked.

"I will," he said. "She's just now with the Bogrovs." And he left her to move on toward the front door.

Other guests came and left. Then a pale Olga joined Elsie and Timofei to say in an upset voice, "Rasputin has taken over in the buffet room! He's lurching drunkenly around. He's already overturned one table and tried to embrace a serving maid. Alex seems unable to manage him!"

Timofei said, "So the wedding party ends in a brawl! The new Russia under Tsar Rasputin!"

Olga was near tears. "He's destroyed some priceless china. And now he's demanding that the orchestra go in there to play for him!"

Elsie shrugged. "What are we to do?"

Timofei said, "Send the musicians to him. They may keep him happy! There's no need for them in the drawing room any longer; he's chased all the other guests away!" And it was true. Only a handful remained. No one wished to cross the path of the man whose whim might destroy them.

"I'll tell them," Olga said and went to deliver the message to the musicians.

Timofei turned to Elsie. "If I were you, little innocent, I would retire to the apartment. That mad monk is liable to go on here until dawn!"

248

She gave the big man a shocked look. "Leave Alex! This is our wedding night!"

"Rasputin evidently thinks the occasion is to honor him," Timofei said with sarcasm.

A harried Count Andre came hurrying out of the buffet room as the musicians passed him on their way to pay tribute to Rasputin. The old man was tottering on his feet. He said, "Thank Heaven the countess did not remain down here to see this desecration. Rasputin has destroyed a fortune in chinaware and turned the buffet room into a pig pen. And Alex, my only remaining nephew, is catering to that monster!"

Elsie said, "He may think he has to. Rasputin is a powerful man."

Count Andre looked ill. He swayed as he stood there. "My apologies, dear Elsie. I swear nothing like this has ever happened before in this house. The name of Martynov is tarnished for all time!"

"Please, Count Andre, don't feel badly on my account," she begged him.

"I did not believe it before," the old aristocrat said. "But now I have seen it happen with my own eyes. Russia is surely doomed!"

He walked unsteadily in the direction of the staircase, a tragic figure. Elsie gazed after him with her eyes moist with tears. She turned to Timofei and said, "You'd better follow him up the stairs. He looks as if he might collapse."

"What about you?" Timofei worried.

"I'll follow. Please go on!" she begged him. And at her bidding, he rushed off to see the old man safely up the steep stairway.

She turned to speak with Olga. But Olga was no longer in sight. And she guessed that as soon as she'd given instructions to the orchestra, she'd left. Perhaps she had some rendezvous with her Feodor, who might be lurking outside. It seemed a pity that the good-mannered young student should be barred from the occasion and the monstrous Rasputin welcomed as a guest of honor. She would have a word to say to Alex about this!

She stood alone in the big drawing room, which now looked tawdry with the remnants of the party being removed by a few silent servants under the direction of a

249

Clarissa Ross

stern Frederick. They all, including the old butler, avoided
looking her way.

It was incredible! She, the bride of the evening, stood in
the big room deserted by all but the servants. Meanwhile,
from the adjoining room, there was wild music, drunken
guffaws of laughter, and equally drunken cheers!

She was weary and felt ill. She hoped that she would not
faint. Slowly and with great dignity, she picked up the
train of her virgin white dress and walked toward the entrance to the room, where Rasputin was holding court.
When she reached the doorway, she stood there very still
and with a look of disdain on her lovely face.

The music went on, and no one noticed her for a moment. Besides the orchestra who had gathered around Rasputin and who was being led by him in tipsy conductor
fashion, there was Alex and perhaps a half-dozen middle-
aged, bearded men in red military uniform—undoubtedly
court lackies who had trailed along with Rasputin.

Suddenly, the wild eyes of the mad monk spotted her.
He ran a hand through his matted black hair and then
shouted some hoarse obscenity at her. The others, with the
sole exception of Alex, roared with laughter! Then they
bent double in their glee and threw their champagne
glasses to splinter on the floor! Encouraged, Rasputin
shouted something else and had the same response.

Then Alex came hurrying across the room to her. He
was tense and white-faced. He said, "I'm sorry. I'm doing
my best. I think you'd better go upstairs."

"Aren't you coming with me?"

"I can't leave him. And if you stay, he might be dangerous to you!"

"Would you allow him to paw me as he did that serving
girl?" she demanded slowly.

"In God's name, this is no time to linger and argue! I
beg you to go upstairs!"

Elsie said, "You invited him, didn't you?"

Alex opened his mouth and then despairingly closed it
without saying anything. She turned and walked out of the
room toward the stairs. Behind her the music and drunken
revelry continued, and she heard Rasputin shouting another of his coarse jokes!

❧ Chapter 20 ❧

TEARS RAN DOWN ELSIE'S CHEEKS, and she fought to not burst into sobs and break down completely. She walked by the stern Frederick in the hall as she made her way to the stairs.

"Good night," the old butler said in a tone of sympathy.

"Good night, Frederick," she managed. "And thank you for handling the evening so well."

"I did my best," he bowed. "You made a beautiful bride, Madam, if you will allow me to be so bold as to say so."

"You are a good man, Frederick," she said. "You have served the family well. Good night."

She moved slowly up the stairs like someone in a daze. The weeks of happiness before the marriage now all seemed to have been annulled. Her wedding night, which had begun so perfectly, had ended in a nightmare! All her old fears and doubts about her husband returned with this evidence that he was still a creature dominated by Rasputin!

The name of Martynov would suffer. Count Andre and the Countess Marie had always held their heads high. But this was bound to cause a scandal. Perhaps they were no more disgraced by the mad monk than the royal family, but people would not hold back their comments as they did about the goings-on at the palace of the tsar.

She reached the landing, which was silent and deserted. For a moment, she waited there hoping Alex might change his mind and come up to join her. But the revelry went on below, and she realized that her hopes were in vain. So she moved on down the shadowed corridor, a pathetic, solitary figure in her bridal gown of white.

She was part way to the door of the apartment before

251

she realized she was not alone. It came to her in some odd, instinctive fashion. There was no sound. But she knew she was no longer alone. She wheeled around expectantly thinking that her wish might be fulfilled, that she would see her handsome bridegroom standing there.

But it was no bridegroom she saw. It was a monk-like figure with a cowl shadowing his face! A gross, overweight man in a black robe was slowly gliding toward her.

She drew back and uttered screams of terror.

As she did so she heard an answering call from down the corridor. It was Timofei who had heard her!

"Timofei! Come to me!" she screamed, backing up.

The figure in the monk's robe hesitated and then turned and fled around a turn in the corridor, and she lost sight of him. She was sobbing and her teeth were chattering as Timofei, still fully dressed, came rushing up to place a comforting arm around her.

"Little innocent!"

"Timofei! I saw him again! The fat monk! He was coming after me! I saw him, and I screamed for you. Then he turned and fled!"

"Where?" Timofei demanded.

"Down there!" She pointed where the phantom figure had vanished.

"I'll see!" Timofei muttered and raced down the corridor and around the turn.

She waited for several minutes before Timofei returned with a frustrated look on his face. He said, "I couldn't find anyone. I'll see you to your apartment."

"Thanks," she said wearily. "What an ending!"

He waited as she opened the door and then stepped inside as she turned on the lights. He went from room to room making sure there was no one in hiding there.

Then he came back to her. "Seems safe enough," he said.

"Thanks for coming so soon."

The young artist gave her a worried look. "I heard you scream. Luckily, I hadn't closed my door."

"I did see someone," she assured him. "It wasn't just nerves."

"I'll accept that," Timofei said. "Where was Alex? He ought to have been with you."

"He is still entertaining his friend," she said unhappily. "He ordered me to come up here by myself."

Timofei eyed her wryly. "Your wedding night."

"My second wedding night," she corrected him. "I think now the entire affair was a mistake."

"You know what I advised."

"I know," she said. "Would you like a good night drink?"

He smiled. "Have I ever been known to refuse?"

"I only have brandy."

"That will do very well, and you'd better join me. You didn't drink much during the evening, and you look pale." He offered this advice as he settled himself on the divan in the drawing room of the apartment.

"I will have one," she said. And she poured out drinks for them and went to him. She sat on the divan facing him. "To happy weddings," she said with a sigh.

"Why not? They're rare enough," Timofei said with a wink and downed a gulp of his drink.

"I was in tears when I came upstairs," she said. "Then I was terrified by that strange figure. Now I find myself drained of every feeling but anger."

"Better for you than fear," he said, studying her.

"Yes. Anger may help me see this through," she said, looking down at her glass. "It seems the problems Alex and I have are not over."

"Profound conclusion," Timofei said, taking more of the brandy.

"I did not expect him to let me down this way."

The big man on the divan said, "I don't want to sound disloyal. But both Basil and Alex seemed to me to have a weak streak, perhaps because of the way they were brought up. Or maybe because in these old families, the blood line gets thin. At least, I don't have to worry about that."

She challenged him, saying, "You hate it because you were adopted, don't you?"

"I need a reason for hating. It helps me. Just as anger is helping you now," he said. "Hatred at being adopted is as good an excuse as any."

She sipped her drink. "You are stronger than the others; yet you waste your talent and drink yourself to death."

"We all make our choices in life. I have made mine."

"And Alex?"

"He seems to have chosen Rasputin over you," Timofei said. "I think he's showing bad judgment, but then it's hard to know about other people."

She sighed. "I suppose I've hung on because I haven't been able to make myself accept that he is weak and something of a degenerate."

"I questioned you about his lovemaking once and you became angry," the big man reminded her. "But I had a solid reason for it."

"Now it seems I'll have to admit defeat. The wedding tonight was a farce. Tomorrow, Alex and I must have a serious talk. Likely the result will be my returning to New York."

"You would be wise."

She stared at him. "You still insist that?"

"I wouldn't if Alex were here now to argue the point with me. But he's down there with Rasputin. I don't think it will change."

She said bitterly, "Prince Serge asked me how I liked St. Petersburg, and I had to tell him Alex had never taken me there."

"Serge left as soon as Rasputin showed up. All the young nobles hate the monk."

"Little wonder!"

Timofei stood up. "I should return to my room. Will you feel safe alone? I could try and find Olga and have her come here to you."

"No. I'll be all right," she said, rising. "Perhaps he'll come in a few minutes."

"I hope so," he said.

Her eyes met his. "You do?"

"Yes," he said in his mocking way. "It would mean you'll remain here in Moscow. And I hate to think of your leaving before I complete my icon."

"Have you really started it?"

"Certainly."

She gave him a weary smile. "I must see it before I leave whether it is completed or not."

Timofei came close to her and took her in his arms. He

kissed her gently on the temple. "Good night, little innocent."

She delayed preparing for bed. And even when she had donned her nightgown, she hoped Alex still might put in an appearance. But he did not come. So, at last, she slipped between the cold sheets of their wedding bed and stared grimly up into the shadows. What would she do now?

Sleep came at last. And she slept restlessly through the night. Her dreams were a jumble, and she could remember little of them. She was awakened by the door of her husband's apartment opening and a haggard, white-faced Alex coming into the room.

He stood at the foot of her bed in awkward silence for a moment. "I have bad news," he said. "My Aunt Marie died at dawn this morning."

It came as a shock to her. Everything else fled from her mind. She threw back the covers and rose from the bed. "The poor dear, old woman," she said, near tears.

"There was no pain. She just slept away, probably worn out. We all knew she couldn't last much longer," he said.

"But she enjoyed it all so last night!"

"Well, perhaps that was the best way," her husband said. He was wearing a black suit and tie, and they enhanced his pallor.

She picked up her robe and put it on. "Is there anything I can do?"

"No," he said. "We have the arrangements under way. She will be buried tomorrow afternoon in the family cemetery."

"I see," she said. Then she gave him a sharp look. "Is your friend still here?"

"Rasputin?"

"Yes."

"No, he and his party took a droshka to Moscow as soon as Frederick brought me word about the Countess Marie."

She couldn't hide her scorn. "I'm surprised he and those other drunkards would have the decency to leave even then."

Her husband's cheeks flamed. "I'm sorry things happened as they did. I mentioned the wedding to him. I didn't actually invite him."

"You will have a hard time convincing me of that!"

"I'm sorry," he said grimly.

"We can talk about it later," was her reply. "The main thing now is the death of your aunt."

"Yes," he said, avoiding looking at her directly. "You will excuse me, won't you? I have the chief responsibility in this business. Count Andre is confined to his apartment, and Timofei has left for Moscow, probably on a drunken binge!"

"He loved his foster mother," she said. "This will go hard with him."

"Yes," he said in the same grim fashion. Alex made no move to come to Elsie or ask her forgiveness. There was a dreadful impasse between them.

She watched him march out of the apartment stiffly. And she found herself again wracked with pain. How could it begin so well and end this way? He was wrong! Was his pride so great that he wouldn't admit it? But then he had come to her before and begged forgiveness and received it. Perhaps he felt this time it was too late. Probably it was.

Elena brought her breakfast on a tray. The petite girl had been crying. She told Elsie, "The staff feels the house will never be the same again. The old woman was kind to us all."

"I know," she said, standing by the table. She had no appetite, but would take the tea.

The maid hesitated, apparently wanting to talk about it. "First a wedding and now a funeral!"

"It is a sad business," she agreed.

Elena suddenly showed anger. "Perhaps if the mad monk had not come and remained all the night, the mistress would not have died."

Elsie sat at the table. "I don't think the Countess Marie knew that Rasputin was here. She went upstairs before he ever arrived."

"But he and those drunken friends of his made such an uproar! You could hear them all through the house. And the mad monk himself ripped poor Anna's dress down to

256

the waist so that her bare breasts were exposed to all in
the room!"

"Yes, I heard about that."

"Worse! Then he tried to fondle them with everyone
looking on! Poor Anna ran from the room screaming and
the cook had to watch over her all the night. She had hysterics!"

"It was a dreadful thing to happen," she agreed. "We
are all very sorry about it. And I shall make it a point to
talk with the young woman and ask her apology."

Elena shook her head. "It wasn't your fault, Madam.
You shouldn't have to apologize. If anyone is to blame, it
is Count Alexander. He was there with Rasputin."

"Never the less, I shall talk with Anna," Elsie said. "We
are all in for a difficult time. You know the funeral will be
tomorrow afternoon."

"Yes," the maid said. "Frederick says we may all attend. And the cook says she had an omen two nights ago.
She saw the ghost gliding along the corridor all in black!"

"Oh?" It suddenly struck her that the cook may have
seen the fat man. The one who apparently was lurking
somewhere near, hoping to attack her. It wasn't a comforting thought.

"I'm staying too long, countess," Elena apologized. "I'll
come back later and do the bed and room." And she left
her.

The first person she encountered when she went downstairs was Sophie. The blonde girl had also donned a black
dress and was emerging from the drawing room.

Sophie said, "Last night it was the scene of a dance, and
tonight the old lady will lay in state in there."

"It is a shock," she said.

The pretty blonde grimaced. "It means I'm out of a job,
although the old man has promised to keep me on. He is
getting so feeble he needs someone to watch over him."

"I'm sure he'll need someone to depend on. And you
know his habits."

"I'll miss the countess," Sophie said. "She was a true
lady. She was a lady-in-waiting at the court of Tsar
Nicholas. Did you know that?"

"Yes."

"Olga is not the same. She will never be at court. And you are an American countess. There is a difference!"

"I realize that," she said.

"Yet the hope of the Martynov name may rest on you and Alex. Your children could be the important link."

"Don't count on that," Elsie said.

The blonde girl moved wearily to look out the window at the dreary day. "Who counts on anything? It is going to rain. There is no future for anyone in Russia any longer. More than ever I want to escape."

"Be sure it is what you want before you make your decision," she warned the other girl.

Sophie turned to stare directly at her. "You don't sound much like a happy bride the morning after the wedding."

She crimsoned. "We have had a sudden death in the family."

"There's more than that to it!"

Elsie said, "All right. If you must bring it up. You know what happened last night."

"The mad monk and his company!" Sophie said. "And Alex remained with him all night, didn't he?"

"Until dawn when he received word of his aunt's death. Then Rasputin and the others drove away."

"Did Alex go up to you?"

"I did not see him until much later, about an hour ago."

The blonde's eyebrows raised. "Interesting!"

"Alex and I will have an understanding after the funeral is over," she said.

"Do you still love him?"

She spread her hands. "Does that matter now? He seems not to love me any longer."

Sophie asked sharply. "What about Ralph?"

"What about him?"

"Do you love him?"

"I'm very fond of him. I wouldn't like to see him hurt," she said defiantly.

It was Sophie's turn to look uneasy. She said, "You still think I might hurt him?"

"I don't know."

Sophie said, "At least we couldn't do much worse than you and Alex, could we?" And with that jeering comment, she went up the stairs.

The Countess Marie lay in state in a rich, mahogany casket in the same corner of the great drawing room in which the orchestra had played. Father Peter had returned to offer prayers for her and lingered to offer solace to those of the bereaved who might need it.

Frederick had arranged a schedule for all the household help and the outdoors workers to come at intervals and pay their respects. Other members of the gentry were already sending messages of sympathy; some had paid calls. The palace, which had pulsed with gaiety the previous night, was cloaked in solemn silence now.

Alex remained in the drawing room near the casket. He and Countess Olga received the visitors as they arrived, chatted with them in discreet tones, and thanked them as they departed. Sophie made herself generally useful. And in the late afternoon, the frail old Count Andre came down and sat in an easy chair near his wife's casket. In this way, he was able to see some of those who came to pay their respects.

For some reason, Elsie felt out of place in the group. For one thing, she—a foreigner—spoke the language of the visitors imperfectly and could not conduct proper conversations with them. For another, she felt her presence was too striking a reminder of the wedding, which had just taken place.

She was badly concerned about Timofei and prayed that he might soon return. She found herself wandering alone into the chapel, which was being made ready for the funeral. She stared up at the icon of the Holy Mother and Son.

She heard a footstep behind her and because she was still frightened from the previous night, she wheeled around with a gasp.

It was only Father Peter. He apologized, "I'm sorry. I didn't mean to scare you."

"My nerves are jumpy!"

"One would expect that," he said.

She felt embarrassed and to make conversation glanced at the icon of the Holy Mother and Child once again. She said, "I was enjoying the icon."

He gazed up at it. "The amazing thing is how differently

259

each artist interprets the Madonna and Child. It is as each visualizes it in his mind's eye."

"Timofei promised his mother before her death he would do a fine icon," she said.

"I hope he keeps his promise," Father Peter said.

"So do I. He is so bitter and cynical. He loved the Countess Marie more that anyone. I'm afraid he may get in some bad trouble."

"Let us pray that he doesn't," the young priest with the black beard said quietly.

She began to pace up and down, twisting her hands nervously. "I'm saddened by the death of the countess. But that is only part of my troubles, Father."

"Yes," he said quietly.

She halted and stared at his kind, young face. "You know Rasputin was here last night?"

"I saw him before I left," Father Peter said.

"Did you talk with him?"

"With Rasputin?" He said it incredulously.

"Father, there are good priests as well as bad. He is a villainous priest, isn't he?"

"He is not a priest, but a monk. And you are right. He is an evil one."

"What would make him become such a scoundrel, Father? He has my husband under his spell. He is leading him into a path of degeneracy!"

Father Peter said, "I do not usually talk about Rasputin. But I will say what I think now. I fear he will bring down the royal family, and all Russia will collapse with them. Mother Russia will lose her religion because of him. And yet no one seems able to halt his wickedness."

"I do not understand it," she said.

"He is a type you can find only in Russia," Father Peter said bitterly. "Gregory Rasputin came to St. Petersburg as a starets, a man of God, a pilgrim monk who lived in poverty, asceticism, and solitude, who plodded from village to village and town to town giving his life to our Lord. We do have many of these holy men who abide by these principles."

"Surely not Rasputin!"

"No! Rasputin is a fraud. But he has a fluent tongue, and his head is filled with the Scriptures. He was born the son of a coachman in the Ural Mountains. It is a place of strange sects and mystics. As a boy Rasputin had a bad fever and is supposed to have made prophecies. The villagers spread his fame. He became accepted as a seer. As a young man he was a rake. He battled, swilled strong drink, and made free with any village girl he could.

"He became a wagoner and his reputation for cruelty and immorality grew with his travels. One of his travels took him to a strange monastery, a place of degeneracy and terror; they claim he became first a member of the immoral group and then its leader. And they say the chief monastery is in St. Petersburg today."

"You're talking about the Skoptsi cult?"

Father Peter betrayed surprise. "Yes. You know about them?"

"Only by name and that they are a strange immoral group out for political power," she said.

"That is enough for you to know," Father Peter said. "At any rate, he became a wanderer and proclaimed himself a man of God. When he first announced his new saintliness, his village priest was shocked. But later, he managed to get an audience with Father John of Kronstadt, through trickery, and that holy man gave him his blessing. This furthered Rasputin's career as a holy man and healer. The manner in which he has tricked the royal family into thinking he is keeping the male heir alive is known to you."

"Yes."

"He has no power over this bleeding sickness of the lad," Father Peter said sadly. "But he has convinced them that he does, and they fear to dismiss him. He has become royal adviser and some say he is the full power behind the throne."

"No wonder he is so brazen. But how can he enlist normally decent men like Count Alexander in his cause?"

Father Peter said, "I cannot tell you, countess. Put it down to the devil. Rasputin has the evil eye!"

It was not all that rewarding a conversation, but at least it gave her the relief of telling her troubles to someone. And she had learned something more about Rasputin. Even the good clergy, such as Father Peter, did not know how to combat the mad monk's evil.

The day wore on. Countess Olga grew tired and went to her apartment to rest for the evening when the majority of callers were expected. Thus far a steady stream of the older folk had come to pay their respects. Elsie took the place of Countess Olga beside her husband. Alex seemed in an odd, depressed mood and talked only when there were visitors.

It was Ralph Manning who brought home a drunken Timofei around six that evening. Timofei could not walk without his arm over Ralph's shoulders for support. And when Elsie spoke to him, he replied in a slurred drunken mumble she could not understand.

Frederick quickly summoned two of the stalwart young manservants, and they undertook to see Timofei up the stairs to his room. The butler told Elsie, "I shall see he gets a warm bath and that everything is done to sober him for this evening, countess." And then the little man hurried up the stairway to supervise the drunken man's treatment.

Elsie faced Ralph in the foyer and said, "We are most grateful to you."

Ralph, still in his overcoat, told her, "I found him in the Metropole bar. He never goes there. It was just a lucky chance that he wound up there."

She said, "Won't you remain for some dinner."

"No," he said. "My carriage is waiting. You have enough to think about without a guest."

Elsie told him, "The funeral is tomorrow afternoon. Do come."

"I will," he promised. "And I'll go in by the casket for a moment now and pay my respects briefly."

She said, "Alex is in there."

Ralph's expression changed. "I'm afraid I have little respect left for him after last night."

"I know."

"How is it with you two?"

"Bad," she said.

"I was afraid of that. And then to have the countess die."

"Sophie will want to speak with you," Elsie said. "While you're inside, I'll tell her that you are here. She is in the kitchen seeing the cook. There has been trouble. Rasputin molested one of the serving maids last night!"

Ralph shook his head grimly. "Tell me no more." And he went on into the drawing room.

She sought Sophie out in the kitchen and told her that Ralph was briefly paying a visit. The blonde showed surprise at this cooperation from Elsie, but at once went out to see the young newspaperman before he left.

Elsie went upstairs, leaving the two to talk in low voices by the door. She was beginning to think a romance was truly blooming between Ralph and the lovely blonde girl.

The evening proved an ordeal. Many callers arrived. Timofei managed to get downstairs, white and trembling but properly dressed and sober. He took his place by his foster mother's casket and politely accepted the sympathy of all who came by.

Elsie did door duty until ten o'clock when the last of the visitors left. Then she said good night to everyone, including a solemn Alex. Tapers burned at the foot and head of the casket of the old countess as she took a last look at her peaceful, old face. Then she went up to the apartment.

She waited for a while thinking Alex might come to her. But it soon became apparent that she would again spend the night alone.

❧ Chapter 21 ❧

IT SEEMED IRONICAL to Elsie that the next morning should be utterly lovely. The Russian spring was in full bloom. The sun was shining, the air fragrant and warm, the snow had vanished. And in occasional spots, green grass and exotic wild flowers were beginning to appear.

And it was one of the saddest days of her young life. In a few hours, Countess Marie would be buried. Then Elsie would face the bleak prospect of having some sort of understanding with the husband who no longer seemed to have any love for her.

Elena served breakfast with the usual portion of gossip added. "Frederick is leading us in procession to the cemetery," she said. "We will walk behind the carriages carrying the family and the chief mourners."

She said, "It is not far away, is it?"

"The burial ground is about a half-mile from the stables," the maid said. "It is a fine day for it. And because the frost is out of the ground, they were able to dig the grave quickly."

"I see," she said.

"Had it been winter the countess would have had to remain in the vault, built in the hill by the cemetery. Then the casket would have been removed for burial when the ground was soft."

"You know a good deal about it," Elsie said as she sat at the table.

"I was a mourner when Count Basil was buried," the girl said proudly.

"Were you?" she said.

"Poor Countess Katrin had hysterics and sobbed all during the burial."

"Sad."

264

"It was," Elena agreed. "And no wonder, Count Basil was such a fine looking, slender young man. What a loss! You've seen his portrait in the drawing room."

"Yes."

"It was a grim day. And who would guess that more was to come," the maid sniffed sadly.

"Life is often a series of grim events," she said, hoping the girl would leave. She wasn't all that hungry, but she did want to enjoy her tea in silence.

"You will see the burial ground," Elena volunteered.

"Yes."

"It's large enough for the family and those of the household staff who wish to be buried there. My old aunt rests there, bless her soul."

"Your family have served the Martynovs for some time, I take it."

"We have, countess," Elena said. "And barring marriage and my having to go to another estate, I wouldn't ask for a better place, although Anna says that what Rasputin did here the other night means she'll be leaving. Her parents won't allow her to be treated with disrespect."

She said, "I saw Anna. And I promised her the Countess Olga would visit her parents and try and make things right. What happened here the other night was most unusual."

That afternoon a small, solemn procession wound its way along the narrow road that led past the stables to the Martynov family cemetery in a clearing in the woods by the bank of the Moscow River. A hearse whose glass sides were draped with elegant black velvet with a golden fringe was drawn by two large gray horses. Two men rode on the high seat in the front of it in shiny black top hats and black morning coats and striped gray trousers.

Behind the hearse was a droshka in which Count Andre, his ancient head bowed, Countess Olga, Count Alexander, Elsie and Timofei were seated. Joseph drove the vehicle and was also suitably dressed for the occasion.

In the next droshka Sophie; Prince Serge and his princess, as representatives of the tsar; and an elderly male cousin from Moscow were the passengers. There were five other carriages in the procession.

Next came Frederick, in top hat and morning coat,

sadly heading the servants and other employes of the estate. They marched behind him in a double line with sober faces as if in the realization that with the old woman, a part of Mother Russia was also being buried.

The burial ground was simple, but well kept. There were no elaborate headstones, but simple marble markers giving the names and dates of the dead resting there. The procession came to a halt at the edge of the cemetery, and the mourners gathered by the open grave.

Father Peter was in charge of the graveside rites. And the bearers of the casket, by the Countess Marie's wishes, were sturdy young farmhands of the estate chosen by Frederick.

Elsie found the occasion a moving one, although she had only known the Countess Marie a short time; she had found the countess a gracious lady of charm and understanding. She noticed that Timofei stood close by his foster father and was visibly shaken by the sad event.

Countess Olga and Alex stood with quiet dignity. Elsie was at her husband's side although they had spoken only a few words to each other during the morning. Prince Serge and his attractive princess were a little distance from them. The servants gathered in a group a short way from the family and the regular mourners.

When Father Peter finished the service and the casket was lowered into the ground, the sun flashed briefly on the shining mahogany casket. It was a fitting last glimpse of the earthly remains of the indomitable old countess.

First Father Peter and then many others approached Count Andre and Timofei before returning to their various carriages. Prince Serge and the Princess spent several minutes with the old man and his foster son.

The prince also had words for Countess Olga and Sophie. He then came to where Elsie and Alex were standing. He took her hand and said, "I deeply regret that such sorrow should so soon follow your wedding.

"It was kind of you to attend the service," Elsie said.

"I am here at the request of the royal family," the prince said. "And I would have come because of my personal admiration of the countess in any case."

He then turned and spoke polite words of condolence to Alex, but his manner was cool, and he wasted no time on it. Elsie knew the prince still must be rankled by the Rasputin incident.

When they were left standing alone, Alex turned to her and said, "I suppose we should get back. Some of the mourners will be remaining for food and drink."

She hesitated and asked, "Where is your brother buried?"

His handsome face shadowed. "I'll show you," he said. And he led her a short distance away to a spot where two neat mounds were marked by a single stone. The stone gave the names and dates of Basil and Katrin. She stood staring at them and wondered what story the two beneath those mounds would have to tell her if they could rise from the grave. Had Rasputin been responsible for Basil's death by a bomb, and had one of the Skoptsi cultists murdered Katrin and made it seem a suicide?

She said, "They were very young."

"Yes," Alex said in a taut voice. But he added nothing more.

Silently, he escorted her back to the droshka. The others were all seated in it and waiting for them. Countess Olga said, "You were seeing the graves of Basil and Katrin?"

"Yes. I have never visited the cemetery before," she said.

"I didn't realize," the Countess Olga replied.

Count Andre sat silently with his head bowed as if in some secret communion with the wife of long years whom he'd left behind. Timofei was fidgeting and looking as if he badly needed a drink.

He said to Alex, "Where is Joseph? Why don't we get under way."

Alex had a grim expression on his pale face. He said, "The vodka will keep. It won't evaporate!"

Timofei shot back, "It does when your friend Rasputin is around!"

Countess Olga gave the two young men a look of entreaty. "Please! Not at this time!"

The tension was broken by Joseph mounting the driver's seat and the droshka rolling on. They circled the cemetery on a road still soft from the ravages of the winter frost coming out of it. For a bad moment, it seemed that the hearse might become rutted down in it and they would all have to wait. But the horses dragged the heavy wheels of the hearse out and the rest of the lighter carriages managed without any difficulty.

Frederick and the other marching servants did not use this road, but waited to follow back along the main gravel road to the stables and palace.

Back at the palace, Elsie found herself involved in what amounted to a formal session of entertaining. The mood was subdued by the conversation, which rambled from the deceased to the events of the day. She particularly noticed that Prince Serge and the princess had not come back to the palace, a further sign of their displeasure with Alex.

Ralph was there along with Jacob Bogrov and his wife. Sophie spent a good part of her time with the three. It seemed to Elsie that Bogrov's aging, stout wife seemed to wear an especially strained expression on her matronly face.

When she and Ralph managed a moment apart from the others, Elsie said, "It was considerate of you to come."

"I wanted to be here," he said. And he glanced across the room where Alex and some of the older members of the nobility were in conversation. "Any change?"

She shook her head. "Alex and I have hardly spoken to each other since our wedding night."

"Incredible!"

"I expect we'll talk tonight," she said. "He has no excuse now to avoid it."

"What are you going to say?"

She shrugged. "I think he is the one who has to do the explaining. If he is determined to carry on under Rasputin's shadow, I have no choice. I will leave him."

"I'd say you are right," the young journalist agreed. "I will keep in as close touch as I can. But things are happening rapidly. I have news assignments that will take me away from Moscow for days at a time."

"Contact me when you can," she said.

"You should know where things stand after you have your talk with him."

"I wonder," she sighed. "Alex and I have tried to settle our differences before. We reconcile, and then we find reasons to quarrel."

"Too bad," Ralph said.

"Yes, isn't it. We could have had such good lives together."

"Maybe there is still a chance."

"I'm beginning to think it a small one," she said.

They were interrupted by Sophie joining them and had no more chance to talk together for the balance of the afternoon.

Because of the late afternoon entertaining, there was no regular dinner served that evening. Timofei left for Moscow before the last guests had said their good-bys. Sophie elected to have a light meal with Count Andre in his apartment. Olga also went to her apartment, as did Alex and Elsie.

Alex in his dark mourning suit stood in the middle of the drawing room of their apartment with a troubled look on his handsome face. She had taken a stand by the window and was staring out at the river, where all signs of ice had vanished. The change had come about quickly. Her back was partly turned to him.

At last he broke the silence between them. "So many things have happened in the last few days," he said.

"I know," she said quietly, still looking out at the river.

"Aunt Marie's death stunned me," he said.

"It was a shock to all of us."

"It was not my wish that the wedding celebration should have ended as it did," he went on awkwardly. "I did not really think that Rasputin would show up."

"But you told him about it."

"Yes."

"Why? What do you owe him?"

He paused for a moment. "I don't think I can explain that to you."

"Do you think he warrants more loyalty than I do? Does he come before me in your life?" She turned to study him as she asked him these things.

He looked like someone in pain. "I had an association with Rasputin before I went to the United States, before we met. I didn't think then that my marriage to you need change my relationship with him."

"You're reluctant to give up his companionship and the orgies he offers his friends?" she said with sarcasm.

"There is a good deal more to Rasputin than being the

master of orgies," he shot back. "Do not underestimate him. He is the most powerful man in Russia. One day he will be the most powerful man in the world."

"I very much doubt that," she said dryly. "He is a charlatan."

"You don't understand the inner man!"

"Nor do I want to," she said. "If you continue to be one of his companions, there is nothing for us."

Alex took a step toward her. "That is unfair!"

"No," she said. "He made use of your brother, and he is dead along with his wife. He wants to use you because you are Count Martynov, one of the aristocracy. But the real nobility of Russia despise him, and they will despise you for turning traitor and joining him. You saw how Prince Serge behaved today!"

"Prince Serge was never my friend!"

"Nor is Rasputin," she said. "He will corrupt you and when he has used you, throw you in discard. I have seen you return here still deep in drugs. I'm terrified whenever you're away that something will happen to you. That you will do something criminal in your drugged state!"

"That is nonsense!" her husband protested.

"I think not," she said. "And let me tell you something else. When I went upstairs by myself on our wedding night, on your orders, the fat man came out of the shadows after me. Only because my screams attracted Timofei did I escape being attacked by him."

Alex looked guilty. "I sent you upstairs because I was afraid Rapsutin might embarrass you further."

"I can well imagine," she said. "But what about placing me in danger from his fat accomplice?"

"I know nothing about that. You probably imagined it!"

"Ask Timofei!"

"That drunken disgrace!" Alex said with disgust.

"There are times when he shows more decency than you," she said. "I know you barely escaped being caught in that raid on the orgy in St. Petersburg. That is why you returned here so soon and still in a half-daze from drugs."

He waved a protesting hand. "Nothing is going to be settled by our fighting about the past. What are your terms for a new beginning "

"Remain away from Rasputin."

"Give me a little time," he pleaded. "A complete break could be very difficult."

"I don't trust him," she said. "He is mad! Dangerous! I fear what he will do to you!"

Alex came close to her. "I love you! You must never doubt that!"

She saw that he was tortured and trembling. The pain in his eyes was real. And once again her heart was touched. She said, "I'm not jealous of any woman. I know you and Sophie had an affair, but that doesn't matter!"

"It ended long ago," he said. "It was never important."

"I'm terrified that Rasputin will involve you in some violence and that he is trying to have his assassins kill me because he knows that I stand between you and his using you."

Alex said, "I will find a way! I must! I care for you as I have never cared for any other living being. If it means an end to the Rasputin business, then I have no choice!"

"Alex!" she responded with a sob.

He took her in his arms and kissed her with great tenderness and later they made love. Elsie had never known him to be more passionate. It was as if all the desire he had suppressed during the days of their quarrel had come to the surface. She could not have asked for a more virile or tireless lover. The grim disappointment of her wedding night was forgot, just a bad memory.

They slept entwined. And on this night of love, there were no grim dreams. Her sleep was childlike in its placidity. Once again she believed that her marriage problems had been resolved.

And once again, she was doomed to a sad awakening. When morning came, she was alone. And as she roused herself in the bed still showing the imprint of where her husband had lain with her, she found an envelope addressed to her pinned on the pillow.

Her throat tightened as she reached for the envelope with a trembling hand. Despair was already surging through her before she managed to rip the envelope open. She fought back her tears so that she might read the message scrawled on a single sheet.

"My Dearest Elsie,
    In the light of morning I know that I have not yet de-

cided which way I shall go. I'm leaving Moscow for a little to try and sort it all out in my mind. There is only you, I beg you to believe that. But there is another decision which I must make. Please be patient with me and remain at the palace until you hear from me. Your loving, Alex."

She dropped the note on the coverlet and placed both hands over her face and sobbed. She was still crying when Elena arrived with her breakfast tray. She at once dabbed at her eyes and retrieved the letter as the maid arranged the tray on the table. If she must suffer, she would suffer in silent dignity. She had learned that much from the late Countess Marie.

Elena hesitated by the table. "I think everything is there, countess."

"Thank you," she said.

"I didn't bring up anything for Count Alexander, as I saw him being driven to Moscow early this morning," the maid said.

"Yes," she said, her head bowed.

"I expect he was catching the early train to St. Petersburg," Elena said. "Do you wish me to draw your bath, Madam?"

"Not yet," she said. "Perhaps when you return for the tray. I can manage."

"Yes, countess," the girl said and started for the door. She halted on the way to add, "Count Andre is very upset this morning. Timofei did not return home last night."

"Oh?"

The maid nodded. "He is often very late, but it is rare for him not to return at all. I'm sure the count is worried about him."

"No doubt," she said. And she remained in bed until the maid left. Then she read the letter once more and cried for a second time.

At last, drained of emotion, she rose and put on her dressing gown. She was having tea when there was a knock on her door. She went to it and opened it to see Olga, fully dressed, standing there.

"May I come in?" the dark girl asked her.

"Yes," she said.

Olga entered the room. "I know Alex left early this morning. What is the story?"

Elsie pulled his letter from the pocket of her dressing gown and gave it to Alex's sister to read. She sat down at the table and sipped more of the hot tea as Olga perched on the edge of the bed and scanned the letter.

Olga finished it and came over and returned it to her. "I'm so sorry," she said. And staring at her, she added, "I can't believe that Alex would do this to you, cause you so many tears."

"I hoped we had reconciled," she said. "Now I think that may never happen."

"He has asked you to wait," Olga said.

She shrugged. "Why should I?"

"I think I would do as he asked if I were in your place."

"You really mean that?"

"Yes," Olga said. "I know Rasputin has some weird hold on him just as he had on Basil. But maybe this time, it will end differently."

"I could become another Katrin," she pointed out. "There have already been attempts on my life. I suddenly feel very lonely for America."

Olga was standing by the window. She gazed at her and sighed. "You know I discouraged your marriage to Alex from the start."

"And I thought you were doing it out of jealousy," she said bitterly.

"No," the dark girl said. "I was afraid of what might happen once Alex returned here. I knew about Basil and his fate. I wanted to spare both you and Alex heartbreak. While he was in America, he forgot about all that had happened here. But when he came back, he soon changed."

"I can't say you didn't warn me. And my Aunt Jane was also gloomy about my prospects," she admitted. "But I loved Alex, and nothing else seemed to matter."

Olga looked at her with questioning eyes. "Do you still love him?"

She hesitated. "Yes."

"Then wait—at least for a little. You always have a

staunch friend in Ralph Manning. You can begin life again if you have to."

She said, "Ralph and Sophie seem to be in love."

"I think he cares more for you. But he respects the fact you are a married woman," Olga said. "Should you decide to break with my brother I'm sure Ralph would declare his feelings for you."

She sat back and stared at the dark girl. "So you think I should sit here and wait."

"It need not be so bad," Olga said. "I will be here. And Uncle Andre. More than ever he will need company. And Timofei, if he ever returns home."

"He will," she said. "I'm sure he drank too much somewhere and couldn't manage to return. He was in such a depressed mood when he left."

"Let us hope he comes back during the day," Countess Olga said. "Otherwise, I shall surely worry."

"Timofei is needed here, especially with Alex gone."

"Without a question," Olga agreed. "My Uncle Andre is ill with worry over him." She moved toward the door. "Will you tell my uncle about Alex?"

"I'll try," she said. "I'm barely over the shock myself."

"You'll have Sophie to work on your Russian lessons," Olga said. "That will occupy some of your time."

The dark girl left, and Elsie finished washing and dressing. There was no phone call from Ralph and she wanted to let him know about her husband's leaving. So she called the Hearst agency in the Hotel Metropole. An apologetic male voice informed her that Mr. Manning had left Moscow for an unknown destination on an urgent assignment.

She then remembered that he had warned her this might happen, but she hadn't expected him to go away so soon. She left her name with the young man at the other end of the line and asked him to have Ralph call her when he returned. Then she went up to Count Andre's apartment to go about the unpleasant business of telling him that Alex had gone away once more.

The old aristocrat was still in his dressing robe and seated in a leather easy chair. Sophie was standing near him and so heard the complete conversation between Elsie and the old man. Count Andre said nothing until Elsie had finished her story.

The old man gripped the arms of his chair so that the knuckles stood out white on his thin hands. "It is that villain Rasputin! The man is a hypnotist! He has cast some sort of spell over him just as he did over Basil."

"It seems so," she agreed.

Count Andre studied her with sad eyes. "What can I say? I am so sorry for you. It is cruel of Alex to bring you here to a strange land and treat you in this manner. He is not a true Martynov. He does not deserve the name."

She said, "Olga thinks I should remain here for a little. She feels it possible he may change his mind and return."

"I dare not advise you, my dear," the old man said. "You must make the decision yourself."

"I know," she said. "And I will."

"This is your home," he went on. "You will want for nothing."

When she finally left the old man's apartment, Sophie followed her out and caught up with her by the head of the curving stairway.

The blonde girl said, "I'm sorry."

"Thanks," she replied.

"To think I once hated you for taking Alex from me," Sophie said.

"Did you really?"

"Yes. But I don't now. I can see that it was the best thing which could have happened to me. Otherwise, it would be me he'd be deserting now rather than you."

"Maybe not," Elsie said. "You might have been able to hold him."

"Never. He cares for you far more than he ever did for me. But Rasputin has him in his grasp. And a lot more along with him, including the royal family."

Elsie said, "I tried to phone Ralph, but he's away on an assignment."

"He spoke of that to me," Sophie recalled.

"Did he say when he'd return?"

"No," Sophie said, but there was an uneasiness in the way she said it that made it seem likely she was being evasive. It seemed clear she would try and keep Ralph for herself if there was any prospect of Elsie vying for his love.

Elsie sighed. "I suppose I'll stay on for a little. If I didn't, I would always wonder if I'd been completely fair with Alex."

"I think he's mixed up in something really vicious," Sophie warned her. "Don't count too much on him."

She went downstairs with this gloomy prediction still ringing in her ears. And the worst part of it was that she knew the blonde girl was very apt to be right. She went into the library and paced up and down for a little trying to settle her nerves.

She studied the portrait of the late Basil and again was struck by how much this younger brother looked like her husband. Then she went over and found a magazine and sat down with it. It was a recent copy of the *Illustrated London News*, and one of the main articles had to do with the threat of a war in Europe. She read the article, which pointed to Germany as the chief threat to peace and studied the rather frightening photograph of a uniformed Kaiser Wilhelm, standing so that his withered arm would not be conspicuous. She found herself debating if that deformity might have something to do with his needless belligerence.

She was still reading the magazine when Olga came into the room with a troubled expression. The dark girl said, "I've just had the most extraordinary phone call."

Elsie put down the magazine. "What about?"

"From the proprietor of some dive along the waterfront. He talked in a garbled fashion, but I gathered from what he said Timofei had been there, or was still there. And he thought he should let us know."

She felt an ominous foreboding of something grim in the news. She said, "What are you going to do?"

Olga gave her a worried look. "I think I should drive in to Moscow and seek out this place and see if Timofei is still there. Will you come along with me?"

"All right," she said, deeply concerned about the big, friendly man.

Chapter 22

THE STREET ALONG THE RIVERFRONT was a wretched one. In the slum section of the great city, it consisted of rows of drab gray hovels, huddled closely together. The street itself was muddy and rutted wantonly from the passage of countless wagon wheels. On the riverside, most of the buildings were supported by shaky looking pilings; few had cellars.

Joseph was at the reins of the closed carriage; now he peeked in at them from the window behind his perch at the front and in a worried voice asked, "Are you sure this is the right street, Countess?"

Olga said, "Yes. It is. The place is called the Seaman's Haven. There should be a sign."

"I'll watch for it, countess," Joseph promised and urged the horses on.

"Timofei enjoys losing himself in these places where he is not known," Elsie said.

"In this area, a life isn't worth a half-dozen rubles," Olga worried.

"And he sometimes is so argumentive when he is drunk," she said. Being involved in the search for Timofei had not been without benefits. To an extent, it had shifted her anxieties from her own personal problem to concern about the artist's absence.

"I had hoped he might change and bring a stop to his drinking with Aunt Marie's death," Olga said. "But it appears he is going to be worse."

Elsie hastened to the defense of the young man. She said, "I can understand his sadness causing him to go on this binge. Perhaps later he will get hold of himself. He could be a great help to Count Andre."

"There are affairs of the estate which only he or Alex

can take care of," the dark girl worried. "I'm afraid if this goes on, you and I will find ourselves shouldering a man's responsibility."

She sighed. "Things have surely happened at a terrifying rate."

Joseph brought the carriage to a halt, then he jumped down and came around to let them out. "Mind your skirts in this mud, ladies," the coachman said. "This is the place."

Olga stepped out first and picked her way across the mud to the wooden sidewalk. Elsie followed her, with Joseph helping her. Before them was a ramshackled building, badly in need of paint, with an ancient sign proclaiming it the Seamen's Haven. The sign had once been bright with gaudy blue lettering on a gold background that was sorely faded now.

Olga gave her a resigned look. "Well, shall we venture in?"

"I hope we find Timofei and can get him away quickly," she said.

"I won't count on it," the dark girl said as she gingerly advanced to the battered door and opened it. The room was large and dark, and at first seemed empty. Then there was a scraping sound from the rear; a door opened and a thin, stooped man appeared.

He came hobbling over to them, and as he neared them they could see that he was rat-faced and sallow with his black hair thinning and matted across his domed head.

"Yes, ladies," he said, his hands clasped before him as if ready to be of service, his body still crouched in that peculiar way. His voice was nasal and unpleasant.

"I'm Countess Olga Martynov," she said. "And this is Countess Elsie. You phoned me earlier about our cousin, Timofei."

"Ah, yes, countess," the bent man said. "A sad business. I thought I should let you know."

"Is he here now?" Olga asked sharply.

The rat-faced man showed surprised on his sallow features. "Didn't you understand my call?"

"No," Olga said. "You didn't make yourself too clear."

"I'm sorry, madam. Very sorry. You see there was a brawl here last night. Your cousin, one of my regulars, I might say, became involved in an unfortunate argument with a seafaring man. We cater to men of the sea, as you know."

"Go on!" Olga said sharply to bring an end to the crouched man's rambling.

"Yes, countess," he said. "I was a seafaring man myself before my unfortunate accident. It left me a bent cripple, as you must see. I was on the prince's yacht, a trusted servant. But no more of that. I have been reduced to running this place."

"What about Count Timofei?" Elsie said, seeing that Olga was too exasperated to speak.

"Well, Madam," the proprietor of the dive said, "He and this seaman went beyond the point of words. Oh, yes! Not that their language wasn't abusive enough! And the next thing I know they are throwing chairs at each other and battling in the middle of the place. Very bad for business!"

"And?" Elsie said.

"The upshot of it, Madam, was this sailor drew a knife. Someone tried to get it from him, but it was too late. He drove it into Count Timofei's chest two or three times. Then he ran out of the place. I thought Count Timofei was finished, but he surprised us all by lifting himself from the floor and dragging out after the scoundrel, leaving a trail of his blood behind him. You can still see the stains of it on the floor, although I scrubbed them enough this morning."

"Where is our cousin?" Olga cried.

The crouched man looked hurt. "I wish I could tell you, countess. The two of them went out back on the wharf. And would you believe it, they continued their battling. And in a flash both of them went over the side into the river. We went out and searched for them, but there was not a sign of either of them!"

Olga gasped. "Do you mean Timofei was drowned?"

The rat-faced man looked wary. "He could be, although I won't promise it. Maybe he wasn't all that badly hurt, although I think he was mortally wounded. It's possible the water revived him, and he made his way off to some other place."

"It doesn't seem possible if he were so badly wounded," Elsie said worriedly.

"I agree, Madam," the proprietor said. "Odd things happen, if I may say so. If that sailor fellow knew he had murdered Count Timofei, he might have decided to swim a distance away with the body and then dispose of it some place else. As long as the body isn't found, there's no proof of murder. And the fact the seaman vanished, too, makes me think that is what happened."

Olga said in a hushed voice, "You're saying that he, or he and some of his friends, managed to get Timofei's body out of the water to bury it somewhere it wouldn't be found."

"Yes, countess, that's about the size of it. But you can't be sure. It could be that tonight Timofei may come walking into my place and none the worse except for some slight stab wounds."

Elsie said, "How strongly do you believe that?"

The man looked wary. "It would be an off chance, Madam."

"I'd say so," she said in a weary voice.

"There's something else," the bent man said. "He left something."

"What?" Olga asked.

"Come in a bit further," he said, hobbling ahead of them in the dark place, which seemed to have no windows at all. He struck a match and lighted a candle on one of the several tables. Then he held it up and pointed at the wall. "See!"

Elsie stared at the wall and gasped. "He did it! His icon!"

Olga said, "I can't believe it. Here! In this place!"

"Worked on it for weeks; drunk or sober, he kept at it. I told him it wasn't a fit decoration for my place, but he wouldn't listen to me. He just said he'd pay me well and now he's gone, and I'll never see a ruble!"

Elsie made no reply. She was lost in a study of the colorful and magnificent icon. It consisted of four sections. Each for a different icon. And each had a gold border around it. In the upper left space Timofei had painted the Nativity of St. John the Baptist, showing the room and eight figures by the baby. In the upper right he had drawn the Nativity of the Virgin, with the room and six figures near the baby. In the lower left, he'd depicted the Birth of Our Lord with the stable and manger and the Virgin and St. Joseph, along with the Wise Men and the midwife. Also there were the animals: the oxen, sheep, goats, and asses. And in the fourth space was the Birth of St. Nicholas, and here, too, was the hall of the palace and the child and many figures besides. The masterpiece had, worked in careful lettering of gold beneath it, "The Holy Children." And it was signed, Timofei Martynov.

A sob filled her throat and she told Olga, "He said he would paint a masterpiece and he has!"

Olga gazed at the delicate artwork covering almost a six foot square section of the dive's wall. Even in the flickering flame of the candle, there was no denying the worth of Timofei's prodigious effort.

She said, "It is truly beautiful!"

The bent man complained, "Now he is gone and it will cost me to paint the wall. I barely make a living here. I'm a very poor man. I cannot afford it!"

Elsie turned to him angrily. "You must not touch the wall!"

"Eh?" He was shocked by her ferocity.

"You heard me," she said. "Do not dare touch that wall. Count Andre Martynov will send carpenters and masons here to remove the section of wall with the icon and replace it in any fashion you like. And he will also pay you well!"

Olga joined in now. "Yes, Countess Elsie is right. It would be sacrilege to destroy that fine painting. I will see that my uncle sends workmen here in the morning, and there will be a worthy payment to you for your trouble."

"Of course, countess." The crouched man showed a smile of greed on his pinched face. "I shall see the icon is not touched. But do not put it off longer than tomorrow. We get a rough lot here. Several times a customer has threatened to mar or destroy it. But always Timofei was here for its protection. I will now have to defend the icon as best I can."

Olga said, "Our word is good. The workmen will be here. And of course I must inform the police my cousin is missing."

"Is that required?" he whined. "They may cause me trouble."

"You could not help the brawl," Olga said.

"I did my best to stop it," the bent man replied.

"In that case, the police can't blame you. My cousin vanished somewhere outside. Do you know the name of the seaman who stabbed him?"

"No, countess," the man looked guilty. "But for a few rubles discreetly offered here and there, the information might be delivered."

Olga gave him a disgusted look and opened her pocketbook. She took a dozen or so rubles from her purse and gave them to him. "Try and have the name by the time the police arrive here."

"Depend on it," the man said, fawning on her as he greedily clutched the money in a dirty claw.

"I want my cousin found dead or alive; but if he is alive, it will mean an extra reward for you," Olga told him.

"I will try and find him. You may count on it. He was my most distinguished and valued customer. A poor place like mine never sees the likes of Count Timofei. He was my pride."

Olga said, "If you wish to honor him, protect that icon until we can have it removed."

"You have my word, countess," the crippled man assured her.

They left the shabby place with little hope that Timofei was still alive. Olga told Joseph the bad news, and he drove them to the nearest police station. The officer in charge listened to their story with a scowl on his face.

He asked, "Why would a member of the nobility frequent such a place?"

"My cousin was a rebel," she said. "He also was ashamed of his drunkenness and chose to go to places where he wouldn't be recognized."

The police official reacted to this with scorn. "His peculiar tastes may have cost him his life. Those riverfront dives are evil places."

"We are well aware of that," she said. "We have paid the owner to try and find the name of the seaman who stabbed our cousin."

"I suggest that it's money lost," the police official said,

annoyance on his bearded face. "Those fellows never talk. It would be worth their lives if they did."

Olga said, "You will investigate it thoroughly?"

"That is our duty," he said.

Elsie asked, "Do you think there is a remote chance that Count Timofei may be alive?"

"There is always a remote chance when the body has not been found," the police official told her. "But if he remains missing, I would not hesitate to have a memorial service held for him."

They left the police station after having received firm promises that they would receive regular reports on the investigation. Olga dropped a broad hint that her Uncle Andre was a close friend of the head of the Moscow police. She also suggested that he was a generous man, and any good results would be rewarded. The police official at once became more interested and polite.

As they were driven back to the palace, Olga gave her a troubled look and asked, "What do you think?"

"I don't know," she said. "I don't dare give up hope."

"Nor do I," she said. "Timofei is a sturdy one. He may have survived the stabbing and killed the seaman. That may be why he remains in hiding."

From the account they had heard, Elsie felt this was most unlikely. The grim truth was probably that Timofei had been brutally murdered and his body hidden away somewhere or burned so that it could not be found. But she knew they were all too low in spirits to want to admit this new tragedy.

She said, "I believe you should present the story to Count Andre in this fashion. It will give him something to hang on to, even if he worries about Timofei being a murderer and a fugitive."

"Better than thinking him dead," Olga agreed, as the carriage rolled on.

Elsie realized they were becoming coconspirators to try and make things easier for the old man. She was coming to understand Olga and have a true affection for her. She said, "And we must go ahead with recovering the icon and bringing it to the palace."

"We can find a place for it on the wall of the chapel," Olga said.

"Why not?" Elsie agreed. "And the excitement of it will be a blessing for your uncle."

"If only that wretched man doesn't let anything happen to it in the meanwhile," Olga worried.

"I doubt if he will," Elsie said. "His eyes shone when you gave him the rubles, and you promised him more money if the icon was preserved safely."

Count Andre received the word about Timofei with more calmness than they had expected. The fact that they stressed he was likely alive and in hiding from the police helped. He was also bolstered in spirit by the news of the discovery of the icon and their plan to have it brought to the palace and installed in the chapel.

The old man ordered them, "Have Frederick hire the best artisans available. I do not want that icon to suffer any sort of harm."

"I'll see to it," Olga promised.

"If only Marie had lived to know about this," the old man said with a smile. "That young scoundrel must have been working on it long before she died."

"I'm sure he was," Elsie agreed.

"It will have a place of honor in the chapel," Count Andre said. "And you say he signed it as a Martynov."

"Yes," Olga said. "I was a trifle surprised."

"He accepted us as his parents in his moment of triumph at finishing the work of art," the old man said. "That is a great satisfaction. If only he is still alive."

Olga said, "You must realize he will be slow to show himself since he may have murdered that seaman."

"If the seaman attacked him first and with a knife, there should be no trouble clearing him in the courts," the old man reasoned.

"No," Elsie agreed. "But he may be afraid." She wanted to keep the old man believing the rebel Timofei was still alive. If truth be told, she also wanted to believe it. The theory she had devised was comforting to her also.

Count Andre said, "See that the workmen start removing the icon tomorrow. Do not delay!"

Now there began a season of suspense and despair for Elsie. She received no reply from Ralph Manning, and when she tried to reach his office again, the clerk blandly told her that he was still away on assignment. Nor did she receive any word from her husband. There was only silence from St. Petersburg.

The police officials made several visits to discuss the disappearance of Timofei. But no headway was made concerning the mystery of what might have happened to him. Elsie was convinced each day that he had been murdered. But for the sake of the elderly Count Andre, she and Olga kept up the pretense that there was still a possibility of his returning.

Sophie was angered by this. She told Olga and Elsie so one afternoon when the three of them happened to be in the sun room at the same time. She said, "That old man is up there dreaming of what he will do when Timofei returns, and you both know he will never return!"

Olga's lovely face was shadowed. "His body has never been recovered."

"So how can we be sure," Elsie said, backing her up.

The blonde's blue eyes flashed scorn. "We all know why. Whoever murdered him cleverly hid the body. The proprietor of that dive told you that."

"I think it is not right to rob Uncle Andre of hope," Olga said. "I, for one, will never do it."

"Nor I," Elsie said.

"You two are not with him as much as I am," Sophie replied with some annoyance. "I'm weary of the pretense."

Olga gave her a scornful look. "Admit it, you always hated Timofei in any case. You're relieved not to have him here."

"His drunken behavior couldn't have been pleasant to you either," Sophie replied.

Elsie said, "Despite his drinking, I liked him. He was basically a good person and a fine artist. The icon he left behind in the bar proved that."

"More waste of time and money, preserving it and bringing it here," Sophie said with annoyance.

"I disagree," Olga replied. "It will give Uncle Andre something to occupy him!"

"I won't complain about that," Sophie said bitterly. "Now his chief activity is having me accompany him to his wife's grave every day. I've had enough of it."

Elsie said quietly, "If you are weary of being here you can leave."

"Perhaps I will." Sophie snapped at her. "Just as Alex seems to have done!" And with a nasty smile for her she left the sun room.

After she was a safe distance away, Olga said angrily, "I find I dislike and distrust that girl more and more. She had no right to say that to you."

Elsie shrugged. "The unhappy part is that it happens to be true. Alex has deserted me."

"Not even a letter from him?"

"Nothing. He has been in touch with his banker to see sufficient money is available for my needs. That is all."

Olga said, "Perhaps you should go to St. Petersburg and find out what is happening there."

"What could I do alone?"

Olga frowned. "There is your newspaper friend Ralph Manning."

"I have not been able to find him," she said. "I'm beginning to wonder if Sophie hasn't something to do with it."

The dark-haired Olga moved close to her and said, "There is something you must know."

"What?"

"Almost every night around eleven, a carriage calls here for Sophie and she leaves the house. I suspect it takes her to Moscow and that she may be meeting Ralph Manning. It is often very late when she returns. Part of her being so irritable of late is likely because of her lack of sleep."

She was shocked. "How long has this been going on?"

"At least two weeks and almost every night. I know because Feodor comes here to meet me. We have both seen Sophie waiting in the shadows outside and quickly getting into the carriage when it comes by."

"Maybe that is why Ralph is ignoring my messages," Elsie said. "He is afraid I'll find out about his meeting Sophie regularly."

"I doubt if he's really out of town. It's just that he hasn't time for both of you."

Elsie said grimly, "Sophie has been determined about him from the start. He offers her as escape from Russia."

"She's forever complaining lately. I think she is on the verge of leaving."

"I thought Ralph would be more wary. But there's no denying Sophie has great charm when she likes."

Olga grimaced. "And she's willing to sell it as it suits her. He's getting no bargain in her."

The conversation left her in a more despondent mood than before. She felt she had been deserted by all those she had counted on. Alex had been the most cruel to her. But she had expected more of Ralph. It was embarrassing to think that he was carrying on an underhanded romance with Sophie and at the same time pretending to be away from Moscow whenever she tried to reach him. And poor Timofei was likely dead.

She had vaguely thought of going to St. Petersburg and searching for Alex. Perhaps there she might be able to fight the influence Rasputin held over him. And Ralph could have been of great help to her. But he, too, had failed her.

Letters came from her Aunt Jane and Uncle Gordon again. She was slow in replying to them because she did not know what to say. She felt that within a week or two, she might be able to let them know that she had given up on her marriage and was returning to America. So she put off writing for a little.

The big excitement in the palace was the arrival of the icon, which had been removed from the wall of the waterfront dive. Now the plaster wall with the painting on it came carefully crated. And the workmen began to cut a square of the same size in the wall of the chapel near the entrance and make ready to place the icon in it.

Count Andre, a little less well than before the death of his wife and the tragedy of Timofei's disappearance, used a cane now. His bearing was not quite so erect, but he was still a distinguished-looking old man. At least once a week some other older member of the aristocracy came to call on him; and these visits always left him restored in spirits.

Sophie continued to look after him in a disinterested fashion, and Elsie noticed the blonde girl made every attempt to avoid her. This, together with her midnight excursions to Moscow, made Elsie certain that the blonde girl was getting ready to leave the country in the company of Ralph.

As the artisans entrusted with the placing of the icon in the chapel wall came to the final, intricate stages of the work, old Count Andre went down nearly every day to

Clarissa Ross

watch their progress. He would sit in an easy chair and direct the operations with his cane.

On the morning when the masons began to cover the plaster line of the insert and make it seem a part of the wall, Elsie was there with him. The icon, with its colorful design and gold borders, was a fine addition to the chapel.

Count Andre's thin countenance was lighted with pleasure as he watched the masons covering the joins with a plaster coat. "Timofei will be delighted when he returns and sees what we have done, won't he?"

She said, "He will know that you appreciate his talent and that will mean a lot to him."

The old man said, "I would call it fine work, even if it were not the creation of my foster son."

"So would I," she agreed.

Count Andre suddenly gazed at her with his sharp old eyes and, with an abrupt change of manner, said, "You do not think him dead, do you?"

"No," she said. And in a sense this was true. The lovable big man could not be thought of as dead while this work of genius he had completed continued to exist.

"Sophie claims that he is."

"Sophie does not know everything," Elsie said.

"You are right," the old man said, gripping the head of his cane grimly. "She is too greedy! Too anxious to look after herself. One of these days she will know a bitter defeat."

"I wonder," Elsie said, more worried about Ralph and what an unhappy relationship with the girl might do to him.

Count Andre was watching the workmen again. And he began to reminisce. "As a lad I remember seeing an icon portraying the Great Martyr of St. George, whom we call Yegory, the Victorious. He had a sword in hand and was on horseback as he went about slaying a dragon. It made a great impression on me."

"And you have remembered it all these years," she said.

"It is still clear in my mind," he assured her with a nod of his white head. "The Miracle of St. George and the Dragon is rarely accompanied by scenes of the saint's life. But in the Tretyakov Gallery there may be seen a sixteenth-century specimen of St. George preaching to Diocletian. In

288

some of the scenes, he is scourged with ox-sinews, broken on the wheel, and tortured with hooks, yet he goes on preaching in prison."

"Does the icon show his death?"

"Yes," Count Andre said. "There are other scenes showing his last miracle when he restored life to a bull belonging to a farmer in Glykery. He was cast into a lime pit and brought some dead to life. Pagans began to embrace his faith. He was beheaded later by his enemies. And the last scene shows him in a dungeon conversing with an angel."

"It would make a colorful collection of paintings," she agreed.

The old man remained on hand until the wall was completed, and Timofei's icon looked as if it had always been there. When he had visitors, he took them to see it, and the work invariably drew praise.

Meanwhile, Elsie had no word from Alex. She found herself becoming more on edge. Several nights she thought she heard footsteps in the corridor outside her door. And on one frightening night, she was sure that some unseen hand had opened the door a fraction as a phantom figure peered in at her. She began to be afraid of sleeping alone in the apartment.

Olga kept her trysts with the young revolutionary, Feodor, and had been attending meetings of the group in which he was a leader. According to her, the situation with the workers and students was becoming more intolerable every day. There were bound to be more uprisings. And they would also be more violent.

The press had come under strict censorship by the tsar's orders, and so there were few references to what was happening. And there was no mention of Rasputin at all, although it was claimed he was now the ruling figure at the court of St. Petersburg. She had relied on Ralph for much of her inside information, but his office insisted he was out of the city somewhere. And so she hadn't talked with him for weeks. Meanwhile, she knew that Sophie continued to be mysteriously picked up by a carriage nearly every night for visits to Moscow. And she had come to believe the blonde girl and Ralph were having an affair.

It was a warm night in early summer, and she had been

especially uneasy. Twice she thought she had heard someone in the hall and had risen to cautiously peer out into
the shadows. Each time she had the frustrating experience
of not being able to account for the sounds she'd heard.

At length she'd managed an uneasy sleep. Suddenly, this
sleep was broken by a thunderous knocking at the front
door of the palace!

☙ *Chapter 23* ❧

THE LOUD KNOCKING was repeated, and Elsie sat up with a start. From outside, she heard the sound of harsh voices and the champing of horses' hooves. She glanced at the clock on her bedside table and saw that it was still the middle of the night. And she tried to decide what might be happening out there in the darkness.

There was more knocking; then she heard the door below open and Frederick's ancient voice as he tried to deal with whoever the intruders were. She at once jumped out of bed and put on her robe and slippers. Her first wild thought was that the revolution might have at last broken with full force and these midnight callers might be part of some revolutionary band.

Surely Olga would use her influence with Feodor to spare the ancient Count Andre. But there was no telling. This might be some other rebel group with whom Feodor had no association. Russia was filled with conflicting rebels, each on their own course.

She went to the door and opened it in time to see Olga, in her robe, rushing to the curving stairway. She followed, and when she reached the entrance foyer she saw a strangely dramatic tableau.

A group of cossacks was there; an officer with a bristling brown mustache and goatee was in charge. Count Andre, in his robe, stood leaning on his cane, and seemed confused. The cossack officer was sternly questioning a nervous Sophie, who had apparently only just returned from one of her nightly escapades, because she was fully dressed and wearing a light cloak.

The elderly butler, Frederick, stood near his master and seemed terrified, while several other female domestics in nightgowns and robes hovered in the background, staring at the stern cossacks in their summer uniforms and caps as if they were visitors from another planet.

Count Andre quavered, "I cannot condone this intrusion of my home!"

The cossack officer saluted him smartly. "I am here in the interests of the tsar, Count Martynov. We know you to be a loyal subject, and we ask your pardon."

"I should think so," the elderly count snapped. "What is the purpose of coming here at this hour of the night?"

The cossack officer said, "We have followed this woman, Sophie Martynov, here; and I have a warrant for her arrest!"

Olga gasped. "For her arrest?"

Sophie's eyes were brimming with tears. "It is all an awful mistake!"

Count Andre moved to her. He said sternly, "This girl is a member of my family. She lives here with us. What can you possibly want with her?"

"A grave matter, count," the young officer said. "She is one of a group of conspirators with a plan to assassinate the tsar!"

"I don't believe it!" Count Andre exclaimed with a look of dismay at Sophie.

The blonde girl said, "Lies! You must save me!" And she ran to the old man and hugged herself to him.

The frail, old Count patted her gently. "Have no fear, my child. We will settle this."

Olga, looking pale and strained, asked the officer, "What proof do you have against her?"

The cossack officer was coldly polite. "We have all the required proof, countess," he said. "We followed her here directly from a meeting she attended. The others have been rounded up and will appear in court tomorrow."

Count Andre stared at Sophie in amazement. "You were in the city tonight?"

The blonde girl pressed to him and uttered muffled sobs. She made no attempt to answer his question.

Elsie knew that the old man, unlike herself and Olga, was not aware of Sophie's midnight excursions. But she, too, was shocked by the charge made by the officer, since it could well mean that Ralph Manning was involved. Surely a mistake had been made. The Russians were extremely suspicious of foreign newspapermen, and this may have led to their frightening charges. She could not imagine Ralph being wild enough to lend himself to any political plot! There had to be some error!

Count Andre held the hysterical girl in his arms and in a pleading tone asked the cossack officer, "Can you not place her in my care? I will be responsible for her appearance in court."

The officer said, "I would gladly do it, count, if it were within my realm. But the charge is too serious. I have strict orders to take her with me."

The discussion continued for a few moments longer. Then it came to the inevitable end. Sophie was dragged away sobbing with a cossack soldier on either side of her, supporting her. As she vanished through the doorway into the darkness, the cossack officer clicked his heels and saluted the stricken Count Andre again.

The officer said, "The girl will appear before the judge in the central division of the Moscow court at eleven in the morning. Perhaps you will wish to attend."

"I shall be there," Count Andre said with stern pride.

The officer vanished, and old Frederick closed the door after him. He then turned to the master of the house and asked, "Is there anything I can do, Count Andre?"

The white-haired man said, "Yes, bring me some hot tea. Enough for all of us and something to go with it."

"Yes, count," the old servant said and went away, herding the stunned female members of his staff who gathered there ahead of him.

Olga said, "Let us go to your study, Uncle Andre."

He nodded. "That would be best."

They went down the hall to the intimate room lined with books. Frederick came in and touched a match to the several logs in the fireplace. The room was always coolish, and they were dressed lightly. The quickly rising flames not only gave them heat, but also some slight assurance.

One of the female members of the staff brought in a steaming samovar of tea and some cakes. No one said more than a few words until after the tea was served.

Count Andrew held his tea cup in his hand and stared sternly across the room at his niece. "Will you explain why

I was not informed about these nightly excursions to Moscow of Sophie's?"

Olga's pale cheeks flushed. "Elsie and I did not want to further worry you."

"I ought to have been told," he said. "I am not a child to be protected."

Elsie said, "It was a mistake. But we didn't think it would end in anything like this."

Count Andre looked stunned. "I have never known Sophie to have any revolutionary sympathies. I would not be surprised if the officer had come for Timofei, or Alex, or even you Olga. But Sophie is a creature concerned only with herself."

Elsie said awkwardly, "Perhaps I can explain."

The white-haired count said, "Please do."

"You remember the newspaper reporter I have had here as a guest, Ralph Manning?"

He frowned. "Yes. Clean-cut young chap."

"Olga and I have reason to believe he and Sophie are having an affair. She went in to the city to meet him every night. A carriage came for her and brought her back. Ralph is a foreign newspaperman, and so may be wrongly suspected of being mixed up in some kind of political plot."

Count Andre listened to her with amazement. "It seems I know little of what is going on. Surely you must be mistaken. This reporter represents a reliable American newspaper service. He could not be guilty of planning to kill the tsar."

"It's very strange," she agreed.

Olga gave her a knowing glance. "I'm beginning to think we have been mistaken. Maybe your Ralph is out of the city after all. Sophie may have been seeing someone else, someone we don't even know."

Elsie nodded. "She might have met somebody at the wedding. It was after that she began leaving the palace at night."

Olga said, "If some political plotter told her he'd get her out of Russia, she'd become easy prey for him."

Count Andre looked from one to the other. "I must get in touch with my lawyer first thing in the morning, and we should all be in court when Sophie makes her appearance before the judge and is charged. Then the truth will come out."

"You are right," Olga said. "We should know in the morning."

None of them slept any more that night. Count Andre had his lawyer on the phone early in the morning and arranged to meet him in court. At ten o'clock, Joseph arrived with the droshka to take Count Andre, Olga, and Elsie into the city. They all sat in somber silence during the drive, not knowing what they were about to face.

Once more Elsie was thinking of Alex and where he might be. She knew he would be shocked to learn of Sophie's plight, but he had left no word with her where he might be reached. And when she had contacted their banker this morning, he had pleaded no knowledge of where her husband was, although Alex did send him written instructions every few days or so from St. Petersburg.

They reached the central court in good time and made their way up the steps of the majestic building. Inside, the lobby was bleak, and there was a scattering of forlorn-looking people apparently on hand to hear the trials of friends or relatives. Count Andre leaned heavily on his walking stick and glared around him in search of his lawyer.

Thomas Kashetsky appeared after a few minutes. He was a nervous, stout man with a pink round face and thinning gray hair. He bowed to them all and directed himself to the old count.

"This is a serious business, Count Andre," he warned him.

"I do not understand it. The girl never had any political views," the count said.

"The information was laid against her by a responsible person," Thomas Kashetsky said. "She will appear in the large courtroom in a few minutes. I think we should take our places there."

Elsie found the building completely lacking in color and full of echoes—of voices, footsteps, and doors opening and closing. It was like a gray nightmare. She was terrified that she would see Ralph standing before the judge along with Sophie and the others involved. It was truly a nightmare, and she was upset to the point of being only vaguely aware of her surroundings and what was happening to her. Olga supported her uncle on one side, and he leaned on his walking stick on the other. The lawyer led the way, and Elsie trailed behind.

They entered the courtroom and took places on a side balcony. The lawyer went down to be near Sophie when she was brought in. The courtroom was well filled, and there was a buzz of voices. Elsie still sat there in a bewildered state.

The judge entered and took his place at the high bench. Order was called, and the courtroom became silent. Officers appeared and with them the prisoners. Elsie saw Sophie looking wilted and ill, and she strained to see if Ralph was with her. But all the faces of the other defendants were strange to her, all except one—that of Jacob Bogrov, Borgrov of the Imperial Ballet!

The charges were read against the prisoners, and she heard only a little of what was said, she was so shaken. At least Ralph was innocent, and also innocent of having an affair with Sophie. It was Bogrov she had been visiting nightly! Bogrov who had been plotting against the tsar.

The lawyer for the prosecution was speaking in a dry voice. "The information was first laid against the defendants by Madame Bogrov. The documents we subsequently found and the confessions made by some of the defendants prove their guilt beyond a doubt. I ask that they be held incommunicado until the date of their sentencing."

"Request granted," the judge said severely. "Take the prisoners away, and let us get on to the next case."

Elsie saw Count Andre's lawyer confer with the prosecutor and that grim gentlemen shook his head. Whatever the request, the reply had been in the negative.

The police led the prisoners out, and Sophie did not even look up. She seemed completely broken in spirit. Jacob Bogrov marched proudly with head high, as if proud of the crime for which he was charged. She and Olga helped Count Andre down the steps to a side exit, and they rejoined the lawyer in the hall.

The lawyer looked defeated. "There is no help for her," he said. "I asked special permission for you to talk with her, and it was refused."

Count Andre showed pain. "What can I do for the poor, misguided child?"

"Nothing, count," the lawyer replied. "These cases are settled quickly. The evidence was damning. Madame Bogrov turned witness against her husband."

"I think I can imagine why," Olga said bitterly.

The lawyer nodded. "She claimed that Sophie Martynov was Jacob Bogrov's mistress and one of the plotters."

"What will happen to them?" Olga asked.

The lawyer said, "They will be sentenced and sent to prison."

"Where are they likely to be taken?" Count Andre wanted to know.

His lawyer spread his hands. "For a crime of this magnitude there is only one possible place—Siberia!"

"Siberia!" Olga said in dismay.

"Tragic," the lawyer said. "There is nothing to be done. You will only make trouble for yourself and family if you attempt to intervene further in her behalf."

Count Andre said, "You have long managed my affairs, and you are not only my lawyer but my trusted friend. Is there no move you can make?"

"None," the lawyer said. "You have others to think of. Be discreet!" Elsie saw the lawyer's glance in Olga's direction and had an idea he knew she was somehow involved with the revolutionists.

They left the central court and began the drive home in a grim mood. Olga said, "She brought it on herself. She counted on Bogrov taking her to Paris with him, and instead she will find herself his companion in Siberia!"

"How long a sentence will they be liable to get?" Elsie wanted to know.

Count Andre frowned. "For treason against the royal family, the sentence will be life. Sophie will be exiled to Siberia for all time, even though she is eventually let out of prison."

"Her youth and beauty will soon fade in the face of the hardships and barrenness there," Olga said. "She will be an old woman in no time."

Elsie said, "Perhaps she will somehow escape."

"Where?" Olga asked grimly. "To the wolves?"

"There is no escape," Count Andre said. "She is dead. We have lost her."

No sooner did they reach the palace than Elsie called the Hotel Metropole in an effort to contact Ralph. Now that she knew he was not having an affair with Sophie, she had no compunctions about trying to reach him.

The young man in the office was more friendly this time. "I'm sorry," he said. "Mr. Manning is presently in St. Petersburg."

"Will he soon return to Moscow?"

"Yes." He paused and then asked, "Are you, by any chance, Countess Elsie Martynov?"

"I am," she said.

"Mr. Manning sent a message for you. He said that he will be in touch with you as soon as he returns and that he will have a good deal more information for you."

"Thank you," she said.

"You will be at the palace?"

"Yes," she replied. "He may call me here."

"I will tell him," the young man said.

She sought Olga out in the dark girl's apartment and told her what she had learned. She said, "I can hardly wait to hear from him."

Olga was pacing up and down in the room and looking bleak. "I'm terrified for Uncle Andre and for myself. I may be the next one to be picked up by the police."

"You are not plotting to kill anyone."

"No," Olga said bitterly. "But we are holding meetings to plan a rebellion, and that is almost the same thing."

"Feodor is careful," she said. "You have had no trouble so far."

"His group works in small cells," Olga said. "And all the members are trustworthy. It was Sophie's affair with Bogrov that proved her undoing. Madame Bogrov had her revenge."

"And a cruel one," Elsie said.

Olga sat in a nearby chair. "The day will come when for my own safety I'll have to leave here and go to another city. What will happen to Uncle Andre then?"

"It would be cruel to leave him."

"Crueler to remain here and have him see me arrested."

Elsie said, "I don't know how long I'll be staying here."

The dark girl stared at her. "Do you honestly think Alex is going to return?"

"He promised me he would let me know," Elsie said. "And he hasn't done that yet."

"Perhaps he'll be like Timofei. Just drop out of sight."

"Timofei is dead," Elsie said grimly. "Sad as it is, we must admit it between ourselves."

"I know," the dark girl said. "If you still hope for a reconciliation with Alex, why don't you follow him to St. Petersburg?"

"I have thought about it," she said.

"Ralph is also in St. Petersburg. You could likely find his hotel. With the two men you care most for there, why are you remaining here?"

She gazed at the dark girl. "There is no good reason, except I'm afraid to go there on my own."

"You would manage," Olga said. "And better for you to go now while I am here to watch over Uncle Andre."

"You think I should go?"

Olga suddenly rose from the chair as if she had an inspiration. She said, "Let me tell you! We have a girl here now from a cell in St. Petersburg. She is returning in a day or two. Why don't you go along with her? She would make a traveling companion. She is very wise and resourceful, one of the leaders of the party. She might even be able to lead you to Rasputin's monastery."

It was a tempting idea. She said, "When could I meet her?"

Olga said, "Tonight."

"Tonight?"

"Yes," the dark girl said. "Feodor is coming to get me at eight. You can come along. The girl's name is Marfa Naratshev."

"Marfa Naratshev," Elsie repeated. "Would she accept me as a companion?"

"She is a very good person," Olga said. "And if I explain you are trying to save your husband, who is also my brother, from that villain Rasputin, I'm positive she will do all she can for you."

"What would I tell Count Andre?"

"Simple," Olga said. "Tell him you are going to visit Alex in St. Petersburg. That will make him happy."

"It will be hard to explain if I fail," she said.

"Worry about that when the time comes," the countess said. "And be ready to leave with me at eight."

Elsie hesitated. "There is one other thing."

"Yes?"

"I'm afraid of sleeping alone in my apartment at night. I have heard footsteps, and there has been no one there. The door opens and closes by itself. And last night before I went to sleep, I thought I saw the shadow of the fat man in the doorway watching me. Then he vanished."

Olga said, "The palace has always been haunted."

"This was no ghost," Elsie argued. "At least I think not. When Litvinov tried to take my life in London, he was very real."

"You think you saw this Litvinov last night?"

"The phantom was grossly fat and in black like Litvinov."

"Or like a shadow playing with your imagination?"

Elsie shook her head. "I feel there was a presence there. I know Litvinov is one of Rasputin's vassals. And I believe the mad monk wishes to destroy me just as Katrin was destroyed. You know Timofei once told me he thought she wasn't a suicide. He believed she might have been murdered by the same cult who were responsible for Basil's death!"

"Who knows?" Olga said with a sigh. "He may have been right. Our numbers grow smaller, first Basil and Katrin, then my aunt and Timofei, now Sophie. One dares not venture to guess who will be lost next."

"I know I'm afraid," she confessed with a shudder. "For myself and for Alex. I have seen his poor drugged eyes after being with those people. They took him to the edge of madness."

Olga said, "Until you leave for St. Petersburg, there is no reason why you should not sleep in one of the bedrooms here in my apartment."

"Would it be thought strange?" she worried.

"The only important thing at this point is your safety," the dark girl said. "You will sleep here."

Elsie was grateful for the dark girl's suggestion. And she was also excited at the prospect of attending the meeting of the student revolutionaries and meeting Marfa Naratshev. Somehow she felt this might be the first step in a successful fight to save her husband from the influence of the mad monk.

She had dinner with Count Andre and Olga. After dinner the old man went upstairs to his apartment. It was his custom now to retire early. As soon as he had left them, Olga told Elsie to meet her on the riverbank out back.

Elsie wore a dark cloak over her white dress to be less conspicuous and was there promptly to meet Olga. They walked along a path, which eventually led to a country road. On the road a wagon with a tarpaulin covering its back was waiting. She did not recognize the young country boy who was driving the wagon, but she followed Olga's example of scrambling up into the back on the straw-covered bottom of the wagon and drawing the canvas over them so they were covered.

The wagon rolled on for some time, and she had no idea where they were heading. By the time they halted, it was pitch black. The young man helped them down from the wagon and she saw they were in a back street of the city. They entered a log cabin and then went down a ladder that led from a trapdoor into the cellar.

In the cellar, eight young people sat around a big table with a lantern and a lot of papers scattered on its surface. Feodor in a peaked cap and blue blouse was presiding at the table. He rose to greet them.

The other young men and women of the group eyed her with suspicion, so that Feodor at once told them, "Comrades, you need have no fear. This is a sister-in-law to Olga, and an American. She has sympathy with our cause."

A big blond youth broke into laughter and said, "Why not? She is an American. And it is the land of revolution."

Olga said, "Elsie is my dear friend as well as my relative by marriage. She has a serious problem, and I have brought her here in the hope that Marfa may be able to help her."

"But I'm returning to St. Petersburg tomorrow," a sturdy, peasant-type girl said from the end of the table opposite Feodor. She had a square face, but she was also pleasantly intelligent in appearance. Her large brown eyes were her good feature. She wore her brass-colored hair braided and coiled in the back.

Olga said, "My sister-in-law's problem has to do with St. Petersburg. We can discuss it later. Now it is more urgent that we get on with the business of the meeting."

Feodor found Elsie a plain chair, and she sat listening and watching, just outside the group of nine now gathered at the table.

Feodor was expounding a plan for distributing pamphlets in several of the colleges. And the other young people made suggestions from time to time. Olga seemed well versed in it all and also made suggestions. The pamphlets had been printed in a secret place in the country and now were ready for distribution.

Elsie marveled at the high spirits of the young people as they planned this enterprise. She knew the risks they would be taking and the severe punishment they would face if they were caught. She glanced around her at the walls of log, packed with what looked like a mortar of mud. The floor was uneven and of hard earth with huge boulders showing in the places where they could not be removed.

The table was battered and of the plainest type. And the lantern providing the only light in the room smoked in an annoying manner. But the faces of Feodor, Olga, and the others gathered at the table were eager; and it was plain that the cause they represented was more important to them than their mean surroundings, or the dangers they faced.

After a good deal of discussion, the meeting officially ended. The young men and women at the table broke up into clusters of two and three. And Olga used this opportunity to bring Marfa over to meet Elsie.

Marfa gave her a bright smile and offered her hand. Her hand was callous and her handshake like that of a man. The girl also wore a man's black trousers tucked in peasant's rough shoes. She said, "So you think I may be of some service to you?"

"It would be kind of you to hear my story," Elsie said.

"Tell her all about it," Olga said. "I have some further things to settle with Feodor and his comrades." And she moved over to join Feodor and the several other men.

Marfa stood facing her. "Well?" she said.

When it came to telling her plight in detail, Elsie did not find it all that easy. Somehow she did stumble out the important facts, ending with, "Olga thinks you may be able to help me find my husband."

The girl with the square face eyed her with some cynicism. "Or perhaps this newspaperman, Ralph Manning. Is he your lover?"

"No," she said, blushing furiously and grateful that the dim light would not reveal her embarrassment. "No! He is my good friend."

Marfa shrugged. "I am not narrow-minded. None of us young revolutionaries are! Does it matter if friends sleep with one another as long as they remain friends?"

She did not feel equal to the question. She asked instead, "Will you try and help me?"

The solidly built Marfa thought it over. "I have enough risks to take as it is. Rasputin is a bad man to try and best!"

"I know that," she agreed.

"And if Count Alexander is enrolled in the Skoptsi, I do not hold out much hope for him, for this group is the wickedest of the wicked."

"They are said to have a monastery in St. Petersburg," she suggested.

Marfa nodded grimly. "I have a friend who knows where it is. He has seen them in their orgies. He could tell you stories which would curl your hair."

"I love my husband," Elsie said, pleading. "If I find him it may not be too late. I have delayed too long in trying to help him."

Marfa gave her a look of resigned good humor. "You sound like a heroine in a Russian novel. And you are an American. I did not think Americans were so sentimental!"

"I need to find him and make a last try to save him from Rasputin," she said tensely.

"All right," Marfa said. "I'll do what I can. I leave for St. Petersburg on the morning train tomorrow." She started to move away and then turned with a grim smile. "And, countess, you'd better change your style of dress. Borrow something from one of your maids. I travel third class!"

⊸§ Chapter 24 §⊸

THE TRAIN JOURNEY from Moscow to St. Petersburg was
one which Elsie was sure she would never forget. Unlike
her previous traveling across Russia by train, she now
faced the hardships of third class. To journey crowded in
a barren car with hard wooden seats was much different
from being in one's own compartment and sipping tea as
you watched the countryside from the privacy of your
own window.

When she had journeyed in luxury, the day-long trip between the two cities had not been difficult to endure. But
covering the same number of miles on the hard wooden
seats with others crowded all around you was a much different experience. But Marfa had insisted that she travel
this way; it was part of the business of keeping out of
sight of the police. Marfa, as a young revolutionary, had
to keep her identity masked from the authorities. Crowded
in with the other peasants in cattle-car-like conditions, she
was just an uninteresting face among a sea of them.

Marfa had warned Elsie to dress like a peasant; so she
had. A borrowed dress and shawl from Elena, plus rough
stockings and shoes, gave her the appearance of a country
girl. Marfa had supervised scrubbing her face hard and
doing her hair in plain fashion. And as a last touch she
had ground her hands in loose earth to make them seem
weathered and calloused and left a good amount of earth
under what had been carefully manicured fingernails.

She carried her belongings in a shawl as Marfa did.
And under the clever girl's guidance had her money in a
tiny bag hung from a string around her neck and hidden
under coarse underclothing.

The spunky Marfa elbowed her way through the railway
car and found them a seat near the very end of it. She let

Elsie sit next to the window while she endured a very old, deaf woman next to her. The old woman promptly dozed off and was awake little during the twelve-hour journey.

"Put the window up," Marfa said. "It's stifling in here."

Elsie fought with the window and managed to raise the lower sash a few inches before they pulled out of the Moscow Railway Station.

She asked the other girl, "Will it be hot in St. Petersburg?"

"Always hot in summer and cold in winter," Marfa said. "And you'll have to get used to daylight nearly all around the clock."

"I didn't know," she said.

"In winter it's all darkness, in summer all light. But you get used to it after a few nights."

Elsie said, "I only passed through the city without stopping there."

"Then you'll have a lot to see," Marfa said with a grim look on her square face. "I've been a student there for two years. I can show you around."

Elsie looked out the window as they began moving through the countryside. There were clusters of birch trees with slanting green leaves and grassy open spaces with wide rivers flowing through them. Russia had a beauty, but its people knew no peace.

"You can smell the Gulf of Finland in St. Petersburg," Marfa said.

"Do you prefer it to Moscow?"

"It is better for me," Marfa said. "I'm doing well at the college, and the boy I love is a fellow student."

She said, "You originally came from the country."

Marfa showed a smile. "Yes. I'm a moujik. I don't mind that. When I first came to St. Petersburg, I worked in a factory to help get money for my tuition. Now I have enough."

"Do the royal family ever show themselves?" she asked.

"Not lately," Marfa said gloomily. "Rasputin keeps them in retreat in the palace. He is a wily one!"

"He attended my wedding," Elsie said with disdain. "I found him appalling. His vulgarity and drunkenness were worse than anything I could imagine."

"The holy man!" Marfa jeered. "And yet your husband let him enlist him in his cult."

"I know how," she said. "He keeps his victims under drugs until he has full control of them."

"I've heard about it," Marfa agreed. "There are whisperings of his orgies all over St. Petersburg. His name is on everyone's tongue, and none has anything good to say of him."

The train moved swiftly, but the journey seemed endless. Marfa asked her to tell her something about America. And this filled in some long hours for them. The train made several halts and at one place they were able to buy milk and some sugar cakes to eat. Marfa claimed they were better than bread since they gave energy.

Marfa said, "I would like to see your New York."

"Maybe you will some day," Elsie said as they had their lunch.

Marfa glanced at the old, deaf woman who was now awake and munching on some crusts of bread with toothless gums. "I have only a little better chance than that one!"

"You mustn't say that. You are getting an education. You will find a place for yourself one day."

The girl with the brass-colored hair smiled. "Before then there will be the revolution. Not likely I will live through it. I will be in the line of battle."

"You are so sure it will come?"

"It has to," the girl said. "Maybe not this year or next, but soon after that."

She said, "Perhaps change will come without violence."

"Never."

They talked about Marfa's childhood in the country. She came originally from a small village outside of Moscow. Now she had been separated from her family for years. She did not regret this, but enjoyed being on her own.

"When I last went back to my village, my family were almost strangers to me," Marfa said. "I could find nothing to talk about with them."

"So you didn't stay long?"

The girl smiled. "Just long enough to visit my grandfather and receive his blessing. Even he had to ask me my name, but then he has many grandchildren."

Marfa had the healthy peasant ability to drop off to sleep quickly under almost any conditions. And she did so now. Elsie wanted to follow her example, but found the heat kept her awake. The partly opened window did not help ease the accumulating warmth and stench of the many bodies crowded in the railway car.

She thought how strange it was for an American girl to be making this journey in peasant fashion, looking like a poor farm girl. If she ever tried to tell the story to her friends in New York, they would be skeptical and think she was making a lot of it up. But here she was, thousands of miles from her native land, playing the part of someone entirely different from herself.

When she had sat in the richly appointed train compartment with Alex on her way to Moscow, she had never dreamt of a return trip like this. Yet it would be worth it if she were able to salvage the life of her husband. If she could rescue him from Rasputin's clutches, it would be worth any sacrifice.

With luck, she might be able to almost immediately contact Ralph His office assistant had given her the name of his hotel. Between Ralph and Marfa, she should be able to find Alex and reason with him. This was her one hope now. She lapsed into a light sleep with all these thoughts going through her mind.

The train came to a jolting halt and she awoke with a start and stared at Marfa. "Where are we?"

"Where do you think? St. Petersburg!" the good-natured girl laughed. "Be careful they don't trample over you as we get off!"

The advice was well given. There was a general push for the exits, with no manners shown by either men or women Children screamed and whimpered as they were almost drowned by the surge of human flesh. Elsie was aided by Marfa taking a position behind her and giving her as much protection as she could by bracing against those following. As it was, Elsie almost fell as she struggled down the steps to the railway platform.

"You did well for a novice," Marfa said.

"What now?"

"Fresh air and exercise," the big girl said. "We walk to the building where I live. You can share my room with me. My boyfriend can move in with some of the other fellows, although I expect he'll want you to give us an hour or so privacy every day or two." Marfa winked at her.

She walked along beside the sturdy girl and said, "I don't want to be a nuisance! I'll likely soon manage to get a room at the hotel."

"Don't worry about it," Marfa said. "We are all for comradeship and sharing. Why shouldn't we put it into practice?"

"If you look at it that way," Elsie said, feeling better and deciding she liked this girl with her country frankness.

They left the busy railway station for the equally busy streets. St. Petersburg was as bustling as Moscow and hot!

They walked a long distance until they came to a street of grimy, three story houses. There were a few small shops scattered along the narrow street, but it was mostly a district of tenements. They halted before a house that looked shabby and identical to all the others. Its door was open, and the aroma of cabbage soup poured out into the fresh air of the street.

"This is it! Home!" Marfa told her in her cynical way. "Come along."

They trudged up narrow, dark stairways to the third floor, hearing many voices loud and low along the way. Everyone seemed to be having discussions or arguments. When they reached the third landing, Marfa opened the first door they came to; and they entered a small room with an ancient double bed, a dresser, and a chair. On the wall over the dresser was a square mirror suffering badly from distortion and a chipped corner.

On the bed lay a bespectacled, young man with dingy brown hair, a plain, long face, and lots of freckles. He was wearing only trousers, his body was bare to the waist and his feet were also bare. He was reading a battered textbook, and when he saw Marfa enter, he put it aside, let out a wild shout of joy and took her in his arms. He wheeled her around several times, babbling happily about all manner of things, then he kissed her over and over again.

Only after that did he turn to stare at Elsie and ask, "Who is she?"

"She's going to be my roommate," Marfa told him as she flung her sack of clothing into a corner.

"I, Boris, am your roommate," he declared, indicating himself with a finger pointed at his bare, rather hairless chest. "I will have no interlopers."

"You can sleep on the floor if you like," Marfa teased him. "My friend is not fussy."

"And where will you be sleeping?" Boris wanted to know.

"In the bed with Elsie," she said.

Elsie protested. "Please don't be upset, Boris. I'm almost sure I'll be staying somewhere else. I can afford a room of my own."

Boris was staring at her, owl-like. "You aren't bad looking at all! And slender! Let Marfa move out, and we can have a fine time here!"

Marfa shoved him backward onto the bed. "A likely thing! You will behave!"

Boris sat on the end of the bed and declaimed for them, "Did you know that the third and last peasant war in the history of feudal Russia was the war of 1773, led by Emelian Pugachev. This rebellion staggered tsarism and serfdom and showed what Russia was in actual fact. I am a student of history!"

"You are an idiot," Marfa jollied him. "But a likable one. Go out and get us some meat and bread and I will make us all some hot tea and we will sit here and I will tell you who Elsie is and why she has come to be with us!"

"I know," Boris said in a melancholy tone as he slipped on an untidy yellow blouse. "The angels have sent her. She is a blessing from the patriarchs of Holy Russia!"

"Go on, you scoundrel! Some meat!" Marfa said propelling him toward the door.

"One day I will revolt!" Boris declared as he went scrambling down the steps.

Marfa laughed and told her, "You see how it is? We are in love!"

"He seems nice and intelligent."

"A fine scholar, but he also likes to play the fool. It

309

may be his undoing," Marfa said, suddenly more serious. "But he is the one who can show us where the Rasputin orgies go on."

Elsie said, "I should phone the hotel and try and contact Ralph Manning at his hotel."

"There are no phones in this street," Marfa warned her. "So you will have to postpone your call until we have something to eat and some blessed tea! Hot as it is, I need my tea! It always cools me!"

Elsie sat on the bed. "Where is the nearest phone?"

"There is a small hotel a few blocks from here. They have a phone in the lobby. I will take you after we have a rest and I explain to Boris why you are here."

Elsie asked, "Is he also a revolutionary?"

"Of course," Marfa said proudly. "The leader of our cell, just as Feodor is back in Moscow. I would not have a friend who did not believe in the revolution."

Boris returned with food for the three of them. They drank copious amounts of hot tea and oddly enough the heat did not seem so bad. Then Marfa quietly told Boris about the mission which had brought Elsie to St. Petersburg.

Boris was different now, serious and very considerate. He sat beside her on the bed and said, "Of course you are welcome to stay here as long as you like. I can bunk with Josef on the floor below."

Marfa eyed him proudly. "I said you would manage."

The young man frowned. "I'm not sure you were wise in coming to our city, countess."

"Why do you say that?" she asked.

"Rasputin is all powerful here. He controls everything from the tsar down. And his agents are everywhere. If as you suggest, he wants to have you killed, you are in much more danger here than you would be in Moscow."

"I had to come," she said.

"I know how you must feel," the young man said. "And I would like to help. But you must be extremely cautious."

Marfa said, "That is why she should continue playing the role of peasant girl and living here. They won't be looking for you in this guise."

"That's true," Boris agreed.

"But I want to talk with my American newspaper

friend," she pointed out. "And I hope to get to Alex and reason with him."

"One thing at a time," Boris advised. "Marfa will find a place where you can phone your American friend. And later I will take you to the house where the Flagellants have their revels!"

Elsie said, "I have been told it is in the Skoptsi cult that my late brother-in-law enlisted. And that is the group Rasputin wants Alex to join."

Boris explained, "The Flagellants are the novice order of the Skoptsi cult. I do not know where the Skoptsi level has its monastery. But I know about them. The leader is a fat monk named Litvinov."

"He tried to kill me in London," Elsie said. "My husband saved me."

"Litvinov has his headquarters here," the history student went on. "And most, if not all, of the high-level Skoptsi are gross, fat men like Litvinov. And they all follow Rasputin's bidding."

"If the holy monk requests a murder," Marfa said with bitterness, "a murder is done. They are his personal guards and servants, dedicated to evil!"

"When can we go to this place where the Flagellants gather?" she asked.

"We can try getting in there tonight," Boris said, his youthful face concerned. "If your husband is mixed up with that crowd, the sooner you get him away from them, the better your hopes of his giving them up."

She and Marfa went out and walked the few blocks to the hotel where she was able to phone the distant luxury hotel where Ralph was registered.

She got no further than the desk clerk. He told her very politely, "Mr. Manning has a suite here, but he presently on a tour of the countryside."

This was bad news. She drew in her breath and then asked, "When will he return?"

"I am not sure," the desk clerk said. "I believe within two or three days. Is there any message?"

She was afraid to leave her name since in St. Petersburg Rasputin was said to have agents placed everywhere. The innocent-sounding clerk might actually be one of those agents.

She said, "I will call again." And she hung up.

Rejoining Marfa, she told her the disappointing news. The sturdy girl with the brass-colored hair said, "Well, maybe it will turn out all right. We can try to locate your husband tonight."

"Yes. It might be easier if I know where he is before I see Ralph," she agreed.

"We'll go back to the house and wait until it is later," Marfa said. "It won't be dark, but the tempo of the city will quiet. It is then the orgies begin."

Boris was reading his history book again. He put it down and listened to what had happened. He sighed. "Too bad. But at least you know he will return in a day or two. You haven't missed him completely."

"No," she said. "What time do we leave?"

"In about an hour," Boris said. "I found a way into the brick house they use by accident. There is a wooden building built tight against it. A friend of mine lives in a room at the top. You can go out through a skylight and cross to the other roof."

Marfa said, "There's no danger. I've been there with him. You just step from one flat roof to the other."

Boris said, "That's it. Now there is a trapdoor on the roof of the house used by the Flagellants. You open it and get down to the upper level of the house. There is a balcony overlooking a kind of big ballroom on the ground floor. That is where they gather to pay tribute to Satan."

"They do their feasting and drinking in another room somewhere down there," Marfa explained. "Then they enter this large room for their rituals."

"We've never ventured further than the balcony," Boris said. "And we crouch low there, so we won't be seen. The one time we were there, we only stayed about five minutes."

Marfa grimaced. "That was long enough."

Boris gazed at Elsie solemnly from behind his glasses. "What Marfa means is that it can be sickening. And it may be especially bad for you if your husband is among them down there."

"Do you think you can stand it?" the sturdy peasant girl asked her.

"I must," she said with grim determination. "At least

once I see what goes on, I'll know what I'm fighting against."

"Part of it," Boris said. "We'll have to be careful getting in there, and we hadn't better stay too long. Someone could come up to the gallery and then we'd be in real trouble."

"I'll do whatever you say," Elsie promised. "You are taking this chance for me."

"It will be just a little trickier with three than with two," Marfa worried. "The worst time is really getting in and out of the building. Once you're crouched down in the gallery watching them you feel fairly safe."

"They're all taking drugs," Boris said. "That helps. They don't pay much attention to anything but the ritual."

She worried, "I don't want you two to get into trouble on my account. I could wait until Ralph gets back and let him take me there. You could give him the directions."

"We were there before just out of morbid curiosity," Marfa said.

"She's right," Boris agreed. "So there's no reason we shouldn't try it again when we have a good reason."

"I'm terribly grateful," she said.

Boris stood up. "Don't thank us until we've managed it successfully. Let's get on our way."

It was now close to eleven at night, and the sky was still bright in an iridescent sort of way. Elsie found it hard to realize it was close to midnight. The three of them quickly made their way along a series of fairly empty streets. The respectable people were at home and in bed.

Soon they were in a different part of the city with better residential buildings. Boris halted and indicated a square, red brick building on the corner ahead. The building was on the right corner and had all its windows shuttered. It had an almost evil look about it.

"That's where they are," he said. "The building above is the one we use to get to it."

"Do we have to use your friend's room to reach the skylight?" Elsie worried. "What if he isn't home?"

"It doesn't matter," Boris said. "The skylight is in the hallway. A ladder goes up to it. And it's the same in the Flagellants' building, you use a plain ladder to get down and then out again."

Elsie asked no more questions as she crossed the cobblestoned street. She was trembling but trying hard to control it. She saw Boris give her a troubled glance and then look significantly at his girl friend.

Marfa, in turn, eyed her uneasily and said, "You're sure you can see this through?"

"Yes," she said, battling the tremor in her voice.

"There's no turning back once we get on that roof," Boris warned her.

"I know," she said.

They entered the wooden building and climbed the stairs. When they reached the upper floor they came to the ladder leading to the skylight, just as Boris had described it. He said, "I'll go first. Then you, countess. And Marfa will come after you in case you lose your balance."

She managed to get to the rooftop without a mishap. Then Boris gave them a sign to step lightly, and they crossed from one tar and gravel flat roof to the other. The lanky student was almost comically cautious in lifting up the other skylight. Then he vanished down the ladder. Her heart in her mouth, Elsie followed him. She was so nervous she had a hard time holding on to the ladder. Marfa came down after her.

They stood in the shadows with the gallery and its low railing just to the left of them and stretching the length of the house. Boris whispered to her, "You go first, so you can get closer to them. That way you'll have a better chance to spot your husband if he's there."

They advanced stealthily with Elsie in the lead. At a signal from Boris, who was third in line, she crouched down so that the railing hid her. She stretched out on the floor and peered into the empty room below as did Marfa and Boris.

The rituals had not yet started. They heard what seemed like organ music from some distant room. Then suddenly a fat man in a black monk's robe came waddling across the room carrying lighted black tapers in silver candlesticks. He placed these on shelves at various places in the room. The lamps that had previously given all the light were approached by the fat man, and he turned all of them low so that the entire effect was one of soft, subdued amber.

314

Elsie watched him and could not be sure whether it was the villainous Litvinov or one of his brothers in the cult. The cowl he wore almost entirely hid his face. His task completed, he waddled out of sight. Then the organ music ended and from the same area could be heard the laughing voices of men and women.

Marfa whispered to her, "I think they are going to start now. Last time we were here, they had already gathered. It was some sight!"

Boris plucked the girl's ample arm and made a gesture for her to be silent.

Elsie was aware of an odor which seemed like incense but not any that she recognized. And she wondered if this was the odor of the drug used by the cultists.

The voices grew louder, and she became more tense. Now men and women in pure white robes came strolling into the big room. She searched the group to try and see if Alex was somewhere among the thirty or so who had formed a loose sort of circle.

She could see no sign of him, and in a way this gave her relief. She badly wanted to find him, but not in this eerie place in this strange company. A moment later her relief was replaced by misgivings. Another group of about six came in to join the circle, and Alex was the first of these to enter with an exotic-looking auburn-haired girl on his arm.

Alex had eyes for no one but the girl. And she seemed as much involved with him. They talked to each other as one of the group moved to the center of the ring. Alex looked thinner and more haggard than when she had last seen him.

Someone put out the lamps and now the room was lighted only by the soft glow of the candles the fat monk had set out. The strange, spicy odor was stronger than ever, filling the air and making Elsie feel dizzy. She looked to see if her companions were reacting to the incense in the same way, but it was now too dark to see them clearly.

The group below began to chant some strange, toneless hymn, which Elsie thought must be directed to Satan. Then they began to revolve slowly about the room as they chanted. At first, the movement was slow and reverent.

315

But gradually their chanting grew louder, and they moved more swiftly.

Marfa excitedly touched her on the arm. "Watch!"

She was fascinated. The dancers moved in a kind of wild abandon now, circling one way and then the other. Suddenly one of the women ran out to the middle of the room and stripped off her robe. She stood there lithe and naked, reveling in her nudity, lifting her arms and moving her hands toward her breasts in an inviting gesture.

There was a loud cry from one of the men, and he threw his robe off, went to the naked girl, and embraced her. Then he lifted her in his arms and they disappeared in the shadows at the side of the room.

It was like a signal for the others. One by one, young women disrobed and stepped naked into the middle of the diminishing circle. Each time a man would also disrobe and join her.

Elsie gave a small moan as she saw the auburn-haired girl flaunt her nude body and a nude Alex go quickly to her and lead her to a spot nearby where their bodies writhed together in a sexual ecstacy.

And it did not end with each having individual partners. They began to exchange and move from one to the other. The room was filled with a frenzy of nude men and women in a chain of sexual interludes, which would eventually find them all linked at some point in the orgy. Moaning, blasphemies, and shrill, passionate cries filled the air!

ఆం Chapter 25 ఆం

ELSIE WAS TERRIFIED she might faint! She had never
known such a carnal experience! Once she had been
shown a special edition of an erotically illustrated *Dante's
Inferno*, and this was all she could think of now! The sexual fantasy she was witnessing grew more intense each
moment! No longer were the nude men and women content with the gratifying of their ordinary desires.

It seemed the drugged participants of the orgy were insatiable. Then she caught a glimpse of the enraptured
face of Alex as he raised up from between the open thighs
of the beautiful auburn-haired girl who had been almost
his constant companion from the start!

Her horror-stricken eyes now had actual proof of what
Rasputin was offering her titled husband and how far in
the morass of moral degeneracy Alex had descended under
the tutelage of the mad monk and his adherents. The
thought that religion should be so twisted as to end up in
rituals like this was almost beyond her comprehension.
And Boris had said this was only the lowest level of the
cult! What went on beyond this?

Her absorption with the writhing bodies below was so
great that for a moment she did not hear the movement to
her left. It was an angry hissing sound from the shadows
over there which quickly alerted her, and she glanced up
from her stretched out position on the floor to find herself
gazing up into the double-chinned evil face of Litvinov!

"Danger!" she cried out.

Her cry let Marfa and Boris know what had happened,
and they jumped up and scrambled toward the ladder that
led to the skylight. She was now also on her feet and following, aware that Litvinov was on her heels. She could
only hope that he was not agile enough to catch her.

Boris had already managed the ladder and opened the skylight. He was bending through and dragging up the sturdy Marfa, who had reached the upper section of the ladder. Elsie was halfway up the ladder, and he was bending as far down as he could to grasp her.

"Faster!" he cried.

"Can't!" she sobbed.

And as she spoke, she felt the hands of the villainous Litvinov clutch her and drag her back. He roughly caught her so that she lost her balance and fell backward onto the floor by him. Her head hit the wall and she knew it was over. There was to be no escape. She blacked out!

When she came to, she found herself trussed in a chair in a dark dungeon of a room. In the distance, she could hear water dripping. There was a small table with a lighted candle on it and another chair in the place. Otherwise, it was empty. The walls were of stone and looked to be of the thickness of a fortress, and the ceiling above her constructed of wooden planks and sturdy beams. The floor was packed earth. She was obviously deep in some cellar room of the sinister red brick house.

Her head ached, and there was a soreness at the back of her neck as she turned to take in her surroundings. She gradually recalled all that had happened leading to her being a prisoner here. She had been watching the Flagellants' orgy when Litvinov had suddenly discovered the presence of her and her two companions.

Boris and Marfa had managed to escape, but she had been captured by the evil cultist and was now a prisoner. She knew that they wanted to kill her and wondered why they had not done so right away. There was a door in the wall almost directly across from her, and this seemed to be the only exit or entrance in the underground room.

The air was stale, the room damp. She eyed the flame of the candle and wished she might get nearer to it to benefit from its heat. Her mind went back to the orgy, and anger against Alex rose within her. Why had he deserted her to return to this sordid life? And he could be sure that Rasputin had a plan and would demand a price of him for catering to his lusts.

Only now that she had been a witness to her husband in

his joining in the Satanic rites did she feel the hopelessness of it all. If he had gone so far with this group, then he was lost to her. As dead to the normal world as his murdered brother, Basil. He had chosen to follow in Basil's footsteps and as a result would be sent on some dangerous mission like his brother in which he would likely meet his death.

She could not save him because he did not want to be saved. She must now accept this. If she managed to escape, she would seek out Ralph and have him help her get back home. She would say good-by to Olga and the courageous old Count Andre, whom she had come to regard as her own family. But then it would be good-by to Russia!

But that might never happen except in her mind. It was all too likely that Litvinov, or some of the other cultists, would murder her. She was a threat to them in trying to take Alex out of the cult. He was valuable to them as a member of the aristocracy.

Alex would likely never know that she had witnessed the orgy, or that she had been taken captive. They would murder her and it might be only later, when he tried to reach her, that he would find out she had been slaughtered. Surely he would turn against the evil group then. Did she have to sacrifice her life to save him? It began to seem so.

She was grateful that Boris and Marfa had managed to escape. She had become fond of them both in the short time she'd known them. And they had taken great risk to try and help her.

Her reverie was interrupted by the sound of footsteps coming down stairs, and then a key creaked in a lock and the single door of the room swung open. Behind it was revealed a monk in a black robe and cowl. The cowl was brought forward in such a way as to hide the monk's face except for its general round contour. She could not tell whether it was Litvinov or someone else in the group.

He carried a tray with bread and a glass of water on it in one hand. With the other, he closed the door behind him. Then he crossed the room in the waddling movement of the very fat and placed the tray on the table.

In a low, hissing voice he said, "I have food and drink for you. I will release one of your hands if you promise to cause no trouble."

"I will behave," she said grimly. "I'm very thirsty, and my head aches."

The fat monk made no reply to this but undid her right hand. She quickly reached out and thirstily drank some of the tepid water and felt better. Her mouth and throat had been parched.

The monk stood a distance away, his side to her so she would have more difficulty seeing who he was. In the odd, hissing voice, he said, "You spied on our novices! You brought this on yourself!"

She said, "If what I did was wrong, what was happening down there was much worse!"

"By your standards," the man said. "They were dedicating themselves to our cause."

"You must let me go!" she challenged him. "My friends will report you to the police."

The monk gave an evil chuckle. "That will do them no good. Rasputin sees to our protection. The complaint will only gather dust on a desk somewhere. No action will be taken!"

"I can't believe that!"

"It is true!"

She felt new despair as she realized this was all too likely. She decided to try another attack. She said, "You have my husband here. He may enjoy your harem delights, but if he learns that you have taken me prisoner, he will soon cause you to regret it."

"Count Alexander Martynov is a dedicated member, although he has not yet undergone The Baptism by Fire. And he will not be informed that you are our prisoner."

"He will know if you kill me!" she promised.

The hissing voice directed at the wall said, "But we will not kill you! You will have an unfortunate boating accident. You will be drowned, and no one will be to blame!"

"No!" she said, panic surging up in her. She knew they were complete in their villainy. She might have guessed they would have some diabolical plan.

"It is your own fault," the soft voice of the unknown monk said. "You came between us and Count Alexander, just as the wife of his brother attempted to hinder us. And so she had to die!"

320

"So she wasn't a suicide!" Elsie said triumphantly. "Timofei told me that."

"Timofei cannot help you," the voice hissed on. "He is long dead. You may consider yourself proud to die for the Skoptsi. Your husband will make a notable priest! Already his name has enlisted new members to the order!"

"I would prefer to rescue him from your filthy order," she said. "I say you are all madmen!"

"We live in a world of madness," the hissing voice said. "We have our women priestesses as well, but you would never bow to the divine will. So we did not consider you!"

"If you're referring to Rasputin, I certainly would not do his bidding!"

"Rasputin is immortal. He will live forever," the hissing voice informed her.

She sank back in the chair, exhausted and ill. In a low voice, she asked, "What can I do to have you change toward me? To have you free me? Do you wish me to renounce my husband? I will if he stands before me and tells me he honestly wants to be one of you rather than return to me."

The fat monk stood there carefully concealing his face. "That would not be a suitable test. He might weaken before your beauty. We cannot risk that."

"You are afraid!" she challenged.

"We prefer to win in these matters," the fat monk said. "So it would be nonsense to take needless risks. And it might be painful to you if your husband turned his back on you as a result of the test."

She said, "So you're offering me a painless drowning. So considerate of you!"

"Your welfare or wishes do not enter into it," the fat monk said as he came waddling around to tie her right hand again.

"How long do I have?"

"We will be removing you within the hour," he said.

"And then?"

"You will be taken a distance from here. You will be placed in a pleasure boat and a simulated accident staged before the early morning."

"You have it all carefully planned," she said bitterly. "I die before dawn."

"Except that we have no actual dawn. It is light all the night. Sometime within the next few days, your bloated body will rise to the surface of the river. There will be a story in the newspaper. Sorrow will be expressed. And Count Alexander will be more ready to dedicate himself to our order since his last link with the lay world has been severed."

He picked up the tray and went to the door, opened it, and went out. She heard the key turn in the lock again and his retreating footsteps as he went up the stairs. She might have known they would be thorough. This was group planning, with every detail checked and no room for error.

No doubt they would also have some story concocted of why she had gone boating. It was a terrifying thought, but maybe they had captured Boris and Marfa after all and they would be supposedly drowned with her—a happy boating party that turned into a tragedy.

She could visualize being taken out in a craft of some kind and held a prisoner under the water until she drowned. Then they would remove her bonds and toss her body in the water along with an overturned boat and perhaps the body of one or more companions. Ralph would be suspicious, but he would not be able to prove anything.

At least she would not have long to wait! He had said within the hour! That was their only generosity. She did not know that the monk who had brought her the tray was Litvinov. She doubted it, since he had worked at keeping his face concealed from her. And there had been that hissing quality about his voice, which she did not indentify with Litvinov.

She thought about her aunt and uncle in New York. The sorrow her death would bring to them and the misgivings and guilt they would feel for having allowed her to make the marriage. But she had been insistent even in the face of Olga's grim efforts to halt her from marrying Alex. In her ignorance, she had thought Olga and Alex guilty of an incestuous relationship. How wrong that had been!

Olga had turned out to be her staunch friend, and Alex had almost cravenly deserted her. Yet she still knew that deep in her heart she felt love for him. Their marriage had been a romantic dream on her part, and she was loath to let it pass. She knew real pain for his predicament now and cursed the day he and his late brother had ever discovered the secret society led by Rasputin.

Now her thoughts turned to Ralph and that in this case she had found true love, with deep feeling on both sides. But her meeting with him on the *Lusitania* had come too late. By the time Ralph had confessed his love for her, she had been Alex's wife. And she couldn't believe then that she'd made a mistake.

When she started to think that her marriage might collapse, she had been certain Sophie and Ralph were having an affair. But she was wrong, because there was no affair.

She had not seen Ralph since before Sophie and Bogrov had been arrested and presumably sent to Siberia. She and Ralph would have so much to talk about. But that was the most futile fantasy of all. She was going to die. She would never see Ralph again. There was no hope.

The candle on the table burned lower, and she feared to think of being there in darkness when it had burned out. The place might be infested with rats, and she was helpless to protect herself. The damp was eating into her bones, and her head was aching badly again.

She closed her eyes and tried to picture that party in New York when the music had been lovely, the night filled with gaiety, and she had lost her heel. This had been the start—when Alex had rescued it for her and taken her over for the rest of the evening. But on that night the grimness of Russia had shadowed the occasion; the news of his uncle's assassination had caused him to leave the party early.

She heard footsteps on the stairs again, coming down, and she judged more than one person was out there. In the next moment the door swung open, and Litvinov appeared with two women in black robes beside him. They wore black shawls over their heads, and their faces were pale with sunken eyes burning with a fanatical light. She judged they might once have been beauties, but they were now haggard looking.

Litvinov said, "We are about to take a journey." He showed a nasty smile on his double-chinned face.

She said, "Your man told me about it."

Litvinov said, "We wanted to prepare you. And you are really rather fortunate. Drowning is not the worst of deaths."

She said, "You will be arrested and executed for this. I am still an American citizen, and I have friends in the embassy with power."

"The question of your citizenship is in question since you are the wife of a Russian nobleman," Litvinov said. "But no one at the embassy can complain of a boating accident in any case."

"They will know better," she warned him.

The fat man gave the two women in black some sharp orders, and they at once came and untied her and lifted her from the chair. But they each kept an iron grip on her arms. She was a prisoner still, held between them.

"Fix on her cape and shawl," Litvinov said. One of the women did this while the other woman held on to her.

"Both myself and each of these good sisters are equipped with sharp knives that we can use in an instant. Will you please keep this in mind," the fat man said with a gloating expression on his egg-shaped face.

"I know your ability with a knife," she said grimly. "I have not forgot London."

"Your husband stupidly rescued you then," Litvinov said. "But he is not here now."

"I'm too well aware of that," she said as the two silent women gripped her firmly between them.

Litvinov went on, "In case anyone on the street at this early morning hour is watching, they will see myself and three ladies sedately entering a carriage. A closed carriage, may I add. And because it is a well-known fact that our cult has a sisterhood, there will not be any surprise noted."

"I can call out," she told him.

"The ladies have orders to place a knife between your ribs the instant you do," the fat man said. "So you will be wise to conduct yourself in a dignified fashion. I happen to be a person who dislikes scenes."

"I appreciate your sensitivity," she said grimly. "It is too bad you are also a murderer."

He smiled coldly. "We are now ready to proceed," he said. "And remember, one sound from you, and it is all over."

She made no reply. But in her mind she decided to wait for what might be the most propitious moment and then risk making a break for it. Perhaps it would come at the other end of their journey. She would pretend to submit to them until she had lulled them into at least a kind of security. Then she would fight hard!

Litvinov lead the way up the narrow, dark stairs; then there was another flight shorter than the first before they came out in a hallway. The two women in black held her securely as they moved toward a side door.

Litvinov opened the door, and the women propelled her outside and down several steps to the brick sidewalk. There was a carriage waiting with its door open and one of the women entered it first, dragging Elsie after her with the second woman following.

In the carriage they sat on either side of her, still keeping her in their steely grip. Litvinov lumbered into the carriage and sat opposite them, his huge body almost filling the entire seat. The driver shut the door and sprang up on the front seat and urged the horses on.

As the carriage began to roll Litvinov said, "If you had taken warning in London, you would not find yourself in this plight now. You should have left the count and returned to America."

She made no reply, but tried to see which direction they were taking. She debated their chances of keeping a firm hold on her if she suddenly jumped up and hurled open one of the carriage doors. Would the moment of shock give her time to escape? She doubted it. There was the ponderous Litvinov to consider. He might somehow bar her way.

The streets were empty because it was just before dawn. But it was as light as day. Yet people were used to this constant daylight of summer and kept their usual hours. It was still a time when most were sleeping.

The carriage rounded a corner and began going up a narrow hilly street. Suddenly, without any warning, a crowd of silent people surged out from the alleys on either side of the street and came toward the carriage. They carried clubs and threw stones and several of them were armed.

Litvinov quickly took note of the situation and opened

the small slot window behind him to scream at the driver, "Lash the horses! Get us out of here! Quickly!"

The fat man did not have time to turn around again before the mob was on the carriage. There was no question of the driver lashing the horses, for he was quickly pulled down from the driver's seat, the horses were unharnessed and the surging mob grasped the carriage by the wheels and turned it on its side.

The women in black screamed out in shrill fear and released Elsie. She braced herself to try and keep from falling to the side with the carriage. A shocked Litvinov grunted and rolled his eyes at her in surprise before his fat hands were upraised and he fell heavily with the carriage. He struck his head and blood spurted from it. He lay still.

At the same moment, Boris opened the carriage door on the upper side and pointed a tiny pistol at the two hysterical women in black. He warned them, "Try to stop her and you die!"

He covered the two women cult members while Marfa came and helped Elsie crawl up out of the carriage.

Marfa's square face showed a smile of triumph. "You knew we would rescue you!"

Elsie hadn't known anything of the sort. She hadn't even thought of it. As she clambered off the carriage, she saw Boris deliberately point the pistol at Litvinov and fire it three times. Then he jumped down and joined her and Marfa.

The crowd was already dispersing when someone shouted, "Police!"

Boris quickly took her by the arm. "Come!" he said grimly.

The street, which had a few short minutes before been empty, was so once again except for the overturned carriage, the horses floundering around in their harness, the driver stretched out by the carriage, and the two women in black still screaming and trying to get out of the toppled vehicle.

Boris led the way down an alley at a fast pace with Elsie and Marfa keeping up with them. They continued on through a maze of alleys, climbing over occasional fences, venturing out into empty streets briefly and then using the alleys for escape again. At last Elsie recognized they were in the street where they had a room in the battered three-story tenement.

They rushed into the house and up the stairs to the room and shut the door behind them. Marfa sat down on the bed with Elsie, breathless, sitting beside her. Boris collapsed into a chair. And the only thing which struck her was that in all the violence, he had managed to keep on his glasses.

Marfa got back her breath and gave her a glowing look. "At least we got to you in time!"

"You were wonderful!" Elsie told the two.

"We couldn't have done it alone," Boris said. "You were rescued by the members of a half-dozen cells. It was a case of student revolutionaries to the rescue."

"What about the gun?" Marfa asked him anxiously.

He produced it from under his blouse. "You didn't think I'd leave it behind?"

Elsie asked him, "What about Litvinov?"

"Three bullets in his head," Boris said. "Unless he's a snake, he's dead."

"He was horrible," she said with a shudder. "They were going to drown me and make it seem an accident. Those two women were members of the cult."

"I guessed that, but I let them live," Boris said. "They are bad enough off just being linked with the Skoptsi."

Elsie said, "Litvinov bragged that the police would take no action in saving me, that Rasputn controlled them."

"I don't doubt it," Marfa said. She turned to Boris. "Do you think they will guess it was the students who saved Elsie?"

"They'll be suspicious of us along with others," Boris said. "I'm afraid it won't be safe for her to stay with us any longer."

Elsie stood up. "I'll leave now. I don't want to get you two in any more trouble."

"We thrive on it!" Marfa said. "There's plenty of time. Sit down while we think this out."

"The police act slow, and they may never link us with what happened," Boris said.

She said, "I have money. They didn't search me or try to take it. I suppose they wanted it found on me in case they set up the false accident."

Marfa said, "I think one thing you should do now is buy some clothes. Get a wardrobe suitable to your station in life. They'll still be looking for you in peasant garb."

"Countess, how many of them know you by sight?" Boris asked.

"I have no idea," she said. "I'm sure there is at least one other of the monks who knows me well. He came and talked with me, but he wouldn't allow me to see his face. He had a strange hissing voice and was fat like Litvinov!"

"They all are fat," Boris said with disgust. "At least the top members of the cult are."

Marfa said, "As soon as the stores are open, I'll go and buy some things for you."

"Thank you," she said.

Boris said, "You should also try the hotel again. If Elsie's American friend is there, I'd say it was time she joined him."

"I agree," Marfa said. She gave Elsie a wise look. "How do you feel about saving your husband now? I mean after what you saw."

She gave the sturdy peasant girl a grim look of distaste. "I don't know that it will be possible. What I saw horrified and disgusted me."

"Those are almost nightly revels," Boris warned her. "So it is easy to see that your husband is caught up in a web of evil."

Marfa shrugged. "I'm not narrow-minded. But how can they go on in that way? No privacy, no respect, just a return to the lowest bestiality!"

"The drugs account for a lot of it," Elsie worried. "But I know Alex is addicted. He was weak when Litvinov approached him in London. I should have known then that I couldn't hold him."

"The best thing you can do is return to America and divorce him," Boris said.

"I made up my mind to that when I was a prisoner in that cellar," she agreed. "But there are some things I must do first. Some people I must see. I cannot leave Russia without saying good-by to Olga and her Uncle Andre."

Marfa gave her a sympathetic look. "You really loved your count, didn't you? It is too bad."

"At least you let me see part of what is going on," she said. "I hesitate to think what else they do."

Boris said, "Better not to think about it."

In mid-morning Marfa went out to buy Elsie some clothes. And the peasant girl also promised to try and reach Ralph on the phone.

Boris went out to a history class at the university, and she waited alone in the room impatiently. It was almost noon when Marfa burst in with a broad smile on her face, her arms full of parcels and told her, "Your American journalist is back in St. Petersburg. You must dress quickly and make yourself attractive for him. He is coming here to pick you up and take you to his hotel!"

·⁙ Chapter 26 ⁙·

THERE WAS ONLY a pan of cold water for her to wash with. It was not enough, and she felt filthy after her experiences as a prisoner in the cellar. Marfa produced some precious hoarded perfume and face powder for her. She changed into fresh underclothing and put on the attractive print dress Marfa had selected.

Marfa eyed her with pride. "There! Now you look more like a countess should."

She turned away from the distorted mirror with the chipped corner and said, "I never want to be called a countess again."

"It is your proper title."

"I have never felt so," she said. "And now less than ever. It reminds me of Alex, and I don't want to think about him."

Marfa said, "You will be safe at the hotel."

"What about you and Boris?"

"Don't worry about us," the peasant girl said. "We have got through some scrapes before."

"Did you hear anything about the accident?"

"Yes," Marfa said happily. "They found Litvinov dead. The two women members of the cult weren't able to give any descriptions, and the driver remembered nothing. The word is that Rasputin is fuming!"

"I'm sure Litvinov was one of his chief henchmen," she agreed.

Marfa had been standing watching the street from the window. And now she exclaimed, "He is here! I will see you down."

Despite her desire to see and talk with Ralph, she was loath to leave the good-natured girl. She said, "You know the phone number at the hotel."

"Yes," Marfa said as they went out to the stairs.

"If there is any trouble, get in touch with me. There will be something I can do to help," she insisted.

"There will be no trouble," Marfa said as they descended the dark narrow stairs. "You are the one in danger. Stay close to your American."

"I will," she promised. "And I won't leave St. Petersburg without seeing you. I want to talk to both you and Boris before I go. We shall keep in touch when I return to America. I shall never forget you saved my life."

"Nothing!"

"It was a great deal!" Elsie said. "And I won't forget."

They reached the front steps of the house, and Ralph was waiting there in a brown, gabardine suit, wearing no hat. He took her in his arms without a word and held her close, as Marfa watched with delighted eyes.

"So long since we parted," he said.

She told him, "This is Marfa. She and Boris saved my life."

"We talked on the phone," Ralph said. "What can I say to properly tell you how grateful I am?"

"Nothing need be said. Get on your way. Carriages don't come to this door every day. Let us not attract undue attention. And keep Elsie close to you; she could still be in grave danger," Marfa said in a rush of words. She kissed Elsie and hurried inside.

"She and the young male student she lives with were fabulous," she told Ralph after they were in the carriage and on the way to the hotel. "I want to see them again and later do something for them."

Ralph kept staring at her. "To know you're alive and safe."

"I came here to find you, and you were away from the city."

"Yes, on assignment. In fact, I've been working with a fellow from the Military Intelligence in London, trying to learn some solid facts about the state of the Russian army. We made a tour of the military installations together."

"I knew something was keeping you away," she said.

"He is staying at the hotel," Ralph said. "You will meet

him. Interesting chap. But I want to know what has been going on in Moscow and why you are here."

"So much," she sighed, leaning back against the seat as the carriage slowly rolled on through the heavy traffic of the noonday St. Petersburg streets.

"Let me hear."

"Alex left me again," she said. "He's here now with the Flagellants' group led by Rasputin."

"How can he be such a weak fool?" the young journalist asked.

"I saw one of their gatherings," she said. "Alex is lost in lust. I'm going to leave him. I know there is no hope."

Ralph took her hand in his. "You're sure?"

"Yes."

"There are some things I will tell you later," he promised.

She said, "And you have not heard about Sophie."

His eyebrows raised. "What about her?"

She told him, finishing by saying, "Count Andre's lawyer said they were being sent to Siberia, and he would try and learn where the prison is located."

Ralph showed distress. "Poor Sophie!"

"One can't help feeling sorry for her. She was so desperate to escape Russia."

"And now she is lost deeper in the Russian wilderness than ever," he said. "Sophie and Bogrov! I didn't suspect them."

"Madame Bogrov soon found out, and she knew that Jacob was one of a group plotting to murder the royal family."

He said, "We really know so little about people."

She went on to tell him about Olga and Feodor and her experiences in getting to St. Petersburg and also about being a prisoner in the cellar of the grim, red brick house.

They reached the hotel and went directly up to the large suite he'd engaged. He told her, "There are three bedrooms. You can have your pick."

She smiled ruefully. "My main wish now is for a bath and after that a good meal and some champagne."

He clapped his hands in the manner of a potentate summoning servants. Laughing, he said, "It is all arranged! You have your bath, while I order us a fine meal. I'm taking the day and evening off, although I did promise to meet Brown, the man from London, for cocktails before dinner. But you can join us."

"Oh, Ralph, it's so good to have you back again," she said and impulsively threw her arms around him and kissed him.

The kiss was returned with feeling. And in a solemn voice, he said, "There must be no partings from now on."

She smiled at him, her arms still around his neck. "You say that, you newspaperman! But I know better!"

Ralph smiled, "We're not as bad as people think."

She went into the nearest of the luxurious bedrooms and left her things. The fixtures in the bathroom were of late design and the bathtub long and deep. Elsie luxuriated in it. She lay back blissfully in the sudsy, warm water, and lost all thought of anything but the sheer pleasure of the moment.

Ralph roused her from her relaxed enjoyment by telling her, "Hurry and put on a dressing gown and get out here. If you don't this meal will be ruined."

She quickly stepped out of the tub, toweled herself in haste and donned the silken dressing gown Marfa had bought her. She pushed back her hair and tied a ribbon to keep it in place. And she thought the gown had a slinky sexiness, which reflected Marfa's taste.

When she entered the living room of the suite Ralph stared at her in wonder. "You've never seemed so beautiful!"

Elsie laughed. "Give Marfa the credit. She chose the dressing gown for me."

"Hurry, the food will be cold." He pulled out her chair and then lifted the top off the silver chafing dish to reveal two plump partridges. He lifted the champagne bottle. "I also have the champagne."

They enjoyed the meal and washed it down with the huge bottle of bubbling wine. Then they sat holding each other's hands at the table in the manner of lovers. And it all at once struck her that this was right, that they belonged together and should be lovers. A strong desire filled her, and she felt that she must tell him of her urgent need of him.

People in love and those who are close to each other of-

ten do not need words to express their thoughts. Ralph
knew how she felt.

He knew yet he said nothing. They rose from the table
as if caught up in a spell and made their way toward the
bedroom she had chosen. He pulled down the blinds and
closed the drapes against the afternoon sunlight. And as he
began to remove his jacket and tie, she doffed her dressing
gown and stood before him in rosy nakedness.

She was unashamed and full of the need for his love.
She wanted him to take her in his arms and press his
maleness to her, caress her and become familiar with the
woman of her, pierce her so that they might lose themselves in the ecstasy so long denied.

He came to her and gently picked her up and carried
her to the bed. How long did their frenzy of lovemaking
last? She had no idea. And she did not care. It was not
long enough She wanted to rest in his arms for all the rest
of her life. With him, there had been a perfection of love
she'd never known with Alex, a peace she'd never found
with the handsome Russian.

They rested until Ralph checked his watch and saw
that it was five. Then they both got up, enjoyed a bath,
then dressed for dinner. There was an easy intimacy between them, a new relationship they had never known before. Being with him seemed right.

When they were dressed, it was close to seven. He told
her, "We're meeting Major Brown in the bar. Don't ask
him too many questions. He's here on hush-hush business
and likes to play the role of mystery man."

She said, "Are you sure you wouldn't rather meet him
alone? I may be in the way."

"No," he said. "I'll be delighted to show you off to him,
pretty American girl, whom I'm going to claim for my
own."

She smiled as he took her in his arms again. "You're
sure? I'm not even free yet."

He kissed her. "You will be, no problem there."

The hotel bar was fairly crowded. An orchestra played
on a small platform near the entrance of the ornate room.
And the headwaiter, who knew Ralph, marched them by
the crowded tables to a table near the rear wall, a distance

from the music, where a stout man in a gray suit was smoking a large cigar.

The stout man, who was also bald, rose and greeted them with a smile on his pleasant face. He said, "Well, Manning, where did you locate this charming creature?" He spoke hoarsely with a decidedly British accent.

Ralph said, "She dropped into my life." And he introduced her by her maiden name. "Meet Elsie Cooper of New York and various points in Europe."

"Delighted," the stout Englishman said. "I am also one of those people who have made my home at various points in Europe. May I ask where you last were?"

"Moscow," she said.

"My favorite Russian city," Major Brown observed as he studied the blue smoke he had exhaled from the large cigar. "No intrigue there such as we have here. I tell you this city is a hive of revolutionists. Did you hear what happened this morning?"

Ralph said, "I'm only a newspaperman. Tell me."

"Well," Major Brown said, "I understand a group of rioting students attacked a carriage in one of the downtown streets shortly before dawn. They overturned the carriage, injured the coachman, and one of the students murdered a monk, who'd been a passenger, with three pistol shots. And all this cruel lunacy went on before the eyes of two sisters of the religious order, who were taken from the scene in a state of shock!"

Ralph showed no betraying expression as he inquired of Elsie, "What do you think of that?"

She knew she must be wary. She said, "It sounds like wanton violence."

Major Brown puffed on his cigar. "Indeed it was. Nothing of that sort ever happens in England."

She said, "What sort of religious order was it?"

The stout man said, "Haven't the faintest idea. Russia is full of weird sects. I can't keep track of them."

Ralph, in an attempt to change the subject, said, "Do you hear that orchestra? They are supposed to be playing tunes of Victor Herbert, but they are only barely recognizable."

"Consider yourself fortunate, young man," Major Brown wheezed. "When I was last on duty in India the band playing for our formal mess functions attempted Gilbert and Sullivan. There never was an Indian atrocity to match their performance."

She smiled. "I supposed other people feel the same way when they hear their native music played by our musicians."

Major Brown glared at his cigar. "Without a doubt! I tell you there's nothing like a Chinese band if you are not a music lover. I listened to one a full evening in Shanghai, and for the only time in all my life I wished I was afflicted with faulty hearing."

She laughed pleasantly but found Major Brown kept staring at her, which made her feel nervous. She had the odd sensation that they had met before. Perhaps it was because he was such a fat man and she had lately, understandably, come to have a fear of fat men!

The conversation went on for a while; then Major Brown paid his portion of the check and excused himself on the grounds of having to go to his room and write a long and detailed report, which must be in the mail for England in the morning. He bowed to her and took her hand in his again. She almost drew back from his moist, chubby grasp.

When the fat man had strolled out, Ralph turned to her and said, "What do you think of him?"

"He's strange."

"No argument about that, but immensely clever. All that odd conversation conceals a quick mind."

She gave a tiny shudder. "He kept staring at me in that odd way."

"Admiring true beauty."

"It wasn't that sort of look," she protested. "And he's so grossly fat. And I've come to have a phobia about gross, fat men."

"I don't blame you for that," Ralph said.

She frowned. "And he made a point of telling us about that business this morning and Litvinov being killed."

"He told it as gossip of the day." Ralph smiled. "He didn't connect you with it in any way. Why should he?"

"I suppose you're right," she said. "Where did you meet him?"

Ralph said, "He came to me and presented me with a

proper set of credentials. He's a key man in the British Secret Service."

"You're sure his credentials were valid?"

"Don't worry," he said with a grim smile. "I haven't been a newspaperman all these years for nothing. I at once made a private check with the British Embasssy here. He is working with them and accepted by them. I understand he spent some of his younger years here in Russia and so speaks the language well and knows his way around."

"Why exactly is he here, and what is your business with him?" she asked.

Ralph glanced around to see that there was no one sitting close enough to overhear them. He said, "I think the orchestra is playing loud enough to cover up what we say."

"Don't tell me anything I oughtn't to know," she said.

"I can trust you," he said. "My boss, William Randolph Hearst, is very much worried about the danger of war in Europe. He feels, and probably rightly, that if there is a war it will become a world war and America will be drawn into it."

"Never!" she protested.

"The chances are greater than you think," Ralph said very seriously. "We couldn't let France or England fall to Germany. And the Kaiser has been preparing for a war for a long time. Russia would be on the side of France and England. The big question in London these days is, how strong is the Russian army?"

She said, "So you are trying to find this out for your newspaper, and he is trying to find out for the British government."

"Exactly," the young man said, looking pleased that she had so quickly grasped the idea.

"And what have you found out?"

"Nothing that was a shock to me. The Russian military machine is as badly undermined as everything else in this unhappy country. The army is riddled with graft, their equipment is ancient or second rate, their officers are badly trained, and the ordinary soldiers aren't even fed well."

"So Russia cannot offer anyone strong military support."

337

"That is what we've discovered," he said. "The navy is even more hopeless. If war comes, France and England will find themselves trying to bolster Russia against the Germans rather than the other way around."

"In the meantime, this country could have a revolution," she pointed out.

"You have seen enough to know that," he agreed. "And war might provide the match to bring the flame of revolution to full peak. Russia could collapse politically, as well as militarily. And this would mean that America would almost surely have to come to the aid of England and France."

"I feel every moment that I'd be happier back home," she said.

"I won't feel easy until I see you on your way. When can you leave?"

"Not yet," she said. "I have some things to do."

He looked at her worriedly. "Is it Alex?"

"No," she sighed. "I have lost him. I know it."

He said, "I will make a date for you at the American Embassy in the morning. We have a man there who is a specialist on Russian secret societies. He is an elderly man and very well informed. I told him about Alex and the Skoptsi, and he revealed some shocking things I think you must know."

"Can't you tell me?"

"I don't know everything," he said. "And what I do know, I would rather he tell you. It's not a nice business and since I hope to win you from Alex, I don't want to discuss it with you."

She stared at him. "Is it so bad? You're frightening me."

"It is not anything we know about in America," the young man said. "Things are different here in these older countries. I will let Professor Adamson tell it to you in his own way."

She tried to question him more, but he would not go on with it. They talked of other things. He hoped he might be transferred back to the New York headquarters of the newspaper syndicate for at least a time. And he had cabled over a query as to whether William Randoph Hearst would wish to personally interview him in New York about the Russian military situation. There was a lot too confidential to be sent through the regular channels. If the New York office decided his employer wished to discuss the problem with him, he would be asked to return to the United States almost at once.

They remained in the bar for a while longer and then went for a short stroll. They listened to some native folk music in a small park and then slowly returned to the hotel. In the suite they talked some more and rested in each other's arms. They spent a night of love and peaceful sleep. When she wakened once in the night she turned, reached out and touched his cheek tenderly while he slept.

They enjoyed a leisurely breakfast, and he arranged for her meeting with Professor Adamson at the American Embassy. He was remaining in his suite in the hotel to write reports and take phone calls. And he had a late morning meeting with Major Brown.

She said, "When will I meet you?"

"When you finish at the embassy, have them get you a carriage and come straight back here. If I'm not in the suite, I'll be down at the bar with Brown."

She hesitated. "I'm not sure I wish to meet him again, especially if I'm in an unhappy mood. And I expect what your professor friend will have to tell me will put me in one of those moods."

Ralph said, "All right. You have a key to the suite. If I'm not here, call the desk and have me paged. I will know it is you, excuse myself from Brown, and come up here." He kissed her to seal the agreement.

Downstairs he placed her in a carriage and gave the driver his pay and the address. She found herself being driven through the central section of St. Petersburg again. It was an interesting city, different from Moscow. When they halted before the American Embassy, she felt safer for seeing a giant stars and stripes hanging from over its entrance. But she was struck by the fact that the building was of Italian style rather than Russian.

Inside she was greeted by an elderly clerk and told to take the elevator to the third floor. The elevator operator was elderly. When she reached the office of Professor Adamson, she found the door open and saw a fussy looking little old man seated at a desk poring over some scattered papers. He did not seem to hear or notice her.

She cleared her throat as she stood in the doorway. And when the wizened, gray-haired man glanced up to gaze at her in mild surprise, she said, "Professor Adamson, I'm Countess Martynov."

The little man, a head shorter than she was, rose at once and came cordially toward her. "I was told you were coming, but I declare I'd forgot. I'm trying to break down a particularly tricky code we've picked up from the Bulgarians, and it is giving me a bad time."

"I'm sorry to intrude on your work," she said.

"Not at all," he told her. "The code can wait. We must look after our nationals. Do sit down, and I will close the door as our discussion is to be rather confidential."

She sat down in a comfortable leather chair but feeling far from comfortable, said, with her cheeks burning, "You know why I am here."

"Yes," he said, settling down behind the desk, which overwhelmed him by its size. He sat staring at her, a pigmy-like figure. He seemed embarassed. Glancing toward the windows, he observed, "We have a good view of the city here."

She followed his glance and saw the great baroque buildings of red and yellow or pale green. There were the familiar onion domes and the golden ones. The spires of large cathedrals shone in the sunlight. She said, "It is a lovely city."

"And a sad one," Professor Adamson said. "I understand your husband has come under the spell of Rasputin?"

"Yes."

"He is not alone. So has the tsarina."

She said, "Count Alexander is the second one in his family to become a follower of Rasputin. The first one was his younger brother Basil, and he was murdered in a bombing."

Professor Adamson said, "There is at least one a week.

"I struggled to stop Alex returning to St. Petersburg, but the hold Rasputin exerted on him was too strong. I came here for a final pleading with him. I secretly observed a session held by the Rasputin group, an orgy in which my husband took part. I was so shocked and ashamed, I almost fainted. For a time, I was a prisoner of these people;

but I was rescued by some student friends and found my way to Ralph."

Professor Adamson's wizened face showed sympathy. "This is a difficult task Mr. Manning has entrusted me with. And I ask that as a married woman you not be shocked, as I will speak to you with the frankness of an older man."

She found herself trembling, but she tried to conceal her upset. She said, "Ralph warned me it would not be pleasant. But he said you were best fitted to tell me, that you are the best authority available on these secret societies."

The old man got up and stood by the window. He stared out at the colorful skyline of the city as he began talking. "The Skoptsi are a disgrace and blight on Russia. But Rasputin has made them his people and so at present they are too strong to fight. They are a secret society which began as a religious group that indulged in sexual frenzies to purify themselves. Today the Skoptsi have become both criminal and political. Their plan is through crime and politics to control the world. They have members scattered in every country, but the main headquarters is here in St. Petersburg."

She said, "I think they wanted Alex and his brother because they belonged to a noble family. And they could use their names to bolster their reputation."

"Without a doubt," Professor Adamson said, gazing at her sadly. "There are three levels in the Skoptsi, the Flagellants, whose revels you have witnessed. The next step is these novices undergoing the Ordeal of the Flame and then moving on to be monks or sisters in the cult. There is again a division of 'The Minor Seal' and 'The Major Seal.' The members of the Major Seal are the arch villains. Litvinov was one of them, and it is a blessing he was murdered."

"Rasputin sees they are drugged, doesn't he?"

"Drugs are administered in heavy doses in the beginning; sexual satiation is also a ploy to weaken the wills. And I personally also think hypnotism is involved," the little man said.

"There has to be something. I know Alex loved me.

341

And it wasn't that he felt more loyalty to Rasputin, but that he couldn't help himself."

"I'm sure you are right," Professor Adamson said. "Let me give you a brief history of the Skoptsi. The bare basis of the group is erotic religious frenzy ending in self-mutilation."

"Mutilation!" she gasped.

"One of the first to preach the Skoptsi cult was a peasant called Andrei Ianov, who was arrested and convicted of having induced thirteen other peasants to mutilate themselves. In this act, accompanied by orgies of singing and dancing, he was helped by one Selivanov. This Selivanov fled to the district of Tambov and began preaching salvation through the Baptism of Fire. He converted others, working them to a wild, uncontrollable frenzy and encouraging them to self-mutilation."

In a small voice, she said, "You are talking about castration?"

"Yes," Professor Adamson said. "By 1775 Selivanov, the revered leader, by now plump and facially hairless, as a result of his eunuchry, was in Moscow enrolling disciples. He was seized by the police, given the knout and sent to Siberia. But the movement spread and Selivanov returned to Moscow several years later and appeared before the mystical-minded Alexander the First. The tsar was dominated by a strange woman who believed in magic. She decided that Selivanov was a saint. This Baroness Krudner arranged for him to be given full freedom and offered him an entrée into the best circles. He numbered among his followers extremely powerful figures. State Councillor Alexei Michaelov Jelanski, a secret member of the cult, castrated himself, and was also a castrator of new recruits."

She gasped, "But I saw these people having passionate sex in a group the other night. None of them was castrated."

Professor Adamson smiled grimly. "You have not heard the full story," he said.

ᦕᶾ Chapter 27 ᦕᶾ

THE SMALL PROFESSOR ADAMSON began to pace up and down by his desk, his hands clasped behind his back, his gray head slightly bowed. He said, "There is a lot more historical fact, which might only weary you. But the grim reality is that the movement gradually became more corrupt, more politically powerful, and more widespread."

She said, "This is why Rasputin decided to use it."

"Unfortunately, it has provided a perfect weapon for him to perpetuate his power and to cater to his own foul immorality. He begins by enlisting selected men and women into the Flagellants' group. When they are mad with drugs, he leads them in sex orgies. The orgies go on so long and are repeated so often that the participants gradually lose their drive for sex. Then they are ready for the next stage in the secret society."

Elsie said, "My husband is being prepared for that now, if what you say is true."

The little man halted in his pacing and nodded. "Yes. These novices, sexually weary, but still wild with drugs, are lectured to by the monks of the society. They are given the Baptism of Fire, which used to mean castrate by fire tongs. Now knives and other means are used. And women of the cult are often the castrators!"

She gripped the arms of the leather chair and tried to fight against fainting. "Horrible!"

"This is not the end," Professor Adamson went on. "There is a second ceremony later on in which there is removal of the entire phallic organ. From then on, these are men apart, with a hatred for normal mankind, driven by an insane ambition for power within their own ranks, kept drugged and under submission so that they are ready for any criminal bidding."

"You say the women are often the castrators? How could they take part in such mutilation of others?"

"Because they are also victims," the old professor said calmy.

"The women," she said with disbelief.

"Yes," he said. "The females expose themselves to an external and internal mutilation that is more appalling than the similar male operation. They become sexless and wildly fanatical!"

She shook her head. "All those handsome young men and women whom I saw in naked orgy will become such victims?"

"Like cattle in a slaughter house," the little man said with anger. "Somehow it must be stopped. But not while these fanatical castrated are scattered through every important office in Russia."

"One would expect that over the years they would die out and their influence would be lost," she suggested, still feeling faint.

"The old recruit the young in their perversion. And some are permitted two children before they submit to the final rites. Unhappily, there is every prospect the group will continue and on an international basis."

"Once they are victims, they cannot turn back."

"This is why Rasputin is able to use them as his puppet criminals so successfully. When you married Count Alexander Martynov, you married tragedy."

She got to her feet and pleaded, "I feel I want to save him. It doesn't matter that he's deserted me, I would like to help him. Is there no way?"

"They tried to kill you for interfering, and more than once," the professor reminded her. "Do you want to take that risk again?"

"Alex cannot understand. He is proud of his body. He would not allow them to mutilate him so."

"You are thinking of him as you have known him," the little man said, "not as he is now. He has been reduced to a point where he can no longer make proper judgments. Likely by now he has been removed to one of the isolated outposts in the country where the operations are performed."

Tears brimmed in her eyes. "I can't bear to think of it."

344

"It is loathesome to us," the professor said. "But brain-washing has been a process used since the start of what we call civilization. It can be used for good or evil. In this case, it is the most despicable kind of wickedness, the destruction of humans. These victims should properly all be placed in madhouses."

She shook her head. "I'm almost sorry I know."

"You understand why Mr. Manning preferred that I tell you."

"Yes," she said. "It's too horrible. I can't accept that Alex will be a victim. I have to think he will escape."

"I know of none who has," the little man said.

"Let me still hope."

"By all means if it makes it easier for you," Professor Adamson said. "We must find our own ways to bear our burdens. I'm sorry to have brought you such pain."

She sighed. "You did as you were asked. And I insisted on knowing."

"I would try to forget this unfortunate marriage. You will have no trouble securing a divorce."

"I realize that," she said.

The little man eyed her gravely. "And I would return to America as quickly as possible. These Skoptsi cultists are a strange, vindictive lot. You were involved in the incident in which Litvinov was slain."

"Litvinov created the situation."

"True," he said. "But the Skoptsi aren't going to see it that way. Even though they have robbed you of your husband and what was a happy marriage, they may still think the debt unbalanced and try to avenge themselves on you."

She said, "I cannot understand such evil."

"Nor can I," the professor said. "Mr. Manning asked that I personally see you in a carriage with a trusted driver and I will."

He was as good as his word, escorting her down in the elevator and out to the waiting line of carriages outside the embassy. He selected a driver and told him the name of her hotel.

All during the carriage ride back to the hotel, she was oblivious of her surroundings. She sat in a stunned state, horrified by the revelations of the little professor. She would rather have heard that Alex would go on with the drugged orgies, or that he had been murdered like Basil for his loyalty to the villainous Rasputin, than that he go on living as a mutilated, half-mad creature.

It was the most diabolical thing she had ever heard of, and she knew why Ralph had been unable to offer her the full truth. She hardly knew how she could even bring herself to discuss it with him. It would be a thing of horror they would try to avoid talking about as much as possible.

The carriage drew up before the Empress Hotel, and she got out and paid the driver. Inside, the hotel lobby was busy as usual. She went directly up to the suite and since Ralph was not there had him paged as he'd suggested. She waited but there was no word from him.

She began to feel uneasy and went to the second floor to the room used as the Hearst syndicate office in St. Petersburg. The young man who was the permanent correspondent there greeted her with a friendly look.

"I'm glad you came down here, countess," he said. "Ralph had a sudden message from Major Brown about something and had to leave unexpectedly."

"I see," she said. "Then he's not likely to be back for luncheon?"

"I think not," the young man said. He had a small mustache and was from Boston. Ralph felt he was an excellent reporter for his age, somewhere in the mid-twenties.

"I'll have something to eat and wait for him in the suite," she decided.

"I'll let him know," the young man said. "I have some good news for him."

"Oh?"

"Yes, his cable to New York has been answered, and he is to be there at the end of the month. I wish I were going."

She managed a smile for the young man. "You don't like Russia?"

He sighed. "It's not so bad. Ralph gets all the action. I stay here at my desk mostly. But I'd rather be home."

"I guess we all would be," she said.

The young man regarded her with interest. "But you have a husband here, don't you?"

"Yes," she said. "I have a husband here."

"So that makes a difference, especially when he's one of the nobility. Russia is no place to be if you're not among the rich."

"It is a place of contrasts," she agreed.

"Have you seen Rasputin since you've been here?"

"No," she said. "I met him in Moscow. I'm not anxious to see him again."

The young man nodded. "Pretty rough character."

"Too rough for me," she said. "Don't forget to tell Mr. Manning I was here."

"I won't," the young man promised. "I intended to try you again at the suite. I've been ringing it regularly. I wanted to give you the message."

She said, "I was kept longer than I expected at the embassy."

"Those characters there take their time," the young man agreed.

Elsie left him and took the elevator to the lobby. She decided that she would prefer to have her lunch in one of the dining rooms rather than alone in the suite. She was depressed and nervous—in no mood for being alone. The things she had heard from Professor Adamson had shattered her. She had not believed that humans could reach such depths of degradation.

She stood in the center of the lobby indecisively making up her mind what she would do. There was a large dining room and a smaller one. She thought that perhaps she might feel more at ease in the smaller one. She was about to turn to go through its broad entrance when she felt the touch of a hand on her arm.

Startled, she turned to see a fat man in the black robe of the Skoptsi monks, with a rope-like tie around the waist of the flowing robe. He wore rough shoes, and his bald head was bare. He had the same ugly, double-chinned face as the dead Litvinov and could have been his double. His small eyes burned with a malicious fire.

"I have been waiting for you, countess," he said in a soft voice.

"Who are you?" she demanded tautly and tried to draw away from him, but he had taken her by the arm.

"A friend."

347

"You are one of them," she exclaimed. "The Skoptsi!"

The fat, ugly face showed a surly smile. "You are quite correct. I am a monk dedicated to our cause."

"Let me go," she said more loudly. People were passing by every minute, but no one seemed to be paying any attention to them. The sight of a black-robed monk and a woman talking was not going to cause anyone concern. But they did not know!

The small, mad eyes fixed on her. He said, "I am Father Adrian and I wish to do you a service."

"What sort of service?"

"The count wishes to see you."

"I do not believe it," she protested.

The fat one said, "You must believe me. The count is about to be removed to a country monastery to undertake initiation into a higher order. It is his desire to see you before he goes. You must know he is making a great decision."

"You mean he is facing mutilation," she shot back.

"The decision is one which cannot be reversed," the fat monk said smoothly. "Perhaps you two should discuss it. This is his wish."

She realized she was suddenly faced with the opportunity for which she'd been praying. A chance to save Alex before it was too late. And now this last minute chance was being offered her. Dare she turn it down? Coldly let Alex go to that fearful fate without trying to reason with him.

She gazed up at the fat face and burning eyes of the supposed Father Adrian. She said, "Where is my husband?"

"Not far away."

"Where?"

"Outside in a carriage waiting for you."

She frowned. "Why won't he come in?"

"It is against the orders of Rasputin that he has left the local monastery. He dare not be seen in a public place like this. He persuaded me to help him because I was a friend of his brother's."

"How can I believe you?" she asked warily. "You people made me captive before and wanted to murder me."

"Not I," the fat man said. "That was Litvinov's doing. And as you know, he is dead. I am only allowed to move freely because I belong to the highest order, the Great Seal!" He spoke proudly with a mad fanaticism that sickened her.

"You claim to be my husband's friend?"

"Yes."

"Then surely you must know that joining your order is wrong for him. He owes his loyalty to me first. He brought me here as his wife."

The fat man smiled grimly. "That is his present torment. I think if you see him, you may be able to help him. I believe the only true happiness is as a Skoptsi. But you may be able to convince him otherwise."

"Where is the carriage?"

"Just a little distance from the door," the fat man said. "I will take you to it. You can enter it and talk to him privately. I will wait on the sidewalk."

It seemed fair enough and to involve a minimum of hazard. She need only go out to the sidewalk with him to see Alex. She could not refuse to offer this last resistance to her husband's planned madness.

She gave the fat monk a grim look. "Very well, take me to him."

"You are a woman of courage and loyalty," the grossly fat man said as he led her toward the revolving door of the hotel.

They went out onto the street, and he indicated a carriage far down on the left and by itself. He said, "He is waiting there."

She hesitated. "You are not tricking me?"

"Surely you must believe me," the fat one argued. "I'm not trying to abduct you. I'm simply taking you to a carriage to speak with your husband in privacy."

"All right," she said.

But she was not sure. The fat man's story was pat enough. But she distrusted the Skoptsi.

The fat monk further caused her distrust by holding onto her arm firmly all during the conversation between them. And as they walked along the sidewalk to the carriage, he still held onto her arm.

She said, "You do not need to hold my arm."

The fat man said, "You might lose courage and go back."

"No," she said. "I want to see my husband."

"He is aware you witnessed that orgy. He is afraid you may be angry with him."

"I am deeply hurt," she said. "But I do not want to see him one of you."

"We are the blessed," the fat man said with a cold smile.

She did not reply. He was too obviously a fanatical madman. They drew near the carriage, and the driver eyed them impassively as they approached. She thought it might be the same driver who had been injured when the students overturned the carriage in which she'd been a captive.

The fat monk opened the carriage door. "Go in," he said, his tone now stern.

She drew back. "The carriage is empty! My husband is not in there!"

"I'm taking you to him!" the fat man said angrily.

"No," she said, pulling away without freeing herself. "That is not what you said! You lied to me!"

"I have a knife," the fat man warned her. "If you don't enter the carriage, I will use it!"

"You wouldn't dare!" she protested, still trying to get away from him.

"Countess Martynov!" A voice called out to her at the same time a smart-looking young man descended from a carriage which had pulled up behind them. The young man had a brown goatee and mustache and wore a gray suit and gray top hat. It took her only an instant to recognize him as Prince Serge Pavlovna, the representative of the tsar who had attended her wedding with his wife.

She cried almost tearfully, "Prince Serge!"

The dapper young man doffed his gray top hat and came up to her and the grimly surprised Father Adrian. He gave the fat man a glaring look and asked, "Is that fellow bothering you?"

"Yes," she said. "He's been trying to force me to go with him."

The fat man spat angrily, "The woman is a liar. Her husband, the count, asked me to bring her to him."

"I don't believe it. He claimed my husband was here in the carriage waiting. He is trying to kidnap me."

Prince Serge had donned his gray tophat and now he placed a monocle in his eye and gave the fat man a scathing appraisal. "You are one of *them*," he said with disgust. "One of Rasputin's black angels!"

"I do not have to listen to your insults," the fat man huffed. "The woman's husband can wait for her until doomsday as far as I'm concerned." He turned and told the driver. "We are not waiting!" And he sprang into the carriage with an agility surprising in one his size and slammed the door shut as the carriage was quickly driven off.

Prince Serge eyed the departing carriage with scorn as he said, "That wicked fellow didn't tarry long when he saw his game was up."

She gave a deep sigh. "I was warned at the American Embassy that I must be cautious. They are madmen! They have Alex in their power, and they won't rest until they kill me!"

Prince Serge registered concern. "Alex has joined those filthy beggars?"

"Yes."

"Then he is done for!"

"I know," she said. "I am sure he didn't send for me. He probably doesn't know I'm in St. Petersburg, and I'm not sure he'd care anymore if he did know."

The handsome Prince Serge stared at her. "You poor girl. Where are you staying? Where did that fat monk find you?"

"I'm staying in the Empress Hotel. He found me there alone in the lobby. I was just about to go to luncheon."

"Let me escort you back there," Prince Serge said.

"I can't take your time."

"I have no pressing engagement," the prince told her. "I suggest we go to the bar and have a drink. You look as if you need it. Then later we might have something to eat."

"I'm trembling," she confessed. "I was in tears when you arrived. Another moment, and he would have had me forced into the carriage."

The prince smiled and guilded her gently along the sidewalk by the elbow. "You see. And they keep saying we princes are quite useless. I shall use you as a witness it is not so."

They went back to the hotel and the prince and she were shown to a pleasant window table in the lounge. He confided to her, "Some of the nobility won't accept window tables, they are so afraid of the many bombings which have taken place. But I like to think I may be one of the more popular princes. Tell me about Alex."

The Prince ordered them drinks, and then she told him all that had happened, ending by saying, "If it hadn't been for the student revolutionaries I would have been murdered."

The handsome prince was amused. "So you have friends to come to your rescue at both ends of the social scale."

"I am grateful to you," she said.

"I knew Basil was a friend of Rasputin's, but I did not hear of his becoming a Skoptsi," the prince said with a frown. "Of course, he was killed in the bombing of the Dvenekno Station and so had no chance to make the choice. I was shocked when Rasputin attended your wedding."

"So was I," she said. "And it marked the turning point, when Alex really chose the Skoptsi before me."

"He had known Rasputin and the Skoptsi before, of course," the prince said. "And much of the time he has likely been drugged. There are some of us who believe that the villainous monk is using the same drug to keep the tsarina compliant and his advocate."

"You are attached to the royal palace?"

The prince sipped his drink and nodded. "Yes. And would you believe it, we hardly ever see the tsar or the tsarina. Once in a while we see the daughters. The tsarevich has had a relapse of his bleeding, and we never see him around any more. In the old days, he was a merry little boy in spite of his illness, and we all loved him."

"Rasputin has managed to keep them behind the barriers of his making?"

"So he can remain in power. And the Skoptsi do his bidding, both in Russia and outside in the other world capitals."

She said, "I'm sure they're strong in London and New York."

"They are everywhere," Prince Serge said. "Some of them act as spies in Berlin. We suspect that they take pay from both sides and are really betraying Russia. Alex is offering an insult to his class by going along with this scoundrel."

"Rasputin wooed him and his brother for their titles."

"Definitely," Prince Serge said with anger. "Because we of the nobility are normally the enemies of the mad monk."

"I have given up hope for Alex," she sighed.

Prince Serge finished his drink and gave her a knowing look. "It is not a pleasant subject. But you realize if he becomes one of the monks he will be robbed of his manhood. Why do you think they are all so grossly fat? They are eunuchs!"

"So I have been told!"

"Rasputin makes sure they have no family life to return to. They must dedicate themselves to him and his evil thirst for power!"

"Is there no stopping him?" she asked.

Prince Serge said, "There is hope. Prince Phillip Yussoupov has sworn to kill him. Phillip is one of the most powerful men in all Russia, richer than the tsar. He usually does what he says."

"I have seen one of his estates near Moscow," she recalled. "Timofei drove me out and showed it to me."

"Phillip has maybe forty estates scattered about Russia," Prince Serge said. "I believe I met Timofei at the wedding. The adopted son of Count Andre and the late Countess Marie. I was later at her funeral."

"Yes," she said. "A large man."

"And an artist."

"Yes," she said. "Inclined to drink too much."

"The fault of many otherwise good men," Prince Serge said. "The count seemed devoted to him."

"And Timofei liked his foster father," she said. "But a tragic thing happened." And she told the prince of the quarrel in the waterfront dive, of Timofei's stabbing and their firm conviction he was dead.

"A sad waste of a talented young man," Prince Serge said. "I would like to see that icon one day."

"It is at the palace," she said. "When you are in Moscow, go and visit Count Andre. He would be extremely pleased, and he will show you the icon."

"Does the old man remain in good health?"

"Very good for his age," she said. "He now uses a cane but he is of strong stock. I think, barring an accident, he might go on another fifteen years and be ninety."

"I'm glad to hear it," the prince said. "The decay of age is the saddest of all things to witness, but it is not likely many of my generation will live to worry about it. If the unrest continues, we shall have a revolution, and most of us will be shot down."

She said seriously, "I don't think the student revolutionists want violence, only change. I'm sure if they could sit and talk with you, you would find there was much in common between you."

"This is the tragedy," Prince Serge said. "We will not get the chance for that. The violent minority will start the great struggle, and the rest of us will be caught up in it whether we like it or not."

"I pray it doesn't happen. In the short time I've been here, I've come to love this country."

Prince Serge smiled. "I am pleased. With all her faults, Mother Russia has a certain quality. If it is lost, the world will never see its like again."

"I admire Count Andre and the Countess Olga."

"I'd forgot about Olga," the prince said. "What about her?"

"She is remaining with her father. She has her problems. She worries about what lies ahead. She is torn this way and that."

"So I have been told," the prince said quietly.

Elsie found herself a little alarmed by the prince's words and the tone of his saying them. Had the word somehow got out that Olga had a revolutionary lover and was a member of the student revolutionary party. She hoped not, for Olga's sake and also for the sake of the elderly Count Andre.

She said, "My own problems are great."

"You will go back to America?"

"Yes."

"It is probably the only thing you may safely do," the

prince agreed. "With Rasputin still holding the high cards and the Skoptsi out to destroy you, there is nothing but constant danger for you here."

"I have a friend," she said. "A newspaperman from New York. His name is Ralph Manning. I'm staying in his suite here, and he is doing all he can for me. I'm sure with his help I'll get out of the country safely."

"I'm glad you have such a friend," Prince Serge said, betraying no surprise at her statement that she was living with the reporter.

She looked directly at the handsome man with the brown goatee. "I do not feel I'm being unfaithful to my husband."

"How could you?" Prince Serge said. "Because of what Alex has done, you no longer have a husband."

"I plan on a divorce as soon as I return to New York."

"Naturally," the prince said. "I shall always be happy that I arrived here today at the moment I did."

"And so will I," she said. "I was to meet Ralph for luncheon. But he was called away on some errand by a British secret service man named Major Brown. I guess it is generally known that he is here acting for his government, although he pretends it is hush-hush."

"I have heard of this Major Brown," Prince Serge said with a slight frown. "He has been visiting our military posts in the guise of a journalist and making a general nuisance of himself."

"I've warned Ralph I don't like him," she said. "But perhaps this is because he is fat. And I identify all fat men with the evil Skoptsi cult."

"Hardly fair," Prince Serge said with a smile. "No, I think your Major Brown is purely a self-important, bungling Britisher."

"Ralph seems to agree with your opinion," she said.

The prince asked, "What about some food?"

"If you don't mind, I'll wait until later," she said. "I'm still upset a little."

The prince explained that he now had to leave. He signed the check, and they left the bar. She led the way from the bar to the lobby and at exactly the same moment Ralph entered by the revolving door followed by the stout

Major Brown. Ralph smiled and came across the lobby toward Elsie and the Prince. Major Brown followed, and she was almost sure his fat face had shadowed with disappointment!

⋖§ Chapter 28 §⋗

INTRODUCTIONS WERE MADE ALL AROUND. Prince Serge was polite and friendly and asked Elsie not to leave St. Petersburg without getting in touch with him and his princess. She promised to phone him, and he put on his gray top hat and moved on toward the revolving doors.

Ralph apologized to her. "I'm sorry, darling. But the major thought he had a lead on a top story, and we rushed off to get the details—turned out to be a worthless tip! There was no story!"

"Bloody awful!" the fat man puffed and moped his sweating forehead with a white handkerchief that he'd retrieved from the jacket pocket of his linen suit.

"I broke my lunch date with you to no purpose," Ralph said. "How did you make out?"

Major Brown fanned himself with his Panama hat. "I'd say she did herself well! She surely has friends in high places. Prince Serge from the royal palace, no less."

She smiled. "He came at a fortunate moment."

Ralph seemed to sense a hidden meaning in her words. He said, "What do you mean?"

"Can't we adjoin to the bar for this reunion," Major Brown said. "I'm thirsty, and I could do with a spot of food."

"I'm pretty parched," Ralph agreed. "What about you, Elsie?"

"I've just come from the bar," she said.

"Companion of the prince! Jolly!" Major Brown chuckled.

She said, "I don't mind joining you. I'll have something light to eat.

Major Brown started for the bar with them following.

"At this moment my idea of nourishment is a gin and tonic!"

Ralph told her, "He's had a rather grim setback. He thought he was onto some graft in munitions. But it fell apart. Now he's trying to bluster it out and make on he isn't let down. I know he is."

"That's part of the game, isn't it?" she said as they followed the major into the big bar with its ceiling fans.

Ralph smiled at her. "For a countess, you're catching on fast."

When they were all seated and served, Major Brown took a mouthful of his gin and tonic and smiled happily. Then he said, "My superior in London has an idea all you wear in Russia are fur hats, overcoats, and galoshes. He sympathized with me for having to endure the freezing weather."

Ralph said, "He clearly has no picture of what it is like in St. Petersburg in summer."

"Wish you'd write a story for the *Times* and educate him. Mind you, it would have to be in the *London Times*. Fellow never reads anything else." He took another swallow of his drink. "Come to think of it, I'm not sure he reads that. Possibly he eavesdrops on someone else reading it in his club."

"The spring was so backward in Moscow," she said. "There was snow and ice when I arrived there."

"St. Petersburg is not Moscow," Ralph said. "Here it's hot summers and frigid winters." He gave her a worried look. "What did you mean about the prince just arriving in time?"

"Simple, my dear old boy!" Major Brown blustered before she could offer a reply. "The prince always does make his appearance at the critical moment. Slays the crocodile, or the dragon, or what have you! Then he whisks the princess off and ruins the whole business by turning into a frog before they can bed."

Ralph laughed at this and said, "Honestly, I think Elsie has something to tell us. I'm interested in hearing."

She looked at him, ignoring the major. "I went down to your office and your associate told me you'd gone out with the major."

"Yes, I left the message," Ralph said.

"I decided to go down and have lunch in the small dining room. I didn't feel like eating alone."

"Good idea,' the newspaper man nodded his approval.

"Not as good as I thought," she said with a grimace. "I went down, and I was almost immediately accosted by a black-robed Father Adrian, one of Rasputin's Skoptsi converts."

Ralph's eyebrows lifted. "I don't believe it. Here in the lobby of this hotel?"

"Yes. Professor Adamson at the embassy warned me I could still be in danger. He was so right."

"What happened?" Ralph asked.

"He took hold of my arm. I told him to let me go. But he wouldn't."

"Why didn't you scream for help?" Ralph asked.

"No one would have understood why," she said. "This fat old monk seemed to be quietly talking to me and touching my arm."

"This is what comes of my leaving you," Ralph said with despair.

"You have your work to do," she reminded him.

"Go on," he said.

"This Father Adrian at once launched into a story that Alex wanted to see me before submitting to his final vows and mutilation. He offered to take me to him."

Ralph said, "That was a ruse."

"I thought so until he told me Ralph was outside waiting in a carriage," she said.

"And?" Ralph was leaning close to her.

"He convinced me Alex was out there waiting. I couldn't lose a final chance to try and save him. I went out to the carriage; but when he opened the door, the carriage was empty. He ordered me to get in and threatened me with a knife he was holding concealed in the sleeve of his robe."

Ralph asked, "Then?"

"I heard the prince call out my name. He had emerged from a carriage just behind us. I let him know I was in trouble. And he sent the monk rushing off alone in the carriage. Then the prince brought me in here for a drink."

"I keep thinking what would have happened if he hadn't

come along and recognized you," Ralph said. "I blame myself. I ought not to have left you alone!"

"Don't think that," she said. "I'm safe and that's all that is important!"

Ralph turned to Major Brown. "What do you say to that?"

The major's fat face and bald head were crimson and covered with sweat. He shook his head in outrage and said, "Bloody nihilists! Such scum would all be loaded up and driven off to prison in England! The empire may have its faults, but we don't tolerate this sort of nonsense." He signaled to the waiter. "Another round for us, at once!"

Ralph eyed her earnestly. "It makes one thing clear. You must get out of Russia promptly."

"I plan to. But I have to return to Moscow first."

He showed upset. "I don't agree."

"I must," she said. "I need only stay a day or two. I want to see Olga and Count Andre and find out if there has been any word from Timofei."

"You know there hasn't been," Ralph said. "You are not safe anywhere in this country, understand that."

"There are personal things I want to pack and take back to America with me," she said. "And I want to make Olga and Count Andre understand why I am going to divorce Alex."

Ralph said, "You could do that by letter?"

"Not in the same way," she said. "And in any case, I have news for you. You're being recalled to New York for a conference with Mr. Hearst personally."

"The reply to my cable arrived?" Ralph said.

"Yes."

"Wonderful!" he said.

"So you'll be leaving in a week or two. I will be safer if I wait for you and we return to America together."

He shook his head. "I might have known you'd come up with a logical argument."

"Of course, it's the sensible thing," she said.

"All right," he told her. "I'll be returning to Moscow for a few days when my work is done here. We'll go back together, and then we'll take the Moscow-Paris express together."

Major Brown was halfway through his second gin and

tonic. "Bloody wonderful!" he said. "I envy you two. I expect I shall be forced to stay in this awful place for the rest of the stinking summer."

Ralph smiled at him. "Think what you are doing for the empire."

"The word will never get beyond my superior. He will take all the credit, while I do the sweating," the major said.

Ralph said, "Today may have been a failure, but most of our other trips paid well. I'll return to America with a lot of information."

"And a lovely young lady," the major beamed at her.

"Without a doubt," Ralph said, smiling at her. She smiled in return, although the blustering major still made her uneasy. She supposed that Prince Serge had been right; he was something of a blustering drunkard.

"I tell you what," the major said. "Let us have one memorable final day for our memory book. One last high time before we all report back to our superiors."

"What have you in mind?" Ralph asked.

"A two hour's journey from here by carriage there is a park, I think it is called Gormky Park. From it you can see and smell the Baltic. There are evergreen mountains, pure air, fantastic gorges, and trout-filled streams. Let us take lunches, a bottle or two of good stuff—champagne and gin are the best—and have a carriage take us up there. We can spend the day enjoying the air and sunshine and exposing our souls. We'll come back refreshed and younger."

Ralph looked delighted. "It appeals to me. I can leave the office by midmorning."

"And you, dear countess?" Major Brown leaned toward her, his face flushed.

She hesitated. "Why don't you two go? It may be too much roughing for me."

"Nonsense!" the major said. "It's a park! On Sundays it is filled with family groups. But during the week we can have it almost to ourselves."

"I won't go without you," Ralph said. "I won't leave you alone again."

She saw that he wanted to make the excursion and wished she could have more enthusiasm for it. She said,

"I'm not exactly in a picnic mood. I am in the midst of a tragedy."

"Undoubtedly," the major agreed. "But one must keep a stiff upper lip and all that kind of thing. You will feel better for a day in the open."

"All right." She sighed. "Is it to be tomorrow?"

"Tomorrow unless it rains," Major Brown said. "I'll hire the driver, get the lunch and liquor and whatever else is needed. Leave everything to me."

Elsie was not enthusiastic about the party, but she knew she could not avoid it. The bright part of it, however, was that it would be the last time she'd have to endure the major—she hoped. She and Ralph would be leaving for Moscow, and they would take the train from Russia from that city.

The three parted. She returned to the suite for a rest. Major Brown headed for the British Embassy to humiliate himself with the admission he'd managed to be cheated out of an important bit of information. Ralph returned to his office on the second floor of the hotel to complete the day's work.

He finished early and went upstairs to find Elsie just out of her bath and in bed. He joined her, and their lovemaking was filled with an extra excitement because of the knowledge that a tragedy might have parted them.

They had dinner in the hotel and went up to the suite later to discuss what they would do when they returned to America. Ralph pointed out it would be important for her to find a lawyer who had some contacts with Russia. She was of the opinion that Prince Serge would be able to help her from within his country. And this was another reason she wished to talk with Count Andre, since the old aristocrat had many friends among the judges of the Moscow courts.

They were in the midst of this discussion when the phone rang. Ralph took it and then turned to her with a warning look on his pleasant face. He said, "It's for you!"

"Who?" she asked, rising from her chair.

"I don't know the voice," he said.

"A man or woman?" she asked, drawing near him.

"A woman," he said. "Be careful what you say."

She nodded and took the phone from him. "Yes, this is the Countess Martynov," she said carefully.

"Elsie!" someone with a familiar voice cried from the other end of the line. It was Marfa.

"Marfa," she said, pleased to hear from the student again.

"We must see you," Marfa said. "We have a surprise for you."

She hesitated. "Can't you come here?"

Ralph was giving her warning motions not to make any promises to meet the girl. But she felt she must listen to her. She owed a lot to Marfa and Boris, and she trusted them.

"What is the surprise?" she asked.

"Not over the phone," she said. "Boris will pick you up at the hotel. He will be very grand tonight. He will actually come for you in a carriage."

"I don't know," she said. "Wait." And she asked Ralph, "What am I going to tell her? She says she has a surprise for me, and Boris is coming to pick me up in a carriage."

"I don't like it," he said.

"But I know I can trust them!" she protested.

He frowned. "You don't go without me. Tell them that."

"You might make them uneasy. They are revolutionists and you are a foreign newspaperman. You might write about them and place them in danger of arrest."

"I won't write anything. I promise," he said.

"I'll see what they say," she told him. And into the phone she said, "My newspaper friend from American says he must come with me, for my safety."

"Doesn't he know you'll be safe with us?" Marfa said.

"I've had another close call. He's worried."

"Another one?" Marfa gasped.

"Yes."

"In that case I don't blame him. He seemed nice enough from the little we saw him. Bring him along."

"What time?"

Marfa said, "The carriage will be at the hotel door in a half-hour."

"We'll be there," she said. And she put down the phone. "They have a surprise," she said. "What could it be?"

He shrugged. "Maybe they've somehow got hold of Alex."

She shook her head. "No, I doubt it."

"Then what?"

She considered. "Maybe it's just a party for me. They are a fun-loving group. I came to be fond of them."

Ralph worried. "They think me an old man."

"Not at all," she said. "You're not more than ten years older than the majority of them."

"I won't mind it," Ralph smiled. "Not if there are plenty of girls. But they might."

She went and pressed herself to him and eyed him teasingly. "Never worry, I'll scare off any girls."

"I believe you would," he laughed.

They went downstairs at the appointed time, and the carriage arrived. Boris jumped out with a smile on his long, freckled face. The eyes behind the spectacles were bright as he said, "It is not often I can treat my friends to a carriage."

After they'd got into the vehicle and were on their way, she asked, "Where are we going?"

"I will not tell you the address because of our newspaper friend," Boris said with a wink for Ralph. "But it is a student coffee house. It's closed for the month, and we are having a combined meeting and party there tonight."

"It sounds wonderful," she said.

"There will be student representatives from the various revolutionary cells all across Russia," Boris said. "It is an important gathering."

"Why are we being honored as guests?" Ralph asked.

"Because Elsie is our trusted friend, and she vouches for you. And because we wish to say farewell before she leaves St. Petersburg."

Elsie said, "I came close to leaving it today in the wrong manner." And she went on to tell the history student of her near-kidnapping.

Boris heard her out and scowled. "I thought when I finished Litvinov those fellows would give up."

"It seems not," she said.

"You need not worry about any of those fat monsters being in our group," Boris assured her. "You will be safe for tonight."

The carriage stopped at the corner of what seemed a dead-end street. They left it and led by Boris walked a distance up the street, then along a narrow alley. At the end of the alley several steps descended to a solid wooden door. He went down the steps and gave a special sort of knock on the door. It was obviously an arranged signal.

The door was opened cautiously by a young man with dark hair and a round face. He saw it was Boris and opened the door wide for them to enter. Inside the place was well-lit with lanterns, although all the windows had been boarded. It was a big room and not too awfully hot, as it was actually part cellar. A crowd of young men and women were clustered about in groups talking enthusiastically. It could have been a fashionable party, except for their shabby dress and that they were drinking coffee rather than liquor.

Marfa emerged from among the clusters of people to come and throw her arms around Elsie and kiss her. "My little sister," the peasant girl said.

She laughed. "Timofei used to call me little innocent!"

Marfa shook her head. "No sister of mine is innocent!" She turned to Ralph and shook his hand. "Remember this is not for the press."

"I'm not here for news," he laughed. "I'm looking for pretty young girls."

"And there are dozens of them," Marfa said. And to Elsie she said, "Not to mention handsome lads. Boris is beside himself with jealousy. I had a hard time getting him to go fetch you."

Boris looked around with a scowl on his face. "Where is that political science student who was being your shadow?"

"He has found another interest, someone from Toblovst! She is not as attractive as I am, but she preaches the same sort of violence he does, so they are now soulmates."

Boris looked disgruntled. "Violence. There can only be so much."

Ralph said, "Have you ever seen a mob returned to control once it has started to riot?"

Marfa's square face showed a reproving smile. "We are getting far too serious. And now the surprise. Do you know who our speaker is tonight?"

"I'll make a guess," she said. "Boris?"

Boris looked sour. "You are right! It should be me."

"Idiot!" Marfa reproved him. "You want to always be the leader. You are president of the group. Isn't that enough?"

"Who is the speaker?" Elsie asked.

"Feodor," the other girl said happily. "Feodor from Moscow."

She gasped. "Feodor here!"

Marfa's eyes were shining. "And not alone! Come with me!" She took her hand and led her down the length of the crowded room, leaving Boris and Ralph behind in some earnest discussion.

Elsie saw Olga before the dark girl saw her. Then Olga turned from the light-haired youth she was speaking with and burst into a delighted smile.

"Elsie!" she cried. And she ran to her and embraced her, tears filling her eyes. They kissed and held each other tight.

She said, "How do you happen to be here?"

Olga said proudly, "Feodor is the speaker for the gathering of all the student cells. This is a big night for us. I had to hear him. Also, I can't return to Moscow."

"Why not?" she asked.

"Things became too dangerous," Olga said. "I know I was being watched. They were just waiting to pounce on me."

"That may be so," Elsie agreed. And she told the dark girl what Prince Serge had said, adding, "He gave me the idea you were under suspicion and it worried him."

"He would be fearful for Uncle Andre," she said. "And so was I. I went to him and told him the truth. He did not want me to leave, but in the end he gave me his blessing. And it will save him from being involved with any dishonor. If I am caught, it will not be under his roof."

"That was thoughtful and kind of you."

"I could do no less."

"How is Uncle Andre?"

"I think he grows stronger with adversity. He has even given up using his cane. He is angry with Alex, and he waits to hear from you."

Elsie's lovely face shadowed. "You have lost a brother and I a husband."

Olga looked as if she might faint. "He is dead! They murdered him as they did Basil?"

"No, but in a way I wish they had. He has joined them—enlisted under Rasputin, become one of the Skoptsi monks."

Olga closed her lovely eyes as if in pain. "Alex was weak. I knew that. But there must have been more to it. They had to drug him to make him submit to such a dreadful thing."

She said, "Drugs are part of it. According to Professor Adamson at the American Embassy, who is an expert on the Skoptsi, they have a strong addictive drug manufactured from herbs which are grown secretly in the Skoptsi monasteries and manufactured by them. It is both hallucinatory and weakening. I saw Alex taking part in a naked orgy with other men and women, all maddened by the drug. But that first phase is over. I'm sure he has been taken from St. Petersburg to some remote monastery where in his most abject state he will be mutilated. After that, he will be brainwashed like the rest."

"I mustn't think about it," Olga said, gritting her teeth. "I loved him so."

Elsie placed a comforting arm around her. "I would have saved him if I could. He made no attempt to communicate with me; and when I tried to reach him, my own life was threatened. They see me as a threat to them, and I'm still in danger."

Olga nodded silently. "There is no reproach due you."

"Now I will leave Russia," she said.

Olga showed alarm. "Not without seeing Uncle Andre before you go! He is alone with the servants. And some of them have left. It will be a dreadful blow to him if you do not at least come to say good-by."

"I'll do that," she said, "I promise. And if Heaven is kind, perhaps Timofei may be returned to him alive."

Olga shook her head. "Never. Timofei is dead!"

"Maybe there is a small chance."

"Never. You were with me and heard what the owner of that dive said. At least Uncle Andre has the icon, and he derives great comfort from it."

"Timofei could have been a great artist if he had applied himself and lived."

"Vodka was his mistress," Olga said unhappily. "To think that Uncle Andre is the only Martynov left in the palace!"

"Poor old man!" Elsie said. "I shall see him in a few days. Ralph is returning to his Moscow office, and I will go with him. I'll go out to the palace and try and make Uncle Andre understand!"

"He is keeping your apartment in readiness for you," she said. "And of course he talks of Timofei returning. One clings to small hopes when one is old."

"He is at least entitled to them," Elsie said. "You must come and talk with Ralph."

They made their way back through the crowd where Marfa, Boris, and Ralph were in conversation with Feodor. Olga's fiancé smiled at Elsie and greeted her warmly.

Elsie told him, "So you are to be speaker tonight."

The tall, young man said, "I have nothing much to say. Events will take care of everything."

"You think it is getting worse?"

"Yes," Feodor said. "Every hour, every day, every week the moment draws nearer when all Russia will be in flames."

She asked, "Will you remain here now that Olga is here?"

"No," Feodor said. "She will find lodgings here, but I will keep on the move. You know they are looking for us."

"Yes."

"As party organizer, I have to travel from city to city, village to village, and address the various cells. I also have to try and bring about the formation of new ones. Our student group must be stronger."

"I wish you luck," she said.

He grimaced. "If I'm caught, it is the knout and Siberia."

"Have you heard anything of Sophie and Bogrov?"

Feodor said, "The lawyer Olga's uncle hired had them traced to a small prison in a very remote section of Siberia. They might as well be on another planet."

"Are they together?"

"No, the men and women are in separate quarters. They may catch a glimpse of each other as they pass on their way to their work duties. That would be all."

Marfa had joined them and she said, "I think they manage better than that. The guards can be outsmarted and any of them bribed, since guards and prisoners share the same bitter hell of the place. I have been told of love affairs that have bloomed up there amid the ice and snow."

Elsie smiled sadly. "I hope Sophie is one of the lucky ones."

"She will have some money," Feodor said. "Olga says her uncle has given the lawyer money to be sent there."

Marfa gave him a meaningful look. "If it ever reaches her. I don't trust lawyers."

Elsie said, "He is an old and respected man. I think it will be all right."

Feodor offered one of his rare smiles. "Not too much talk about lawyers. It happens I am one."

"I didn't know," Marfa said. "My apologies."

"Not needed," he said. "I'm aware of the limitations of some of my profession. And I have only had my degree a few months, so I'm truly hardly a lawyer."

Elsie said, "Be good to Olga. She is a wonderful girl. She has given up much because of her love for you and for Russia."

"I appreciate her," Feodor said with a warm glance at the dark girl who was still arguing with Boris and Ralph.

"I will keep in touch with you somehow," she said. "Maybe we can send our letters to the news agency here and Ralph's associate will see they get to you and to us."

"It sounds like a good idea," Feodor said.

Boris left Ralph and Olga to come to the tall, youthful lawyer and say, "Time for you to speak, Feodor!"

"So soon?" he said.

"Yes, it's getting hot in here. Get to them while they are still cool enough to have enthusiasm." Boris shoved him toward a big wooden table, and Feodor got up on it and raised his hands for silence. It was amazing that nothing more was needed. The clusters of students at once ceased their talking and turned their young, earnest faces toward him. Elsie felt a choke in her throat at the sight of all those attractive, believing faces.

"Comrades," Feodor said with warm emotion in his pleasant voice and a glow on his plain face, "we are gathered here tonight to decide what we may best do to further our cause. There are with us two young Americans who are true friends of Russia. And so I shall begin by quoting a famous American who firmly believed in freedom, a freedom we do not know in Russia. His name was Thomas Jefferson and he said: 'The tree of liberty must be refreshed from time to time with the blood of tyrants. It is its natural manure!'" He paused as loud cheers rose up all over the dark, cavernous room.

Elsie listened with tear-brimmed eyes. She was leaving them all in this moment of despair, those she had come to love, and the man she had loved and lost. Soon it would be only a nightmare memory for her. But what lay ahead for these people?

gathered here tonight to decide what we may best do to...
further our cause. There are with us two young Russian...
who are here friends of justice and we I shall begin by...

◆§ Chapter 29 §◆

THE NEXT DAY WAS WARM, bright, and thoroughly suited
for Major Brown's picnic excursion. Ralph had a hasty
breakfast with her and hurried down to his office on the
second floor to clear up any work that needed immediate
attention before he left for the day's outing.

She lingered in the suite until the last moment. She
chose a light dress and a matching scarf and a broad-
brimmed straw hat to guard against the strong sunlight.
She was still sentimental from her reunion with Countess
Olga the previous night. It had been wonderful to see
the countess again—also a little sad.

Of course, Olga had made her decision, and no doubt it
was the proper one for her. Feodor was talented, his speech
before the students had proved that. He had spoken in a
strongly emotional fashion and had the young men and
women with him all the way. He was clearly destined to
be an important leader in the student revolutionary party.

Fortunately, Olga would have Marfa and Boris to keep
a careful watch over her when Feodor was away organiz-
ing the various cells of resistance of the youth movement.
The great tragedy would be if anything should happen to
Feodor, and he was always in danger of a violent death
from the authorities. But Marfa would stand by Olga; the
peasant girl had proved how resourceful she was.

Olga had been as horrified as Elsie at the macabre waste
Alex had decided to make of his life. She knew there had
been a strong bond between this sister and brother, so that
the pain Olga felt was almost as great as she knew as the
wife of the handsome young count. But Alex made his
choices.

She stood at her window gazing out over the multicolored rooftops of St. Petersburg, trying to convince her-

self that the sensible thing to do was erase Alex from her mind. Forget that he had ever existed. But that was much easier to do in theory than in fact! She had deeply loved her Russian count and entertained a dream picture of their future together in this distant, exotic land.

It surely was not her fault it had not worked out? Yet, could she wholly blame Alex? He had been confused and shocked by his brother's murder. He shared with the revolutionaries doubts about his country's future; yet he could not join them. Rasputin had offered another way. And Rasputin had played on his lusts, his weakness for sexual excesses. He had already had a taste of this kind of abandonment to immorality before they'd met. The seeds had already been sown.

Alex had tried to fight his nature because of his undoubted love for her. He had stopped Litvinov, Rasputin's most powerful aide, when Litvinov had attempted to kill her. But in the end, Alex had lost his freedom of will to lust, drugs, and the evil hypnotic influence of Rasputin. Now he undoubtedly would be recuperating from his castration in some remote country monastery, still maintained by drugs to accept his mutilation.

Her marriage had ended in so repulsive and terrifying a manner that she would find it diffcult to offer the truth about it to even her closest friends. Enough to say that Alex had dedicated his life to an evil secret society and had deserted her. The courts in the United States need be told no more. It was enough to gain her freedom.

The phone rang and it was Ralph, he said, "I'm ready. We can meet the major in the lobby now."

"I'll be right down," she promised. "I can't say I'm looking forward to it."

Ralph chuckled at the other end of the line. "Well, we won't see him after today. Comfort yourself with that. We move on to Moscow tomorrow."

"That is what is sustaining me," she said.

When she reached the lobby, Ralph was already there and chatting with Major Brown. Ralph was wearing a light suit and a straw hat and the major was dressed in a khaki outfit of shorts, short-sleeved blouse and the type of light khaki helmet worn by officers in the Indian Army. He looked very much the British colonial. He also looked more massively fat than ever.

The major greeted her with bluster and a beaming admiration. "My dear countess, you look stunning, much too grand for a simple country picnic."

She smiled. "It is a thin material. I'm sure it will be comfortable."

"I think you look just right," Ralph told her and once again she gave thanks for the chance meeting which had brought them together.

Major Brown eyed them with approval. "Tomorrow you'll be on your way to Moscow and then to America. I envy you two young people."

Ralph said, "Is the carriage ready?"

"Yes, it is. And so is the lunch, and I have plenty for us to drink," the major confided with a wink. "So proceed, troops. We are on the way to the objective."

They soon left the busy streets of the city behind for the lazy, narrow roads of the countryside. They kept driving higher into the hills; the sun was stronger, the air much more pure. The major had chosen an open droshka for the excursion. And despite her reluctance to go on the trip, Elsie began to find herself enjoying it.

The major pointed out the various landmarks and knew the names of the churches and the small villages. He kept up a flow of conversation more entertaining than that of the average tourist guide. She began to see him as a pathetic, lonely figure eager for company—a fat man assigned to a secret, unpleasant job in a foreign land and longing for his own people and country. She realized she had been too hard on him.

They passed village children who waved and shouted at them. Some of them ran after the droshka and the major threw them coins. They laughed with delight and scrambled for the small treasures in the road, lost in the wake of the carriage wheel's dust.

"Good people," the major said, "the ones on whom Russia will eventually depend for its salvation."

Finally, they reached the park. It seemed to be completely deserted except for them. They left the carriage at a place reserved for vehicles and horses. The major gave the driver a bottle of some sort of liquor and asked him to wait. Then the stout man led them along trails through the woods, which led higher up into the mountains.

They finally reached a peak point that had been cleared for the use of picnic groups. It gave a view of the tall mountains all around and there were wooden tables, roughly finished, set out on an area of flat rock. There was a very precarious path down from the flat rock surface which led to a swiftly running stream in a deep gorge. The drop from the rocks down would be at least a hundred and fifty feet.

"Kings of all we survey!" Major Brown declaimed with a boyish enthusiasm, which was partly from a large amount of brandy consumed from a flask along the way. "I wish I could think of some proper quotation from Kipling to match the occasion."

"It's beautiful," she exclaimed. "And so peaceful!"

"Just the distant sound of the rippling brook far below," Major Brown said.

Ralph had carried the basket with the lunch. "Now we have only to enjoy ourselves," he said, as he sat the big basket on one of the tables.

Major Brown sat down on a bench and took another deep drink from the silver flask he carried in his hip pocket. His face was beet red. He held the flask up. "Anyone need this medicine?"

"Not yet," Ralph said. "I'll have some champagne later."

"So will I," she agreed, holding onto the brim of her straw hat as the breeze caught it.

"Not ladylike to drink from a flask in any case," Major Brown said with a wink as he screwed on its top and returned it to his hip pocket. "My weight is what undoes me. I confess that walk up here exhausted me."

Ralph said, "Well, going back won't seem so bad."

The major nodded. "Before I forget it, I must take a photo of the occasion. Then I shall have it enlarged and framed and place it in my flat in London to remind me of this blessed day."

She laughed. "I didn't know you were a photographer."

"Have to be able to do a bit of it in my line," the major said as he removed the white cloth covering the basket and began digging into it.

Ralph said, "You wouldn't guess that St. Petersburg is only a few miles away. We could be deep in the interior of the country."

"I know," she agreed.

Major Brown looked up from the picnic basket, his fat face redder than ever. "Blast!" he said.

"What now?" Ralph asked, moving from Elsie to the fat man.

"I'm a blooming idiot!" Major Brown fumed. "Went to all the trouble to pack my camera and accessories and then stupidly left it in the carriage! And I'd so counted on having a photo of us!"

Ralph laughed easily. "No problem about that. I'll go back and get it for you. It won't take me longer than twenty minutes."

Elsie said, "I don't mind the walk. In fact, I enjoyed it. I'll go along for company."

Ralph turned to her. "No! Stay here and enjoy the view and get the lunch ready. We can't leave the major here alone."

The major said, "I'm never alone as long as I have a drink handy. But I would enjoy the company of the countess. I'll tell her of the time I met the late King Edward at a garden party. Good story if I do say so myself."

Ralph gave her a good-humored glance. "You see! You'll be royally entertained, and I'll be back before you know it." He started for the path in the woods.

Major Brown called after him. "The case should be on the floor of the droshka out in the open. I don't think that driver chap would take it. Gave him enough vodka to occupy him in any case."

Ralph halted at the end of the woods to say, "I'll find it." And then he vanished along the path.

Elsie knew it was nonsense, but she suddenly felt uneasy at being left alone with the grossly fat major. It seemed that her fear of the Skoptsi had extended to all fat men. She would have to fight this phobia on her part. She busied herself with the lunch basket, finding the plates and utensils, while the major strode along the edge of the cliff enjoying the view. She found it difficult to talk with him when they were alone and so waited for him to take the lead.

375

Presently he glanced at her. "Don't fuss about with those dishes, dear girl! I beg you to come here and join with me in enjoying this magnificent view."

She hesitated at the table. He was on the very edge of the cliff and being so near the dizzying drop made her nervous. She said, "I have a bad head where heights are concerned."

"Nonsense!" he said. "Nothing will happen to you. Stand back from the edge. I'm here to protect you. From this point one can see for miles!"

Reluctantly, she crossed over near him. And now she began to tremble a little, and she felt ashamed of her behavior and hoped he wouldn't notice. She tried to avoid staring down at the depths below by gazing at the distant mountains. She said, "They are glorious and still snow-tipped despite the heat we have in St. Petersburg."

"They never melt," Major Brown said, staring at them. Now he turned to her with sympathy on his fat face. "I know that there are things which never change. Such as the love which, despite this tragedy, you must still feel for your husband. I do not mention it before Ralph for obvious reasons of good taste. We British put good taste before good sense!"

She was surprised at his turn of conversation and found herself staring at him. She said, "I cannot bear to think of what Alex has done, so I have decided I must forget him!"

Major Brown said, "That is one way. Think of another. I have done some investigating of the Skoptsi in my work as an intelligence agent."

"You have?"

"Yes," the big man said earnestly. "And there are those who claim the Skoptsi do good in their own way."

"I cannot imagine how!" she said.

"They have been placed in the care of Christian monasteries and converted whole monasteries to their teachings, despite the horror with which they had been viewed on their entry. The Skoptsi have endowed churches, paid large sums of money to priests and officials, and become regarded as benefactors by large numbers of people."

"Nothing they do can make up for their creed of self-mutilation. That is fanaticism!"

Major Brown sighed. "The riddle of the power of the

Skoptsi may be found in the self-destructive urge that rests deep within most of us. Alex must have had it. There are religious people who believe that self-mutilation is a step to the attainment of mystical insight. Only those who suffer gain the secret knowledge."

With a growing sense of fear, she realized he was talking like a different person, orating like someone in a strangely, elated state. His eyes had taken on that mad, burning light which she knew so well.

"How do you know so much about the Skoptsi?" she asked, taking a step back.

"Because, dear countess, I happen to be one," Major Brown gloated. "I am of the Great Seal and it is my duty to remove you. Rasputin has ordered that Litvinov must be avenged!"

"No!" she cried and tried to get away.

She didn't manage it. He was too quick for her. He had her by the arm, dragging her close to the edge of the precipice. Breathing heavily, he gasped, "It will only take a moment! You go over the side!"

"No," she cried, struggling.

He held her firmly. "I shall report the tragic accident to Manning! You stepped too close to the edge. And I'll quietly suggest it may have been suicide for the loss of your husband!"

She sobbed, "He won't believe you!" And struggled more as the fat man propelled her to the very edge of the rocks. Below, more than a hundred feet, the water seethed over jagged rocks!

"He will never suspect me. I'll weep a little when we go down and retrieve your broken body," the major said with insane glee.

She was at the edge, the ground started crumbling under her. He gave her a shove; but as he did, she managed to shift the weight of her body so that instead of dropping over the cliff she fell heavily against the major. He had been ready to see her drop far below and was caught completely by surprise. The impact of her body made him lose his own balance and it was he who went over the side with a high, chilling scream as she toppled down on the rocks, perilously close to the brink, but still safe.

The major's fearful cry as he fell to his death rang in

her ears. She did not dare move. She thought she would be ill; then she blacked out.

She was a distance from the edge when she came to, and a shocked Ralph was bending over her. "What happened? I found you on the cliff's edge in a faint! Where's the major?"

She gazed up at him, still with her mind in a cloud. Weakly, she said, "Down there!"

"The gorge?"

"Yes."

"Good God!" Ralph said in a low voice. "I thought he had been drinking too much, but I didn't guess there was any danger."

Now she was gradually coming around to herself. She lifted herself on an elbow. "He wasn't drunk," she told him solemnly.

"Then what?" Ralph asked in amazement.

"As soon as you left he began to lecture me about Alex."

"About Alex?"

"Yes. I thought it strange! He began to tell me the good the Skoptsi cult did. He took on a strange mood of elation."

"He must have been very drunk."

"Not with alcohol," she said. "With fanaticism! He admitted he was a Skoptsi convert on the level of the Great Seal and that he had been ordered by Rasputin to murder me as revenge for the death of Litvinov."

Ralph stared at her. "The major was a member of the British intelligence. I was at his embassy with him. I have seen his papers."

"He was also a spy infiltrated by the Skoptsi. He tried to push me over the cliff. By a freak accident he went over rather than me."

"What will we do?" Ralph said in alarm. "Will they believe your story?"

"I don't know and don't care," she said wearily. "You can say it was merely an accident."

Ralph shook his head. "I must report the facts to the British Embassy. No telling what double-spying he has been up to. I have a responsibility."

She let him help her to her feet. "He planned to tell you

378

I went too near the edge, that it was an accident, or that I did it because of a broken heart over Alex."

He looked at her in shock. "So it was all carefully planned. The picnic and leaving the camera behind."

"He had to get you out of the way."

"And he did the same thing the other day when he made me break my luncheon date with you and led me on that wild goose chase. You would have been captured again if Prince Serge hadn't come along."

"I saw that the major seemed upset when you returned and he saw me still at the hotel," she said. "But I kept telling myself I was being silly, that he couldn't be one of them."

Ralph gave her a knowing look. "Still, he almost betrayed his eunuchism. He was groosly fat."

"Many men are who don't belong to the Skoptsi," she said.

"The Skoptsi have a different look," Ralph said grimly. "I should have recognized it. But I was convinced he was a harmless old army officer." He went to the cliff's edge. "Let the body stay there. The authorities can get it."

"I think I'd prefer that," she said. "I still feel ill."

Ralph came and put an arm around her, "I'll take you back to the carriage and we'll have the driver return us to St. Petersburg as quickly as possible."

She said, "What about the basket of food and drink?"

"Let it stay there," he said. "They can get it when they come for the body."

He helped support her as they made the journey back through the woods. She was still faint. The driver was too drunk to question much about the missing third passenger. Ralph sternly told him to drive them back to the Empress Hotel as quickly as possible.

On the drive back, Ralph said, "This may keep us longer in St. Petersburg than I'd planned. There will be an investigation, and we won't be able to leave until it is over."

"I know," she said.

"And you must never leave the suite without me," he warned her. "And I'll ask a police guard at the suite's door. Rasputin will be more determined to settle with you than ever after this."

She knew it was true, and yet it seemed that the mad

379

monk should be satisfied. Litvinov and Major Brown had only been killed because they had first attacked her. She had lost her husband to the cult without ever having known the insidious nature of the terror she was battling.

That night she hardly slept at all. Ralph was kept busy on the phone. And the following day, she and Ralph made a request appearance before a solemn official of the British Embassy. He was a tall, gnarled man with thinning gray hair and a bulbous, purple nose. He had the weary air of one who has been too long in foreign service.

His name was Commander Reginald Wheatley, and he was the second in charge at the embassy. Ralph and Elsie sat across the desk from him while he regarded them with an owl-like expression.

He said, "First, may I offer the apologies of his majesty's government to you, Countess Martynov. We now have learned without question that the service was harboring a member of the Skoptsi."

"You didn't know until this happened," she said. "I can't blame you."

The commander rubbed the side of his purple nose. "Unhappily, we feel otherwise, my dear lady. Members of our MI division undergo severe tests. It appears that Major Brown was not a member of the Skoptsi when he first joined the service. He thus had a clear record as far as we were concerned."

"I was with him a lot," Ralph agreed. "And I did not ever have reason to supsect him."

"Nor did we," the commander said. "His reports have been helpful, presuming they are correct. I think they are, but I also think he was using the information he had about the British military strength and passing it on to Rasputin."

"That would be expected," Ralph agreed.

"A physical examination of his recovered body revealed he was, if the lady will pardon me, most brutally castrated. And not too recently according to the medical evidence. And in his rooms we found correspondence with Rasputin and his agents in a hidden wall safe. So the doubt is settled."

"I was neatly tricked," Ralph said bitterly. "And I think your service should be wary from now on."

"Be sure that we shall," Commander Wheatley promised them. "I'm afraid I shall have to ask you to remain until next week for the official investigation."

"We haven't much choice but to remain," Ralph said, "although it is dangerous for the countess to remain in Russia."

"I know that," the British officer said. "And I will make sure you have adequate protection from the Russian police."

"Thank you, sir," Ralph said, rising.

The commander was on his feet to see them out. He said, "I don't think you'll be sorry to leave Russia, countess."

At the door, she hesitated and said, "Yes and no. There are people and things here I will miss. But the country is in such a chaotic state."

"My government is very concerned," the commander said with a frown. "If the evil power of Rasputin could be broken perhaps a proper government might be established. If only the tsar could be reached by the proper politicians, a revolution might yet be avoided."

Ralph said, "From what I know, I wouldn't count on it."

Commander Wheatley smiled bleakly. "I have my wife and family living here, you know. I have asked for a transfer to Sweden. I hope that I may get it."

They left the British officer on this note. And now the period of waiting became trying on them. Despite the police protection she had, Elsie was continually fearful for her life.

Feodor had already left on his tour of the student cells. But Elsie and Ralph had Marfa and Olga twice as their dinner guests. On their last evening together, Olga made no mention of Alex at all, althought there was no question the dark girl still fretted about her brother. Nor did Elsie mention him.

Olga seemed most concerned about her Uncle Andre. She said, "When you see him urge him to leave Russia. I have tried and he won't listen to me."

Elsie asked, "Why should he listen to me?"

"It will be another person urging him," Olga said. "And he has always liked you."

Elsie said, "I can picture him hard to convince. Russia is all to him."

"The flood is coming," Olga warned her. "Nothing will halt it! And unless he escapes before it happens, he runs a good chance of being killed defending his property."

"You think it that certain?"

"The one thing uncertain is the date," Olga said. "If he leaves before anything happens, he can escape with his life and enough of his wealth to live on."

"He would think that cowardly."

"Cowardly or not, many of the noble families have apartments in Paris at this moment. And many of them have removed their valuable jewels to Paris vaults if they have not managed to salvage rubles. He should do the same."

Elsie smiled at her sadly. "You are torn between your family and your dedication to the cause."

"Other than you, Uncle Andre is my only family left," she said.

"You forget about Sophie."

"A distant cousin. A young woman who loved herself better than anyone else. I cannot fret about her."

"Do you think she is alive?"

"In Siberia it is always a question. But knowing Sophie, I would be likely to bet on it," Olga said.

Marfa turned from talking to Ralph to ask her, "When do you leave for America?"

"Probably in ten days or sooner," she said.

"Boris would like you to send him some books," the peasant girl said.

"Gladly."

"I have a list," Marfa said with a smile on her square face. "There are quite a few. Boris has no consideration for his friends." She handed Elsie the list.

Elsie scanned the list quickly and gave it to Ralph. She said, "We'll have no trouble getting the books, but will the authorities allow Boris to have them?"

Ralph looked up from the book list. "I'll have them sent to the office downstairs. I'll explain to my associate. Boris can pick them up there."

"Wonderful!" Marfa said happily. "He will be delighted."

"Are you going to marry?" Elsie asked her.

The peasant girl shrugged. "I like him better than any other man. But first there is the cause. I will make no plans until after the chaos. If we are alive then, who knows?"

Ralph reached across the table and took Elsie's hand in his. "I'm not by any means that patient. As soon as Elsie is free I want her to be my wife."

"What about you, Olga?" she asked.

For the first time a shining happiness showed in the dark girl's eyes. "It is a secret. We have lied about it. But I can safely tell you, my friends. Before we left Moscow, Feodor and I were married by Father Peter in the presence of Uncle Andre."

Elsie was thrilled. "In the chapel?"

"By Timofei's icon," Olga said. "I shall always remember it."

"I'm happy for you," Elsie said. "You must let us give you some sort of present."

"The present I would value more is your spending a night at the palace and talking Uncle Andre into leaving," the dark girl said.

Elsie turned to Ralph. "May I?"

"Only if I stay at the palace also," he said firmly. "I won't let you spend the night there alone."

"Uncle Andre knows you," Olga told Ralph. "He will not mind having you as a guest. In fact, he will welcome you."

So it was settled. In the several days that remained of their stay in St. Petersburg, Ralph and Elsie were witnesses against Major Brown at the British Embassy and were guests one evening of Prince Serge and his wife in the prince's palace. The young noble was shocked about the business of Major Brown and depressed about Rasputin's continued control over the royal family and through them, the government.

At last the morning came when they were free and took the train to Moscow. Elsie's mode of travel was again that of the privileged. She and Ralph shared a compartment and dined in the elegant dining car. She knew she should be completely happy, but she was still apprehensive about returning to Moscow and the palace of the Martynovs.

Chapter 30

In Moscow, Ralph and Elsie took another suite at the Hotel Metropole. New York was already keeping the Atlantic cable line hot with queries about the strange death of Major Brown. Ralph replied that he would offer the whole story of the Russian events in full when he talked with the head of the syndicate.

Elsie found herself glad to return to a city with normal days and nights. She almost welcomed the darkness of this early autumn in Moscow. The leaves were beginning to fall and rustle across the brick sidewalks, and other signs of the approaching winter were in the air. But she enjoyed this older city with its Kremlin inner city and the architecture more typically Russian. The golden domes and onion tops of the cathedrals and buildings pleased her. She even was glad to hear the pleasant clamor of the many church bells.

Ralph was deeply involved in office work. He had a good deal to do to catch up with all the paper details before he turned the assignment over to a newcomer and left for New York. Because of this, Elsie did not rush out to the palace to see Count Andre, but remained in and near the hotel.

She was not so fearful in Moscow, although she knew danger might lurk for her there as well. But the royal palace and Rasputin were a day's train journey away and all the seething intrigue of the Baltic city seemed part of another world. Yet the shadow of the Skoptsi hung over her. The terrifying experience with Major Brown had brought her close to collapse.

On her second night in Moscow, she and Ralph dined at a famous restaurant near the hotel. She waited until they were finished with their meal and having coffee and brandy to discuss the problem of visiting Count Andre.

She said, "I must go to the Martynov palace. I promised Olga I would."

Ralph's handsome face showed concern. "I wish it could be avoided."

"It can't."

"Why?"

"For one thing I have some personal jewelry and other things there I want to get," she said.

"And?"

"I must talk with Count Andre and beg him to leave Russia," she reminded him. "I told Olga I would try and coax him to leave before any violence takes place."

Ralph said, "He won't listen to you."

"I must at least try."

"Have you written your own aunt and uncle in New York?" he asked.

"Just briefly," she said. And with a gesture of despair she added, "I can't explain in a letter. I can't tell them everything even when I see them."

"But you have let them know you are returning?"

"Yes."

"And alone?"

"Yes. I said Alex was kept here by other problems."

He looked grim. "I guess that explains it as well as any way."

"That is why I made the letter brief."

"What about me?"

"I spoke of meeting you. That you were assigned here."

"So I won't be too much of a shock for them?"

She smiled. "You needn't worry. I can manage it."

"I don't want them to think I helped break up your marriage," he worried.

"They won't," she said. "And I hinted there was a possibility you might be returning to New York on the same liner with me."

"That was a good idea," he said with some relief.

She smiled. "My people will like you. And they'll be so happy to have me back in America, they won't care who I marry!"

"Not very flattering," Ralph said.

"I know I'm marrying the best man in the world for me," she said. "But it will be a little while. There's the divorce to be settled."

"A few months," he said.

"It could be longer," she warned him.

"I hope not," he said.

"So much for New York and our plans," she said. "My main concern now is that I must visit the palace and spend at least a night with Count Andre."

"You're really fond of that old man."

"He is a true aristocrat," she said. "And probably the last generation of his kind."

"If a change comes it will be people like Marfa, Boris, and Feodor who will take over," Ralph said. "And the great problem is that they have no tradition, unless you count a peasant tradition."

"You're forgetting Olga," she said. "There are bound to be many Olgas and male counterparts of her among the new revolutionaries. They will keep the cause civilized."

"Let us hope so," Ralph said grimly, glancing around the elegantly appointed restaurant with its oriental trappings and crowds of wealthy patrons. "I don't think there will be much of this."

"Perhaps not," she admitted. "But more important things may take its place."

Ralph said, "I'll try and get free of work tomorrow and take you out to the palace."

But when the next day arrived, he was still occupied with some unexpected new business. So they made a compromise. He told her, "You go out to the palace, and I'll join you later."

"When?" she asked.

He shrugged. "That depends on when I receive some cabled information I'm waiting for."

"At least try and make dinner," she pleaded with him. "The count will be hurt if you don't come."

Ralph kissed her and with a smile said, "I'll keep in touch by phone. If I don't make dinner, I'll be there for brandy."

"I know," she said with a sigh. "And if you don't make it in time for brandy, you'll arrive by midnight."

"It won't be that bad," he promised her.

So Elsie journeyed to the Martynov palace alone. As she sat in the dark interior of the carriage taking her to the great estate on the outskirts of Moscow, she thought of all the experiences she had known since arriving in Russia as a bride. It did not seem possible that so much had happened in so brief a time. Nor that so many of the principals in the drama could be dead or as good as dead.

Every time she let her mind rest on Alex, she knew an intense pain. She knew she would suffer this secret sorrow for a long while to come and she must conceal a great deal of it from Ralph. But she had been in love with Alex, even though he was now lost to her.

She remembered the afternoon when the Countess Marie had been buried and the strange, haunted look on the face of her husband when he'd gone to stand by the grave of his brother Basil. Was it then when he had made up his mind to return to St. Petersburg and the sexual excesses Rasputin held out to him there?

It was all a puzzle to her and probably would remain so. Did Alex believe, like the mad Major Brown and the others, that through the ordeal of mutilation he would achieve certain mystic powers, be one of the special group to rule the world? The sexual orgies preceding this grim business were a good-by to physical sex. Now in his drug confused mind, he would expect to move to a higher spiritual plane. Obey the monk Rasputin and commit the most atrocious acts without having to feel spiritual blame because he had already paid. It was a false surmise!

It was late afternoon when she reached the grounds of the palace. Most of the trees still had their leaves, so the palace was hidden by a mantle of surrounding green. The river was clear and looked beautiful in the background. She felt that she much preferred Moscow with all its rigors to St. Petersburg.

The coachman brought her suitcase to the door. She rang the bell and after a long while the door was opened by the wizened old Frederick. His wrinkled face first registered surprise and then pleasure.

"Countess!" he exclaimed. "We did not expect to see you again!"

She smiled. "Well, I'm here, Frederick. Welcome or not!"

"Of course you are welcome," the old butler said, taking her bag and showing her in. "You plan to stay for a little?"

"Overnight at least," she said. "And I have a friend coming later. You may perhaps remember him, the American newspaper man, Ralph Manning."

"Yes, indeed I do remember him," Frederick said. "Was he not a guest at your wedding?"

"He was," she said. "He will also be remaining overnight."

"Your old apartment is ready and waiting for you," Frederick said. "Count Andre has always insisted you would return."

"How is he?"

"Very well for his age," Frederick said. "The Martynovs are given to live long and with some vigor. He is having his afternoon nap now."

"Don't bother him with the news I'm here until he wakens," she said.

"Just as you wish, countess," the old butler said, leading her up the familiar broad, curving stairway and carrying her small bag along.

They reached the apartment, and her eyes became wet with tears. She turned away to hide them as the old man went about opening the drapes and fussing with everything to make sure she would be comfortable. He placed her bag on a small table and stood gazing at her with admiration.

"You look rested, countess," he said. "Elena is still in our employ. She will bring you up fresh towels and some soap. I think everything else is in order."

"Thank you, Frederick," she said, over her first moments of heartbreak. "It is good to see you again."

"Thank you, countess," Frederick said. "We were all shocked and sorry to hear that Count Alexander followed in his late brother's footsteps and chose to desert you and follow that scoundrel, Rasputin!"

"It was a tragic thing," she said quietly. "I'm trying to make myself forget it, but it is not easy."

"I know, countess," the old man said. "And forgive me for bringing it up. But we all want you to know our sympathies lie with you."

"Thank you, Frederick," she said. "I'll rest a little until Count Andre awakes and can receive me."

The butler left and she unpacked. It gave her an eerie feeling to be in this room which she and Alex had shared as husband and wife. She wished that Ralph would join her soon.

Elena came with the soap and towels and the usual amount of gossip. The girl curtsied before her and said, "How wonderful to have you home again, countess."

She managed a smile. "Yes, it was my home for a fairly long while."

"It still is, countess," the girl said. "The house has been lonesome of late with only the old count here."

"I'm sure it has."

"Many of the staff are gone," Elena said. "We only have one stableman and one carriage now. The two horses barely get enough exercise as Count Andre seldom leaves the palace."

"Countess Olga is no longer here," Elsie said.

"No," Elena said. "And a good thing. The cossacks came to question Count Andre, but she had left. I do not like those fellows. I think they meant to arrest the poor countess."

"It was wiser for her to leave," Elsie said.

"Is Count Alexander returning?" Elena asked.

"No, at least not for a while."

"And Miss Sophie was sent to Siberia. The old count has money and gifts delivered to her, although whether she gets them in that far-off place is a question."

Elsie said, "No word of Timofei?"

"He is dead," Elena said promptly. "The old count refuses to admit it, but Frederick says that he knows it and prefers to make us think that he doesn't."

"Tragic," she said. "I liked Timofei."

"We all liked Timofei," Elena said, smiling in remembrance. "And he could drink more vodka than anyone."

"Well, that is life," Elsie said. "It does not always turn out the way we expect."

"No it does not, countess," Elena said unhappily. "I expected to be married and on another estate by now, but the scamp I was betrothed to ran off with the scullery maid."

"I'm sorry," she said.

"No good will come to them," Elena vowed. "I hear they have fled to Rumania, and no one is happy there!" With that bit of wisdom she left.

Elsie took a bath and changed her dress. And by the time she completed fixing her hair, Frederick came with the news the old count was waiting for her.

Count Andre looked older, and yet in an odd way he looked less feeble. And she was pleasantly surprised that when he rose to greet her, he did it without any effort or use of the cane, which he'd formerly depended on. He took her in his arms for a fatherly kiss and then surveyed her at arm's length with a jovial expression on his lean face.

"You look better than when I saw you last," he said.

"So do you!"

"I am better," he said. "My arthritis has left me, and I feel ten years younger. I give credit to a new doctor who has taken over poor Orlov's practice. You knew that Orlov was dead?"

"No," she said.

"Very sudden," the old man said. "But this new fellow is excellent, and he has done a lot for me."

"That is apparent," she said.

"I knew you would return. Let us sit down together." He led her to a love seat.

She said, "I have seen Olga."

"How is she?" the old man said. "You know that she is married."

"Yes. And that you gave her your blessing."

The old aristocrat shrugged. "It was better. She would have married him anyway."

"He is a fine young man, and he loves Russia in his own way just as you do in yours."

Count Andre showed pain. "But our conflicts will destroy Mother Russia!"

"I do not think so," she said soberly. "It may change, but it will not be destroyed. Olga knows what is happening in the underground. She begs that you leave here and go to Paris before the revolution begins."

"Never!" he said. "It is my place here!"

"It will do no one any good if you are killed and all your wealth taken," she warned him.

"There is my son, Timofei," Count Andre said. "I cannot leave until he returns. His icon awaits him here, and so do I. It would be Marie's wish."

She touched his arm. "Dear Count Andre, I feel as if you were my true uncle. I beg you to accept that Timofei is dead and leave here while you still have time. Olga thinks it is only a matter of months now before everything explodes."

"I must wait for Timofei," the old man said firmly. "How long will you be with me?"

"A night or two at most," she said. "I'm going back to America."

The old man nodded solemnly. "Because of Alex deserting you?"

"Yes."

"It was a mad thing for him to do. He knew what happened to Basil and Katrin. Yet he gave himself to the cause of that wretched Rasputin, brought him to this house to disgrace it, and turned from you, his beautiful wife."

She looked down at her clasped hands. "I tell myself he became mad. The drugs and sexual excesses Rasputin exposed him to drove him insane. It is the only way I can bear the pain of it."

"You are showing wisdom, my child."

She smiled wryly. "Timofei used to call me his little innocent."

"Timofei was the best of them, and I will not believe he is dead," Count Andre said, his ancient voice almost breaking on the words.

Elsie quickly said, "There is a young man coming here to stay. He is going back to America with me. You remember, Ralph Manning, of the Hearst syndicate?"

"Of course," Count Andre said. "He will be most welcome." Then he took her hand in his and said. "Will you marry him when you are free of poor Alex?"

"That is my plan now," she said. "I'm very confused."

"You may well be," the old count said. Dusk had settled on the room and he stared off into the shadows. "You know this palace has always been haunted."

A chill streaked through her. In a voice with a small tremor in it, she said, "I have heard rumors, the legend."

"Of Nicholas the wife murderer," Count Andre said, still gazing off into the growing darkness. "This house is full of phantoms. Lately, I have heard things I can't explain. Once I thought I heard a voice which resembled Basil's."

"Basil is buried in the family cemetery."

The old man nodded. "I saw him lowered into the grave. Yet, I swear that once late at night, I thought I heard him calling to someone in the hall."

She said, "Perhaps it was a dream."

"And then I have seen figures in black. Figures that appear and then vanish before I can distinguish who or what they are. I tell myself it is because I am so lonely. And that is probably it. When you are alone too much you begin to imagine things."

Elsie still experienced that eerie chill, as if a skeleton hand was on her shoulder. In a taut voice, she said, "It happens to many people. Once, when I was living here, I thought I saw a phantom figure, also in black."

"It is a strange old house. A place of grim memories for me now. Alex has disgraced the family by joining the Skoptsi! If Timofei would only return, I would not take much urging to leave it and all its phantoms and ghostly voices."

"I think you should leave anyway," she said.

"Will your friend, Mr. Manning, be here for dinner?" the old count asked.

"He should have phoned by now," she said worriedly. "I'll call him and see."

She went downstairs to use the phone in the lower hall, aware of every dark shadow in the old house. The mention the old man had made of ghostly voices and figures had badly upset her, and she was more anxious for Ralph to arrive than ever. She called his office at the hotel.

"When will you be here?" she asked.

"When the cables arrive. I have to wait," he told her. "They will need an immediate reply. I can't leave until they come."

In a low voice, she said, "Hurry! This place frightens me now."

"The count is there?"

"Yes."

"Have dinner with him, and I'll be there as soon afterward as I can," Ralph promised.

"It's dark. I'm afraid!"

"You'll be all right," he consoled her. "You have the old man for company until I get there. I'm sure to be there by ten."

"Ten!" she said. "He'll be in bed long before that!"

"I'll get there as soon as I can," Ralph said wearily. "If he goes to bed, have one of the maids keep you company until I arrive. You don't have to be alone."

She put the phone down with a feeling of despair. Ralph didn't understand that every minute that passed made her more panic-stricken. She felt every shadow she passed held a menace for her, and it was a house of shadows! The servants lighted the lamps, and she and Count Andre sat down alone at the great dinner table.

The old man had worn evening dress for dinner as in former days. She had on a suitable gown and sat at his right. As the servants poured out champagne and began to serve the first course, he said, "I'm sorry Mr. Manning could not be here to join us."

"He also regrets it; but he will come as soon as the cable he is waiting for arrives from America," she said.

Count Andre nodded. "At least I shall see him at breakfast. I must confess I retire early. You will not mind waiting for him alone?"

"No," she said nervously, although she did very much mind.

They had a fine dinner of pheasant and then remained at the table for coffee and brandy since there were only the two of them. Toward the end, she saw Count Andre's head slump on his chest as he nodded over his brandy, his lighted cigar still between his fingers on the table.

Frederick gave her a knowing look and retrieved the cigar so it would not burn the tablecloth. The old count woke with a start, consulted his gold pocketwatch and said to her, "You will excuse me, won't you, my dear?"

"Of course," she said. "I'm going up to my apartment to freshen up. I expect Ralph to be here soon."

They paused in the hallway, and once again she

expressed her admiration of the painting of the young Basil, which hung in the living room near the entrance. She said, "He was handsome and much like Alex in looks."

"Yes," the old man said. "I think that is why I never had an artist do Alex. The two were almost identical in appearance."

They made their way upstairs and parted at the landing. She pretended to be at ease, but as she walked down the dark corridor to her apartment, she couldn't help trembling at the thought of the ghostly voices and figures the old count had mentioned. Of course, they were products of a lonely old man's aging brain. They had to be illusions—nothing more. But still!

She prayed that Ralph would come soon as she entered the apartment. Elena had lighted the lamps and drawn the drapes, and the bed was turned down. She stared at it and decided that on this night Ralph would have to sleep alone in the adjoining bedroom. She could not share this same bed with him, not this bed in which she and Alex had once known such perfect love.

"Remembering?" The voice was hollow like an echo, yet familiar. And it came from near the dresser behind her.

She wheeled around to find herself staring at a haggard Alex who was standing close to the dresser in the black monk's robe of the Skoptsi cultists.

Tears sprang to her eyes. "You!" And she went to him, standing opposite him before the dresser.

"Yes, I came back," he said in that flat voice, and she saw his eyes were changed. They held the burning madness of the Skoptsi. "We are staying here for a little. Hiding here if you like. He enjoys coming back and doesn't want my uncle to see him!"

"Who?" she asked in terror, thinking he was truly mad.

Alex fixed those gleaming, fanatical eyes on hers. He said, "I cannot help still loving you. It is a sin—against my vows. But you can join us. You can become one of the sisters."

"No," she protested, falling back against the dresser, clutching it with her hands for support.

"I can no longer be husband to you," he said in a hoarse whisper. And with a quick movement he lifted the black robe to reveal his nude body beneath. Where his maleness had been, there were only ugly red scars— jagged red remnants of the flesh which had been his pride and known union with her!

"My God!" she whispered in horror and lifted a hand to her eyes to spare herself the sight.

"I can be your brother. Join us," he urged her, taking a step closer to her as he let the robe fall back in place. "We have great powers!"

"Fool!" This was another voice, one she had never heard before. She looked over her husband's shoulder and saw a fat figure entering the door from the hallway. He came closer, and she knew this was a Skoptsi because of his gross overweight, the strange walk, and the malevolent, fat face with trembling double chins.

Her horror was doubled by the fact she knew this was what time and his eunuchism would soon do to Alex. Alex turned to the newcomer and seemed afraid of him. And it was at this moment that she realized the fat Skoptsi was known to her. Known to her by his portrait which he no longer resembled to any degree! It was Basil, the brother of Alex who had supposedly died years before.

She gasped, "You are Basil! You didn't die!"

"Only to your sinful world," the caricature of Basil said in a lisping voice.

"Then it wasn't ghost voices the old man heard," she said in awe. "It was you two hiding here."

The fat Basil nodded. "And how fortunate that you should return."

"She will join us," Alex told his brother.

"Never!" Basil said. "You are a fool to believe that. Rasputin wants her dead. And she deserves to die; even now she is waiting for that newspaper man to arrive. I heard her telling your uncle."

Alex turned to her, the mad eyes staring at her. "Is that true?"

"What does it matter?" she sobbed.

"Kill her!" Basil ordered him in his high-pitched voice. "She must die!"

Alex came toward her like a robot creature. His hands lifted and he sprang at her to clutch her throat. At the same instant her hand found a steel letter opener on the desk and instinctively she used it as a dagger to protect herself. She screamed and plunged it into him as his hands tightened on her throat!

The steel blade found a true target. Alex gave a small moan and slumped down to the floor, the handle of the knife still sticking from his chest. The fat Basil at once knelt by him and removed the blade. Blood gushed out, and Alex opened his eyes for an instant of agony, moaned softly again, and his eyes closed as his head fell to one side.

Basil got up slowly, incredible even in his rage at what had happened. He looked at her. "You've killed him!"

Basil's fat face was pale with hatred. "Twice my brother! And you killed him! But never mind! You will die in the same manner of Katrin!"

"No!" she screamed and, dodging past him, made for the door.

He was on her heels. She raced out into the corridor and made for the landing, her screams ringing through the old house. Basil did not turn or attempt to hide. He was beyond this in his present rage and madness. As she reached the landing he caught her, and his fleshy hands quickly found her throat.

She tried to scream and couldn't. And she knew it was over. Then just as she was losing consciousness, she saw the ghost of Timofei, a thin Timofei with a black patch over one eye. The phantom of the big man was coming from the direction of his foster father's room, and old Count Andre came behind him. She knew she was hallucinating and that soon she would lose all consciousness and die from lack of breath.

But it didn't happen. The Timofei with the black eye patch was real! He seized the fat Basil and worried him like a giant, fat rat before he threw him down the long, curving stairway. Basil rolled like a fat, broken doll to the very bottom.

Timofei picked her up and said, "For once I'm sober and on time, little innocent."

She chose that moment to faint. And when she came to, she was in the bedroom Olga had used. Ralph was there; so was Timofei and the elderly Count Andre.

She opened her eyes and looked up at the old man. "You were right! He did come back!"

Count Andre took her hand and said, "It was a miracle. He returned only a half-hour before we heard your screams."

"Alex?" she whispered, her throat still sore and hoarse from Basil's attempt to strangle her.

"Dead, and better for it," the old count said. "Basil's neck was broken in his fall down the stairs. I have already talked on the phone with our local magistrate. He understands and is sympathetic. The police are not controlled here by Rasputin as they are in St. Petersburg. The Skoptsi are regarded here as dangerous madmen and violators of the law."

So it came to an end. A few more days in Moscow, a grim examination in the court, a solemn double funeral in the family cemetery and it was over. The original coffin in which Basil had supposedly been buried those years before was exhumed and was found to contain rocks. Alex had known all along his brother was not dead but a Skoptsi monk and the murderer of Katrin.

Timofei had been living in exile in Paris, where he'd made his name as an artist. He was proud of the icon in the chapel. He agreed with Olga, and he privately told Elsie before she left the palace, "I will get my father out of here!" He now had come to regard the old count as his true father. Elsie knew the Countess Marie must be happy in her grave.

Once again, she and Ralph were in a snug compartment on the Moscow to Paris Express. Ralph kissed her gently as the train glided out of the station on the beginning of the long trip, which would eventually see them aboard a liner on their way to New York. They said nothing, but held hands. She closed her eyes and thought about it all.

She could really be sure of nothing at this moment but her love for Ralph. She could not foresee that they would be happily married and have a son, Timothy, and a daughter, Olga, who would one day visit and marvel at a new Russia unlike the one their parents had experienced. Was it better or worse? Who could say for sure? Russia always presented a puzzle.

She did not guess then that Prince Yusupov would

Clarissa Ross

make good his word and kill the evil Rasputin. And with
Rasputin gone, the evil Skoptsi would lose much of its
power. She had no idea that a world war would touch off
the flame of revolution in March 1917, just a few years
hence. And that the royal family would be slaughtered and
Russia never the same again.

She would have been happy to know that the venerable
Count Andre and Timofei left Russia before the revolution came. That Timofei became a noted artist and earned
enough for them to live well. That he married a refugee
countess and so produced an heir for the old count of
truly noble blood. Count Andre died at ninety with Timofei
holding his hand and a young Count Andre happy in his
playpen in a neighboring room.

Elsie could hardly have guessed as she sat in that train
compartment thinking about the future and with her eyes
closed that when she saw Sophie and Jack Bogrov again, it
would be after a second world war when Ralph was a sen-
ior reporter at Potsdam and Bogrov was an aide of Stalin.
They were all much older. But Sophie was still an attractive woman and a social figure in the new regime.

When Elsie and Sophie had come face to face at one of
the social events attending the Potsdam Conference, Sophie had given her a superior smile and said, "Of course, I
remember you. It was very different in those days, wasn't
it?"

"Yes," she said quietly. "It was."

Elsie had no idea at that moment in 1913 that tragedy
and great success lay ahead for Countess Olga. She could
not know that Feodor would be killed during the revolution and that Olga would desert Russia, first as a refugee
in France and then in America.

The Countess Olga line of perfumes had become a
success throughout the world. Olga lived in New York and
was an ornament of chic society, but she never married
again although she had a number of interesting male es-
corts. She saw Ralph and Elsie often and was godmother
to their daughter, Olga.

The last couple whom Elsie would meet, although this
was far in the future indeed, were Boris and Marfa. They
came to New York as important members of the Russian
delegation to the United Nations.

Ralph was doing a special series on the meetings for the *New York Times* and met them first. He then took Elsie to meet them in the corridor outside the conference room one March day. By this time Ralph was balding and Elsie had decided to let her hair go gray, although Countess Olga, who remained her dark-haired self, declared this nonsense.

Still Elsie was glad of it when she came face to face with a buxom, gray-haired Marfa and a stooped, scholarly looking Boris whose thinning hair was competely white.

Marfa embraced her as warmly as ever with tears in her eyes. She said, "How long it has been and how good to see you!"

Elsie said, "Ralph tells me you and Boris have important duties here."

Boris nodded and with good humor told her, "We are all part of history now."

"Olga is here," Elsie told Marfa.

Marfa nodded. "Yes, I will see her." Then in a lower voice she said, "See, coming up the corridor."

Elsie glanced and saw that a group of dark-clad statesman were advancing to enter the main conference room. They were conversing earnestly and paid no attention to them. She would have recognized their language as Russian, even if she had not also recognized the central figure of the group as Molotov! The group passed on.

Marfa gave her a knowing glance and bent near to whisper. "It is rumored he is the last powerful Skoptsi. I do not know."

"I wonder," Elsie said gazing after him, a chill of remembrance taking over in her.

The two women moved a little aside as Ralph and Boris went on discussing some phase of the conference. Marfa sighed and said, "Of course you remember sometimes."

"I remember," Elsie said in a quiet voice. "How is it, Marfa, was it all worthwhile?"

"Some is good, and some is bad. Boris, who was always a history student, thinks it is to be expected. He claims that man is not capable of a perfect society."

"I wonder," she said. And she glanced into the conference room where Molotov was still visible. She thought of the Skoptsi and this made her remember Alex. Since it was New York, she thought of Alex on that night when she had her heel rescued by him, when he had been a true prince charming and she had been his princess! Lost so soon! Tears glistened in her eyes as she looked at Marfa, and she was touched to see that Marfa's eyes were also bright with tears. And she thought, dreams die hard.